Surrender to Ruin

Sinclair Sisters Series
Book 3

CAROLYN JEWEL

CJEWEL
BOOKS

Copyright

cJEWEL BOOKS

About Surrender to Ruin

Her beauty is divine. His heart yearns for another. Will attempted revenge result in true love?

Emily is the last unmarried Sinclair sister. For all her spellbinding beauty, she's never been able to clear a certain man from her head and her heart. He's made it clear there's no hope, and now he's about to marry her best friend.

The Earl of Bracebridge knows how to hold a grudge. The former prizefighter turned disreputable nobleman hoped to marry Emily's sister until she was forced to wed another. After his hopes for a suitable marriage are dashed once again, he seizes the chance to settle the score with Thomas Sinclair—by eloping with Emily and consigning them both to a union without love.

Emily knows Bracebridge loves another, but every time they're alone, sparks fly. Can the Earl get past his heartbreak to realize the perfect woman didn't get away—she's already his wife?

Surrender to Ruin is the long-anticipated third book in the Sinclair Sisters historical romance series. If you like unmistakable chemistry, sizzling romance, and potent regency drama, then you'll love the next chapter in Carolyn Jewel's heart-pounding series.

Books by Carolyn Jewel

HISTORICAL ROMANCE SERIES

Sinclair Sisters Series
Lord Ruin, Book 1
A Notorious Ruin, Book 2
Surrender To Ruin, Book 3

Reforming the Scoundrels Series
Not Wicked Enough, Book 1
Not Proper Enough, Book 2

Other Historical Romance
How To Find a Duke in Ten Days Anthology
Dancing in The Duke's Arms Anthology
An Unsuitable Duchess from *Dancing in The Duke's Arms* Anthology
In The Duke's Arms from *Christmas in The Duke's Arms* Anthology
Christmas in The Duke's Arms Anthology
One Starlit Night, novella from the *Midnight Scandals* Anthology
Midnight Scandals Anthology
Indiscreet
Scandal
Moonlight, a Regency-set short(ish) story
The Spare
Stolen Love
Passion's Song

PARANORMAL ROMANCE

My Immortals Series
My Wicked Enemy, Book 1
My Forbidden Desire, Book 2
My Immortal Assassin, Book 3
My Dangerous Pleasure, Book 4
Free Fall, Book 4.5, a novella
My Darkest Passion, Book 5
Dead Drop, Book 6
My Demon Warlord, Book 7

OTHER PARANORMAL ROMANCE

A Darker Crimson, Book 4 of *Crimson City*
DX, a *Crimson City* Novella

FANTASY ROMANCE

The King's Dragon, a short story

EROTIC ROMANCE

Whispers, Collection No. 1

Dedication

To Miranda Neville.

Acknowledgments

To all the readers who have written to me over the years asking about this book, your emails meant the world to me. Thank you. And thank you for your patience.

Thank you Gopal Rachagorla for giving me permission to use your name for one of the characters in this story. I'm so glad we had the opportunity to work together, even if it was on separate continents and different time zones. Ah, those late night (in the US)/early morning (in India) deployments. In fact, a big shout out to the whole database team, including everyone who was on-loan from time to time: Venkat, Nachiket, Arathy, Sai Kiran, Surendra. All of you are awesome, and I am glad to have worked with you.

To Carolyn Crane, thank you for reading drafts more than once. I know there were times when it hurt. You are awesome. To editor Bev Katz Rosenbaum, thank you for your insights times three.

As ever, thanks to my sister and my son for being wonderful people. Thank you, Bella for not eating my shoes . . . recently. Smudge, Fudge, and Caesar, you are missed. To the Frieda who was such a wonderful friend to my uncle Marion, and then to all of us, thank you. Welcome to the family, Maybelle.

Chapter One

Rosefeld, near Bartley Green, England, 1821

EMILY STOOD BY the door with her breath caught in her throat, and her heart shattered all over again. Momentarily paralyzed, she watched her dog gallop across the entry. The leash bounced and curved like some demented snake as Frieda headed for the stairs and the man who stood there.

"Frieda. No!" But her ungainly adolescent dog, intent on making a new friend, did not stop. Frieda was also, perhaps fortuitously, unable to safely negotiate the marble floor. Her front legs splayed and propelled her into a four-footed spin that ended with a crash into the bottom step. She scrambled to her feet and shook herself off, panting and wagging her tail hard enough to move her entire body.

The Earl of Bracebridge remained on the stairs, his attention on Frieda, as was wise when a large dog whose bark was a cross between a bay and a bone-chilling snarl was heading straight for one. Thank God for Frieda, for Emily needed time to master her feelings and the brutal realization that her heart was as yet unhealed. Oh, heavens above, how could she still ache like this?

Emily leaped for the trailing leash, but Frieda bounded up the stairs. For all her size and bloodcurdling noise, the dog wasn't snarling or threatening in any way. She wriggled with joy.

Emily had last seen Bracebridge over a year ago. They had met—her fault, all her fault, that meeting—inappropriately alone. Their usual escalation toward unrecoverable disaster had ended with harsh and brutally honest words from him. Devastating words. He'd kissed her yet again, then the embrace had spun completely out of control. His hands had been underneath her skirts, on her bare skin. She, to her everlasting shame, would have allowed him anything. Anything at all. But he'd stopped. Pulled away and told her, in no uncertain terms, that he would never love her, that she must not have any expectations of him.

Without exaggeration, the encounter had crushed her heart to nothing. She recognized her responsibility for that outcome. She did. He loved her eldest sister, not her. He would never love anyone but Anne. How could his heart not be broken beyond anyone's ability to repair it?

Anne had been forced to marry the Duke of Cynssyr, one of Bracebridge's closest friends, when everyone, Emily included, had expected a match between Anne and Bracebridge. The fault for that lay squarely with the duke. On that infamous night when Anne had been dosed with laudanum, the duke had been found in her bed. His claims of mistake changed nothing. Anne and Cynssyr had married the next day.

Frieda woofed again.

Emily just missed regaining the trailing end of the leash, allowing the dog to reach Bracebridge and rear up on her hind legs. Her front paws landed on his chest. Frieda was heavy, strong, and intent on licking his face.

"Good day to you, too, milady." Bracebridge rubbed the dog's ears, then gently pushed her back to all four paws and down the last of the stairs. At least he wasn't angry; Emily was grateful for that.

Emily tried for the leash again, but the moment Bracebridge was off the stairs, Frieda reared up to attempt another face-lick. "Honestly, Frieda! Down!" Emily missed the leash yet another time. He had yet to fully register her presence and truly see her. In the instant when he did, she watched with dismay as his smile vanished and his eyes turned hard.

How utterly humiliating that her stomach was full of butterflies. She would absolutely not let him see that nothing had changed for her. "Oh, drat, Frieda. Behave!"

"Down," he said in that dark, unyielding voice that never failed to send a shiver down Emily's spine. The dog did not precisely obey, but she did return to four legs. He grabbed the leash near where it fastened to her collar and pulled the loose end until he had the strap firmly in hand.

Emily was relieved, not to her credit, by this excuse to delay or defuse what was plainly going to be an uncomfortable and awkward encounter. She'd never intended to fall in love with anyone, but one day, not long after

Anne was married, she'd seen him walk into a room, and all these feelings had simply appeared and refused to be dislodged from her heart. "I beg your pardon, my lord," she said.

He didn't immediately respond to the first words spoken between them in over a year. Yes. Thank goodness for Frieda.

"She hasn't ruined your coat or shirt, has she?" Besides being monstrously large, Frieda had the worst traits of several breeds; a deerhound's wiry coat, but greyish-brindle instead of a solid color, the floppy ears and jowls of a bloodhound, a mastiff's girth, and the tendency to slobber of all those breeds.

"Not at all." He crouched and rubbed Frieda's ears. She pressed the top of her head to the center of his chest and wagged her tail hard enough to move half her body. He glanced up, and Emily caught the fading edge of his frustrated look. If she told anyone just how bad things had got with Papa lately, she'd be forced to leave the Cooperage to live with one of her sisters. If that happened, Bracebridge would have to give up his friendship with her brothers-in-law.

"I came to see Mary and the children," she said abruptly, the heat in her cheeks a further reminder that she was not anything like sanguine. Mary, Lady Aldreth, was wife to Baron Aldreth of Rosefeld and the second of Emily's three sisters. The four women had endured a great deal when they were growing up. Their mother died when Emily was quite young, and Anne, still a girl herself, had stepped in to run the household in the face of their father's utter inability to manage anything himself.

"Did you?" Bracebridge said with understandable skepticism. He didn't know—no one did—that Papa was drunk most days or that if she forgot to lock her door, he'd come in looking for something to convert to ready cash. She'd quickly learned the only safe hiding place for money to pay the taxes and put toward the most pressing bills was in a tin box she kept buried at the southern edge of the property.

"I did not know you were here," she said. Unfortunately, for the past three days, Papa had been in one of his states. She'd spent her time taking Frieda on long walks or hiding in her room with the door locked. "I'd have stayed away otherwise."

Given that her sisters were married to men Bracebridge called friends, the best and most obvious way to avoid him had been to remain at the Cooperage with her father. She was not deluded enough to believe he had not himself declined invitations likely to bring him into contact with her. She'd done the same.

Her persistent and unreciprocated love was a hopeless case. Some people refused to overlook his disreputable past, most notably and painfully her own father, who had banned Bracebridge from the Cooperage shortly after Bracebridge first offered for her sister. Of course, he had not been Bracebridge at the time. No one had expected he, as the youngest of seven boys, would inherit.

She was not privy to the details, but Bracebridge's late father had all but disinherited him when, as a boy, he refused to join the navy or the army. Thereafter Bracebridge had supported himself as a prizefighter and, soon after, as the owner and operator of several enterprises, the nature of which were the subject of scandalized whispers.

"I suppose meeting again was inevitable," he said carefully. He maintained his prizefighter's physique to this day, and though his style of dress was always austere, she liked that about him nearly as much she liked his size, his sense of humor, and that air about him that suggested he was about to do something wicked and did not care what anyone thought.

He gave Frieda another pat, then stood. He smiled—not warm, but not unfriendly—and she ignored the spark of attraction that shot through her. His eyes were inky black, his hair the same color, all unruly curls, and his nose was slightly crooked. He wasn't a handsome man, but when he walked into a room, everyone stared. He took effortless command by presence alone.

"I suppose so." She stayed where she was and prayed she looked composed, even though she wasn't. She would not have blamed him if he'd refused to speak to her. Through no fault of his, her feelings had become engaged, and he had not returned them. She had reacted strongly to him from the very day they met, when she was a girl scarcely old enough to guess there might be something more behind her admiration of him.

"Good afternoon then, Em." He flinched, and she ignored his use of the too-familiar diminutive.

"My lord." She curtseyed with the formality due an acquaintance of his status, rather than someone she had known since she was a girl. She had no choice but to be done with him. "Have a pleasant outing."

A year ago, the tension between them would have destroyed any possibility of either of them walking away unscathed from the encounter. She was, she wanted to believe, now better able to moderate her behavior with him.

"Thank you."

The coldness of his reply stirred up old hurts, but she had vast experience suppressing emotions she did not wish to display. He had no way of knowing she was determined to overcome her feelings for him. He surely and understandably believed he was still in danger of unwanted emotion from her. She ignored the tiny, resentful voice in her head that said he bore some responsibility for what had happened.

"Forgive me, Miss Sinclair. I did not mean to speak so curtly to you."

Miss Sinclair. Emily understood the need for distance between them. All the same, his formality was a blow. Which did she prefer? A too intimate address or one that was too formal? She hated both.

"I have an engagement this afternoon," he said.

She steeled herself. True, she had meticulously avoided him for more than a year, but she wasn't a fool. He'd been to Bartley Green several times in the past months, and she'd long ago guessed the reason. She summoned a smile of the sort she had perfected with dozens of men who needed to be discouraged. How ironic that she must use that skill now, when she was dying inside. "With Miss Glynn?"

Clara Glynn was Emily's dearest friend. She hated herself for wishing she was wrong about them. Clara deserved to be happy, and so did Bracebridge.

"Yes." His relief was a knife across her heart. "I'm to meet Miss Glynn and her brother."

"Please give them my regards." She was astonished by her poise. What an actress she was.

"I shall," he said.

"Frieda. Dear dog, do come here." She clicked her tongue several times, to no avail. Frieda sat on his feet. She looked at the dog, her heart aching with affection. "Be so kind as to hand me her leash, would you, my lord? I'll hold her so you may escape in safety."

"That seems an odd name for a dog."

She did not want this cool, remote acquaintance. She wanted the heat of his touch, the shiver of his eyes on her, looking at her as if she were the only woman in existence. Except that had never been true for him. She'd misinterpreted everything. "I think the name suits her."

"Frieda." He shook his head. "Was it Aldreth or your sister who chose that name? Or one of the children?"

"I chose the name." More proof that he held her in low regard. He considered her frivolous, vain, and spoiled, and most of that was true. She would trade her beauty in an instant if doing so would grant her but half the character of any of her sisters.

"Indeed?"

"Frieda is my dog." She held out her hand for the leash, but he didn't give it over.

She was twenty-two compared to his thirty-four, but that wasn't an insurmountable difference to her. It had been for him. The whole trouble was, she'd never been attracted to men her own age. She'd only ever wanted him.

He continued to hold the leash. She had the awful feeling he was debating whether to invite her to accompany them on their walk. God, no. She'd never survive watching him court her best friend. He settled his weight onto one hip and slightly hunched his shoulders to make himself shorter, as he so often did with women who were not tall. Clara was a more comfortable height for him.

"She's a splendid dog," he said.

"She certainly fancies you."

A quick smile appeared on his mouth, froze in place, then vanished. The distance between them took on a weight she did not entirely understand. "Mystifying, isn't it?" he said.

Oh, another mistake. Resolutely, she ignored the past that lived in that statement and prayed he would, too. She wasn't the same person she'd been a year ago. She was wiser now.

"To be sure, my lord." The sooner she extricated herself from this conversation, the better. She held out her hand for the leash, but infuriatingly, he did not give it to her. "As you see, Frieda is as beautiful as she is well behaved."

He patted Frieda's head. "She's good natured."

"And loyal and brave."

"Admirable qualities, all."

The front door opened as he was extending the leash to her.

Harry Glynn entered, followed by his sister, and Emily's heart fell to the very end of the earth. Clara stopped a few steps from the door and looked between Bracebridge and Emily. Bracebridge smiled at Clara with a fondness Emily had never seen from him except where Anne was concerned. He deserved to be happy.

"There you are, Bracebridge," Glynn said too heartily. "We thought you'd forgot us, but what better reason for delay than a beautiful woman?" He clapped a hand on Bracebridge's shoulder.

She only just managed to restrain Frieda from attempting to greet the Glynns with kisses. "Down, Frieda. Down." She was delighted when the dog obeyed. "Stay." While she had the chance, she went to Clara and kissed her cheek. Kind, generous Clara was the very best friend one could have, and she was absolutely the sort of woman Bracebridge ought to marry. "How lovely to see you."

Clara briefly squeezed Emily's hand. "I say the same to you."

"Miss Sinclair," Glynn said in a softer voice. "You are perfection, as always."

"Thank you." She had always treated Harry Glynn with the familiarity that came with a lifelong acquaintance. She had never encouraged his recent admiration of her. He was too close to her age and, well, not Bracebridge.

Glynn patted Frieda on the head, and the dog gazed at him as if the sun rose and set on his broad shoulders. "You mustn't leave us to fend for ourselves, Miss Sinclair." He knew the trick of keeping a hand on Frieda to prevent her jumping on him. He grinned. "What a propitious meeting, for here you are, cloak and hat already donned for an outing on this beautiful autumn day."

"I came to see the children." Mary and Aldreth had three, two boys and a girl. "Bracebridge was on his way out whilst I was on my way in. He was detained by meeting Frieda. You know how she must make a friend of everyone new to her."

"We aren't going far," Glynn said. He snapped his fingers, and Frieda came to attention. Her tail thumped against Bracebridge's thighs. "You see how she anticipates an excursion."

"She's already had a walk from the Cooperage to here. Besides, I haven't seen the children in an age."

She must have convinced everyone she hadn't a care in the world, for Clara said, "Well, Harry and I haven't seen *you* for an age. Join us, won't you?" "Come, Miss Sinclair," Glynn said. "My sister is correct. We've not seen you in too long."

"Please?" Clara squeezed her hand again, and Emily's heart sank. If she refused now, she would seem childish and petty.

"Please do," Bracebridge said when she caught his eye. His request *seemed* genuine.

"Very well, then. Frieda and I should be delighted." She looped Frieda's leash several times around her hand, then extended her other arm to Harry Glynn. Though he was not as tall as Bracebridge, he laid proper claim to six feet. Emily scarcely reached his shoulder. Why couldn't she return his affection? He was tall, handsome, and good-natured, yet in all the time she'd known him, he had never made her insides shiver.

Outside, Frieda pulled Emily several paces ahead until she was well ahead of the others. She walked briskly, doing her best to control excitable, gigantic Frieda, all the while excruciatingly aware she was using the dog as an excuse to walk alone. Harry caught up with her from time to time. He did so, she knew, to give Bracebridge and Clara privacy.

At one point when Harry had fallen into step with her, she picked up a stick and waved it just out of Frieda's reach. "Tell me," she said, "have you ever seen such a sight as Frieda with her ears flapping and her tail wagging?"

"Unique among canines, I dare say." Harry had helped her rescue Frieda when she was a starving, aggressive young stray living in the alley near the Bartley Green livery stable.

"She's growing into a monstrously large dog."

"You've an affinity for the monstrous," he said gently.

Those soft words defeated her utterly, and she found she had to swallow several times against the lump in her throat.

"Why not let Frieda off her leash? It would do her good to exhaust herself."

"Oh, no!" she said without thinking. "She might run away. What if she does and cannot find her way back?" Her fear was unreasonable, but it was also unshakeable.

"That is unlikely," he said.

"She doesn't always come when she's called." She held tight to Frieda's leash while she and Harry walked side by side in a silence that was no longer comfortable. She wanted badly to look behind her at Clara and Bracebridge and, eventually, she could not resist. She looked. Clara was laughing at something Bracebridge had said to her. He was smiling, too.

Harry sighed. "There's no shortage of women who like what he has on offer."

"Mr. Glynn, I—I am sorry. Forgive me for my thoughtlessness." She faced him and immediately regretted doing so because she could see Bracebridge and Clara walking slowly, arm in arm.

He was courting her. Clara, her dearest friend. What sort of awful person was she to wish that were not so?

"I hope you do not misunderstand what I'm about to say." Harry took Emily's arm and turned her around. "I don't mean to give you hope where there is none. I meant what I said about Bracebridge and other women. He has a savage charm that appeals. But not, I worry, to my sister."

"I don't care what anyone says about him." No one knew that three years ago, shortly after Anne's marriage, Emily had seen Bracebridge without a stitch of clothing. The incident was burned into her soul. Him very deliberately getting out of bed and standing in front of her, daring her to faint. Savage charm, indeed. "That is in the past. He's not a prizefighter anymore."

"No, not that." Harry meant a good deal more by that oblique denial than he was willing to say to her. She supposed his disapproval had to do with the source of Bracebridge's personal wealth.

"I mean no disrespect," she said, "but I sincerely hope your mother does not intend to interfere." Few people disapproved of Bracebridge more than Clara's mother and, naturally, one of them was Emily's father. Emily disagreed vehemently with all of his detractors, and she held tight to that anger because it helped soothe her hurt and jealousy.

Harry did not immediately reply, but when he did, it was thoughtfully. "She'll interfere. She cannot help herself. But the fact is, Lord Bracebridge has asked for and received my permission to court Clara."

She stared at the path ahead. Her happiness for Clara and Bracebridge was dwarfed by her abject misery. Harry was the head of the family since his father had passed away. So, yes, Bracebridge would apply to Harry for permission.

"I'll manage my mother. But now I have a question for you." His tone went from avuncular to something too intimate.

"Oh, Harry, no."

"Do you know what Bracebridge told me to do?"

She did not want to know. She shook her head to discourage him.

"He told me that if I wished to engage your affections, I should tell you I find you beautiful beyond words and that I love you with a mad passion."

She refused to cry. She absolutely would not.

"You see how badly he underestimates you," Glynn said softly. "Sinclair women are immune to flattery."

Emily tossed her head. She was an expert at smiling, no matter the circumstances. "I adore being told I'm beautiful."

"You hate it."

She tossed Frieda another stick, throwing it just to the length of the leash. They watched in silence while she destroyed the stick in two bites.

"Consider this: I understand where your heart lies. Call me a fool, but that state of affairs cannot last, not without encouragement. Not past his marriage. We could grow old together, you and I."

The weather was fine. Blue sky, only a hint of a breeze. "With your mother?"

"I would not have her in my household. Mama must live at Withercomb surrounded by her memories of our father and her iron hold on the society of Bartley Green. You and I can make our home elsewhere. Far from here." He gestured. "Far from your father. Far from the Earl of Bracebridge."

"I cannot leave Papa." That was a lie. How could she marry Harry Glynn when it meant she would regularly see Bracebridge? However far away they went, one saw family on holidays and other occasions. It was inevitable. She simply could not bear the idea of having to pretend her heart wasn't broken.

"The sentiment greatly behooves you. Clara feels the same loyalty toward our mother. However, I will not allow your father to live with us any more than I would permit my mother to do so. My willingness to support his more objectionable habits is already nonexistent. But he won't starve, and I promise I shall keep a roof over his head."

"Your confidence in my character is misplaced," she said.

"I think not." He sighed. "I am not foolish enough to make you an offer yet. But I don't want to see you spend the rest of your life looking after your father. Not after the way he's treated you and your sisters. I do indeed mean to speak ill of him." He pressed her arm. "If your situation becomes intolerable, you must inform me. I'll have us in Gretna Green as soon as possible."

"An elopement?" She laughed.

"Marriage is a permanent solution to your difficulties with your father."

He was right, of course. Marriage was her only escape from her intolerable situation at home. But she needed a husband who would also provide her an escape from Bracebridge. Who, though, would marry her, only to give up the considerable advantage and influence of her connections to her brothers-in-law?

Chapter Two

ALDRETH'S BUTLER APPROACHED BRACEBRIDGE and, in a low voice, said, "A Mr. Gopal Rachagorla is downstairs asking for you."

Bracebridge sat straight. He and Aldreth were in the breakfast room, about to go fishing, so it was still dark out. A caller at this hour was reason for concern. The last time Gopal had been obliged to fetch him back to London, the authorities had been threatening to shut down Two Fives.

Two Fives was a gaming hell at 55 St. James's Street, London, that he continued to operate in direct partnership with Gopal. He'd transferred the others to Gopal shortly after he was invested with his title.

"He says his business is urgent, my lord."

The timing of Gopal's call could not have been more unfortunate. Leaving Rosefeld now, and so abruptly, would not advance his case with Clara. He was anxious to have the uncertainty of Clara's affections for him resolved. He put down his tea. "May I use your study?"

"You may, of course." Aldreth dabbed the corner of his mouth with his serviette. Aldreth and his wife had met Gopal several times, seeing as Gopal often dined at Bracebridge's London home. "Tell Mr. Rachagorla he is welcome to stay for as long as it pleases him. Lady Aldreth and I should be delighted to have him as our guest."

"I'll extend the invitation." To the butler, Bracebridge said, "I'll see him immediately. You'll bring us tea and something to eat?"

"My lord."

Once in Aldreth's study with the door closed, Bracebridge assessed his friend's state and was relieved to see no sign of agitation. Good. Good. The last thing he wanted was a scandal for Mrs. Glynn to get wind of. He took a calming breath. "Two Fives remains open for business, I trust?"

"Yes." Gopal walked to the window and gazed out. The sun was just barely tinting the horizon pink and orange amid the grey. Gopal knew nothing sensitive could be said until the servants had come and gone, and so his first remark was banal. "It's lovely here."

They'd come far in their decade-long friendship. In those early days of struggle, neither of them had leisurely watched a sunrise, and if they had, it would not have been from the inside of a centuries-old house like Rosefeld.

A sunrise view was hard to come by in Cheapside. At the time, Bracebridge had been determined to prove the truth of every accusation his father had thrown at him. That he was incorrigible, disrespectful, a reprobate, and a disgrace to the family, among other choice epithets leveled at him. At the time, Gopal, only recently arrived from India, had found himself at loose ends after his employer's bride objected to Gopal's presence in her household. He had wandered down the same street where Bracebridge, then plain Mr. Devon Carlisle, had been looking to start a fight. Gopal had dissuaded him from that foolishness.

"There'll be refreshments soon," Bracebridge now said.

"Excellent." Gopal turned from the window. He was a tall, slender man, younger than Bracebridge by five or so years, well-formed and handsome.

As usual, his friend was impeccably dressed. Though he sometimes wore garb native to his country, he typically wore English clothes, as he did today, and with an élan all his own.

He'd known Two Fives was a going concern the day he saw a gentleman in what he privately referred to as the Rachagorla waistcoat. The style was distinguished by close-fit silk in bright colors, exquisite embroidery, and a slightly higher collar than most. Nothing outlandish, but enough for a discerning eye to notice. No man of fashion could hope to succeed in the Rachagorla waistcoat without a perfectly tied neckcloth. Gopal's, of course, was perfection itself.

"Sit, please." He did so himself, but Gopal returned to a contemplation of the view. Their meeting had been fortuitous, and their friendship unstinting. Because of Gopal, Devon Carlisle had become a wealthy man. Bloody richer than a military career would have made him, and sooner, too. Gopal often reminded him that they were wealthy because of their partnership, and this, he had to admit, was true. They had different yet complementary talents.

"I could gaze for hours at such a view," Gopal said. Though he retained the accent of his homeland, his English was impeccable. He had adapted to life among the English. He was literate in the language and fluent in society. He looked a gentleman, spoke softly and kindly, and possessed a ruthless streak to rival Bracebridge's own.

A footman entered with tea and a selection of dishes, and they fell silent while the repast was set out.

"Stay then. Enjoy the view. They'd be delighted if you did. I hope you will consider it." He'd be glad if Gopal were to stay to celebrate his engagement and see the door close on his broken heart.

"If I am able, yes." The footman departed, and Gopal served himself tea. Bracebridge declined more for now.

"Stay for luncheon, at the very least."

Gopal took a sip of tea and brushed a lock of black-as-night hair from his forehead. "That would be agreeable."

"Assuming we don't both make an immediate return to Town, I look forward to that." He was now sanguine about Gopal's presence here. If this were something dire enough to require his presence in London, Gopal would already have told him. Still, whatever had brought him here must and would be dealt with. "If Two Fives is open for business, what brings you to Bartley Green?"

"My friend." Gopal shook his head and drank more tea. His waistcoat was peacock blue with gold and silver embroidery—a thing of beauty. Gopal's striking looks were suited to the embellishments of fashion. For himself, Bracebridge did not see the point. "I am not certain I ought to have disturbed your leisure, and at such an hour as this." He arched an eyebrow and cocked his head, a half smile on his mouth. "Have you news for me?"

"Soon, I hope." Gopal's vague words were intended to ask whether Bracebridge had news of an engagement. He relaxed even more. *This* was friendship: Gopal wanting to share in the happiness of an event that would transform his life yet again.

Gopal bowed and helped himself to a slice of toast, asking, "Nothing for you?" Bracebridge shook his head. "May you find happiness in her answer."

"I hope you'll stay. I want to introduce her to you."

"I should like that very much."

He imagined Gopal raising a glass in a toast of congratulations along with Aldreth and his wife. Emily, too, for that matter. He sincerely hoped they were past their difficulties. That was an end to be wished for: to be friends with all the Sinclair sisters. "Now, then." He settled himself on his chair. "You are here. The reason must be important, or you would not have come all this way."

Gopal finished his toast, then drew a packet of papers from the slim case he'd brought with him. He placed the papers on Aldreth's desk. "Behold." He flashed a grin that had devastated women wherever the two of them traveled. Bracebridge did not doubt the devastation continued. "Whether with dismay or pleasure, I cannot say."

Bracebridge walked over to have a look. The packet consisted predominately of scraps of paper, half sheets of foolscap, a bill of fare, a portion of a pamphlet, and several sheets of the letterhead provided by Two Fives for the convenience of gentlemen required to document their debts. "What are these?"

"The reason I have come all this way and perhaps delayed whatever fate is to befall you here. Please." Gopal set a finger on top of the papers. "I beg you examine them, my lord, for then the reason for my visit shall become plain."

True, as it turned out. All too true. The papers were a collection of vowels signed by one Thomas Sinclair of the Cooperage, Bartley Green. Ten pounds, twenty, fifty. Five hundred. Over a thousand. Three thousand pounds. Another for nearly as much as the last. "I hadn't realized he was playing as deeply as this."

"Nor I."

The bill of fare fell to the floor, reverse side up. When Bracebridge retrieved it, the numbers written on the page shocked him. "Bloody sodding—"

"I took the liberty of acquiring these from the various persons who possessed them." Gopal pulled over a chair and sat, elbow propped on the arm, while Bracebridge continued to scan through the documents. "Just over eleven thousand for them all." He evened out his cuffs. "It was necessary to offer more than fair value to secure them all. However, the majority are from Two Fives."

"Understood." Bracebridge counted the notes. More than a dozen, double that, even. Thirty-bloody-seven, in fact. As he arranged them by date, he asked, "Acquired how recently?"

"Over the preceding three days." Gopal smiled in that way that implied no good for anyone, and leaned close to select another of Sinclair's notes. "This convinced me I must act immediately."

Bracebridge let go of the others and took the paper Gopal held. A chill slid down his spine as he scanned it. Damn, damn, damn. Gopal had been right to come here with this. "I'll repay you, of course." Gopal would not have used business funds for this, not unless he'd had no choice, and with this amount, he may have had to. "Do you need a bank draft, or can it wait until I'm back in Town?"

"It can wait."

The document Bracebridge held was on Two Fives letterhead, dated four days ago. It bore the signature of Thomas Sinclair and signed over the Cooperage to the bearer. Concerning enough on its own, but there was more, far more.

Bracebridge returned to ordering the notes by date. The bulk of the debts had been incurred in the preceding six weeks, but the oldest was eight months ago. In all that time, Sinclair, with a daughter still at home and dependent upon him, had been to London at least once a month, if not more often, losing money he had not repaid.

Bracebridge stared at the stack of notes. Emily lived with her father, yet, to his knowledge, she'd said nothing about this. Not a word to anyone, and it was a certainty that if she had, he would have heard about it. Apparently, however far gone Sinclair was, it was not far enough gone to affect the most spoiled of his four daughters. "What's the gossip in Town?"

"Until now, remarkably dull."

Personally, he didn't give a fig if Sinclair was bankrupt. In fact, he'd take satisfaction from the man's personal ruin. But he'd do anything to spare Anne unhappiness and the loss of the Cooperage. She would be devastated. Not to mention that, like Gopal, Bracebridge saw malign intent in what amounted to a staggering set of losses at a gaming hell everyone understood was connected to him.

The authorities generally looked the other way, but certain sanctimonious members of society publicly decried the fortunes lost at such places as

Two Fives. They filled the papers and magazines with screeds calling for the end of businesses whose sole purpose, according to them, was the ruin of the country's youth. Mrs. Glynn was among the most vocal objectors. It was no secret that she held him in some degree of contempt.

Gopal's actions had solved only one dilemma. The question they faced now was how quickly the gossip would spread from London to Bartley Green and, specifically, to the ear of Mrs. Glynn and her ilk. Bracebridge easily imagined Mrs. Glynn's pleasure at hearing rumors that he had deliberately ruined Thomas Sinclair. He had no doubt such rumors would soon be circulating. The question was how damaging that would be to his hopes of marrying Clara Glynn. "Thank you," he said to Gopal. With the notes in one hand, he stood. "How can I ever repay you for this?"

"My friend." Gopal put a hand over his heart. "You would do the same for me."

"Without question or a moment's hesitation." They clasped hands tightly. "I am indeed fortunate in your friendship."

"And I in yours."

Bracebridge returned Sinclair's notes to the case and tucked it into his inside coat pocket. "Now, I shall beard the lion in his den. Whatever happens, I shall have that satisfaction."

"Is there any chance the man's silence can be bought?"

"Vanishingly small, I fear. His hatred for me matches mine for him." He took a step toward the door. "In the meantime, enjoy your visit."

If he was right and Sinclair had acted out of spite, then it was likely too late. He'd have sown seeds of rumor in fertile soil. It might already be too late to prevent gossip, but either way, Bracebridge was going to take a great deal of satisfaction from telling Sinclair who held his notes.

"I should be back before luncheon. I hope you stay. Lord and Lady Aldreth will be disappointed if you do not, as shall I."

On this way out, he met Harry Glynn coming up the stairs behind Aldreth's butler. Glynn held his hat and riding whip in one hand. He was not smiling. "My lord," Glynn said with a bow. "We must speak."

Chapter Three

E MILY TOOK A deep breath. Her father needed only moments to upend her life, but as usual these days, he was oblivious to her distress and dismay. She wanted to leave. To run away, to shut herself in a room, lock the door, and never come out.

Papa headed for the bell pull. "I'll have Mrs. Elliot show him in."

"I need a moment, if you don't mind." She forced herself to smile when he came back to kiss her cheek. She was shaking, quite literally shaking. Had he done this to Lucy, too? To Mary and Anne? Had they felt as helpless as she did when he had attempted to engineer marriages they did not want?

"You must not keep him waiting, my girl." The *him* in question was Mr. Walter Davener. She'd seen him arrive three quarters of an hour ago and hadn't thought much of it until Papa had summoned her here.

"No, Papa." Her thoughts kept slipping around what Papa expected of her and slamming up against what she wanted. To escape, yes. But with Walter Davener?

Anger surged back, overwhelming all else. Papa had arranged all this without once speaking to her about whether she wanted to marry anyone at all. As if she meant nothing to him except as a means to pay his debts.

He moved past her while she wondered whether her next breath would come. She stared into the chimney glass without seeing her face. Her hands went through the motions of adjusting her hair. No one would think anything of her delay.

"There's nothing amiss with you, my dear," Papa said.

She pretended to be absorbed by her reflection, turning her head side to side. She did not care what she looked like. "I'm not perfect," she said with more calm than she felt. Papa was as proud of her beauty as if her looks belonged to him. She was expected to be vain. "I can't possibly be seen like this. Please, Papa. You can't send him in here with me looking like this."

In the mirror, she could see her father scowling. If she did not make eye contact, she could pretend nothing had changed. She set the tip of her slipper against the fender and pushed until it hurt. The pain distracted her from her father and focused her thoughts. Was she really going to do this? Could she really spend a lifetime with that man? "He would not like to see me in such disorder."

Her father shoved his hands into his coat pockets with a mulish expression she knew too well. She gazed at his reflection, heart-hurt and angry at the same time.

With every year older she became, she understood more clearly what Anne had known for years and had tried so desperately to prevent. Time and again, Papa's actions had caused serious, lasting harm to her sisters—to Mary, to Lucy, and up to and including the disaster that had led to Anne's own marriage. Mama would never have let this happen. She would never have allowed her beloved daughters to be treated with such disregard for their happiness.

He adjusted the collar of his coat, a familiar gesture that no longer tugged at her heart the way it once had. Before her, there had been Anne, Mary, and Lucy. He could not be unaware of the harm he'd caused *them*. He couldn't be. He'd meddled with their lives, and it was only the most fantastic of luck that had given her sisters' marriages to men they'd come to love. "You would have married Cynssyr in a heartbeat," he said. "Do not tell me you object to a man whose wealth may well exceed even the duke's."

True. She would have. But not because she wanted to be a duchess. She'd only ever wanted to marry Bracebridge, but she would have married Cynssyr because it would have meant some measure of safety for Anne and Lucy. What a foolish girl she'd been. She still was. Bracebridge was going to marry Clara, and Emily didn't even have the cold comfort of such a union being a poor one.

At least if she married Mr. Davener, she'd never have to see Bracebridge again. Almost never.

"My dear. I mean to call at Rosefeld to announce our delightful news." He grinned.

"What? Today?" Her heart clenched.

The corner of his mouth twitched. "He is impatient, and I agreed there was no reason for delay. He has a special license, my dear! Think of that!"

"I wonder why he wants to speak to me at all." But the dryness of her tone was lost on her father.

"Naturally, he wishes to secure your positive response and pay his respects to his future bride. Everything is arranged. We have an appointment with my banker, and all the rest is settled. There is no reason not to have everything done before dinner."

"Is that what you told Lucy?" The accusation bubbled up from deep inside her, raw and aching. When had he ever worried about any of his daughters? "Or Mary?" She covered her face with her hands until she'd regained control of her temper. She reached into that dark closet and grasped the truth hard. To her father, she was but the means to an end. Nothing else.

"I don't expect you to understand, my dear." She recognized that tone. It came from the bottom of a bottle where Papa lived these days. "But this you can and must know, you ungrateful wretch. A man with four daughters to marry off had best cultivate men of rank and fortune. Men like Walter Davener."

She clenched her hands and lifted her face to his. "Other fathers do not ask their daughters to marry men they scarcely know and have reason to dislike, and I dislike *him*. Exceedingly."

"What use are you if you won't do your duty? It's high time someone else took on the expense of keeping you in fripperies and frocks. Not to mention that damned monster of a dog. You're nothing but a burden to me. There's a constant hole in my pocket from keeping you here."

Never mind that Cynssyr and Aldreth had paid for her clothes or that anything she spent on herself came from funds she'd been hoarding for years. "True, you have the expense of my room and board, but who runs your household, Papa? Who sees the bills are paid from what little I can keep back? Who begs and pleads with every merchant in Bartley Green to extend us a little more credit? It isn't you."

"I'll have no disrespect from you." His lip curled. "You've never cared for the history of the Sinclairs."

"That's not so!"

"—or for the memory of your mother."

"No. No! That's not so."

"You cannot possibly know what we lost when she died." His voice broke. "You've never cared what happened to me or the Sinclair name."

"Papa, no." She'd been so young when Mama died that she remembered her grief more than anything else, yet the soothing calm of her mother's voice remained part of her. The loving kisses, the scent of her perfume, how safe and adored Emily had felt. She remembered that, too, and every day of her life, she'd wondered what her mother would have thought of her, her sisters, and their father.

"If you did, you would have been born a boy."

"That's absurd." But he was too drunk to understand anything but his building rage.

"You cannot understand what it means for a man to have a son to carry on his name. You're a useless female. What good is your beauty if it doesn't buy me anything?"

Her stomach clamped down hard on itself. She was almost angry enough to marry Walter Davener just so she'd never have to see her father again.

"How dare you consider for even a moment rejecting a union that keeps the house your mother so loved in the hands of a Sinclair—your dear mama's own grandchild!"

No argument she could summon would change his mind or the facts that had brought her to this moment. No argument existed that made her matter more than a son to inherit the past and bring it into the future. There was nothing more she could say to him. She was beloved only while or if she was of use to him. She turned back to the mirror and adjusted her hair with hands that shook.

"If he leaves because he's grown tired of waiting for you, you'll have no place in this house," Papa said. "I'll turn you out and have the doors locked and barred against you. You're no daughter of mine if you don't."

Her sisters were safe, she told herself. They were married, and Papa could no longer harm them. "Five minutes," she said. "Tell him I'll see him in five minutes."

"There's a good girl."

She gripped the mantel until he was gone. While she counted to a hundred, she stared at her reflection. She hated the face she saw there. Despised it. "I am strong," she whispered. "I am. They all say Anne is the strong one, but I am strong, too. Stronger than they guess."

The door opened, and Mr. Walter Davener entered. She forced herself to turn and smile at the man.

"My dear Miss Sinclair." He bowed and began talking and talking and talking, and then silence fell. He cleared his throat. "You are overcome."

"Yes." He was exactly as awful as he'd ever been. He bored her. Not one original thought came from his head. He was dismissive of her, interrupting her constantly to explain the simplest of concepts as if she hadn't a brain in her head. If she married him, she'd want to murder him before the year was out.

Mr. Davener headed toward her and she moved behind a chair and gripped the top edges. "Your beauty moves me to poetry. 'From the heavens she has been made, a maid Divine.'" He whirled a finger in the air. "'Made' as in fabricated or born of man and 'maid,' m-a-i-d, as in you. I've been searching for the proper rhyme for 'divine.'"

She clutched the chair harder. "Repine. Recline. Line, sign, its homonym, syne, vine, kine, mine, nine, pine, dine, fine, tine—though that would be difficult to make fit—wine."

"O'er hill, dale and—" He waggled his eyebrows at her. "Vale."

"That does not rhyme with divine."

"Verses, my dear girl. Verses have meter and rhyme—"

"Yes, Mr. Davener. I am aware. You were saying?"

"I trust your father, good man that he is, has explained everything to you. The reason I am here, that is."

Her throat closed up.

"I am absolutely delighted. What children we shall have, you and I. You remain overcome, I well understand. Take a moment to reflect upon your good fortune." He sat at the desk and took out a sheet of paper, pen, and ink. "I shall write to my esteemed uncle informing him of my happy news." He signaled a flourish in the air over the paper. "When I'm done, I shall dictate to you your greeting of delight to him. Please do use your very best penmanship."

She kept smiling, and when it was her turn to write, she scrawled the letters to near unreadability.

"Now, my dearest love, I have some business with your father, but when I return, it shall be with the vicar." He patted his coat pocket. "I can only imagine your delight at the prospect of becoming Mrs. Walter Davener."

Chapter Four

BRACEBRIDGE REMOVED HIS HAT when Sinclair's housekeeper opened the door. He nodded at the woman. "Good day, Mrs. Elliot."

"My lord." She curtseyed but did not move aside to admit him.

"I've business with Mr. Sinclair," he said. He had no quarrel with her. Indeed, she'd always struck him as highly competent.

She winced. "I'm not to let anyone in, my lord."

A reprehensible part of him wished Gopal had been less conscientious about Sinclair and his debts. Bracebridge would have stood by happily while the bailiff evicted the man on behalf of whomever the new owner of the Cooperage would have been. "I'm afraid I must insist."

Mrs. Elliot's eyes widened. She believed Bracebridge would make good on the implied threat, and that was all he needed: her conviction that he would have her employer on the street. In truth, no matter how satisfying the idea, or how darkly he glowered at Mrs. Elliot, he could not. How could he, when the man he so despised was also Anne's father?

"My lord." She curtseyed, one hand clutching the side of the door. "I cannot allow it."

"I'll see him now or fetch the bailiff." He softened his tone. "Step aside, madam."

She backed away with a wary shrug. "Milord."

Upstairs, a door slammed. Mrs. Elliot froze when Sinclair's voice rang out: "What is the meaning of this?"

Emily's father appeared at the top of the stairs, impeccably dressed as always. He clutched a goblet in one hand and dangled a dark green bottle in the other. He took a long drink from the goblet and emptied it before he sloshed the contents of the bottle into it. "You," Thomas Sinclair said as he headed down the stairs, his attention on Bracebridge. He lurched to one side and hit the railing hard, though he managed to steady himself. "What are *you* doing here?"

Sinclair looked substantially older and more dissipated than the last time Bracebridge had seen him. Now that he was close, though his clothes were as fashionable as ever—the man was wearing a Rachagorla waistcoat, for God's sake—Bracebridge noted that his neckcloth was askew and his shirt collar was uneven on one side.

"As if you don't suspect the reason."

"Lord . . ." Sinclair drank half the contents of his goblet. "Bracebridge." He descended the last few stairs, then bowed slowly and with too much care. "You are not welcome here."

Bracebridge had enough experience with angry drunks to know to position himself in front of Mrs. Elliot; drunks like Sinclair always went after the weaker. "Sir."

"You." Sinclair pointed at Mrs. Elliot. "He is not to be admitted. Were those not my clear instructions? That blackguard purveyor of sin and despoiler of Britain's most honorable sons is not to be admitted to decent homes. *This* is a decent home."

"Yes, sir," Mrs. Elliot said with a panicked look at Bracebridge. "But—"

"Not to be admitted to the house." He emphasized each word and then gestured at the ceiling. "Is this not the house?"

"Yes, sir."

"Mr. Sinclair," Bracebridge said. "I insisted."

"I shall deal with *you* presently." Sinclair returned to Mrs. Elliot. "You are discharged. Be gone before the day is done. Tell that pretty scullery maid Nancy or Betty or Daisy or whatever her name is that she's promoted into your place." He made a shooing motion. "I'll not tolerate insubordination *and* inadequate service. It's too much for a gentleman to bear." He said that last bit with a look at Bracebridge intended to imply there was only one gentleman present.

"Mr. Sinclair—" The woman's chin firmed.

"Out!" He reeled into the wall again and knocked a small watercolor off kilter. "I'll have you arrested for trespass."

"You haven't that right," Bracebridge said. He might not throw the man out, but oh, how he would enjoy this. He intended to have every ounce of satisfaction to be extracted here.

Sinclair's watery-eyed glare pierced him. "I'll dismiss any servant I please." He snapped his fingers. "I might dismiss the entire staff, and it would be no business of yours."

"Yes, as to that." Bracebridge then addressed the housekeeper. "Pay him no need. His threats of prosecution for trespass are empty."

"Get out of my sight!" Sinclair waved the bottle. "Both of you. I won't have either of you in this house a moment longer. Conspirators, the lot of you."

"He's discharged me a dozen times," Mrs. Elliot said in a low voice. "Tomorrow he won't remember."

"No whispering!" Sinclair attempted to go around Bracebridge to reach Mrs. Elliot. "If you've something to say, say it to me directly, or I'll call you a bloody damned coward."

For years, Anne had taken the brunt of this man's anger, constantly protecting her younger sisters from his vituperation. The thought of every moment she'd been forced to accept his blame and disregard still made his heart ache. He wondered how often Emily had been alone here with her father in this condition. He prayed to God it was not often.

Bracebridge planted himself in front of Mrs. Elliot. "I would be obliged, ma'am, if you convinced Miss Sinclair to remove to Rosefeld at her soonest possible convenience." He did not want Emily here. Not with her father like this. "Before then, even."

Mrs. Elliot put a hand over her heart, stricken and pale as snow.

"Here now," Sinclair said. "What's all this whispering when I've told you not to? Plotting against me like the blackguard you are." He jabbed a forefinger at Bracebridge. "You've had it in for me since I sent you packing for having the gall to think you could marry a Sinclair."

To Mrs. Elliot, Bracebridge said, "I promise I shall handle your situation, whatever that may be. You and the staff may apply to me. If it comes to the worst, I'll see all their wages are paid. My word on it."

Sinclair slammed a hand against the wall hard enough to rattle one of the gilt-framed mirrors. "I said, get out!"

Bracebridge tipped his head toward the housekeeper. "Leave us, Mrs. Elliot. Please."

With a glance at Sinclair, she fled down the back stairs.

The moment she was gone, Sinclair sneered at him. "If you do not leave my house, I'll have you thrown out."

Now that Mrs. Elliot was downstairs, he no longer had to mind his language. He meant to enjoy every moment of this. "You haven't the right to throw me out."

"The devil, you say. This is *my* house."

"As we both know, that is not so." He savored the procession of reactions as they appeared on Sinclair's face. "It is my right to evict you from the Cooperage."

Sinclair drew back, just sober enough, thank you, to understand what Bracebridge was saying. What wouldn't Bracebridge give to crush this man's heart the way Sinclair had crushed his? "The Cooperage is now mine."

"Impossible."

He smiled. "The deed came into my possession earlier today."

Sinclair blanched, and his upper back banged against the wall. "Impossible."

"Two Fives isn't the only hell under my management." He scratched his chin but continued to smile. He blessed Gopal for having the wit to buy up those debts and all the new ones, then come immediately to inform him. "As you've been so busy telling others, I encourage gentlemen to lose all the money they have when they gamble at one of my properties. Not coincidentally, the house often finds it advantageous to buy up debts."

The other man poured more wine, but only a few drops splashed into the goblet. He focused on Bracebridge, eyes crossed and red-veined. He leaned back and blinked several times. "You won't put me on the street."

Bracebridge shrugged.

"Nor send me to debtor's prison. None of my girls would allow that. In fact, I don't believe you have got the deed. Davener bought it up, not you."

"If you thought Walter Davener would remember anything more complicated than his name, you were mistaken." He withdrew the case Gopal had given him and opened it enough for Sinclair to slide out the note relating to the Cooperage. "I believe *this* is the relevant document."

Sinclair focused on the page. Red crept up from his neck to his cheeks. "Get out."

"Mind your tongue, Sinclair," Bracebridge drawled with pure satisfaction. "This is no longer your property. Should you elect to stay, you'll find I am an unforgiving landlord."

"You are a disgrace to your father's name."

His anger receded. He'd had his heart broken before and survived. Sinclair's insults were nothing compared to that. He tucked the case back into his pocket. "I'm sure he would agree with you."

"You aren't fit to wipe the mud from Anne's shoes. You weren't before, and you aren't now."

"The Cooperage is mine," he said evenly. "If you were wise or sober, you'd worry about how you'll pay the rent."

Sinclair heaved the empty bottle at him, but Bracebridge dodged it easily. Glass shattered against the wall behind him and peppered his back. Sinclair was sliding fast into the final years of a life that had been crumbling for years. Bracebridge had no sympathy. "I'm not the only gentleman to be ruined at Two Fives."

"No, sir. You are not."

Sinclair fiddled with the middle button of his waistcoat. "I'll have your money before the end of the day."

"From Davener?" He snorted. "Why would he give you that kind of money?"

He put a finger alongside his nose. "I have my ways."

"Best hope matters are in motion. I cannot guarantee I'll be in a mood to sell to you. Or Davener. Or anyone else."

"You'll not accept payment on a debt of honor?" The lines around his mouth deepened. "I ought to have known."

"It's not a debt of honor now. It's merely a debt to be paid in due time." Bracebridge waited until he had Sinclair's attention. "In the meantime, the Cooperage is mine."

"Guttersnipe."

He managed not to laugh. "Send Davener my way. If he forgets, my attorneys will contact you regarding the disposition of the property and the terms of your continued residence here." He put on his hat. "I'll take my leave by wishing you merrily to the devil."

"This time tomorrow, you'll regret those words."

He was halfway to the door, but at that, he turned. "I doubt it." He looked Sinclair up and down. "You've already done your worst."

He closed the door firmly on his way out. He was halfway to his gig when the front door opened and a voice rang out from the portico. "My dear Lord Bracebridge!"

He turned and saw Walter Davener, of all people, start down the front stairs at the same time a groom drove Davener's carriage around the corner from the stables. Emily came down the stairs behind the man. She had Frieda on a leash and looked to be dressed for travel. His gig blocked Davener's gilded monstrosity from the front stairs, so the groom brought the carriage to a halt behind Bracebridge's rig.

"My good fellow." Davener was all smiles as he headed for Bracebridge. Behind him, Emily stopped at the bottom step. Her expression was absolutely unreadable, until she turned her head to one side and he saw indisputable evidence of recent tears. What was this? Bracebridge tried to catch her eye, but she steadfastly refused to look in his direction. What the devil was she doing stepping out with Davener?

The man had barely half the brains a sheep needed to stand in the rain, and he knew for a fact Emily did not care for Walter Davener. He'd made a notable pest of himself last season, to the point that the betting books had been full of wagers about which of Emily's brothers-in-law would take Davener in hand and propose that his attentions be directed elsewhere immediately.

"You may be the first to congratulate us."

"Oh?" He shot a look at Emily, but she was staring at the ground.

"I am the happiest man in the entire world," Davener said. "For I have secured the hand of that most beauteous of maidens, the Divine Sinclair."

"Emily," Bracebridge said. She did not look up.

"Pray, my lord," Davener said in ringing tones. "Do not address my bride-to-be in such familiar terms. It won't do. Not at all."

Bracebridge opened the door to his gig, then held out his hand to her. "Come along, Em." That got her attention. Her eyes were wide and as blue as the sky. "The dog, too."

"What is the meaning of this?"

Bracebridge put a hand on the gig door and held it open, his other hand still extended to Emily. "You don't want to marry him." He'd had his differences with Emily Sinclair, and he had deliberately withdrawn from all but the coldest of interactions with her, but that did not mean he would leave her to something like this. Not with those tears. "Whatever your father said to make you think you must do this was pure nonsense. Get in. Anne shall never forgive me if I allow this travesty."

The world froze while Emily refused to meet his gaze. Her tear-stained cheeks told a tale, didn't they? He waited, and it occurred to him that she might actually go through with this. Say what you would about her, she was loyal to her family. To a fault.

"Whatever his threats," he said, "whatever hold he has over you, I shall make it right." He held out a hand. "Come."

She took a breath, their eyes met, and she practically ran to his gig, Frieda at her side.

"Miss Sinclair," Davener called out in a confused voice, "that is the wrong vehicle. Pray come this way."

She urged Frieda up and inside, and followed with an immodest flash of ankle and calf, and no assistance from Bracebridge.

"This is entirely out of order, Miss Sinclair." Davener advanced on her, but Bracebridge caught his arm and held him back. The other man twisted to get a look at Emily. "This is no time to be driving out with another man. We are due at the vicarage! We shall be late."

Bracebridge tightened his grip on Davener's arm. He had an almost irresistible urge to connect his fist to the man's chin. "She's not going anywhere with you."

Davener lunged toward the gig. "My love!"

Bracebridge let go with an upper cross that connected soundly with Davener's jaw. The man hit the ground like a sack of dead rats.

Chapter Five

E MILY FROZE WHEN BRACEBRIDGE vaulted into the gig. The world had become fragile, and she feared it would shatter if she so much as breathed too hard. Mr. Davener remained on the ground, motionless. None of the servants, her father's or Mr. Davener's, moved or uttered a word of protest.

"Papa is at the window," she said quietly.

"To the bloody devil with your father." Bracebridge gave his pair a light touch of the whip, and they were off, leaving Walter Davener stretched out on the ground.

She looked behind her when they reached the curve of the driveway before it went straight to the road. Mr. Davener remained supine, though one of his feet twitched. One of the servants was heading to his aid. "You hit him awfully hard."

Bracebridge shrugged.

"I'm glad you did." She stayed turned around on the seat until Bracebridge directed his gig around the corner, and her last glimpse of the house disappeared. "I don't suppose I shall ever go back," she said.

"I expect not."

If she could have her way, she would live with Lucy, but unfortunately, the sister with whom she was closest was too newly married. Anne it was, then. She loved all her sisters, including Mary, but she was least pleased by the idea of living with Mary and Aldreth. She and Mary had never got on. They were too different, or perhaps too much alike.

She patted Frieda's head. Her heart continued to beat too fast, her hands shook, and her stomach was one huge knot of anxiety. "This is her first ride in an open carriage."

"She is an excellent traveler."

Emily settled onto the seat as he headed the gig toward Rosefeld. "Suppose Mr. Davener comes after us?"

"I'll hit him again, that's what."

"He's bankrupt," she said. "Papa, I mean to say. Not Mr. Davener." It was a thirty-minute drive from the Cooperage to Rosefeld, which was why she almost always walked, since it was half that time through the fields. She took a breath, to little calming effect.

"I am aware." He stared straight ahead.

Her heart gave an unwarranted leap at the thought that Bracebridge had come to her rescue. Nothing in their past supported such a conclusion. "Why were you at the Cooperage?"

"I had urgent business with your father."

"Does he owe you money?"

He let out a breath. When he spoke, he sounded oddly amused. "In a manner of speaking, yes."

"I am sorry to hear that, for he won't repay you."

With an inscrutable look at her, he said, "It happens that I am the new owner of your ancestral home."

Oh good heavens. Emily swallowed hard. "You? But Papa said it was Mr. Davener." Her anger took root again. "He lied to me?"

"Until this morning, I was unaware of the change in your father's circumstances and mine." He patted his upper left chest. "I came the moment I was presented with the deed to the Cooperage. So, no. The charge of lying cannot be laid at his feet, in this case. Until I arrived, I'm quite sure he believed Davener had taken care of matters."

For several seconds, she considered the implications of what Bracebridge had said, the first of which was that this had nothing to do with her and everything to do with Anne. "You came to crow over him, didn't you?"

He chuckled. "I won't deny that."

"Was it satisfying to tell Papa?"

"It was."

She leaned the back of her head against the seat and stared at the sky. "I don't blame you. I'd want to do the same, were I in your position." She straightened. "You really have the deed to the Cooperage?"

"Yes."

His answer shook her to the point where she was nearly incapable of speech. She pressed her head to her knees, shaking at the thought of what her future might have been.

"Em?"

After several deep breaths, she sat up. "I know you did not intend it, but if not for you, I might this very moment be standing before the vicar with Walter Davener. You were correct. I did not wish to marry him."

"I confess, I took no small satisfaction from connecting my fist to his chin."

"Does Aldreth know about the Cooperage?" He must, she thought. Surely, Bracebridge would have told him.

"Not yet."

They'd reached the point where they would make the turn toward Rosefeld. For some reason, Bracebridge pulled the rig to the side of the road. He stared at the reins clenched in his hands. "You'll never be safe from him. Not until you're married."

"Are you suggesting I ought to have married that awful man? No. Believe you me, you did me a very great turn, whether you intended to or not."

"May I ask why you did not refuse? That would have been more like you than the meek acceptance I saw from you at the Cooperage."

She picked at a snagged thread on her cloak. He wasn't asking in a disapproving manner. "I tried. That is, I did say no, but he wouldn't let up, and then Mr. Davener came in with all his ridiculous, dreadful poetry and, well, I can tell you, I was going to tell the vicar I refuse to marry anyone at all, for heaven knows Mr. Davener wouldn't listen to me any more than Papa does. And then you hit him, and it wasn't necessary." She smiled, and it felt like the first true smile of her life. "I thank you for your timely assistance."

He turned his head very slightly toward her. "Is there anyone you'd marry?"

"No." What a miracle. They'd gone nearly twenty minutes without arguing.

"Not even Harry Glynn?" he asked.

"No. Especially not Harry." She stroked Frieda's head. "My lord, I have had a wretched, wretched day. Why are we sitting here?"

In the ensuing prolonged silence, she resigned herself to frustration. At last, he answered. "I'll take you to Scotland."

"Scotland," she said, thoroughly confused. She rearranged the sentence in her head, substituting words she'd misheard for ones that made sense. Sainsbury? Salisbury? The Cotswolds? Constantinople? America? "I beg your pardon?"

"You heard me."

Very well. She *had* heard correctly. But she remained so confused, she did not respond to his intentionally vexatious tone. "For what possible reason?"

He cocked an eyebrow with that devil-may-care look that had so attracted her from the start. "The same reason any other couple hares off to Gretna Green."

Her breath stopped, but no. Not that. *That* was impossible. And yet, she was filled with the same giddiness that had overcome her all those times she'd imagined he'd say such words to her. "Forgive me," she said as coolly as she could. "I do not comprehend you."

With exaggerated and infuriating patience, he said, "I propose to take you to Scotland and, there, marry you."

She blinked. "What about Clara?" He glanced away, but too late, for she saw bitterness in his eyes, and her heart disintegrated. "But why? Brace-bridge, what happened?"

"I have been firmly told there are no circumstances under which I shall be permitted to marry Miss Glynn."

Emily was momentarily stunned to silence. "What? Clara never said that."

"No," he said in a weary voice. "Her brother did."

"That can't be. Why would he? You've been courting her for months."

"His objections arose today."

"Was it because of something Papa did?" His silence made her heart drop to her toes. "What did he do? Tell me. Tell me, Bracebridge. What lie has he told?"

"He's let it be said that I intentionally bankrupted him."

She let out a sharp laugh. "As if Papa needs any help with that. Of course I know about him." She was done with her silence on the matter. Before the end of the day, she would be with one of her sisters, because under no circumstance would she return to the Cooperage. "What happened?"

Emily listened with an ever more painful knot in her stomach as Bracebridge set out what had happened, including several details her father had omitted in the tale of woe he'd spun for her. A dozen reactions whirled through her, variations of dismay, anger, and sorrow. When he was done, she put a hand on his arm. "I am so sorry. For you both. Clara cares for you. I know she does. Can this not be repaired?"

He squeezed the reins and looked directly at her with dead, black eyes. "Scotland. Yea or nay?"

"You don't want to marry me," she said calmly. Was she truly refusing an offer of marriage from him? It seemed unreal she could do so. A dream. "You don't."

"You must be free of your father, or you'll end up married to someone worse than Davener."

"You've gone mad."

One corner of his mouth curled. "I am at liberty to assist you in your escape."

"You can't be serious." A year ago, less than a year ago, she would have told him yes without a moment's hesitation. Those words lay between them, those hurtful words he'd given her, and even after a year of reliving and reinventing his meaning, she knew he'd told her the truth. He did not love her.

He grasped her arm just above her elbow and drew her close. She was too shocked by the contact to pull away, and for several seconds she stared into his eyes and fell straight into the abyss of her attraction to him. She had always reacted to him like this. Always. She shivered.

"I assume it's true you don't wish to marry Davener or someone like him." He reached for the compartment beneath the seat and took out a blanket. He unfurled it and spread it over her lap. Since they both knew the answer to that, she didn't bother with a reply. His eyes held hers, pulling her in.

"Why? Tell me why, Bracebridge."

His gaze held hers, and his smile was truly terrifying. "Revenge."

She swallowed heard. "Against me?"

"Your father. He'll be enraged when he hears what we've done."

Her heart beat so fast, she wondered whether she might faint for the first time in her life. "God in Heaven," she whispered. "Won't he?"

He grinned, but it was a smile that turned her cold. "He'll never recover from his most beautiful and last unwed daughter marrying a man he despises. The very man whose life he intended to ruin."

The bloodlessness of his reasoning robbed her of words. She had no doubt of his sincerity. None at all.

"Marry me, and your father and the likes of Walter Davener can hang in the wind."

"You aren't in your right mind."

There was not an ounce of warmth in his eyes, the way he held himself, or his voice. "I am. Believe you me, I am."

She could not catch her breath, and for several seconds she was convinced she could not hear. But then the sound of the wind through the trees filled the silence. He adjusted his greatcoat and, without thinking, she brushed away a brown and lifeless leaf clinging to his sleeve.

They said nothing while a wagon passed heading north. When they could speak in normal tones, Bracebridge sounded as if he were discussing the weather. "You and I understand each other as well as any two people can."

An ocean lay between the words he was saying and the meaning she wanted them to have. She tipped her chin to get a good look at his face. His eyes were so dark, she could scarcely tell the difference between his pupils and his irises. Her father had destroyed his hopes not once, but twice. First Anne and now Clara. It was not right or fair.

"Come now," he said in a voice intended to beguile.

Her heart lurched horribly, as all her stupid, girlish hopes flooded back despite knowing better. She'd spent a year convincing herself she no longer loved him, and in the space of a breath, he'd returned her to that awful state of unrequited love.

He could be hers. Bracebridge could be her husband, and she could love him as any wife ought to love her husband, and no one would take her aside and warn her not to wear her heart on her sleeve. No one would tell her she should not love the man she'd married.

"You are absolutely certain you cannot repair this break with Clara?"

"Even if I could, perhaps I should not." He released a breath and stroked Frieda's dome of a head. "I am not capable of loving anyone but Anne," he said gently. "You know that. You'll never expect me to fall in love with you, for you know it cannot happen." He waited a long moment before continuing. "I wish I were different. I wish I were a better man than I am, but my heart is not mine to give."

"No," she said, only no sound emerged from her throat. She tried again. "No."

"Marry me," he said, without any sign of admiration or affection. "Marry me knowingly. No compliments from me I would not mean. Just truth. Marry me, and I shall have the coldest revenge possible, and *you* shall forevermore be safe from your father's machinations."

His low, smooth voice melted her, drowned her, pulled her under forever. He offered her what she'd longed for in her most private moments. How could she possibly tell him no?

"Well?" he asked. "What do you say?"

She needed to think and could not. He moved and for a moment, only a moment, she thought, *There, it's over. No more of this nonsense.* But he wasn't done destroying her.

"Marry me, Em." He tapped the fourth finger of her left hand. "Even for the Divine Sinclair, countess isn't too far a comedown."

He meant this, and she hadn't the will to refuse him.

He bared his teeth in a joyless smile. "Give me the satisfaction of knowing I've repaid your father in kind. Tit for tat. He took your sister from me. I'll take everything that matters to him. The Cooperage and you."

Her heart flew away with her breath, her hopes, and her sense. He meant it. For all the wrong reasons, he meant it.

"Say yes," he said with an awful amusement, "and where you are concerned, your father's pockets are permanently to let." He shifted on the seat. "Which is it to be, Em? Rosefeld? Or Gretna Green?"

Chapter Six

S HE'D LOCKED THE DOOR, which was no great surprise. He'd left Emily in their room at the coaching inn to see to his horses and rig, arrange the hiring of fresh cattle for tomorrow, and take Frieda for a much-needed walk. That last Emily had agreed to only after he'd pointed out that the dog needed exercise and relief. He'd had to swear on his soul he would not allow her to escape.

His various tasks completed, he took a brisk walk with Frieda. He'd been sitting for too many hours not to feel a need for physical exertion. Frieda had no trouble keeping up, and he rather fancied she'd be equally able to accompany him on one of his longer training breathers. Like him, Frieda was big, ungainly, and hellishly strong. She was also enthusiastic and affectionate.

Back at the coaching inn, he and the dog bounded up the stairs to the rooms he'd let. Two servants were there setting out the meal he'd ordered for them while Emily looked on. He kept Frieda on a short leash because she was equally intent upon making friends with the servants and snatching the roast they'd just set down.

Emily stood by a small table, hands behind her, looking serene and painfully beautiful. She curtsied. Too late for regrets for either of them, though, oddly enough, he had few. Perhaps even none. "My lord."

Yes, of course. They must maintain the fiction that they were already a married couple. "Good evening," he said. "My dear."

His married friends were familiar, if not demonstrative, with their wives. He could do the same with Emily. When he approached her, there was an audible metallic *thunk* when she leaned against the table. He hadn't intended to kiss her, but he did, a gentle press of his lips to her cheek. He breathed in the faint scent of lavender. At the same time he kissed her, he reached around and took the poker she had concealed. He returned it to the andiron. He could not help a smile at the idea of her gripping that poker, fully prepared to commit mayhem in defense of her person.

Since he did not dare release Frieda while the servants were here, he next put the dog in the bedchamber and closed the door, much to Frieda's vocal dismay. He dropped his valise by the door, and hung his coat and hat on the nearby pegs. "My apologies for the delay in returning to you."

"I wasn't the least bit worried." She made a face at him when he glanced at the fireplace.

"Always a pleasure to travel with a fearless woman."

She smiled fondly at him, and even he, who considered himself, if not entirely immune to her, at least highly resistant, had a moment's shock at the impact of that smile. But she, too, was playing a role—and playing it beautifully.

The younger of the two servants caught sight of her smile and stopped in his tracks. He gaped at Emily until his colleague gave him an elbow in the ribs. The servant was young, yes, practically a boy, but he ought to know better than to stare like that at any woman.

Emily turned her attention to the desk. She'd placed her hat there and spread out the ribbons to dry; it had begun to rain during the last hour and half of their northward drive.

The younger servant continued to gaze at her. "An angel," he said slowly. "The most beautiful angel I've ever seen."

Emily kept her back to the room, to all appearances unaware of any of them. A deliberate withdrawal. While Emily was absorbed in ensuring the ribbons of her hat would be dry by morning, Bracebridge escorted the servants to the door. He handed each a coin before he shut the door after them.

The moment he shot the bolt, Emily turned around. Well. So. Yes, a woman of her beauty attracted notice, but it had been plain even to him that the youth had made her uncomfortable. For the first time, he wondered whether she found such attentions unwelcome. What a peculiar position to find himself in. All this time, he'd assumed she would be insulted if she were not admired. "He ought to have been better behaved," he said.

She shrugged, her expression smooth and untroubled. There'd been a time when he'd never doubted what she was thinking. Now he had no idea, and that unsettled him.

He released Frieda from the bedroom, inordinately relieved by the distraction of her frantic greeting of them both.

While he was busy rubbing the dog's belly, he said, "There should be something for her, Em. Would you mind?"

She found the plate of raw meat he'd ordered and set it on the floor. "There, darling dog."

Bracebridge was struck by how well and truly his life had changed. Emily Sinclair was now his responsibility. No matter how little they had in common, their lives were permanently entwined. "Give me a moment to wash up."

She sat sideways on a chair, by turns watching Frieda and him. He flicked raindrops from his sleeve and withdrew his pistols from his pockets. He never traveled without them. He did wish he'd delayed leaving on this trip long enough to bring Keller, his valet, with him, but that would have meant a return to Rosefeld. An elopement would have been infinitely more difficult.

At the smaller table, he pushed her hat aside to make room for the weapons. Three letters slid from underneath the hat and onto the floor.

"Oh," she said too quickly. "I'll get them."

Since they'd landed near his feet, he stooped to retrieve them. For several seconds, he stared at the direction written on the topmost letter. He glanced at the other two as well, but those were unexceptional since they were directed, respectively, to her sister Mary and to the Duke of Cynssyr.

The silence filled with the soft *shush, shush, shush* of him tapping a corner of that first letter on the others. "I believe," he said at last, "that I am within my rights to ask. Why are you writing to Mr. Harry Glynn so soon after agreeing to marry me?"

She was unperturbed, so it seemed—a face of angelic innocence. Was she pretending to be unconcerned now the way she'd pretended not to notice the young servant's reaction? Rather than answer him, she crossed to the desk and lifted her hat to reveal several more letters. She picked them up. "Aldreth, Thrale, Lucy, Anne, Clara. I wrote anyone who might be of assistance if I found myself stranded here. Including Mr. Glynn."

The edge of his mouth twitched down. "Why would you be stranded?"

She neatly stacked the letters and held out her hand for the ones he held. He tossed them onto the table. They slid across the surface. One of them came to rest against the butt of one of his pistols. "Em." He had no idea what to make of this and, therefore, no idea whether he should be amused or offended or something else entirely. "Why would you be stranded?"

"Misfortune." She returned his three to the stack and squared all of them. Though she had her back to him, she turned her head toward him. The line of her cheek was devastating in its perfection.

He folded his arms over his chest. "What sort of misfortune?"

Once again, she spread out the ribbons of her hat, adjusting them to avoid them coming in contact with his guns. "You might not have returned."

The idea of his leaving her here was so ludicrous, he laughed out loud. "Did you think I would prefer to sleep in the stables? I promise you, I have little fondness for a bed of straw."

She continued to smooth out the ribbons. It was something of a shock to realize she was quite serious. However inconceivable it was to him that he would abandon her, she believed he might.

"But, no," he said slowly, "you cannot have thought I would prefer to sleep in the stables. You wrote eight letters and expected you might be obliged to post them." He drew a sharp breath. He knew her too well and not at all. "I took Frieda with me. Did you believe I would abandon her, too?"

"Certainly not." She clasped her hands behind her back. There was nothing in her expression or the way she held herself to suggest she was anything but calm and possibly amused. He'd seen her like this dozens of times, surrounded by admirers whose adoration she appeared to accept as her right. Did she? "It's plain you are fond of her. I'd never have let you take her otherwise."

"You believed I would abscond with your dog?"

"I was uncertain which was the worse result." She licked her lips, the first sign he'd seen so far that she was discomforted. "Stranding me with Frieda or stranding me without her."

He still did not know whether he was offended or chagrined that she would believe him capable of such a thing. Perhaps both. They had been at loggerheads often enough that she might be justified. Might be.

"You feared I would abscond with your dog and leave you to whatever fate might befall a young woman alone? Strike that. You thought I had more concern for your dog than you?" By God, she did. He had no idea what to make of that. Yes, he was offended. But he could not blame her, not entirely. And if he were to be honest with himself, there was blame here for him.

She released her hands, and he was distracted by the ring on her fourth finger. A quick-witted deception on her part, for it was merely the ring she always wore, turned around as if it were a wedding band. "You're being willfully obtuse."

He took a mental breath. He would never speak so roughly to any of her sisters, nor any other young lady of his acquaintance, as he was prone to doing to Emily. "Enlighten me. Please." Still, he did not sound kind or patient. "I mean that sincerely."

She glanced away, then faced him and replied so forthrightly he decided he must have imagined he had wounded her feelings. "You like Frieda better than me."

"You can't be serious." But no, no, this was not how he ought to behave with her. Not now. Not under these circumstances. Those words, if said to him in such an incredulous, scornful manner, would have offended *him*. He cocked his head in a tight nod of acknowledgment. "Forgive me. Please continue."

She made fists of her hands. "Your abandonment of me was only one of several possible misfortunes I considered."

"My God, you *are* serious." Very well. He was offended, for she appeared to have no understanding of the insult she'd dealt him.

"You were gone over an hour."

"I had a great many things to see to and your dog to exercise." The Emily he knew was frivolous and reckless and vain, and that was not the woman he faced now. "I would not leave any woman like that. It's unimaginable."

She shot back, "And I am not an idiot."

"I did not imply that you are."

"You did. Of course you did."

"How? In what way?"

"Oh, that *is* insulting. I am aware of your low regard for me. You made that perfectly clear. Or do you believe I hadn't the wit to understand you?"

She meant that day in Emmer's Field, when they had been so near to unrecoverable disaster. Her intensity was something to behold. She was nothing like Anne or Clara. Where they were cool serenity, Emily was fire.

"You were perfectly clear, my lord, and I did understand you."

"I am corrected then, and I apologize yet again. But why those letters?"

Her eyes were chips of icy blue stone. "How much better is your revenge if you leave me here, doubly ruined?"

He bristled. He could not help it. He was justified in the reaction. "You wrote those letters in the belief that I planned to abandon you?"

"Against the possibility that you would." She tapped the letters while she scowled at him. "When so many things can and do go wrong, preparation for contingencies and alternatives prevents an even worse outcome."

"I should like to know what, exactly, was your plan tonight if I had snuck away with your dog."

"To post my letters immediately upon discovering my predicament warranted doing so."

He'd never have guessed she was capable of this sort of war planning, and he was at once impressed and insulted. "And then?"

"If no one came in three days, and if I was without funds, I intended to walk to Bartley Green. Assuming I was not in jail."

"In jail."

She swallowed once. "You have paid for tonight's accommodations, but how would I pay for lodging over multiple nights? People are jailed for such offenses."

"Not people such as you." He snorted. The very idea was ludicrous.

"No? Yet I know for a fact that when one is owed money, it is exceedingly disagreeable to learn that you will not be repaid." She twisted her garnet ring. "I would have sold this to pay for tomorrow night's room. If necessary, I was prepared to sleep outside while I awaited responses to my letters."

"My God."

"Think what you will of me, but I considered the possibilities and planned accordingly." She gripped the edge of the table with one hand. "I was prepared for the worst. Do you honestly think I would do nothing until the innkeeper came knocking on the door, demanding to be paid from funds I do not possess?"

"As if anyone would ignore your request for help. Shed a few tears and men bend to your will."

"How lovely you assume I possess such powers as that." She gave him a hard stare. "Jail is a penalty I had rather not risk."

"Your mind is an absolute labyrinth."

"To be clear, my lord, I believed that last to be very unlikely." For half a second, her voice trembled, but she mastered herself. "My goal is always to consider the worst outcomes and be prepared for each. Such a habit has stood me in good stead." She reached into her pocket and withdrew a mesh wallet. "I have these funds because I knew better than to hide my savings at the Cooperage. That was Lucy's mistake."

She referred to that infamous day when Sinclair had stolen the present Lady Thrale's savings and spent every penny on a new carriage and horses.

"There are consequences for a lack of preparation or for trust not warranted by fact or experience. I have this ring—" she held up her left hand "—only because I was wearing it the day Papa removed the contents of my jewelry box. I learn from my mistakes, you see, for I never again put my valuables where he might find them."

The picture Emily was painting of her life at the Cooperage disturbed him—: her sister's stolen money, the offhand reference to her father having taken her jewelry, the fact that she, like her sisters before her, had hidden money and valuables away to guard against financial disaster.

"All that might be so," he said, "but *I* have not abandoned you."

"Not yet."

"I shall not. You may trust in that."

Her mouth firmed, and she squared her shoulders. "I do not trust anyone."

"What have you ever encountered in your life that would lead you to believe the world is such a dark and dismal place? If you were stranded here, you would be inundated with offers of assistance at your first murmur of distress. As we speak, there must be fifty men who would give their lives for nothing more than a smile from you."

"Would they?"

"Of course."

"People lie all the time, if not in words, then in deed. Gentlemen admire my appearance; they do not admire me."

"There's no difference." He gestured at her. "Look at you."

"Others overlook my defects at every turn. They are kinder to me than to others, simply because of my face. My appearance does not warrant better treatment. As to being stranded, you know as well as I that it's happened to other women. Just last month, a woman appeared in a village claiming to have been abandoned. Everyone was kind to her, offering every comfort and amenity. Only, as it happened, she was not whom she said she was. Given that this story has appeared in several publications, I feel it is possible no one would believe a similar story from me." She sucked in a breath. "In any event, the innkeeper has a right to be paid for the rooms he lets, and while I have some funds, I doubt I have enough to pay for my food and lodgings for three or four days *and* post to Rosefeld."

"Emily, this . . . I—"

She waved him off. "It's not necessarily that you would leave me, it's what might happen if you did. Perhaps that makes no sense to you, but it does to me, and that's what matters. I cannot be easy unless I am prepared for the worst."

"I'm forced to question my own sanity, for I understood that."

She went still, and he saw he had offended her. "Pray do not condescend to me in that manner."

"I apologize."

She stayed as she was, motionless, the very picture of unconcern, yet as he watched her, he had the most peculiar feeling there was more beneath that perfect exterior than appeared. He shook himself, for that was nonsense.

"I shall do better in the future." He fetched his valise and placed it on the table beside the washbasin. Emily had evidently already washed up since there was moisture at the bottom of the basin. He poured in fresh water.

He was alone with the Divine Sinclair, a woman he'd lusted after since the day he'd begun to rebuild his life after Anne's marriage. He and Emily were to be married. This, no matter what Emily thought, was fact. He was done denying himself. Done. "You will not be stranded anywhere. I'm insulted you think so."

"You might have been set upon by thieves or murdered or kidnapped."

He retrieved his shaving kit and set it nearby. He missed Keller's expertise, but he was capable of managing for himself; in the days when he'd been Mr. Devon Carlisle, impoverished and disgraced younger son, he and Gopal had played valet for each other. "I think it unlikely I would have been murdered or lost."

"Why do you have those pistols?" she asked in a calm voice.

He put his hands on either side of the washbasin and bent his head. "I am compelled to point out that preparedness—" How on Earth did one counteract such an astonishing conviction that the world was a perilous place and that no one, himself included, would protect her? He took a deep breath and gave in. "Never mind. I concede your point."

"Thank you."

He unbuttoned his waistcoat and loosened his neckcloth and shirt. He set aside the linen. He could not get his mind away from her fear that she would find herself abandoned. Except . . . except, if one were to look at the situation solely from her point of view, she was right to wonder about his sincerity. He had told her revenge was his motive. He had told her bluntly he had no interest in her, and he had avoided her for more than a year. What reason had she to trust him? He looked at her over his shoulder. "I would never leave you in straits. I intend to marry you."

"No one intends to be robbed or murdered."

"Again, point taken. However, I hold out hope of convincing you I shall do everything in my power to see to your safety."

"Yes, my lord," she said softly.

Only then did it occur to him that she was as unsettled as him by the reality of their flight to Scotland. Emily understood that the nobility of Lord Bracebridge was but a veneer, and one too easily pulled away. The man beneath that shell was no gentleman, and she knew it. Devon Carlisle had been a prizefighter, was a past owner and operator of three brothels, and to this day maintained his interest in a gaming hell. Moreover, he had not always treated her as a young innocent to be protected from one's baser urges.

Devon Carlisle had wanted to fuck Emily Sinclair for going on three years. He still did. She was right. She wasn't safe.

In silence, he washed his hands and face, then the back of his neck and his upper chest. Deftly, he prepared the lather and spread it over his face. He stropped his razor, and when he saw her interest in the process, he turned and addressed her in a calm manner. "As to being set on by murderous thieves," he said, "even without pistols, I've a fair chance of defending myself."

"I'm sure so."

He turned back to the stand and the provided mirror. He drew the razor along his cheek and continued shaving. He cleaned up and rearranged his clothes until he was Lord Bracebridge again, gentleman and nobleman. She did not need to deal with Devon Carlisle tonight or ever.

When he was done, he joined her at the table where their dinner awaited.

"Down, Frieda," she said when the dog came to investigate. Her command had no effect, though eventually, with a sigh, Frieda lay down by his chair. They ate in silence, and he, for one, was grateful. If they were silent, they would not argue.

A tap on the door interrupted them. Frieda perked up. "Excuse me," he said.

"Of course."

He dropped his napkin on the table and answered the door to a maid with an armful of the clothes he'd requested. "Ah," he said. "Thank you. Your promptness is appreciated." He slipped a coin into the servant's hand. He closed and locked the door one-handed. Lacy trim from one of the items he held flipped up and touched his chin. "I took the liberty of asking for additional garments for you. I hope they'll do until we are able to retrieve your belongings from the Cooperage."

"How thoughtful. Thank you." She was so smoothly gracious, yet he now distrusted his ability to correctly divine her mood. No doubt she was, even now, planning what to do if her clothing became lost or a fire obliged them to decamp without any of their effects.

He looked through the items as he walked. "A clean shift, serviceable stockings from the looks of them, a petticoat. They'll do for now. No gloves." He frowned. With the weather turning as it was, she needed a better pair of gloves than the cotton ones she had been wearing when she walked out of the Cooperage.

He returned to their meal once he'd put the items on the bed. He poured a small amount of wine into a glass for himself and tasted it before filling hers. The stone in her ring caught the light from the lantern when she picked up her glass. He nodded. "What was your plan if your ruse was discovered?" He waggled his fingers at her hand.

"To say I had recently reduced." She turned the ring back and forth. "So loose it constantly turns."

He leaned against his chair and stretched out one leg. His boot knocked against her foot, and he drew his leg back.

Their meal had been excellent, the wine better than decent. He was feeling quite well, thank you. "Your pardon. With chairs like this, there is no comfortable position for a man my size."

"That's no more your fault than I am at fault for being shorter than you."

At least they were not arguing. "I suppose not."

"Do you hurt?" She touched the hand he'd used to punch Davener and his pulse leaped, both because of her touch and because of the unintended ambiguity of her question. The answer was yes. Yes, he hurt. His soul always ached, even though there were days he did not recall why.

"Some." He examined his hands. The tops of his knuckles were scarred. A long, thin scar extended across the entire back of his left hand. Across that landscape, bruises darkened his skin. A small cut, though no longer bleeding, hurt whenever he moved his fingers. He'd had much worse. "It was worth it to have laid out Davener like that."

"I imagine his chin hurts a good deal."

His response was a laugh.

"I am sorry."

"As you say, not your fault." He moved his fingers and embraced the pain. He had touched her with his hard-worked hands. His arms had been around her shoulders, his breath warm against her ear, balancing them on the precipice of ruin. "I am inured."

"When do you intend for us to depart?"

He looked away from his hands. She had left Bartley Green wearing a practical wool spencer and a lightweight wool traveling gown. She could be clad in canvas, and she'd still take his breath away. "The earlier, the better," he said.

"Very well."

He pushed his chair back an inch or two. "We'll drive for as long as there is light. Longer, weather permitting. If we change horses often and limit our stops, we may expect to be on the road fifteen or sixteen hours at least. I want to reach Scotland no later than three days from now."

She nodded.

The open bedroom door was no safe place to look, but what was he to do when just past her shoulder, he could see a corner of the bed? "I'll wake you in time," he said.

Her eyebrows arched. "Tell me when you want to leave, and I'll be ready in time. I always am."

"Four." He crossed his arms over his chest. Emily was several years younger than Anne. He remembered meeting her—a girl, for pity's sake—and thinking Anne would have her hands full when that girl was old enough to join the adults. "In the morning."

She bristled. "You don't believe I can awaken at will."

"I doubt my own ability to awaken in time." He was alone with Emily Sinclair. Alone, with all the social barriers gone.

"No, you don't."

She was right, and he found that annoying.

"If you think I need an hour to be ready, you are mistaken. Twenty or thirty minutes is sufficient."

"Very well then. But I'll carry you out to the carriage in your nightrobe if you are not prepared to leave."

Her fork clinked against her plate. "See if I'm not."

"Then I hope you'll awaken me in the morning." Reprobate that he was, part of him entertained the possibility that they'd still be awake at four in the morning.

"We ought to drive straight through until we are in Scotland and our business there is done."

"Not even I am prepared for a trek that brutal."

She pushed her food around her plate. "No stopping for anything not absolutely necessary."

How many plans were spinning through her head? What to do if she overslept, or if he did, or if they both did. Or if the horses bolted. What if there were no fresh horses available after all? "Em," he said.

"Yes?"

He pushed away the remains of his dinner and gave in to Devon Carlisle's basest nature. "Will I sleep on a chair tonight?"

Chapter Seven

B RACEBRIDGE'S QUESTION PARALYZED HER. She could not answer him, because there was no safe answer. Then words tumbled out, all in a rush, without her able to take in enough air to steady herself, and they weren't remotely the right ones. "I want so badly to be at home. In my room with Mrs. Elliot to bring me tea and bread and my own maid to dress me."

He cocked his head.

Oh, heavens. She wanted to disappear. She was tired and on edge, and now she'd said something that could only reinforce his poor opinion of her. "That's how I want to imagine home. Just Mrs. Elliot."

Bracebridge replied with unexpected gentleness. "We've had a long and tiring day full of the unexpected."

She did not want him to be kind. How could she live if he was kind to her? She wanted—needed—the safety of his disdain, and now it was gone. Underneath the table, she clasped her hands so hard her fingers hurt. She forced herself to release her grip. "I never want to see him again. Anne only sees him because of me and her sense of duty, but she's as frustrated and angry as any of us. The same for Mary. I don't think Lucy intends to see him again. I know I shan't. He's done enough."

She struggled to maintain her calm. He wanted to engage in intimate relations. Tonight.

As the silence lengthened, she exhaled slowly. She wanted to know what happened beyond kisses and embraces. She wanted. Wanted.

Bracebridge stood and held out his hand, and she stared at his fingers, her stomach a knot of pain. He flashed that sinister, wicked grin that always made her heart fly away with her breath. That look was full of secrets kept from proper young ladies and lines never crossed.

As if there were nothing shocking about his asking where he would sleep, he said, "Shall I be your lady's maid tonight?"

She held herself still. What if she'd misunderstood him? Thoughts whirled through her head too fast for her to examine but for these few facts. He could have arranged for one of the tavern maids to assist her tonight. He could have taken adjoining rooms. He could have said nothing at all. He could have left the bedroom to her without ever raising the subject. He could have. He should have.

Why hadn't he?

Shall I be your lady's maid?

"Does your silence mean the chair is my bed tonight?" His voice was deliberately light, completely the opposite of how their exchanges usually progressed. He spoke to Anne that way. Not her. "Never fear if it is. I've slept in worse places and been more uncomfortable than I would be here."

She touched her napkin to her lips, then dropped the linen to the table before she rose. She had no idea what to say. She knew what it was like to be in his arms. To have his mouth on hers. Every time she was near him, she was aware of him, the size of him, the way he was so at ease with his body. She wanted him.

"Bracebridge," she managed to say.

He gave her a lopsided grin as he came around to stand beside her. "I'll borrow a pillow and a blanket, if I may, and be up before you in the morning. There's no need for you to sleep in your clothes, though. I'll help you ready yourself for bed." He held out his hand. "Nothing more."

She turned his hand palm down and gently kissed his knuckles. "I'm sorry you were hurt because of me."

He did not speak or withdraw his hand. Not right away. He turned his hand over and, two fingers under her chin, tipped her head up. All the air in the room disappeared. His kisses had been brutal, savage, and overwhelming, and she wanted more of that. She wanted to know what lay on the other side.

She'd often wondered whether he understood the potent effect he had on women. She was now certain he did; he was far too confident of himself.

He trailed a finger from the point of her chin along her jaw. Tomorrow did not exist. There was no future to be ruined, no family to be shocked. There was only Bracebridge and right now.

Forever fixed in her mind was the truth that wicked, improper, ruinous-to-know Mr. Devon Carlisle was also one of the kindest, most generous men she'd ever met. He was a gentleman and a nobleman, but to her, he had always been larger than life, compelling, and impossible to ignore.

"I can be charming when I put my mind to it," he said.

When he said *charming,* he meant *seductive.* "So you say." She prayed her flippant reply was not a mistake.

"True enough," he said with a low laugh. "I don't suppose you've seen much charm from me, but even with this face, I promise it's true."

"Yet I find you unbearably attractive."

He tipped his head to one side. In the shifting light, his eyes seemed darker than black. He let out a short, soft breath, and she was off balance again. She had no idea whether it was even possible for her to withstand a deliberate seduction. How, when she did not want to?

"I'm too tall for you."

A thrill shot through her at his low comment, uttered as if he did not believe what he'd just said, or else meant something else entirely. "You're not too tall. I am too short."

His appeal, she'd long believed, lay in the expressiveness of his face and in the passion of his eyes. Well. Also in his size and brawn and his crooked nose. "What other nonsense is stuck in your head?" he asked in a silky voice.

"I like your rough looks." She had his full attention, and she was melting inside, surrendering already.

"What else?" he asked.

"Your eyes are outlandishly beautiful."

"Outlandishly beautiful, you say?"

"They are soulful and expressive. Your eyes always make me wonder whether you are thinking thoughts you should not."

"Do you wonder that now?"

"Yes." She pressed her palm to the side of his face. His cheeks slashed hard, and his nose was permanently crooked from having been broken one time too many, and she adored that too. "Your mouth is stern most of the time." Tenderly, she passed a finger over his lower lip and his soft mouth.

That touch was an intimacy she'd never dared before, and he permitted it. At last. At last. "The shape fits perfectly with the rest of your face and your so-outlandishly-beautiful eyes."

He pitched his voice to a rougher tone. "No woman ever went to bed with me on account of my eyes."

"You're a fool if you think that."

"One contradiction of me after another." His amusement was just evident enough, and she thanked the heavens for that.

"Your mouth puts me in mind of kissing you, and I don't care what you think of me for that. It's true. Long before I knew what kissing was like, I dreamed of kissing you. You call yourself a brute. Since I find you beautiful, it stands to reason that either you are wrong or I like a brutish man." She stroked his cheek again. "Tell me whether you think it matters which it is."

The room—the entire world—shrank to just the two of them. His amusement vanished. "Do not say such things to me if you mean for me to sleep on a chair tonight."

Smiles were a talent of hers. Numerous gentlemen had declared undying love after just one smile from her. "I don't, my lord."

Bracebridge took her hand in hers. "Come to bed with me, Em. Now."

"Yes," she said. "Now."

He led her to the bedchamber and closed the door before Frieda could follow. Inside, he crossed to the fireplace and crouched to add more coal.

She stared at his broad shoulders. Twice she'd seen him stripped down to his bare skin. The first occasion had been not long after Anne's marriage, when she'd gone to his townhouse because Anne was missing and someone had to fetch him to help find her. The less Emily thought about that day, the better. She'd never meant to interrupt him in a moment of such intimacy.

The second had been when she'd followed Lucy to a private boxing exhibition between him and Lord Thrale. Both men had been peeled off, and though there was much to admire in Lord Thrale's physique, Bracebridge had transfixed her. He still did. That was the day, the infamous day she would have surrendered all to him and he'd told her he could never love her.

He finished at the hearth and stood. The muscles of his thighs flexed and relaxed.

"Bracebridge, I—" None of her feelings had changed. He walked out of her line of sight. She couldn't move or speak. Bracebridge. Bracebridge. He would kiss her again and touch her, and her body would respond. He would tear her heart to shreds.

The sound of cloth rustling disrupted her paralyzed state. He'd taken off his coat and draped it over a chair. "Yes, Em?"

He did not *want* to marry her. Not the way he'd wanted to marry Anne or even Clara. His love for her sister was the sort of emotion that came but once in one's lifetime. Papa had never loved another woman after Mama. Bracebridge loved Anne like that. Completely and without reservation, with the whole of his heart and soul. Emily loved Bracebridge that same way. She wouldn't be herself if she did not love him.

She blinked until she'd mastered the tears that threatened her composure. He'd ruined her the day she and her sisters had arrived at Bracebridge's country estate with the expectation that Cynssyr would offer for her and rescue them all from their father, and that Bracebridge would make an offer to Anne. Her moment of irreparable ruin had come when Anne had emerged from their carriage, and his smile was his soul lit with love. She still grieved for his losing Anne when he loved her so deeply.

Somehow, he'd managed to stand behind her without her realizing. He rested his hands on her shoulders. He was not wearing gloves. His bare fingers were warm from being so near the fire, and his breath warmed her cheek. "We'll be married soon. Two days with a little luck. Three at the most."

She fought for calm when he swept two fingers across the nape of her neck. With the contact came her body's recognition of him that always left her so stubbornly unwilling to retreat. Whenever he touched her, she came alive and wanted more. She wanted to follow where that thrill took her. Oh, how she wanted to, even if it meant disaster and a heart that could never be put back together.

They were not married, and she did not care in the least. Tonight, tonight at last, she had hours with him instead of the minutes they'd snatched before. One night. One night with him was worth the ruin of her life.

He unfastened the first hooks of her gown. It wasn't the same as her lady's maid undressing her. His hands were bigger, and he took his time. "So many fastenings to manage," he said in a voice as dark and dangerous as his eyes.

Bone-shaking desire filled her—subsumed her. His fingers brushed her skin wherever he bared it. They were alone here, and he had unfastened all the hooks down the back of her gown. She tried to speak, but the words lodged in her throat.

"Come to bed," he whispered. His hands tightened on her shoulders as he leaned against her—or maybe he drew her back. "With me."

"What would you do . . ." she began in a trembling voice. "What would you do if I told you I want to wait?"

He released her, an abrupt disengagement, and she turned around. She would not cry. Would not. She refused to humiliate herself with him. But now that they were here, at the very moment, the enormity of her desire for him and her fear that she would be crushed by how hopelessly she loved him was too much. Too much. She met his gaze because she owed him that.

"What would you do?" she whispered.

His eyes were fathomless pools of black, and she was lost there. She always had been. "Nothing. I would do nothing."

She had to tilt her chin to look at him. "What if you change your mind?"

"About what? Doing nothing?" A furrow appeared between his eyebrows. "You have my word on that."

"Not that." She spoke too fast. "I did not mean that."

"What did you mean, then? Leaving by four? I won't change my mind about that either."

"You're willfully misunderstanding me." The room was shrinking by the second. She was so wound up now, she could scarcely think.

"How? For I can tell you, I do not understand where this conversation has gone."

"I mean about me. What if you change your mind about marrying *me*?"

Several emotions flickered across his face. She took a step back, but not far enough to prevent him from closing the distance between them. He cupped the side of her face. "I would not leave any young woman ruined because of my actions or inaction." His voice turned hard. "Make no mistake, before the end of the week, you will be my wife. Nothing but death will prevent that. Nothing."

Outside the door, Frieda whined once.

"What if I change my mind?" she asked.

"About this or about marrying me?"

"Either."

At his sides, his fingers flexed and relaxed. "Have you?"

She backed away, a mass of conflicting emotions. "I don't know. No."

He held his breath a moment, then released it slowly. "I cannot take you back to Rosefeld as you are now. Not after a night spent on the road. The damage to both our reputations is done. All we can do is live with our regrets."

"You know how it is between us. And while that may have changed for you, it hasn't for me."

"That hasn't changed," he said.

If ever he guessed how desperately she loved him still, he would know exactly her weakness. He would know that love had lived in her without encouragement, an emotion as one-sided as it was unreasonable. He would pity her for such abhorrent weakness. Or worse, he might never notice.

She spun on her heel and faced the fireplace. Her head was full of images of him crouched before the fire, a physically powerful, confident man. Her thoughts whirled with no place safe for them to land. "Something might happen."

"Yes," he said with wicked amusement in his voice. He was breathing up all the air, taking up all her senses. "Perhaps the moon will crash to Earth. Do you require time to write letters informing loved ones of your plan in such an eventuality?"

She looked over her shoulder at him. "Do not make fun."

He lifted his hands in a warding-off gesture.

"The perils of our situation are unequal," she said. "Should something prevent us from marrying, *your* life will not appreciably change."

"Point taken."

"It's not as if we are bound for Scotland no matter the obstacles to our passionate love." She faced him. "Nothing holds us together but spite."

"Spite?" he said, eyebrows arched.

"For Papa. For me." How was it possible she wanted two things in such fundamental opposition? It was not possible to be with Bracebridge and protect her heart.

He considered that for several seconds. "I am not a forgiving sort. That's a fault I readily confess."

"He never meant for Anne to marry anyone at all. He meant to keep her at home, caring for him the rest of his days. He'd convinced her that was all she deserved. Anne! Anne, the best of us all. How could any of us forgive him for that? I haven't."

He looked thoughtful. "Did you agree to marry me out of spite?"

"I don't know. It's likely."

"You don't know?"

"If it was spite, it was for Papa, not you." She extended one arm; the other she needed to hold up her loosened gown. "I am not a dutiful daughter. I've tried and failed to be better than I am. I cannot set aside my resentment of him. I hate him for what he did to you and Anne. Mary and Lucy, too. He oughtn't have done that."

"We have that opinion in common."

"I'm not good and gentle and loyal like Anne. Anne never resented Papa the way I do. She never plotted her escape even if it meant leaving him with no one to care for him. I thought I could be like Anne and be a dutiful daughter. But with every day that passed, I grew more and more resentful."

Her breath hitched, and she needed a moment to be sure she could speak over the lump in her throat. "Sometimes," she said, "I hate him as much as you do. More. I think sometimes I hate him more, and what good daughter hates her father? And now . . . now . . . He wanted me to marry a fool. That foolish, foppish, dandy Mr. Davener, who has never had a thought more complicated than what color waistcoat to wear. He's not half as amusing as he believes, and he never reads. Is it any wonder he writes the most wretched poetry? I can't marry a man who struggles to make a decent rhyme. I shan't. Not even for Papa. Not even if it means he loses the only home I've ever known. I'd rather be ruined than allow Papa to win. So you see, I am the most despicable woman possible."

"Hush, Em." He stepped close and put his arms lightly around her, and she was enveloped by him, the warmth of his arms around her, the scent of him, the unyielding hardness of his arms and chest. "You are many things, but you are not despicable."

She curled her fingers in the lapels of his coat and bowed her head. She was shaking. Trembling like a leaf.

"Had I been a dutiful son, I'd be in the army or the navy. You and I have disobedience in common." He stroked the back of her head. "If I fault you for that, I must fault myself, so no more talk of obedience to one's father. I only wish I had a counterargument for your fear that the moon might make a crater on the earth before we reach Scotland."

"You haven't one, because there is not one." She was losing her wits. Every last one.

He kept his arms around her. "Allow me to point out that if the moon does come crashing down, it will surely kill us both."

She swallowed. "I—you—the two of us. Bracebridge." She grabbed his hand and held it in hers. "Please. Even if I was . . . If something should happen that prevents us getting married—you would not want that ruin upon you. I know you would not." She squeezed her eyes closed and tried to find some measure of calm.

His reply was low and amused. "Do you fear I'll perish before we arrive at Gretna Green?"

She did. She absolutely did. Unreasonably so.

"Killed by passion, perhaps?"

Her eyes flew open, and she saw the smile that had accompanied his mirthful tone. "Don't say that. Don't ever say that. Awful things happen. They do." Her voice fell to a whisper. "Mama died. Your family died. Lucy's first husband. Anne very nearly died. Terrible things happen. They do. All the time, and to people I love."

He brought her close. "I am sorry for your sorrows. And I am touched that you have given so much thought to mine. But surely we are both grateful that Anne is with us still. Safe and unharmed." He hesitated. "And deeply in love."

"Yes," she said, even though she hated that Anne's happiness had come at Bracebridge's expense. "Yes. That's so."

"Well, then." He rubbed a hand up and down her back. "Don't allow your worries to rattle about in your head until you're forced to write a dozen letters. Share your cares and worries with me. Our married life shall be well served if you do. We might find we get on rather well."

He could have poked fun at her. She was grateful he hadn't. "Everything is so . . . upside down now." She craned her head back to look at him, and her knees were not steady at all. "The most fantastic scenarios take hold of me, and all I can think of is, what shall I do if the very worst happens?" She drew back, out of the circle of his arms. "Miss Emily Sinclair, tragically killed on her way to a scandalous elopement."

"Neither one of us shall die." He gave her a very slow smile, so wicked there was very little left in her head but him. "Not in the way you imagine."

"No one can promise he'll live even to the next moment, let alone until tomorrow."

"Do you fear some slip of a girl will open that door—" he pointed "—and find me naked between the sheets?" He held her gaze. They both knew he referred to the day three years ago when she'd burst into his bedroom to find him with a married lover. "In bed with *you*, this time."

"Don't." She gripped the front of her gown. "You know why that happened. You know. Besides, if anyone were to burst in here, it would be Aldreth or Cynssyr or Thrale. Or the innkeeper to accuse us of fornication."

"Not fornication," he said wryly. "In any event, I assure you, if it happens that we are interrupted, whoever it is will not shoot me." He was standing close again—when had he done that?—so close, and she wanted to kiss him and let the world fall away. "Your brothers-in-law would be here with a special license and an escort to the nearest parson."

"Bracebridge, I—"

"You and I—" In a sharp motion, he lifted his hands, stiff fingers spread. "We light sparks."

His confession shook her mind free of thoughts of disaster. "It's like that for you, too?" she asked softly.

"I've spent months avoiding you because of it." He took her hand in his. His skin was warm. "There's desire between us. Passion. Lust." He bent to her, and for a numbing, blinding moment, she thought he meant to kiss her.

Then he did.

Chapter Eight

H E DREW EMILY closer. She wasn't Anne. She wasn't the woman he loved, but Lord, she was exquisite, all golden hair and smooth skin, with a figure to bring a man to a painful cockstand. Now that she was in his arms again, kissing him again, lust consumed him as if he'd never trained himself to ignore her.

She did know how to kiss. More specifically, she knew how to kiss him, and he bloody well knew that was his doing. She'd learned from him.

His body settled into a state of arousal he hadn't dared allow himself for more than a year. In this regard, she brought out what most would say was the worst in him.

She pushed free of his embrace, cheeks pink, and her breath coming hard. He released her, but as she stepped back, he gently caught her arm. Right now, he wanted more than anything to take Emily to bed, even knowing their feelings were unequal.

He was done resisting her. There was no longer any need to do so. After all, he hadn't taken her back to Bartley Green. An insistent refrain hummed through him. *She is to be my wife. She will be my wife. She shall be my wife.*

"Stay with me," he said in a voice thick with passion. "Please."

"I don't know what to do or say, or how to behave." She swallowed hard. "This is madness, Bracebridge. Madness. You don't want this. Not with me."

He'd been unkind to her, he was aware of that. He had said harsh words to ensure he did not ruin both their lives when he had not been prepared for the consequences of seducing her. Scandalous words came to mind. Words one did not say to a lady. He did not love her, but he did want her, badly. He cupped her chin in one hand. "There will be no disaster."

"You don't want me. You don't. You told me so."

"I've always wanted you." Reprehensible, unthinkable words stayed just there behind his lips. He was a brutal man, and she'd implied she liked that. He had brutal words to say and, God help him, he wanted to know whether she'd like that, too. "Why do you think we came so close to scandal so often?"

"Because of me."

"Do you think you got into my arms all by yourself? There was always the two of us."

He saw the moment she gave in to what they both felt, and it was remarkably arousing. The blue of her eyes was all the more piercing because of the inky black of her lashes, a trait she shared with Anne. How had he never noticed that before? "Come here," he said.

She did.

"All my life, I've been warned about this." Her voice was amused and frustrated and desirous. "'You'll come to no good, Emily Sinclair, if ever you permit a man to touch you.'" Her eyes fluttered closed, and she winced. Those words had come unbidden, thoughtless, hurtful. There was nothing equal about their positions. Their past left her vulnerable in a way he was not.

"We're ruined, the both of us." He kissed her once, briefly, and he was pulled into that peculiar, seething whirlpool that was so dangerous to his control. *This* was why he'd avoided her for over a year. What he wanted to do with her and to her was a poor reflection on any man's notions of honor. Even his. "You're to be Lady Bracebridge."

"What a horrible fate," she murmured.

He stepped closer and kissed her the way no man should ever kiss a young lady to whom he was not married. His thoughts fogged around the edges. Somewhere in there was considerable danger for them both, but he'd asked her to marry him, and she'd said yes, and they were here for the night in this room. Alone.

She placed her hand over his midsection. She'd never been shy with him when he was behaving inappropriately with her; she wasn't shy now. Emily— reckless, passionate, joyful Emily—was the woman his body desired beyond all others, and as a consequence, he was hard. More, now that her hand was sliding lower. He kept one arm around her waist and pressed his palm to the side of her face. "May I stay?"

"Yes," she breathed, pliant in his arms, surrendering to her own passion. The Divine Sinclair, unattainable, perfect, was his. "Yes, do."

He walked her backward toward the bed with her still in his arms. This woman had consumed his erotic life for months, and he was struggling not to give in to very selfish desires. He could not allow this to be only about him, but Lord, he'd dreamed about fucking her for months and months—years, if he were to be honest. He'd crossed lines with her, had been perilously close to ruining her. Now there was no reason to avoid her, no reason to hold back.

He sat on the mattress and slid backward until he leaned against the headboard. There was history between them. Kisses and caresses that should never have happened, indisputable knowledge of incendiary physical compatibility. "Here." He bent his knees. "Between my legs."

She lifted her skirts high enough that she could come near without the material getting in their way. Bracebridge focused on his arousal and the immediate future that included her hands and the fascinating possibilities of what they would do to him.

"Closer," he said. She complied, on her knees still, and his arousal became his entire existence. He put one hand on her upper chest, a caress that turned reverent. A year of avoiding her. A year—and more—of denying himself this. "Such soft, delicate skin."

He waited for some prideful acknowledgment of her beauty, but she whispered, "May I touch you?"

"Please."

She drew a finger across his cheek and then beneath his lower lip. His stomach dropped a thousand miles when she dipped her head to his and kissed him. Nothing in the world existed but her and the desire eddying around them.

He opened his mouth under hers and joined the kiss. She was so delicate, she seemed the sort of woman a man like him would break apart, but she wasn't. She'd said she liked that he was rough. The question was whether she would also like a lover who sometimes abandoned finesse.

Her mouth was soft, so soft, and then eager, then carnal, and she took control of the kiss. He was more than happy to follow the pace she set. She kissed divinely, erotically, and when his hand wandered from her shoulder to the front of her gown, she adjusted herself to give him better access. Her gown wasn't loosened enough, despite his stint as her lady's maid. He worked at more fastenings.

She leaned into their kiss, took things a little farther between them; tongues became involved, and the longer they kissed, the more he wanted flame to come from whatever spark it was that made her his physical match. He flattened his palm against the upper curve of her chest. His arousal increased, and he wouldn't have thought that possible.

He drew back enough to put a few inches of separation between them. He held her face and stared at her mouth and gave in; after all this time, he accepted his desire for her without wishing it wasn't so. "What I want from you isn't decent."

The side of her mouth quirked up, and he left himself open to that flirtatious, inviting smile. "Not even a little?"

"No." He was fair out of his mind. "I've no wish to shock you."

"I'm sorry to hear that, my lord."

Lord. Lord, she would kill him. "Don't say such things if you don't mean them."

She ran her other hand down his torso to the waist of his trousers. "Shock me, my lord."

"I've never undressed a proper young lady before."

"Never?" A smile danced in her eyes, and his imagination leaped ahead to the possibility that she would embrace relations with him without reservations of any kind. She seemed to possess absolutely no shyness. There was nothing coy about her at all. "Shocking, indeed," she said.

He drew his hands as far down her bare upper back as he could reach, and she arched toward him. "Such a pretty thing you are," he whispered. For a slender woman, her figure was lush. "Mine to spoil."

She understood what he meant by that, for she laughed. His hands wandered more, and when the side of his finger brushed the outside curve of her breast, he leaned in and whispered, "Let me ruin you tonight."

Her eyes were dazed with passion, but there was awareness there too. "You said yourself, we are already ruined."

He pushed at the tangle of her clothes and managed to expose a good deal of the right side of her torso, exposing her stays and chemise. She took a breath, then let go of her grip on the fabric. He tossed aside her gown. She did not move, and there was defiance in her stillness. He was in no condition at the moment to puzzle that out and so did not. He slid a hand over the curve of her, and her breath hitched.

"Do you like that?" The need for barriers between them was gone, gone, and gone. Gently, he plucked her nipple through her chemise and absorbed her reaction to that. His, too. Touching a woman as responsive as her was heaven. He did the same again and elicited another hitch of her breath, a tightening of her skin, her nipple coming erect under his finger.

They had all night. *He* had all night to fuck her. He trailed the tip of his finger over her. "Answer me."

"Yes," she said on a quick intake of breath. "I do like that."

"I want to see your body," he said. "Laid out nude for inspection at my leisure. At the same time, I want to be inside you when you are without all these clothes you have on. I want to touch you. I want my mouth on your skin in places I've not yet touched." He put his lips by her ear and kissed her there. He was half-gone already.

"I think you should do whatever you like," she said.

He slid his palms along her thighs, downward toward her knees. "You slay me," he said. "You've no idea."

Her nipples were taut, and there was nothing he wanted more than to bare her so he could lick and taste and touch. He put his hands over her breasts, as much as he could with her only half-undressed. Her soft flesh filled his palms. "What a delicate woman you are."

"No. No. Please, no." Emily made a noise of frustration and yanked at her corset.

"No, what?" With a bit of fumbling, he managed to unlace her and pull the garment away from her.

"Don't treat me as if I'll break," she said, all fire and passion. "I want you to be crude. You say you're a beast." She pressed one hand on the headboard above his shoulder and with the other ran a finger along the top of his cheek. "You're not behaving like one, and I want you to."

He pulled her forward, closer, closer, one arm hard around her waist. If she wanted crudity, he was the man to satisfy her. "If you like fucking half as much as this, I might not survive."

Her wild, satisfied smile sent his arousal into dangerous territory. He'd said an unforgivable word out loud, and she wasn't offended. She put her hands on his upper arms. "More of that," she said. "More. You said you'd ruin me. Keep your promise, my lord."

"I am a man of honor." He put one hand over her breast and his mouth on the other, and she was so soft, and her reaction to him was so completely arousing, he was beyond hard.

"Oh, my," she whispered, her breath coming in short gasps. She arched toward him.

He licked her from her nipple upward to her collarbone, then whispered, "I can't wait until you scream my name." He worshiped her breasts, her shoulders, and damn, but he wanted her. All of her, crudely, slowly, tenderly, brutally, however it happened. He held her gaze, and she stared back just as directly. He watched her dark, dark lashes come down, then slowly lift.

"Will you let me touch you?" she said.

"Do."

God help him, he had not anticipated that she would put her hand on the front of his trousers, but that was exactly what she did.

"You're hard," she said.

"From want of you."

"Do you like being in such a state?" She locked gazes with him, and he knew all this was deliberate on her part, and he responded to that. Indeed, he could be crude.

"Very much."

She unfastened his trousers' top button, then fixed him with a gaze that scorched. "May I?"

"I'll perish if you don't."

"I've wondered what a man is like in such a state."

"A natural curiosity."

"I am exceedingly curious."

"I offer myself up for your satisfaction."

She released a second button. "I've only the vaguest of ideas about all this."

"Your instincts are excellent so far. Pray continue."

When she had enough buttons opened, she got her hand around him and, between the two of them, he ended up with his prick exposed. She wanted him crude? He would be that for her.

"I want you to use your mouth on me," he said. In his imagination, he'd said those words to her more than once. Now he was saying them out loud, demanding, desirous, already anticipating orgasm.

The play of emotions across her face as she looked at his member fascinated him. That odd stillness was back, and once again he wasn't certain what to make of it. "Like so." He demonstrated the motion and the grip he liked, and she was not the least bit shy about holding him. Or stroking him. "Em. Lord, Em." He forced his eyes open and saw her staring at him, that is, at his cock in her hand, with an expression of absolute focus and reverence. "Don't stop."

She took him in hand again, and he groaned.

"I enjoy giving pleasure where I can."

He wrapped his hand around hers and stilled her stroking. "I'll warn you again. I am a brute. In fact and at heart."

"Yes," she said slowly, and with a smile that left him wondering whether he'd spend in her hand. "You are." She tightened her fingers around him. "But I've warned you, I like your brutish ways." She drew back after some minutes, though her fingers remained around his cock. "Tell me what would please you best."

"Your mouth."

Her focus returned to his sex, and that slow smile wasn't from a woman offended. Not in the least. "You'd like that?" she asked. "My mouth on you?"

Bracebridge was fully aware this was the moment he could resist his baser nature. He could stop this now.

He curled a hand around the nape of her neck. "Yes."

"You'll tell me how?"

"God, yes." He shifted on the bed, and then she did what he lusted after. He had no words. None. In frantic silence, he showed her exactly how he wanted to be fellated. His cock in her mouth, his foreskin drawn back. "Your tongue," he managed to groan out.

Before long, he had his hands up and clutching the headboard while he gave himself over to the moment. Wicked. Unbelievably arousing. She used her tongue and her hand and her lips, and he was powerless to do anything but surrender completely. His climax shattered him and reduced him to an incoherent shout.

He came slowly out of his fog of completion and saw a private, satisfied smile on her mouth. Slowly she lifted her gaze and said, "I liked that."

He hadn't the wits to speak yet.

"I liked having you in my mouth." She was utterly genuine. "The taste of you. The way you cried out."

At the moment, he was in a state of sexual repletion that convinced him the world was a most excellent place to be. If the moon crashed down on them now, at least he would die a happy man. "Well now."

"Have I shocked you?"

He let out a laugh. He ought to be shocked. He ought to be appalled he'd allowed her to do such a thing. "What a question."

"Am I wicked for wanting to do that again?"

He bent one knee and leaned the inside of his thigh against her side. "As wicked as I am for allowing it." He tightened his hands on her. *This* was what came of his lust for her, for a woman whom he did not respect enough to treat like the lady she was.

He did not care. He didn't. "I promise you, the favor shall be returned." He drew her close for an open-mouthed kiss that made him think he'd soon be hard again.

Emily Sinclair. His. The woman every other man wanted was in bed with him. He ought to have known she'd not be shy or reticent.

Before long this kiss, too, devolved into desperation. Desperation for her beauty and her openness to him, his body, and her pleasure. She hadn't merely complied with something he wanted. She'd bloody enjoyed it, reveled in it. He slid off the bed, naked. They'd been here before. Him naked, her not.

Emily stretched out, her back against the pillow where his head had been, and this time she stared at him with an appreciation that changed his mind about the need to sleep at all this night.

Chapter Nine

꧁✦꧂

BRACEBRIDGE DIDN'T LOOK away from Emily. No man in his right mind would, for she lay on the bed like an erotic dream come to life. Her clothes were in disarray, tapes unfastened, her corset on the floor, pettiskirts rucked up nearly to her knees. One of her garters was missing. Her hair, which he'd loosened, had come entirely undone. She continued to look him up and down.

"Bold, aren't you?" he said.

"Should I not look at you?"

He lifted his arms away from his body. He trained almost as hard now as in his fighting days. His body was a weapon, his muscles defined and hard. He'd never been a wiry fighter like Bill Richmond. He was more on the scale of Jim Belcher or Devil Wilcott, shy of Belcher's science and without Wilcott's blinding speed and perfect technique. He was strong, though, faster than most and with excellent bottom and wind, as the pugilistic crowd liked to say of a fighter with endurance and control of his breathing.

Emily took a handful of her skirt and lifted one knee. "When I look at you, I feel like I'm stepping onto thin air with nothing to stop me from falling."

He sat on the side of the mattress and put a hand on her bent leg, just below her knee. He moved his hand upward, sliding his fingers around to the inside of her thigh. "When I look at you, I feel you have too many clothes on."

Her mouth curved in a smile. "Compared to you, I do."

He reached the apex of her thighs and slid two fingers along her sex. "You're wet."

She blinked twice and went quite still.

"It means I've aroused you. The same way my hard prick means you have aroused me."

With her assistance, he stripped her of the rest of her undergarments. Everything gone: garters, stockings, chemise. Naked, she lay still, with a quietness that made a barrier between them. He was both frustrated by it and grateful for it.

He drew his fingers from the base of her throat down the center of her torso, then back to cup one breast. "Magnificent."

She caught his gaze and held it. "I know what you're thinking."

"What?" He had his hand between her legs again. She was hot and wet, and she had adjusted to give him access.

She sat up and dislodged his hand, and if she hadn't moved closer to him, one hand on his chest, sliding down, then up, he'd have been annoyed she'd stopped him from feeling her sex. "You think I'm too delicate for a brute like you."

He curved his hand around her waist. Her skin was astonishingly soft. "You're a young lady of society. Coddled and cosseted from the day of your birth, spoiled by everyone who meets you because you're this." He pressed his hand to the center of her upper chest, then slid his palm down. "Perfection."

"While you are a disreputable, reprehensible beast, my lord."

"Compared to you."

She was kissing his chest, touching his stomach, following the ridges of muscle. "I know what else you're thinking." She drew back. "It ought to be out in the open."

"Why, when I'd rather be doing this?" He leaned over and took her nipple into his mouth and sucked hard. Her chest rose with her intake of breath.

"I can't think when you do that."

He cupped her. "No? That's a shame."

She put her hands on either side of his face. "You resent me because I'm not Anne. In fact, I think you hate me because I'm not."

His heart skipped a beat. Jesus.

She was right, though. "You have her eyes."

"Mine are blue."

He touched the side of her eye. "The shape is the same. Your lashes are dark like hers."

"Yes."

"Sometimes when you smile, you remind me of her. But you're nothing like her."

"Not at all." She leaned close and kissed the bulge of his biceps, then his pectoral.

He wrapped her hair around his hand and pulled her head back. Not enough to hurt. He was careful of that. "Your hair isn't the same color."

"It's not."

"Anne is taller. She's gentle, always so gentle. So kind. She was always kind to me when I was a man no lady ought to know. She's the finest mind of any woman I've met, and she's loyal to a fault. She was a mother to you and all your sisters."

"She was, and we loved her for it."

"You aren't her."

"Tell me how much you hate me." She straddled his lap, and he put his hands on her bottom, either side. "Say it and be done with it. It changes nothing for me if you say what I already know."

He was hard and aroused by her ferocity and the perfection of her. "I hate that I want you like this." He pressed his mouth to her shoulder and kissed her there while he worked his finger around to her sex. He bit her, not enough to break skin, but enough to make her gasp. He gripped her hard, and she sucked in a quick breath. A moment later, he pushed her onto her back and splayed himself over her, palms flat on the mattress on either side of her. Words poured out of him, a river of despair. "I hate that you're beautiful. I hate that every time I see you, I betray Anne because I want you."

"Most everyone wants me," she said without a hint of pride. "And some of the ones who do are married men who shouldn't want any woman but their wives. There's nothing special about you feeling that way."

"No," he said. "There's not."

She curled a hand around the back of his head. "I know," she whispered. She held him close, but he pushed away. He did not want sympathy. Not from her. Never from her.

He used one leg to push one of hers aside to make room for himself. He was so hard, so aroused, so full of anger and heartbreak, he was rougher than he should have been. She smiled and tightened her grip on his shoulders. They'd been almost this close to disaster once. He'd had one hand on her thigh and the other on his breeches' buttons, and the Lord only knew how he'd managed not to ruin both their lives that day.

"Do it now," she said in a low, fierce command.

He shoved inside her in one long, hard, savage thrust, into softness and heat, and he told himself he would not continue in this way. He would be gentler, soon. So soft, and already orgasm hovered, promising him the oblivion of sexual release.

She made a small sound, a gasp, a catch of her breath that wound through him. She tensed, and by the time he remembered that, yes, this was her first time, she'd relaxed. She arched toward him. "Devon," she said while he stopped moving. "My God, Devon. My lord. Do that again."

He fucked her. There wasn't any other word that sufficed. He tried to start slowly, but she caught on quickly, and she held him tight and put her mouth by his ear and said, "It's all right to hate me."

He reared back, and she did something with her hips, once, then again, and God in heaven, she was fucking him in return. He kept his weight on his palms and matched himself to her motion, harder, a little harder, and he had the wit and presence of mind to be sure he brought her along with him.

He didn't have to chase his orgasm, and he'd long ago stopped thinking about slender, delicate Emily Sinclair. Their intercourse was not polite or delicate. Together they were crude and raw. She came first, but he followed only moments later, a release that shattered him because he'd found his sexual match and because it was Emily, Emily, who was forbidden to him.

He came hard, so hard, he found bliss.

Afterward, though. Afterward. He sat up, legs hanging off the mattress. Her words echoed in his head, relieving him of his guilt, accepting his anguish as if she didn't deserve better. "What have I done?" he said to the room. "Emily, what have I done to you?"

The sheets and blankets slid around her as she sat up and put a hand on his back. "Nothing. You've done nothing."

He turned just enough to see her face. Guilt annihilated him. "Don't forgive me for this. Don't ever."

"Too late."

"Why, when I've consigned you to a life without the possibility of love?"

Chapter Ten

T HEY REACHED GRETNA GREEN the morning of their fourth day on the
road. Twenty minutes later, she stood beside Bracebridge at the
blacksmith's shop. The anvil priest gave them a sloppy smile and took a drink
from a flask he'd withdrawn from his coat pocket. He winked at them both,
then at Frieda, whom Emily had convinced to sit quietly.

"Hurry," Bracebridge said with a glance at Frieda. "It won't last long."

Panic scrambled Emily's thoughts and turned her stomach into a hollow,
acid pit. She struggled to regulate her breathing. Her life was about to change
completely.

"You're not the first impatient groom I've had here," the priest said, "and
you won't be the last."

Another couple waited across the room, arms around each other, both
smiling. They made a handsome couple. While Emily tried not to stare, the
gentleman brought his future wife close and tenderly kissed her cheek. When
they separated, the other bride gazed into her lover's eyes, leaning closer and
resting a hand on his chest.

"Get on with it," Bracebridge said in a voice that sent a chill through the
room. He brought Emily closer. "I intend to marry this woman."

"Go on, then," the priest said to Emily.

"I declare my intention to marry this man."

"About blessed time." The priest laughed out loud, then completed his
register, handed Bracebridge a barely legible certificate, and it was done.
They were bound in matrimony.

Married. Her stomach turned somersaults. She was married and, by God,
this was both a miracle and the biggest mistake of her life.

The couple across the room started toward the "priest," but not before the gentleman brought his love to him and kissed her again.

To Frieda, the couple's approach was a certain sign of a new friendship. The dog whined and wriggled with enough forward motion to nearly pull Emily off her feet. For that reason, she was entirely unprepared when Bracebridge leaned over her. He pressed his mouth to hers in a quick, light kiss that landed nearer her ear because she had been unprepared and distracted.

"Let's be off, then," he said without any acknowledgment of the awkwardness. He reached over and took the leash from her. It was just as well, for he put Frieda on his far side, and when she attempted to get around him to greet her new friends, he simply leaned into her and bumped her away with a sharp, "No!"

At the door, Emily gave a final glance over her shoulder. The other lovers were before the anvil priest, their arms around each other's waists. The woman rested her head on his shoulder. They had become husband and wife in the time it had taken for Bracebridge and her to cross the room. "May you have a hundred years of happiness together," she said softly.

The young woman heard her and smiled at them with unadulterated joy. "Thank you, ma'am." She curtseyed. "I wish you the same."

Bracebridge opened the door, and they exited to find the clouds ominously dark and the air sharp with cold. He increased his stride toward his rig, and she did the same to keep up. The boy Bracebridge had hired to watch the horses came to his feet on their arrival, and more coins exchanged hands.

"Up you go, girl." Bracebridge lifted the leash. After all their days on the road, Frieda had learned how to jump in. When the dog was settled, Bracebridge assisted Emily, then took his seat. In silence, they began their return south.

Those dark clouds kept their promise of wet. An hour past Carlisle, a light rain began to fall. Before long, the drizzle became a steady beat.

The rain continued more-or-less unabated until four days later when they reached the Nottinghamshire inn where they'd passed the first night of their journey north. The post was just leaving as they arrived, obliging them to wait for the courtyard to be clear. Emily covered her ears at the din of the departure: blaring horns, shouting, and all the noise of a carriage full of passengers and their luggage.

Their journey south was remarkable only for the fact that they did not argue. They shared a bed at night, and though she was as giddy as ever when he slid between the sheets with her, there was none of the passion of that first night. In the main, everything felt . . . perfunctory, and she did not know how to break through to him, or even whether she should.

Once the spectacle of the departing post was at an end, Bracebridge directed them to the interior courtyard.

Though it was not raining at present, it had been recently, for gutters continued to flow, and water dripped from trees and eaves. Bracebridge opened the gig door for her, helping her down while reaching for the umbrella he'd bought.

Like Frieda, Emily was now an experienced traveler under adverse conditions. She jumped from the step to save him the necessity of touching her and took back the umbrella. "Thank you, my lord." Frieda jumped down, too, landing in a puddle she then lapped at. Bracebridge extended his arm to Emily, but she avoided the contact by putting a hand to her low back and arching. "I'm battered head to toe."

There. She'd broken the intractable silence of the past two days.

He acknowledged that with a nod. "The weather was no help."

What a relief. The Battle of the Long Silence was over. Those were the first words they'd exchanged in the past twenty-four hours at least.

"It's been a long day."

He nodded. Ringlets of black hair were plastered to his cheeks and temples. She resisted the temptation to push that wet hair off his cheeks. He would not appreciate fondness from her, of that she was certain. He gazed steadily into her eyes without any sign he cared what she thought or how she felt. "I must see to my cattle."

She gave him a small curtsey, gripping Frieda's leash in one hand and her umbrella in the other. The very best wife. "Shall I order you something hot to eat?"

But he'd already turned away, hand raised to catch the attention of one of the grooms. A young man already had a hand on the traces, intending to take the rig to the stables and change the horses for Bracebridge's original pair.

Emily hesitated. He hadn't actually told her to wait for him. Nor had he asked her to go inside without him. Did that mean his business with the horses would be brief enough she ought to wait here with Frieda?

Bracebridge took their bags from the boot. Along with the umbrella, he'd also bought her a pair of gloves, a warm, thick cloak, several useful and much-appreciated toiletries, and a valise of her own. Uncertain whether she ought to wait for him, she tapped the tip of the umbrella against the paving stone. She could always leave the matter undecided by taking Frieda for a walk. Before she could, however, the tavern door opened so hard it rattled windows.

A tall gentleman in a heavy greatcoat exited, unconcerned with whether he might have damaged the door. He took three steps into the courtyard, then broke into a run. Her stomach dropped to the bottom of the earth when he shouted, "Bracebridge!"

Aldreth.

Bracebridge had not heard him. He remained with his back to the inn, focused on the groom. She stepped into Aldreth's path, but so intent was he on Bracebridge, he did not see her. Frieda, torn between the opportunity to greet Aldreth or rejoin Bracebridge, shivered with indecision.

She called out, "My lord!"

Bracebridge gifted her with one of his dead expressions, but then he saw and heard Aldreth. Too late, though. Her brother-in-law grabbed Bracebridge by the shoulders. He looked wrecked, near panic. "Is Emily with you?"

Bracebridge pushed him gently away. "She is."

"Where?"

Bracebridge extended his hand in Emily's direction with a subtle *come here* motion of his fingers.

Aldreth whirled, then he saw her standing with her umbrella in one hand and Frieda's leash in the other. Her mouth went dry, and her stomach hollowed out. In three strides, he stood before her. He threw his arms around her at the same time she tried to curtsy. Her umbrella clattered to the ground. Frieda greeted him like a long-lost friend, wiggling, barking, and practically dancing.

"Thank God you are safe. Thank God." He took a step back and fired off a series of questions. "Where have you been? What were you thinking? Your sister has been beside herself with worry from the moment we learned you were missing."

His relief and anxiety brought home more of the consequences of her marriage. Aldreth and her sister had been worried, legitimately and deeply so. What had she done? Regret and guilt threatened her composure. She took her time retrieving her umbrella. By the time she'd straightened, she was confident she presented her usual self. "Good day, Aldreth."

"Where did you go? Why so far away?" He gestured at the coaching inn. "Tell me, please, please, that you did not take the post here. Were you attempting to reach Cynssyr? He's not in Wales. He's at Satterfield. If you meant to escape your father, you could have come to Rosefeld. Good God. I've been so worried!"

"I never intended to worry anyone. I do apologize for that. To you and Mary."

"And everyone else who did not know where you were." He hugged her tight again, clutching her as if he thought she might vanish from his arms. He set her back a half step but kept a firm grip on her shoulders. He looked at the dog, still wriggling with joy. "Frieda. Sit."

Frieda did no such thing. Emily tugged on the leash and managed to distract the dog by rubbing her ears. The groom Bracebridge had been talking to was adjusting the bridle of one of the horses still hitched to the gig, listening avidly.

"Mrs. Elliot came to Rosefeld," Aldreth said.

"You know about Sinclair and Davener, then?" Bracebridge said in a bored tone.

Aldreth shot a look at Emily then returned his attention to Bracebridge. "Once Mr. Rachagorla provided additional details about what transpired, I had my suspicions."

"I did not want to marry him," she said.

"All the more reason, Emily, for you have to come to Rosefeld rather than haring off to Wales. In any event, I went to the Cooperage to fetch you, only to be told you were not there, nor were you with the Glynns or with anyone else, nor at home when I returned to the Cooperage several hours later. And you"—he pointed at Bracebridge—"were also nowhere to be found. Mr. Rachagorla thought you might have returned to London, as did I, to be honest."

"Plainly not," Bracebridge said in a wry tone.

Aldreth waved his hands. "Not that it matters. I cannot possibly repay you for your quick thinking. Thank God you intercepted her on her journey to Wales. I shudder to think what might have happened had you not. Allow me to repeat, Emily, that Cynssyr is *not* in Wales. I don't know what you were thinking." Aldreth lowered his voice. "I would not have permitted your father to force you into a marriage you do not want." He turned to Brace-bridge again. "How far had she got before you caught her up?"

"Not far," he replied.

"Not far?" Aldreth frowned. "How could it have been not far? Was she here all this time?" His gesture included the coaching inn. "Is that it, Emily? You've been here all along?"

"No, Aldreth."

He lifted his hat, then resettled it. "I don't suppose it matters much. Good God, it's been a week. If not here, where have you been? You could have traveled to Wales and back in the time you've been gone."

Again, Bracebridge extended a hand to her. This time, she took it. "Wales," he said with a dark smile. "Or Scotland."

"Yes, but—" Aldreth looked at her, then at Bracebridge. "Scotland?" he said slowly.

"Yes." One corner of Bracebridge's mouth twitched, and he brought Emi-ly closer. "Gretna Green, to be specific."

Silence bore down on them, and Emily braced herself for a storm. "You are married?"

"My lord," Bracebridge said with a glance at the inn. "Shall we go inside to discuss this?"

"You've married *Emily?*" Under different circumstances, Aldreth's confu-sion and disbelief might have been amusing.

"Yes," she said because Bracebridge only shrugged, and Aldreth clearly had not caught up with actual events.

Aldreth blanched. "If this is a jest, I tell you I am not amused. It's unbe-coming of you, Emily, and Bracebridge—*you* ought to know better."

Bracebridge shoved his hands into his greatcoat pockets. "Let's not dis-cuss this here, my lord."

Aldreth glanced at the groom too studiously examining the bridle of the lead horse. His eyes had turned to chips of blue ice. His hand on her shoulder tightened. "Indeed."

"After you, Lady Bracebridge," Bracebridge said when they reached the tavern door. He took Frieda's leash from her and opened the door.

Moments later the three of them were in a hastily evacuated private din-ing room that smelled of beef, boiled potatoes and old beer. The table glistened with the aftermath of a hasty cleaning. Aldreth stood sideways with one hand pressed flat to the wall. He surveyed her head to toe, then pointed at the table. "Sit. Both of you."

Bracebridge did not comply, and neither did she. Frieda, however, oblivious to the tension, sat.

Emily's dread of the coming lecture ramped up. Her brother-in-law was rarely angry. He was everything a gentleman ought to be: well-mannered, honorable, and dutiful. His character was unassailable, and he had always been unfailingly kind to her. She would go to her grave never understanding why she'd fallen in love with Bracebridge instead of Aldreth, who had for so long drawn the hopes and dreams of the young ladies of Bartley Green.

"Good dog," Emily whispered.

"Emily," Aldreth said softly. "Is this true?"

She sat down. Aldreth was the brother she'd never had, then her sister's husband, and he had taken all the Sinclair sisters into his heart, and—she'd not realized until now how grateful she was to him for his kindness to them all. And now she was married, and he was so obviously disappointed in her and distressed.

Bracebridge unbuttoned his greatcoat and sprawled on the other end of the bench from her. "You may not interrogate my wife."

Aldreth's mouth thinned, but he did not look away from her. "Your objection is noted."

"We were married four days ago. In Gretna Green," Bracebridge said.

Aldreth looked to his right, then his left, then at his feet. "What have you done?" he said in a low voice, and Emily wasn't entirely certain whether he was talking to her, Bracebridge, or himself.

Bracebridge reached for her hand. She squeezed his fingers, then regretted the impulse. Too late. Done. No matter what she thought or wanted, her life was in Bracebridge's control. She forced herself to breathe slowly. Sheer madness had possessed her to agree to marry him over the anvil, and now the courses of her life and his were forever altered.

His fingers curled around hers, and that careless touch, which she knew had no meaning other than to have Aldreth take notice, nevertheless made her heart turn over. Even through her gloves, his touch thrilled. "I married her. You require no information but that."

Aldreth released a shuddering breath as he turned to the wall and propped his hands against the plaster surface. He kept his head down while he took several more breaths. At last, though, he turned around to address Bracebridge once again. "How far had she got when you overtook her?"

"You should have seen him, Aldreth," she said. "He hit Mr. Davener on the chin, and Mr. Davener went down. Outside the Cooperage. If it hadn't been for him, I would have had to make a terrible scene at the vicarage."

"Em," Bracebridge said. "You needn't tell him anything."

"You weren't going to marry Mr. Davener."

"Of course not."

Aldreth stared at the ceiling for a count of five. "You could have brought her back to Rosefeld."

"I could have."

He spread his fingers wide, as if resisting the temptation to make fists. "Why?" he whispered. "Why, when you do not like her?"

Before the conversation could go a direction that would likely lead to unforgivable words, she said, "I, too, am grateful to Lord Bracebridge." Was that a lie? She wasn't certain. She pressed her hands flat to the table. Bracebridge had bought her the gloves she wore: grey kid, soft as butter. "However," she said softly, "though I am not unaware of the circumstance you mention, it does not signify." How she wanted that to be true. "Bracebridge and I understand each other perfectly."

For too long, Aldreth stood silent. A flurry of emotions passed over his face. Frustration, relief, and pity. Then he looked straight at Bracebridge and said, "You did this for Anne."

Bracebridge lifted Emily's hand to his lips and kissed the back of her hand, but he had one eye on Aldreth while he did. "My reasons are irrelevant yet fully satisfactory."

"What if he did?" she asked. Both men were taken aback by her vehemence. "Do you imagine me unaware of that?" She pushed to her feet. "I've had enough of the two of you talking over me as if I don't exist. Bracebridge is satisfied with his reasons. I am satisfied with mine. Please believe that is true."

Aldreth took another deep breath before he replied. "I have only ever wanted the best for both of you. You are aware, you say. Then you must also know my opinion is that two people whom I love dearly have made a bad bargain."

Ultimately, Aldreth was right. And both of them knew it.

Chapter Eleven

B RACEBRIDGE PUT HIS HANDS around Emily's waist and swung her down from his gig one last time. He ignored the sizzle of attraction. Aldreth's conviction that this marriage would be unhappy for them both had sunk into his bones as undeniable truth. Anne was the woman he loved, not Emily. All the beauty in the world did not erase that fact. Lust had nothing to do with love.

She understood that, for as soon as her feet hit the ground, she stepped out of his arms and shook out her skirts. She'd traveled just as far and as hard as he, yet he saw no sign of distress or exhaustion in her. It seemed unfair that God would create a woman who could travel from one end of England to the other with no maid and almost no luggage and manage to look effortlessly perfect. Which she did.

Despite the travel-worn clothing, despite her obvious exhaustion, Emily Sinclair was constitutionally unable to look anything but exquisite. Even without the services of a maid this morning, she'd done something fetching with her hair. One of the filigreed combs he'd bought her at an early stop on their return glittered in the curls piled atop her head.

Emily looked around in silence. "As beautiful as ever."

"Thank you." They were at Corth Abbey, his home in Sussex, bought with the proceeds of his misspent youth and early adulthood. He was not at all certain he'd done the right thing bringing her here. Corth Abbey was his domain. Everything here was exactly to his tastes and preferences. His private and personal estate. Part of him resented her presence here already, and she'd yet to set foot in the house.

He reached into the gig for Frieda's leash. He pushed the door open wider to give the dog a clear view of the jump to the ground. As he did this, one of his grooms hurried around the corner from the direction of the stables. He extended one arm to the woman he had married, took Frieda's leash in the other, and smiled at her. "Shall we?"

She nodded, and he headed for the stairs with Emily on one side of him and Frieda on the other. Change must inevitably come, even to Corth Abbey. Whether he'd married Anne, Clara, or some other woman, he would have brought her here to the home he loved. His resentment was unfair.

"Given your preferences," he said, "I expect you would prefer to live in London. I have no objection to that."

"What preferences are those?"

"Yours. You love society."

She snorted, and that took him aback.

"Wherever you are in London, visiting acquaintances or family, you flit from amusement to amusement as if a moment of rest or reflection would cause you untold grief."

She stopped walking, as did he. Frieda promptly sat on his feet. "Allow me to point out that you have never seen me in any setting but a social one."

"I've seen you organize games for children and adults alike. When we were at Blackfern, I thought you'd run your legs off the way you were dashing about with the children."

Blackfern was Thrale's property, which he and the entire Sinclair family had once visited together. He'd lost his head with her yet again during that visit. One minute they were in the midst of yet another dispute—he couldn't even recall about what—and the next he'd taken her in his arms. He did not remember what they'd been arguing about, but he did remember the way he'd kissed her as if she were the only woman left in the world.

When Bracebridge managed to free his feet of Frieda's considerable bulk, they resumed walking, while the dog went to sniff something interesting near the bottom of the stairs to the front door.

"I like children," she said. "I especially enjoy entertaining my nieces and nephews. I don't often see all of them at the same time." Frieda strained toward the stairs, and Emily grabbed his hand. "Don't let go of the leash!"

"You know very well I shan't."

His butler, Pond, opened the door, and they hurried up the stairs. Behind them, a groom was driving the gig around the corner. The moment Bracebridge saw just a glimpse of the foyer, a sense of ease came over him. Lord, it was good to be home where everything was exactly as he preferred.

Pond, a short, dignified, white-haired man of sixty, hardly taller than Emily herself, had been born and raised in Hinderhead, the nearest village to Corth Abbey. He'd been the first servant Bracebridge hired here. When his father's butler had resigned rather than stay in the employ of the new Lord Bracebridge, he'd put Pond in charge of the London house without a moment's regret, then or now. From then forward, Pond followed him between London and Corth Abbey. "Welcome home, my lord."

A footman stood at attention near the back stairs, wearing one of the suits Bracebridge provided his staff in lieu of powdered wigs and frock coats. He'd be damned if he put his servants in livery. That was a tradition he was glad to let die. If he wanted to be reminded of his father, he could go to the London house on Cavendish Square.

Frieda, ecstatic to meet yet another friend, wriggled around Pond's legs. She could not reach the footman, though she tried. Emily closed the door while Pond pressed a hand to Frieda's haunches until she sat.

"Miss Sinclair." His butler addressed Emily with genuine pleasure. "How delightful to see you again. Are your esteemed sisters here, too?"

Manifestly, he and Emily had arrived in advance of Keller and Bracebridge's letter informing Pond of his marriage. Bracebridge stood to one side and reassessed the homecoming he'd imagined. Instead of a household warned in advance that there was now a Countess of Bracebridge, he faced the considerable bother of relaying his news and seeing that there were rooms for Emily.

"Thank you, Pond," Emily said smoothly. "I am equally delighted to be here. You've recovered from your painful knee, I hope?"

"I have. Thank you for inquiring, miss. The poultice you recommended was most efficacious."

Where had that information come from? Not only her recollection of Pond's name, but also her knowledge of his once painfully swollen knee. She would have encountered Pond on her previous visit to Corth Abbey as well as at the Margaret Street house on Cavendish Square, so the opportunity had certainly been there. All the same, he was surprised.

"I am happy to hear that," she said. "Our housekeeper swears by that poultice. I mean," she said with an uncertain glance at Bracebridge, "in Bartley Green. Mrs. Elliot at the Cooperage."

"Please convey my gratitude to her, Miss Sinclair," Pond said. "I have used that poultice many times since, for myself and others."

Bracebridge cleared his throat and said, "Pond."

"My lord?"

"She is no longer Miss Sinclair."

Pond broke into a wide grin. After Aldreth's less than enthusiastic response, Bracebridge was relieved that someone, anyone at all, was pleased by his news. "This is a joyful event, indeed!" Pond headed for the now-closed front door. "Is your husband outside? What are we to call you now, Mrs. . . ?"

"Carlisle," Bracebridge replied dryly as Pond opened the door, looked out, then closed it.

Emily yanked on the back of Bracebridge's coat and murmured, "That is bad of you, my lord."

"Mrs. Carlisle?" Pond turned, his hand on the door, frowning as if he were trying and failing to recall who the poor fellow was.

Bracebridge straightened his coat and said, "Less confusion all around if you address her as Lady Bracebridge."

"Lady Bracebridge?" Pond said with confusion.

"Yes," Bracebridge said.

The butler blinked several times. The footman standing at attention gaped. "Lady Bracebridge?" Pond said.

"As in my wife," he said.

Emily tugged on the back of his coat again.

Pond regrouped and bowed to her. "My apologies, Lady Bracebridge. I was unaware of this felicitous event."

"Of course you were, Pond." She took his hand in hers and pressed it. His butler melted. "In fact, you are among the very first to know of our happy news."

"My lady." He withdrew his hand and bowed again. "Please accept my heartfelt congratulations."

"Thank you so very much."

"My lord." Pond turned to him. "Words fail me."

"We seem to have arrived in advance of my letter to you. Keller must have been delayed in leaving Rosefeld. I had assumed he would arrive before us."

Emily's smile was absolutely dazzling. "It was . . . an unexpected event that came about . . . while—"

Her beauty was so unworldly that even Bracebridge briefly lost track of what she was saying.

"It is a great shock, I know. Thank you so much for your good wishes." Emily stooped to stroke Frieda's head. "But there are more introductions necessary. This is Frieda. She is my dog, but you'll find her love for Bracebridge knows no bounds."

In one stroke, Emily had cemented her place here and declared herself as fiercely loyal to him as she was to the dog of whom he'd become so inordinately fond.

"A very fine creature she is, Miss—Lady Bracebridge. We welcome her to Corth Abbey."

"Thank you." She maintained her smile. "There is one thing I hope you can assist me with."

"At your service, milady."

"Can you recommend a woman of suitable character who could do for me? Just until my maid arrives from Bartley Green. Not unlike my lord's valet, she was delayed in leaving."

"All shall be handled to your satisfaction, milady." If Pond thought there was anything untoward about the two of them arriving without their personal servants, he did not show it. Then again, Pond had been with him from his days as the disreputable Devon Carlisle. He'd seen more shocking things than this.

"That, my dear Mr. Pond," she said, "goes without saying. I am happy to employ whomever you recommend."

Frieda let out a woof that echoed in the foyer. The dog had ceased any attempt at pretending to sit; Pond was now her intimate acquaintance. Frieda pressed against the butler's legs then sat on his feet, looking up at him with an adoring gaze.

"Bracebridge," Emily said brightly and too quickly. She held out her hand for the leash. "I'll take her out. She's been such a good girl all these days."

He handed over the leash, aware of what Emily had already realized. The household did not know he was married, and therefore, could not possibly have prepared any rooms for her. If she went for a walk, the servants would have time to address the issue.

A still-smiling Pond bowed. "I'll have tea waiting upon your return, milady, and the lady's rooms made agreeable, though I hope you will understand if it takes a day or two to bring the rooms to standard."

She put a hand over her heart and beamed at him. Pond flushed. "You are a treasure. An absolute treasure. I have no worries whatsoever. Everything will be splendid."

"Thank you, milady. All of us here at Corth Abbey are happy to see to your every comfort. Whatever you desire, you have only to inform us."

"You are a dear man. Thank you."

They'd not been here even five minutes, and already she had his butler wrapped around her little finger. To be fair, though, she had not done it with one of her stunning smiles, though her smiles had certainly advanced her cause. Rather, she had remembered Pond's personal circumstance. It was well done of her.

Though he'd handed over Frieda's leash, he took it back. If they were to get on as husband and wife, he ought to act the part in front of the servants. Besides, there was no harm in knowing her better. "I'll accompany you."

Pond hurried to open the door for them, practically glowing with pleasure.

How many men had Bracebridge overheard discussing Emily Sinclair? Dozens. Most of those conversations had centered on her beauty, but not all of them. He had dismissed praise of her character as being the more deluded opinions of her coterie. Now, he had to admit he might have been wrong to do so.

He headed out with Frieda beside him and Emily a step behind because she'd paused to say something more to Pond.

"Thank you, Lady Bracebridge." The affection in Pond's response was unmistakable. Softly, he closed the door after them.

Outside, Emily caught up with him. She was exquisite, all that golden hair, those piercing blue eyes, and the way the delicate lines of her face combined. No wonder men lost their heads over her. He, too, could be counted in that number. But he had never entertained the possibility that she was more than her beauty. For the first time, a sliver of doubt lodged in him. He did not care for the feeling. "You must be as exhausted from our travels," he said because he could think of nothing else.

"No more or less than you, I daresay." She shook her head. "It isn't necessary, you coming with me."

"I don't mind."

"Go on inside, Bracebridge." She reached for the leash, but he did not relinquish it. "Honestly, I've been here before and know the immediate grounds. Frieda and I shan't go far, and only long enough for Pond to air out my rooms and change the sheets."

He looked at the sky. "Not a cloud to be seen. Let's enjoy the sun while we may."

"Very well, my lord." Emily set off at a pace that approached a run. That's how she was—always moving, never sedate if she could help it.

When he caught up, she patted the dog on the head, and he said, "You certainly made an impression on Pond. I do believe if you told him the house needed a moat, he'd be off to Hinderhead to buy shovels."

"A moat." She faced the house and shaded her eyes. "A moat would be lovely. I wonder why you didn't think of it sooner."

"If we're to have one," he said, "we must also have fish and swans, don't you agree?"

She threw her arms wide. "All that *and* a dragon!"

He laughed. "A dragon would be required."

"Knights in armor riding enormous war horses." She turned around and walked toward the edge of the lawn. "Pike the size of your arms!"

This must be considered a good start. They weren't arguing; quite the opposite. Had they a real marriage, based in respect and admiration, he might whisper words of love and encouragement about their future as Lord and Lady Bracebridge. A husband who cared for her might hold her hand or tuck her arm under his. Any other husband might lean in and give her a kiss. Laughter was a start, but it was not enough.

As they headed through the trees along the path that led to a meadow to their right, he cast about for a less fanciful subject. "You've added Pond to your legion of admirers."

Her chin came up, and her mouth curved into a smile that could have inspired DaVinci to paint angels in her image. Perfect. So perfect, her beauty hid her every emotion. "I've done no such thing."

Frieda let out a loud bark and ran to the end of the leash. Bracebridge reeled her back. That done, he lifted one hand, palm out. How long before they learned to converse as a married couple? He was afraid the answer might be never. He knew so little about her and even less about holding a normal conversation with her. "As you do every man who meets you."

She fell silent, and that quiet was familiar from much of their journey to Scotland and back.

"Emily."

"Yes?"

"I had considered us staying in London." How to say this to her when so many possibilities had been roiling in him since Aldreth had expressed his doubts? "But I thought it best for us to be away from society whilst our situation is so new to us."

She bent to pick up a stick, an action that caught Frieda's rapt attention. She drew off one glove and peeled off a strip of bark. "Because?"

"We do not know what rumors there are about us. Speculation has surely begun. I don't expect Mr. Davener to keep quiet. Nor your father, who I fear has likely already told at least three different tales about our marriage. Since we are newly wed, no one will remark if we remain here."

"I'm surprised you care what anyone thinks. You never have before."

"I care now that I am your husband."

Her gaze flicked to him, full of doubt. Again he felt the stirring of physical admiration for her. Other than that first night, he had kept their relations subdued. But they *were* married. He could take her to bed whenever he pleased. Tonight, even. In his own bed. Or hers. Without any worries about needing to be on the road at some ungodly time of the morning.

"I should like some private time to learn how to be a married man."

She peeled more bark off the stick. "Have I any choice?" She pressed her lips together. "You know I haven't. Whatever you decide, I must accept. Don't pretend otherwise."

"I'm not pretending anything."

"Yes, you are." She dropped the stick and headed back to the house.

"Emily."

She continued walking. Frieda whined, and he looked at the dog that his wife had rescued from a cruel and short life, and he found that he too couldn't bear to think of her starving.

Emily turned a corner, and he hurried after her. "Emily!"

She faced him with an untroubled expression that by now alarmed him. "Don't pretend you like me. Don't pretend you think this marriage will succeed. For pity's sake, at least consider the worst possible outcome."

"That I'll go mad?"

"That is farther down the list."

"I'd list it first or second."

She did not laugh, though he'd hoped to relieve the tension with the remark. She looked at the ground, then back at him. "What does it matter? Do what you will, my lord. It doesn't matter what I think."

Chapter Twelve

S OMEONE TAPPED ON the door to the parlor where she'd gone to avoid a confrontation with Bracebridge. She was far too on edge to deal with him without saying words she would regret. He'd brought her here, to Corth Abbey, a place that would never be her home because, the moment she stepped in, she'd seen what she hadn't those years ago. He had made this house into what it was for Anne. Not her. Anne.

Corth Abbey was a beautiful estate. One wanted to stay forever in such idyllic surroundings. Trees surrounded the house, with its reddish orange brick and its slate grey roof. And every square inch of the house and every acre of the property was a reminder that the former Emily Sinclair would never be the woman Bracebridge loved.

From the other side of the door, a woman called out, "Lady Bracebridge?"

Lady Bracebridge. She stared at the polished surface of the desk where she sat. The paper before her bore the Bracebridge crest. She'd intended to write her sisters, but she couldn't write the truth, and she did not want to tell them lies. Instead of writing, she sat alternately staring at the wall, the floor, and the blotter. She'd filled two pages with sketches of Frieda or the view out the window. Those were now ashes in the fireplace.

Lady Bracebridge for how long? Until the day came that she wasn't. If he had any sense, he'd divorce her and put them both out of their misery.

Whoever was at the door tapped again. "Milady?"

He'd never divorce her because he'd never allow a hint of scandal to touch Anne, not if he could help it. What a fool she'd been, letting girlish dreams override that truth. What a fool she'd been to dream for even a moment that Bracebridge would ever fall in love with her.

"Come in," she called out.

The young woman who entered was a year or two younger than she, freckled and wide-eyed, with dark brown hair and a warm smile. Even in her despondent state, Emily liked her immediately.

The young woman curtseyed. "I'm Maggie, your ladyship. From Hinderhead. I've come to do for you until your proper maid arrives."

Emily was very good at convincing others she was happy, and she had no doubt she would do so now. "Good afternoon, Maggie. I am glad to have you here."

The young woman pressed her hands together. "Pond says you've been traveling several days."

"Forever, it seems." Good, good. Days of travel were an excuse for her lack of enthusiasm, weren't they? "I'm exhausted."

"I can only imagine," Maggie said. "When I heard, I thought sure you would be longing for a bath. I ordered one as soon as I arrived. I hope you don't think that's too bold of me."

"Not at all." She wanted the familiarity of home, and Mrs. Elliot bringing her tea, and the privacy of dinner in her room, yet what a relief it was not to be at the Cooperage. No matter what happened with her marriage—whether she lived here, pretending for the rest of her life that she and Bracebridge cared for each other, or alone at some other estate—she would never return to the Cooperage. Never. Emily put away the paper and stood. "I should adore a bath."

Maggie grinned at her. "Shall we, then?"

From her previous visit here, Emily knew the location of the rooms that would be assigned to the mistress of the house, but even if she hadn't, Maggie knew the way. As they came in, Maggie said, "May I ask, ma'am, if you know what they've done with your trunks?"

Emily pointed at the valise Bracebridge had bought for her and that happened to be visible through the open door between the bedchamber and this anteroom. "There was a mishap, and that's all there is just now."

"Oh, you poor thing!" Maggie went into the bedroom and picked up the valise to look inside. The young woman frowned. Yes. Well. There wasn't much inside, was there? "His lordship will remedy that soon, I'm sure."

Would he? Emily had no idea. She might soon know the answer, for she wasn't convinced her father would send her things on to Corth Abbey.

Maggie took out the brush and comb Bracebridge had bought for Emily. "Will you come into the dressing room, milady?"

She did. Maggie put her brush and comb on the dresser top then brought out the bottle of lavender water Bracebridge had also purchased for her. Maggie quickly emptied the valise of its other, meager contents and put them away in the wardrobe. "I'll do what I can with what you have, if you don't mind waiting a bit to be dressed after your bath."

"Not at all." Emily would happily wait a year without leaving this room.

"I'm good with needle and thread. Now, come sit here." Maggie stood behind Emily when she'd taken a seat at the dressing table and began taking pins from Emily's hair. When she'd found the last one, she picked up the brush. She had a light, deft hand. "What a lovely color your hair is, milady. Like gold."

"You will find, Maggie, that I do not care for compliments." Emily half turned on the chair and smiled to mitigate the impact of what amounted to a remonstrance. "I'm vain enough as it is."

Maggie continued brushing Emily's hair, though her cheeks were flushed. "Congratulations on your marriage."

"Thank you."

"The whole of Hinderhead has been wondering when his lordship would marry. Some were convinced he never would, what with him being so . . ." Maggie cleared her throat.

"Dignified?"

In the dresser mirror, Maggie's smile turned impish. "Yes, milady. Dignified. Mrs. Duncan hoped he'd wed one of her daughters, but she's the only one who thought that might happen."

Emily closed her eyes and savored this moment of repose. But for the hollow malaise of her stomach, she could almost imagine she was home. "How did you meet his lordship? If you don't mind my asking."

Emily could pretend to be happy. She could. She would. She must, for as long as necessary, pretend there was nothing unusual about her marriage. Still with her eyes closed, she said, "Lord Bracebridge has been acquainted with my family for some years. Since I was a girl."

"Has he? What took him so long, then?"

Emily looked at Maggie and saw nothing but curiosity. Her eyes drifted closed again. "He loved my eldest sister, but she married someone else."

"Ah." Maggie repinned Emily's hair without further conversation. What a relief that Maggie knew when silence was better than chatter.

Her bath was soon ready, and Emily luxuriated in the water. Somehow, despite this being a household of men, Maggie had procured jasmine oil for the water and had added just the right amount. Emily remembered the jasmine soap from her previous visit, each new bar imprinted with the coat of arms of the Earls of Bracebridge.

Afterward, Maggie helped Emily into a fresh chemise and a too large robe. Thus clad, she crawled between the sheets of the bed where she and Lucy had once whispered secrets to each other, never dreaming that Anne's life and theirs were about to change forever. She fell asleep almost immediately.

Maggie woke her in time to dress for dinner. While she had been sleeping, Maggie had cleaned her gown and, miraculously, obtained several new garments: a mantle, a cashmere shawl, silk stockings, and new linens. She'd even had time to stitch a monogram in one of the chemises: the letter *B* surrounded by roses.

Maggie dressed Emily's hair in a loose style bound with a blue ribbon but primarily held up by the combs Bracebridge had bought for her. "There, milady." Maggie took a step back to inspect the result of her work. "Quite respectable, I think."

Emily did not bother looking in the mirror. "Thank you."

When she entered the anteroom where she'd been told Bracebridge was waiting, he was standing at a window overlooking the back portion of Corth Abbey. Even with the hollowness that had taken over her, she shivered at the sight of him. She liked his size, his wild, dark curls, the breadth of his shoulders.

"During the day," he said, turning partly toward her, "the view is spectacular."

"Is there any here that isn't?" She seemed to have stumbled onto the correct response, for he smiled. "I have always thought Corth Abbey was a beautiful property."

He tugged on the bottom of his waistcoat. He wore a fresh suit in the somber colors he preferred. Tonight was fawn trousers, a charcoal waistcoat, and a starched neckcloth. Looking directly into her eyes, he said, "Already you've made changes here."

She stiffened and came up with nothing when she cataloged what she'd done since she'd gone upstairs. The answer was nothing but bathe. Did he mean Maggie? Had Maggie done something he objected to? The clothes she'd procured? Having a bath brought to her?

Emily maintained her smile. "If you mean Maggie—that's the girl Pond found for me—I assure you, your quarrel is with me, my lord. Anything she's done, she's done at my direction."

He pointed to a vase of roses on a table near where he stood. "There have never been flowers in this room before."

Given that she'd made no such request, the flowers must have been Maggie's work or Pond's. Whoever it was, she wasn't about to let Bracebridge blame any of the servants. "My apologies." She went to the bell pull. "Since you object to them, I'll have them removed."

"Emily," he said.

He was too big, too vital. How had she not seen that before, that a man like him could only overwhelm her? She turned, sick with tension, absolutely sick with it, but she smiled as if she weren't.

"I do not object."

Here was another difference between her and Anne; her eldest sister possessed a well of patience. *She* did not, and she refused to even try to be Anne. She knew her own flaws too well to think there was any hope of success in that. "Then why address me as if you do?"

"Forgive me." He looked abashed. "A poor attempt at humor." He took a step back. "The flowers are lovely. I'm pleased the staff thought to put them in here."

She drew a steadying breath with little success. "These past days. It's been . . . difficult. I fear I have temporarily lost my sense of humor. But only temporarily, I hope." He did not look comfortable at all. What an awful mess this was. "I don't know how you expect me to behave. I don't know anything, and . . . and . . ." Oh, this was all just too much. Too much. "I thought you were angry with me."

"No."

She sank onto a nearby chair and covered her face with her hands until she was certain she could speak normally. Her chest was tight with an excess of emotion that would not be suppressed. "It's too much!" she said. "Too much. I cannot bear this. Not any of it."

"What?"

"This. Everything." How dare he look so confused? As if he did not know what a mistake they'd made. As if he did not resent her presence here. "This is your home, not mine."

"All this over my jest about the flowers?"

His dismissive tone focused her anger, a perverse sort of lifeline. "No. Not over flowers." She sat straighter. "Unlike my sisters, I do not bear my burdens in silence. You shall learn that about me. I am surprised you haven't already."

"That is demonstrably untrue." He bit off his words. "You most certainly do bear your burdens in silence."

So it began. The littlest thing set them to arguing. "You are laughably wrong, sir."

"Whom did you tell about your father and what you endured over the last year? Was it Aldreth you told? Cynssyr? Thrale? One of your sisters, perhaps? Or was it no one at all?"

"What difference does it make?"

"The difference between this marriage, another marriage, or no marriage at all."

She gripped the sides of her chair, sick with the realization that he was right. "You blame me."

He paced along the windows, shaking his head. "No. No, Em. That's nonsense."

"Is it?"

"Have you forgotten it was I who proposed to you?" He stopped a few feet from her, eyebrows drawn together, but she met his gaze evenly. "Had you told anyone about your father, things might not have come to this pass, true, but I proposed this marriage to you, not the other way round. I'll take that blame, Em."

"Do whatever you like."

"Come now." He smiled in an infuriatingly encouraging manner. "No more talk of blame. It accomplishes nothing. We must learn to get on better, you and I."

"Get on better? How? I don't know how to behave with you, Brace-bridge. Not as myself, for plainly that would be disagreeable to you."

"That's not so."

"I cannot be Anne. I'm nothing like her. I'd fail if I tried, and you'd hate me more for yet another failure."

His cheeks turned a faint pink. "I do not expect that of you."

"You're lying and think I'm too stupid to know."

Pond came in to announce dinner was served, and they fell silent. She was hideously aware of Bracebridge staring at her as if she had snakes instead of hair.

"Thank you," he said to Pond. "We'll be in straightaway."

Once Pond left, she said, "All this time, I have been asking myself, what would Anne do? She would know exactly the words to use to smooth all this over. But I am not her. I am not. I'm nothing like her."

His black, black eyes were on her, and she was dizzy with lust for him. He'd not touched her in days, not really. The difference between that first time and all the others was too marked. She could not stop thinking about that one night. One night of heaven. Once. Only once, and never since.

"I haven't asked you to be anyone but yourself."

"No, but you wish I were anyone but me."

"I have no desire to quarrel."

"Nor I." She bent her head to her lap until she'd mastered the emotions churning through her. "Forgive me. I am tired and out of sorts, and . . ." She straightened, waved a hand, and let it fall to her side again. "I do not mean to be difficult. Truly, I don't." She rubbed her face and let out a long sigh. "Tomorrow will be a better day. I promise you."

"For us both," he said softly. "I, too, am tired and out of sorts. I apologize if I made you feel unwelcome here. I did not intend that."

She pressed her palms together and lay the outer edges of her first fingers to her nose, as if she were praying. Oh, thank goodness, she was too weary for tears. She dropped her hands and stood. "We can only do our best whilst circumstances keep us here."

He nodded once and held out his hand. "Shall we?"

Thankfully, dinner was an informal affair. They managed to get through the meal while discussing the weather, Frieda, and whether Maggie would suffice until Emily's maid arrived. The weather was fine. Frieda was asleep upstairs. Yes, Maggie gave excellent service.

At one point, she put down her knife and fork and said, "It's lovely to know that tomorrow I am not required to rise well before sunrise for another grueling day of travel."

For the first time, Bracebridge smiled naturally. "I share your pleasure in that. I shall rise early, though."

"By habit?"

He patted his stomach. "I have a regimen of training. In fact, I meant to ask if you mind my taking Frieda with me on my morning breather."

She knew she ought to say yes but could not bring herself to do so. "She might run away."

"I shan't be careless with her. You know that."

"Yes, but suppose she escapes? Through no fault of yours."

"I've told the gamekeeper about her. Nothing untoward shall happen. Unless you account her coming home tired as being undesirable."

"I suppose not." Bracebridge liked Freida. She knew that, and yet the thought of him taking her with him filled her with panic.

They were coming to the end of their meal, and Bracebridge helped himself to several slices of the cheese that had just been served to them. "On my honor, I shall not allow her to escape. She's young. She needs exercise and I wouldn't mind a companion. She'll learn the property." He waited for her response and, when none was forthcoming, said, "I did not lose her on our recent travels. She's a most excellent dog, as, of course, you know."

"Indeed, sir. She is."

They sat in silence while she gathered herself. "May I take your silence for assent?" he asked.

"Very well." Inside, she howled with the fear that Frieda would encounter some disaster. She might escape, or run away, or, upon being allowed to run free, be shot by a hunter or gamekeeper even with Bracebridge's warning. "Take her with you."

"I shall keep her close, I promise you."

"Thank you." She knew her worry was exaggerated, but she could not stop; she could only live with her fault.

A few minutes later, Pond brought in glasses and a bottle of champagne arranged in a bucket of ice. "Thank you, Pond," Bracebridge said. "You may go now." He reached for the bottle and turned the label toward him. "I obtained this just a month before the war ended."

"You were not able to sell it?"

"This is from my private stock." The bottom of the bottle made a dull, crunching thud in the ice when he replaced it. "I always kept back several cases for myself and friends."

"Cynssyr and Aldreth, you mean."

"Among others, yes." He poured a dash of champagne into a glass for her and substantially more for himself into another. As he extended hers, he said, "Join me in a toast?"

She took the glass from him. "Thank you."

He watched the fingers of her left hand. She curled her fingers around the stem of her untouched champagne.

He lifted his glass and tipped it toward hers. "To the future."

"The future." She touched her glass to his. *The* future. Not their future. Not to happiness. *To resignation* seemed an awful toast to make. She took a tiny sip.

"You do not like it?"

"On the contrary. This is delicious."

He gestured toward her glass. "You are a married woman now. You may have more, if you like."

There was much wrong with their marriage, from the reason they'd gone to Scotland to how little they had in common, but she would go forward with the truth between them. "I do not care for spirits."

"May I ask your objection?"

She rested her hands on her lap, out of his sight. "Because of Papa."

"Ah." He stared into his glass. Bubbles rose toward the surface. "Do you mind if I do?"

"Not at all." She straightened on her chair. She was going to lose her mind from the tension of being alone with him, with no idea how to behave or what to expect of their first night here. She opened her mouth to make an excuse and return to her room.

Bracebridge stood and said, "You are a generous soul. Thank you." She nodded and told herself he did not intend to look at her as if she were already naked. She wished she were. She wished *he* were.

Then he held out a hand and said, "Lady Bracebridge, shall we retire?"

Chapter Thirteen

O VER THE PAST several days, he had learned to distrust his wife's pleasant, gorgeous smile; she was quite the actress. Bracebridge drank the last of his champagne and set down his glass. He had no hope of interpreting her expression. Either she was truly pleased with the state of the world or not. He had no notion which was true, but he suspected the latter.

On impulse, he took her hand in his. She went still. Their eyes met, and the outer edges of his restraint and good sense blurred. He could sweep aside the remains of their meal and make love to his beautiful wife on the table without the guilt of seducing an innocent or ruining reputations.

He passed his thumb over her wrist. He shouldn't. He should not subject her to his lusts. "Emily."

"My lord?"

Well, then. He wouldn't. They were done with traveling, but restraint was still required. She was his wife, not his mistress. She was young and so intensely beautiful, and he did not trust himself to treat her with respect. "How far we've come from when I first met the Sinclairs of Bartley Green."

She smiled, but there was no light in her eyes. He was learning how to look past the perfection of her features. "Indeed," she said.

"Not Mr. Devon Carlisle any longer."

A smile flitted around her mouth. Breathtaking. "I rather liked him."

"That rogue?" He'd always been aware of her beauty, but a man in love, as he was still with Anne, could admire another woman's looks without considering action. After he'd emerged from the depths of his grief over Anne's marriage, he'd lost his restraint with Emily. He'd kissed her more than once, and then came that day, that infamous day when he'd come within inches of being obliged to marry her.

He'd spent years making himself deserving of Anne, yet he had reverted to his old ways at the first serious temptation. Out of anger. Out of despair. Out of resentment that after losing the entirety of his family, he'd also lost the woman who had filled the hole in his heart.

"Mr. Carlisle was kind to me." Her tongue darted out to touch her lower lip, and he thought about that night on the road when he'd indulged his lust. Oh, but her mouth. Her mouth on him, and the way she'd groaned. The way she'd felt, the soft warmth of her, that quick intake of breath, the shattering pleasure when he came inside her.

He kept his attention on her lips and imagined more of what they'd already done and many things they hadn't yet. "What of Bracebridge?" He filled the question with carnal suggestion. Because he was a wicked man. "Do you like him?"

The moment stretched out, then something in her sparked, and she looked him up and down. He had no doubt whatsoever regarding what she was thinking now, and his body responded. "My lord." One side of her mouth curved up. "I like him very well."

Once again, he was speared by eyes the color of the sky. Thick, inky lashes made them bluer than anyone's eyes ought to be, as divine as everything else about her. He poured more champagne but stopped with the glass halfway to his mouth. "Do you object to my drinking?"

He expected her to demur, but what she said was worse. She said, "Have I that right?"

"You have the right to tell me what is disagreeable to you." He put down the champagne. Whatever their future, however long it lasted, she had that right, but she did have a talent for confronting an issue straight on.

"Are you cruel when you're drunk?"

His heart twisted up. The reason for her question was at the Cooperage in a bottle that had shattered against the wall by his shoulder. "I don't believe so. I hope I am not. No one has complained that I am."

She fiddled with one of the buttons on her gloves. "It's not my place to say what you may do or not."

That sounded like pure resignation, and the Emily he knew never resigned herself to anything. He tapped the tabletop. He did not know her. Not the way he knew Anne. This exchange had become something that mattered more than it ought to. Take one conversational path and the distance between them would remain. Take another and he might well meet whoever she was inside. "Was your father violent?"

Her eyebrows drew together. "In the main, Papa is blind to my flaws. That is, until recently. He thought I would marry Mr. Davener, but I knew I never would. I am not that sort of daughter, and now he knows."

"You persist in not answering my questions."

"You asked me about Papa. I answered you." She tilted her head just so, all innocence and delightful confusion. "Did I misunderstand you, and you meant something else?"

Here was that wall around the core of her, disguised with smiles and practiced charm. He might circle the perimeter and never find a way past. He said, "Did he ever strike you?"

"He'd never do such a thing." Her smile transformed her from a serious-minded stranger into the Emily he knew—thought he knew—open and easy to read, careless and carefree. The wall was there, though. And she'd stood behind that impenetrable facade.

He would not be misdirected like this. "He threw a bottle at me."

"Did he?" Her eyebrows arched in a careless fashion, but there was tension in her shoulders.

"He missed."

"He was not in his right mind, I'll warrant. Throw something at you, of all people. He could not possibly have understood what he was doing."

"He was not sober at the time, but I believe he knew exactly what he was doing and why. Therefore, I wonder whether he ever behaved so with you."

"He never threw a bottle at me." She rested a hand on his upper arm, and her touch threatened to obliterate the resolve that had kept him from repeating that one night of lust. "You took me to task for not answering your questions. Rightly so." Her smile dazzled. "I realize I have not answered your first question."

As a diversion, this was tactical genius. He was completely diverted, for he knew exactly what she meant. "Which was?"

"Whether we ought to retire," she said slowly. "To which I reply, yes, my lord. We should."

He stepped closer to her, drawn by her inconsequential, entirely innocent reply that wasn't innocent at all. When she did not retreat, he kissed her,
a soft touch of his mouth to hers once, then again. And another kiss from
which he did not disengage.

She relaxed against him with a sigh, a capitulation that sparked his
arousal and turned his best intentions to ash. She made love as if the world
would end any moment, as if there were no one else in the entire world but
him.

He drew back, not much, and said, "If we do not go upstairs now, we'll
not leave this room for some time."

Her smile in return was pure, mischievous joy. "Let's not scandalize the
staff on the first day."

Never once had he imagined walking the corridors of Corth Abbey with
Emily at his side and a destination of the nearest available bedroom. But he
was doing that now, and their destination was the rooms intended for the
mistress of the house.

He opened the door to her suite and immediately brought up the lamp
on a table by the door. Across the room, the fire glowed. These rooms had
never been used for their intended purpose, but now he was a married man,
and he was here with his wife.

Emily walked in farther, turning this way and that, touching furniture. A
young woman he recognized from Hinderhead appeared in the doorway to
their right. The girl saw him, and her eyes opened wide. He presumed this
was the servant Pond had hired for Emily. He liked her looks. She seemed
friendly and open. And discreet, for she curtseyed and retreated, the door
closing after her.

He remained where he was and watched Emily turn in a slower circle,
taking in the entire room. She ended by facing him with a ravishing smile. "I
have always liked the colors here."

"Please feel free to make whatever changes and improvements you like
here. Pond will see to everything." A vase of white peonies, fragrant white
roses, and pussy willow branches sat on a table to Emily's right. The arrangement was enormous and striking. He was glad Pond had thought of it.

"Thank you, though I like the room just as it is."

"You may change your mind tomorrow."

"I might."

He strolled to one of the interior doors and opened it. He'd put a good deal of time and effort into making Corth Abbey a home that others would admire and want to emulate. He had succeeded, but with Anne ever in his mind. The boudoir.

She hurried after him. The chimney glass went from the mantel all the way to the ceiling as it did in every room. The mirror reflected light from the lamp the servants had left and from the candles in sconces. "I've never had a boudoir before. Well, once when we were in Wales with Cynssyr. I felt quite the grand lady."

He stepped aside so she could examine the room at her leisure. There were flowers here, too. Roses and carnations this time. She stopped before the vase and touched one of the roses before moving on, and it stuck in his head that she liked the flower. That particular kind of rose in that specific color.

Was that true? Was that something Pond knew about Bracebridge's wife that he did not? What else was there to know about her that he did not?

He wandered away, thoughtful, and opened the door to a smaller withdrawing room. She'd followed him out and now peeked into this room. He brought up the lamp in here, too, brightening the shelves of books.

"Oh," she said softly, very much to herself. "I'd forgot how lovely this library is." She walked to the floor-to-ceiling shelves and inspected the volumes.

"If you had rather it be a withdrawing room—"

"A withdrawing room?" she replied without looking at him. "I should think not." She ran a finger across the spines of several of them. "You chose these with Anne in mind, didn't you?"

He did not answer straightaway, though she was correct. Then again, perhaps it was not surprising for her to guess he'd had Anne's sensibilities in mind at the time. "No doubt you have different preferences in reading."

"Not as vast as you imagine."

"I suppose I deserve that pert answer."

"You do." He could not see her face since she had continued along the shelves, head cocked as she read the titles. "So many of my favorites." Her finger paused on one on the books. She took it from the shelf and stroked the front. "*Waverley* was a favorite of ours. We took turns reading it to each other. I must have read it myself a dozen times. Then one day, it simply wasn't on the shelves anymore. I accused Mary of taking it. She denied it, and we had the most awful row. Only later did I discover that Papa had sold it." She turned around, the book in hand. "A great many books went missing like that."

"Anne told me."

She nodded as if the loss of those books meant nothing. He could not reconcile her blithe reaction with words that implied she'd keenly felt the loss. Yet her mouth curved in a perfect smile he'd seen a hundred times; careless, perfect, unassailable. She held the book to her chest. "The subscription library in Bartley Green did not always have what I hoped to read, but we made do." She headed for the door. "I am very glad to find *Waverley* here. It's like coming across an old friend."

He followed her out, but before she was halfway, she turned and gave him a look that made him picture the two of them naked and between the sheets. Primarily him, poised over her with carnal intention.

"And so," she said. She was teasing. He was almost certain of it. "I shall retire with a familiar and well-traveled companion."

"Emily," he said, drawing the word out low and soft. A seductive tone he'd used on other women, but never her. Until now. "*I* shall be your companion tonight."

Everything changed, and he could not fathom why or how, but it was as if she'd removed a mask and allowed him to see what lay beneath. There was some change in her eyes, in the angle at which she held herself: a softening, and more than a little of the spirit that had so often driven him to distraction.

Instead of facing a spoiled young beauty, he stood before a woman who knew precisely what she wanted: him. She wanted him, with his imperfect face and the body he kept honed to a weapon. Not Bracebridge, but Devon Carlisle, that depraved and wicked soul.

This was all those moments when he'd lost his head, him kissing her the way no gentleman should ever kiss a young lady, him backing her against a wall when her family was a mere two rooms away, him putting her on her back in a damned woods, within inches of ruin, him taking her to bed on their way to Scotland. All that, wrapped up in right now, and their marriage.

Chapter Fourteen

H E EXTENDED HIS HAND, unable to untangle his emotions from his sexual reaction to her. The two things might well be one and the same. There remained a chance he could restrain himself.

Emily remained by the table, one hand resting on the polished surface, the other still holding the book tight against her chest. Such stillness in her despite that breathtaking smile. He drew close and brushed the back of his fingers across her cheek. Her thick, inky lashes fluttered down until her eyes were half-closed. "Such silky, smooth skin."

Still with her eyes half-closed, she put down her book.

He pulled one of the combs from her hair only to discover it had been used more than decoratively. The mass of her hair loosened. When he pulled the other comb free, the rest tumbled to her shoulders, held up in place by a ribbon and a few pins he quickly removed. A darker gold than Anne's silver-gilt hair, thick and soft in his hands. The intimacy unmoored him, edging him past restraint.

He searched through her hair, finding and discarding pins. There were only a few more. Carefully, he freed a spray of tiny violet silk roses, much bedraggled from rain and wear.

While she did not precisely relax in his arms, she lifted her face to his. He stared at her, bemused and aroused, until she said, "Make me forget how badly this could go wrong."

"If the moon crashes down on us, that's God's will. But, I tell you, there's no better way to die than in the throes of passion."

A smile appeared on her mouth, and she leaned against him. He kissed the top of her cheek. He was going up in flames, and he embraced the conflagration. He kissed the edge of her mouth next, a feather-light kiss, then her lips, and she was soft in his arms, so soft.

Never mind the tension of the past several days. Never mind his doubts and misgivings. Sheer lust occupied him now. He continued to hold her head between his hands as he walked backward toward his countess's bedroom. She wasn't the woman he loved, but she was bloody well the woman he lusted after more than any other.

He kissed her several times as they went, in between whispering words no gentlemen should ever use with a lady. "I adore your mouth," he said. Another kiss, open-mouthed, with her leaning into him, taking and accepting. "I want my cock in you."

"As do I," she said without a shred of shyness.

"You'll have that."

They ended up near a wall, and he slapped his hand on the surface to balance them. He kissed her again while imagination and reality fueled his lust. He put his hands on her shoulders, and she wrapped her arms around his neck, and his heartache over Anne ghosted away in surrender, occupying a different space in his heart.

They were almost to her bedchamber. If they'd taken another few steps to the right, they'd be at the door. He took her hand and pressed it over his erection. They'd been here before. Poised to commit the sin of fornication. "I'll have this in you again. And again." The words came in a needy rasp. He braced his forearms on either side of her head. "Say it."

"What?" she asked, eyebrows drawn in, but there was a teasing lilt to the question. She knew. She knew, she knew, and she wanted to play.

"The word for that part of me I shall put inside you." He leaned his pelvis against her. "You know the word. I want to hear it on your lips. I want to remember the sound of you saying it when you have your mouth on me."

Her eyes were drugged with passion and curiosity and eagerness, and when she looked at him like that, he considered the options if they learned the bed was too far away. Any of them seemed a likely outcome.

She lay a hand over his groin. "The word for this, do you mean?"

"Yes." He pulled her close, and her fingers curved over him. "Say the word."

"Your trousers' front?"

He laughed. "One word."

"Is 'manhood' the word you mean?"

Oh, but she was saucy. "Not that one."

She pretended to be confused, and he laughed again, pressing his hips toward her. "Privity?" she said.

"There's another I wish to hear you say. You know the word. I've said it to you before."

She smiled, and this time there was no stillness in her eyes. The door to her was open, nothing withheld. He had but to walk in. "Cock, do you mean? Is that the word you wanted to hear?"

"You say it divinely." He was enthralled with the way her mouth moved when she pronounced the syllable. "You cannot imagine how wonderful it is for a man to have his cock inside a woman." Another kiss, this time to her upper chest. "Most especially inside you."

"You're the only one who knows that."

"Warm and snug and bloody damned blissful."

"It's blissful for me, too," she whispered. Her eagerness banished the bleakness that had lived in him for so long. He maneuvered them toward the door, stretching out one arm to open it. Once it was, and they were inside, he used the back of his boot heel to close the door. He whirled around to get them closer to the bed.

Aldreth could go to hell with his insistence that he could only make Emily miserable. She was *his* wife. She had agreed, eyes open, to marry him, knowing all the reasons she should not, and was there not something noble in that? Marrying a man despite his flaws, loving him regardless? Even if their feelings were unequal, that did not mean they could not get on. Whatever else was wrong between them, Emily Sinclair had always been his champion.

He brushed the mass of her hair over her shoulder and kissed the exposed side of her neck before he started on the fastenings of her gown.

So many layers of clothing. He wasn't careful, despite knowing she had almost no clothes here. If necessary, he'd send her maid into Hinderhead to buy replacements for whatever could not be repaired.

With her back to him, he regained some composure. Not enough, though. Not nearly enough. One woman's clothes were much like any other's. The basic tasks were the same. He wasn't an oaf when it came to undressing bed partners in need of such services. He pushed away her gown, separated from tapes and hooks and fastenings.

She sighed, low and replete, the sound of a woman in the arms of her lover. She looked at him from over her shoulder, heartbreakingly beautiful. She wanted him. She always had. Broken nose, unhandsome face, his rough life before he became Bracebridge. All of it.

He put his mouth by her ear as he slid a hand from the back of her neck to the side. "Beautiful."

She froze.

He kissed her ear. This time, he would be gentler. No anger. No impatience, just a night of sexual play. She tipped her head to give him access. "So beautiful," he murmured.

"Thank you."

Was that disappointment? It made no sense, so he dismissed the possibility. She'd heard such compliments hundreds of times. Like all the other men who'd praised her beauty, he meant the compliments. They were indisputably true.

"Unoriginal, I know." He started on her corset and quickly lost patience. The girl Pond had engaged for Emily would have to deal with the results.

When he dropped her corset to the floor, she bowed her head. Slowly, her fingers curled at her sides. He put his hands on her shoulders and slid them down her arms and turned her to face him. She looked away, then at him, into his eyes with such longing and uncertainty that his heart turned over.

He did not want to see her so vulnerable to him. He did not want to be reminded he had the power to devastate her, as losing Anne had done to him. Another kiss swept away the moment of poignant melancholy, burned it to ash.

"You'll tell me what you like," he said, half plea, half demand. "I'm nearly out of my mind."

She met his gaze with a forthright stare that spiraled him back to a world of pure lust. All else vanished. "I adore everything you do when we are like this." She draped her arms around his neck, leaning against him. "Be as brutish as you like."

The request wound him up tight. "Anything, everything you desire." He grabbed a handful of her shift and drew it up and over her head. The fabric unevenly exposed her knees, thighs, her sex. She only just got her arms up in time.

Bodies were made to fuck and be fucked, but even he, inveterate reprobate that he was, was momentarily stunned. How could he have forgot her unearthly perfection? He stood entranced, lost to desire, to her beauty. He put his hands on her shoulders and slowly drew them down. He stepped in and just to one side and continued to stroke her. "Allow me a moment to properly worship you."

"Tell me," she whispered. "Tell me everything."

He cupped her breasts. "These in my mouth, under my hands, against my body." He touched the outside of her thigh. "Your legs wrapped around me. My hands holding your lovely round backside. Your shoulders." He curved one hand around the side of her hip. "You moving with me." He pulled her close, one arm around her waist, his hand sliding over smooth, silky skin. So warm and soft and curved. He drew his other hand from her shoulder to her lower back. "So soft." He backed her toward the bed, a four-poster with the curtains tied back with tasseled ropes. She was stunning against that background of grey. "Help me undress."

He meant that as a question, but the words came out as a demand.

"But of course, my lord." She began with his neckcloth. He was distracted through the entire process because he kept looking at her body, touching her, bending to kiss one shoulder, then the other, or to draw a hand along her side. At one point, he dragged a chair close so he could toss his clothes on it. At it. Whatever didn't land on the chair joined her clothes on the floor. He pushed his braces off his arms and shoved his clothes off the chair so he could sit and pull off his boots and stockings. He dropped them on the heap of their clothing. The rest came off quickly enough.

"I want to look at you," she said when he was nude.

He lifted his hands as he stood. "Look all you like, but I'll not complain if you touch me."

There was deviltry in her eyes when she brushed her fingertips across his chest. Her attention flicked downward. "You seem bigger now."

He dropped his head back and took a deep, steadying breath. "Your powers of observation astound me, Lady Bracebridge." Those last two words slid across the familiar wound of his heart, then slipped away to live with the rest of his regrets. He took himself in hand and grinned at her. "I am bigger now than when we came in here."

"It's—"

"Massive?" His language was shocking. Ought to be shocking with Emily a lady born. Right now, the beast in him didn't give a damn about delicacy or gentility. He wanted her primed for him, ready to accept all his depraved and pent-up desire.

Her smiled turned arch. "I adore your body. The way you're shaped. My heart races just from looking at you. Touching you might kill me dead."

"I'll die with you."

She set her hands on his chest. "Such hard muscles." She smoothed her palms over him, lingering on his abdomen. "You *are* magnificent."

He was twice her size and more than double her weight; he was fully, even massively, aroused; and she responded to all that he was. He held her face in one hand. "We'll fit and fit well."

"Miraculous." She was teasing him, deliberately. He adored it.

She tried to hide a smile and failed, then gave up the attempt. "You are impressive, indeed, my lord." She spoke with such innocence he was briefly convinced she had no idea what she'd done to him. The flicker of amusement in her eyes gave her away, and his arousal ratcheted up. "I want to worship your body all night."

"All night?" The urge to put her on her back and himself between her legs crashed over him. "I promise you, I shall make every attempt to satisfy that worthy goal. But tell me, please, what would you do during those hours of adulation?"

"Touch you. Kiss you." Her fingers slid over his belly, alongside his cock. For half a breath, the side of her finger brushed his shaft. The look she gave him set his blood on fire. "Accept you."

Jesus. He was gone. Absolutely gone. He filled his hands with her hair and kissed her long and hard while he simultaneously moved them toward the bed. The scent of lavender rose from the sheets when he pulled them back. Clean and still warm. He slid into bed beside her, turning and pulling the covers over them in the same motion.

"Tell me what you like, and I'll tell you the same." He draped one leg over hers, a hand propped on the mattress just above her shoulder.

"Everything you did before," she said. "And everything you did not dare." She curled one hand around his nape, and he fell, fully and willingly, into his desire for her. "All that rogue Mr. Devon Carlisle wants of me. Everything Bracebridge does not."

Her use of his name stripped him of guilt. He'd reformed, was a man better than he'd once been, but she had never rejected Devon Carlisle. Never once, even though her father disliked, disdained, and disapproved of him. He pressed a kiss to the top of her shoulder. "I'll grant you that wish."

"You are generous indeed, my lord."

He laughed, then pressed several more kisses inward along her collarbone before asking, "Do you like that?"

Remnants of a smile lingered on her lips. "I believe I do."

"Believe? Is that all? I must search for a spot that suits you better."

"If you must, my lord. I shall not gainsay you the attempt." She brought him closer, holding him tight as she arched against him.

He breathed in the scent of lavender from the sheet and a trace of jasmine from her skin. His senses were full of her, of the softness of her, of her curves against him, and of his longing to be inside her. He drew a hand down her body and shuddered with anticipation. His fingers slipped between her thighs, so slick with desire.

She pressed upward, rising to his touch.

"Have I found something agreeable?"

"You have," she breathed. "You have."

Beneath the covers, he settled a hand on her hip. She was naked. He was naked and in bed with Emily Sinclair. He was going to lose his mind. "My heart is pounding. Can you hear it?"

She shook her head. He took her hand and pressed it to his chest. He sat back, letting the sheets slide down his back. "There. That's because of you." His attention fixed on her breasts. He touched the curves of her and watched, with great satisfaction, her eyes go hazy with passion. "Do you like that?"

She spread her fingers wide. "I like looking at you."

He leaned back farther and put his hands on his spread thighs. "For your pleasure, Lady Bracebridge."

She sat up, and that was a magnificent sight. He gazed at her, transfixed, his pulse racing with anticipation. She trailed a finger along his rib where a jagged scar the width of a man's fist angled slightly downward. "What happened here? I suppose you got that in a mill."

"I did."

"Did it hurt?"

"A ribber from the only battle I had no chance of winning."

She passed a fingertip over the scar. "Were you outnumbered?"

"The Devil Himself hit me." The Devil Himself was none other than Devil Wilcott, her sister Lucy's first husband.

Her attention flicked to his face, curious. She'd been quite young when her sister married, and he did not actually know how much she knew about that scandalous marriage.

"He was bigger than I, and a better fighter. I wouldn't have had a chance at any time, but I faced him when I was far too raw. I hadn't the science or the experience to come away without a memento like this."

"You poor man." She leaned in and pressed her mouth to the scar. Her breath warmed his skin, and his entire being centered on her. He smoothed a hand along her side, then up enough to cup one of her delicious breasts. He brought a finger over her nipple, and she looked up at him with those astonishing clear blue eyes, so darkly lashed. "Do that again."

"Tonight, I oblige your every desire." He was harder than felt safe.

Her eyes closed, and her lips parted, and that was in itself an aphrodisiac, no less of an arousal than having her breast in his hand, her nipple beneath his fingers, between his fingers. He tugged and was gratified by her moan.

Her eyelids fluttered up, and once again he was lost in those pools of impossible blue. He set about kissing every inch of her, learning what made her gasp and moan. By the time he was kissing her breasts, he was half-gone himself. For a moment, he feared he was being too rough with her, but she moaned his name and twined her fingers in his hair until he had to lean back to take the edge off his urge to be inside her, now, this moment.

When he had control of himself, he put a hand on her stomach and drew his palm downward. She lifted one knee in a restless motion, and he curved his hand over the back of her thigh. He stared at her body. Long legs, well-shaped and, God, the dip to her waist, the flare of her hips. More curves than he'd expected from so slight a woman. She put a hand on her belly beside his other hand, then slowly, watching him from beneath her lashes, slid it over her mons.

"I wasn't gentle with you before, and I ought to have been."

"Why?"

"I promise you, we'll come to know each other and what we like and how we like to . . ."

She pushed him so he looked at her face. But she wasn't angry. With a wicked grin, she said, "You are thinking perhaps of a certain word used in the poetry of the Earl of Rochester?"

He tipped his head to one side. "Rochester."

"I like his poetry better than Byron's, I'll have you know."

"You would, wouldn't you?"

"Say the word," she whispered. "Lord Rochester's favorite. I want to hear you say it."

After another pregnant moment, he said, "Fuck."

She drew a breath, and he was scandalized and aroused that he'd said the word to her, even though she'd led him there and he'd gone willingly. She was seducing him, this night seduced him, and he was eager to be ruined.

In a low, languorous voice, she said, "Will you tell me something?"

Gold curls fell over her shoulders and his heart felt so full, he briefly closed his eyes against the sight of her. But there was no escape from this cascade of emotion that must be kept at bay. With every breath he took came lavender and jasmine and an undertone of Emily. He dared not meet her gaze for fear his eyes would hold even a faint reflection of what he felt. "Anything."

"How many hundreds of virgins have you despoiled?"

"My God. What kind of question is that?"

She laughed softly, a sound that eased his fear. "Approximately," she said. "A round figure is sufficient."

He settled his hips against hers. "Fewer than a thousand, I reckon."

"Less approximate than that."

He pretended to consider the subject. "More than none."

"More than none, you say." She stroked his chest. "I can't have been the first."

He slid his mouth down her shoulder, and when he came to the side of her breast, he explored for a bit. "My dear—" *My dear* was a dangerous phrase all on its own. What did he mean by that? *Dear Emily? Dear wife? Brat? My dear God?* He settled on the safety of humor. "My dear no-longer-virgin bride. You were my first virgin fuck."

"I don't believe you."

"Nevertheless, it's true." He took her nipple in his mouth.

"I cannot think when you do that."

He lifted his head. "No? What of this?" He slid his fingers along the inside of her thigh. "Can you think when I do this?"

"There are no thoughts in my head but those of you."

"Believe whatever you like about me, but know my past indiscretions are just that." He pressed a hand to her cheek until she was looking at him. "Past. The only information you must have tonight is that when I put my member inside you—"

Her eyes widened. "Cock, do you mean?"

"Yes, I do mean when I put my cock inside you."

She slid her fingers between her legs, another of her devastating smiles flitting around her mouth. "Here?"

Lord help him. He squeezed his eyes shut until colors burst behind his eyelids. When he opened them again, her hand was still between her legs. "Have you ever touched yourself?" His breath hitched. "I cast no blame if you have. I find that arousing."

"Have you?"

"I have," he said. More than once while thinking of her. Something he ought not to tell her, so he kept that behind his lips.

"Tossed off, do you mean?"

"Where did you hear *that?*"

"That's no answer."

"Take it as a matter of faith that I am an unrepentant sinner."

"You *are* wicked," she said.

"I shall be wicked again in the future." He was used to the volatility of the two of them. He recognized the heat and fever that had stamped their previous encounters on his soul, so hurried and desperate. "Answer me this time. I insist. Have you?"

"Yes." She met his gaze full on. "I have."

He stroked down her side again and stopped very close to her thigh.

"I thought of you," she said.

He took away his hand, but his fingers lingered on her thigh. "Show me," he said.

"Show you what?"

"You," he replied. "Touching yourself."

She rested a hand on his upper arm and curved her fingers around him. The echo of her voice centered itself in his belly. "No proper lady would do such a wicked, sinful thing."

"You—" He elongated the word. "—are a right proper lady." Even to his own ears, he did not sound a gentleman. Devon Carlisle or Lord Bracebridge, both men were wicked sinners. He dipped his head close. "I want and desire you to touch yourself while I watch."

His focus stayed on her face so that as she returned her hand to her sex and did as he asked, he saw the subtle changes that told him she was deeply affected. He turned his head to look. Lord, but his wife was a fetching sight.

He watched her fingers and committed to memory what he learned about how she brought her body to pleasure. He'd do the same to her soon. She sighed, eyes closed, and shifted her hips. She wasn't the least bit shy or reserved, was she?

"Are you thinking of me now?" he asked.

"Yes."

He had never been more aroused by a single word in all his life.

Chapter Fifteen

T HE MOST ASTONISHING SIZZLE of need shot through her when Brace-bridge brushed his fingertip over the curve of her breast. Need filled her—no, it emptied her out, scooped her hollow, and put her body firmly in charge of her immediate future. She needed him to touch her. She needed to experience more of this. More, more, and more of him touching her, eliciting these feelings.

Are you thinking of me now?

She could think of nothing *but* him. For the past year, she'd constructed barriers around her heart while she learned to live in a different world, and now all that discipline and strength had been for naught.

"Are you?" he asked again.

She pried open her eyes, and the moment their eyes locked, she was gripped by the conviction that she must experience everything now, for if not now, perhaps never again. While he watched, her fingers moved along her sex in a familiar rhythm. She was at present so slick and full between her legs, she wondered whether she was too aroused to conclude.

"Don't stop, Em."

She closed her eyes and, as she so often did, imagined him staring at her body, perceptive, soulful eyes sliding off the curves that made the shape of her. With affection, with regard. Perhaps his hand was poised to touch her. He was enthralled, impassioned, eager to be with her instead of admiring her beauty alone.

Too much. Too much pleasure, then she settled into the quiet and pushed away her certainty that he would see only what did not matter. In her imagination, he would kiss her gently, and she would kiss him back. They were in the bedroom of his London townhouse, the one where he set up his mistresses, and she was in that wide bed, and he was with her, whispering that he adored her and no one else.

She hit that near peak and pressed harder, pushed her hips toward her hand, slipping away, then returning, and—so close. She was so close.

"Stop," he said, and so deep into her fantasy had she fallen that he startled her. He grasped her wrist and pulled her hand away from her sex. Her eyes popped open to see him staring at her.

Instantly she was as far from climax as she had been close just moments before. A sob of frustration rose. The sensation of completion to come faded away. "I hate you for that."

He leaned nearer, and she was buried by a sharp and terrifying realization that this was the real Bracebridge with her, not the man she pretended he was. His tongue ran along his lower lip. "I want to finish you."

He kissed her several inches below her navel. Just once. His mouth lingered there, warm and soft, then the dampness of his tongue. Wherever their skin touched, the side of his arm, the side of her leg, his torso, she was struck by how impossible this was. This wasn't the remote lovemaking that had filled her with such recent despair.

Then he shifted and rearranged his body between her legs. He hooked one arm around her thigh and explored her sex with his other hand. From one moment to the next, she had no guarantee she would ever draw another breath. For all she knew, this would be their only such encounter. This time might be the last.

She abandoned herself completely. His fingers stroked along her, and in the wake of that contact, sparks of arousal grew to flames. She was slick, all her sensations focused there. He stroked harder, and a sigh escaped her mouth. Her sigh became a moan, became his name.

He kissed her where he'd had his fingers, and a wave of pleasure lanced through her. He sent her wholly out of her mind. Before long, she gasped for breath, close, so close to a shattering release, she did not care about decorum or what was proper or anything but how she felt right now. She pressed a hand to the back of his head and lifted her hips to his mouth.

He stopped. The beast. Horrible, awful man.

"No, no." Her entire body strained toward the completion he'd denied her. She shuddered, seeking the peak she could not reach and feeling it slip away. "No, Bracebridge, no." She reached for her sex, but he caught her wrist in a light grip and pressed a kiss to her palm. Her eyelids were unbelievably heavy, but she opened them. Her heart and breath caught again. "That's not enough. Please. You cannot stop now."

"But I have." He kissed her palm again, his tongue tracing a lazy whirl.

His smug reply brought up her much-lamented habit of answering too quickly. "No decent man would treat his wife so abominably, I am sure."

The moment the words passed her lips, she regretted them. Too late. Far too late. They were said, and now he must be reminded of all the reasons she was not the woman he wanted.

He stayed between her legs, though, and she held her breath. His lips brushed the inside of her thigh, once, then a second time with the damp warmth of his tongue on her skin. "Madam," he said with a tone so prideful there was no mistaking it or his amusement. "Are you begging me to continue touching you?"

Dignity be damned. He had shown her a glimpse of paradise, and she wanted that promise kept. "Finish me the way you said you would." His grin was infuriating and devilish and the most arousing thing she'd ever seen or imagined. "Please."

"Very well." He began again, and with that, she became a creature with no reason for existence but responding to the demands of her body.

The tension of her encroaching climax pushed higher and higher, and his mouth and tongue were magical and wicked. He devastated her. She hadn't known it was possible to feel like this. Pleasure crested, and there was a moment in which she thought she could never, ever reach the other side of this pleasure, and then she did. She fell and fell and fell, and she relaxed herself into the next crest, and his tongue pushed her into mindlessness. In this world he had given her, there was no breath, no sound, no sight, only exquisite pleasure.

When she had her breath back, he slid upward along her torso until he was over her. He kissed her fiercely and lowered himself to her, sliding one arm beneath her neck. His fingers tangled in her hair, along with the weight of his body, holding her beneath him. She could but be pliant in his arms, she was so boneless with pleasure. His mouth ravished hers, and she fell into that, too.

Their kiss was different this time. There was none of the guilty, worried, flushed anxiety of their previous kisses. They weren't in danger of discovery or in the middle of an argument. The edge of his resentment was gone. She wanted to commit all this to memory, this night of her life when she could pretend her dream had come true and there was nothing before her but life with a man who loved her in return.

He kissed her with a sort of desperation, though she must surely be misinterpreting that. Tongues touching, exploring, and all the while his body moved over hers, a rolling pressure of his hips against her. He bent one leg to the side so his weight was partially taken by his knee.

Surely, she would be forgiven if she allowed herself to believe he wanted and needed to be close to her for more than her appearance. What was the harm in believing, for a while, that he yearned as deeply as she did?

"Come inside me, Bracebridge," she whispered. "Please."

"Mm. Yes. Soon." He cupped her breast in one hand, fingers pressing into her. She wondered whether it was possible to lose one's mind from desire. She was very close to finding out.

"Bracebridge." She wasn't a fool. She had observed the connection between parts of her body and pleasure. Therefore, her reaction to his suckling of her wasn't a complete surprise. Only the nature and intensity of it. Her eyes fluttered open, and even though she was prepared to see him, her breath hitched to see her imagination come to life. The dark, wild curls, eyes sleepy with wicked promise. Bracebridge. Not imagined, but real.

"Em," he said. He trailed kisses from the bottom of her throat to the top of her sex. Briefly, his fingers settled over her, and she was ready to feel that all over again. Instead, though, he resettled himself over her, hip to hip, and nudged apart her thighs. His expression changed from what she recognized as admiration of her to something else that made her breath stop and her heart pound.

She was glad of her beauty, then, and she was so rarely glad of that.

He stroked three fingers along her upper torso at the same time he pressed his hips against hers so the condition of his male part was unmistakable. She danced her fingers along the top of his shoulder. The muscle there was heavy and hard. She slid a finger downward along his biceps. Equally unforgiving. She could touch him all night and never have enough.

There wasn't anything in the world except the two of them, and right now she did not want the world to include anyone else. She touched his shoulder, gaze fixed on his face as he settled himself over her, his cock between her legs. Anticipation tightened in her belly, a swarm of lust and anticipation all tangled together.

He released a breath, then said with a heart-stopping smile, "I have wanted to fuck you since—you know when I mean."

"Do I?" She did know. That day she'd walked in on him with another woman.

"I should not have done—anything that happened between us. I knew better. I should have done as you did and pretended there was nothing untoward."

"You were worried about Anne. We both were."

"I could not stop thinking of you. I was angry and hurt, and there you were, so innocent and beautiful, and you risked everything for Anne's sake." He pushed into her, a hand underneath her hip with gentle upward pressure. She knew the goal of that and lifted her hips toward his, and he was fully inside her. She drew in a breath. He stayed still, and all her breath rushed to her upper chest and throat. She raised up one leg and let out a groan of pleasure.

"Magnificent," he whispered. "Divine." He moved in her, and she was nearly out of her mind. His lips parted, and his inky eyes lost focus. Her fingers gripped his upper arms hard. The sound he made was pure satisfaction.

Yes. God in heaven, yes. Him inside her like this was the most intimate, astonishing, life-altering experience of her existence. He pushed deeper in. "Yes," she said. "You inside me, yes. This, this, please, more of this."

Slowly, he blinked. His eyes were a thousand miles away, then he was back. With a smile, he put his mouth by her ear. His hips pushed against her, and he shuddered once as he went deeper inside her. "I'll oblige you as best I can."

She bowed upward, meeting his thrust. In response, he raised his torso, weight on his hands, elbows straight, and withdrew, and that, too, was bliss she gave in to. He pushed inside again, withdrew, then drove in harder, focused on her. A question hung between them. Once again, a shiver of disbelief shot through her, but in between that, the thread of her own need vibrated.

"Em," he said softly, a breath of air, with the diminutive of her name carried along. "Em."

"More," she whispered urgently, holding him close, cleaving to him, meeting his every thrust. "I shan't break. I'll tell you if I want something else." She understood how they fit together, and she matched him, reacted to him. The pressure of him inside her was delicious, and desire unfurled in her and became a promise of approaching passion.

He'd slowed his strokes, some longer now, and she groaned; at the peak of each of his thrusts, she arched her hips into him and found a sliding roll of her hips that brought him in harder.

His breath rasped hard, and he shook his head once. Curls fell over his forehead and cheeks. Once again, she watched his eyes go from unfocused to intent on her. He pushed in harder and deeper. He was moving in her harder and faster, and she would die from this pleasure.

"Yes," she said. "Yes, that. You're a brute," she whispered. She ran her palms upward to his shoulders, then down along his chest, not to push him away, but to touch and caress. He lowered himself to take her mouth again. She lost herself to the heat of their mouths and tongues and to the friction of his cock inside her, the sense of fullness.

This was Bracebridge she was with. Beautiful, brutish, forbidden Lord Bracebridge. A dozen images flashed through her head. All the times they'd put propriety and decency at risk, the way her body came alive around him, and now his naked cock was inside her, and she was fast losing her ability to think of anything but their conjoined bodies. There was an edge of anger there, and panic bubbled up. She tightened her arms around him and turned her face away from his.

"Emily," he said. He stopped moving, though he was inside her. "Look at me."

She did, her face perfectly arranged, proof against anger or recrimination or regret.

He braced an elbow on the mattress above her shoulder, his forearm curled around her head as he pushed in again, harder this time. "Emily, Emily, you'll slay me with pleasure."

She looked into his face, relieved to see a wicked light in his eyes. He grunted once, then pulled back, slowly again, then forward. God, the circle of his hips nearly did her in. This was a soul-slivering cleaving of him to her. He drew his hand from her shoulder to her elbow and then down her hip as far as he could reach.

There were words somewhere in her head, but she could not remember how to speak. He thrust harder, eyes closed, and she watched his face. They settled into a rhythm, harder and faster.

"You're all right?" he asked at one point.

"Stop asking, it's vexing. I want you like this, only more. Stop worrying. My God, you'll ruin everything if all you do is ask me if I'm all right. I'll tell you if I am not."

"I exist to please you, madam." He tightened his fingers in her hair and pushed in harder than before.

She responded in kind. Too many people told her she looked fragile and delicate, but she wasn't. Not at all. "More of this," she said. "More." She put her hands on either side of his head and stared into his face. His expression was a mixture of ferocity and drugged passion. "I won't apologize for liking this. I shan't. I never shall."

He pried his eyes open. "Don't."

She smiled in a slow, lazy manner, but her fingers tightened in his hair as she arched against him. "As hard as you like." She pressed her head back, then reached up and yanked away the pillow. "As you did before. Harder, even."

He pinned her wrists to the mattress. "Like this?"

"Be a brute." She gasped at his next thrust. Desire was the shape of his mouth, the sound of his breath, in the way he strained to stay close. She brought up one knee when he sank deeper this time, and a moan tore free from her, too. She was devastated by pleasure. Devastated, beyond anything. She freed her wrists from his grip and put her hands on the back of his neck. She angled her fingers upward and into his hair and met his body with hers, locked her gaze with his, and demanded, "Are you sorry it's me and not some other woman?"

"I'm not sorry for bloody anything." He shoved away another pillow and held her hip and slammed into her, then again with his arms straight, palms to the mattress above her shoulders.

She lifted her other knee and met his next forward push with an upward press of her pelvis, hard enough that her breath became a groan. "Yes, my God."

He drew another moan from her. She held him tight against her, one leg around his waist. "Emily, Emily."

His throaty groan sent a shiver through her.

"Divine, perfect Emily." He moaned, an inarticulate sound, and the motion of her hips matched his, and her pleasure ratcheted to the point where she wasn't sure she could endure more. "My God, you even fuck divinely."

She slid into wildness when he covered her breast: His fingers gripped her, then released. He swept his thumb over her nipple, and she gasped. He drew completely out of her and said, "Wait, devil take it, wait."

"No. No, why have you stopped?"

He turned her over and grabbed her hips and pulled up, a quick motion, frantic even. He put his hands by her shoulders, one arm around her waist close to her hips, holding her back hard against his torso. His erect sex pressed against her low back. "Allow the tension to recede," he rasped. His hips continued to move against her, slowly, enough to keep her close to the edge. "I promise you, I promise us both, the pleasure will come back redoubled if we deny ourselves a little now."

He leaned back and ran a hand over her bottom, then once along her sex, one finger, then two. "So soft inside. Shall I have you like this? Shall I offend if I take you . . ." He set his cock to her entrance and pushed in. ". . . like this?" She pushed back, and he slid deep into her. Every part of her longed for more wildness. "You little—" He thrust hard. "—brat."

This. This. She was ruined forever.

"Again," he said. His fingers tightened on her hips as he pulled her backward into his thrust. "Again."

He changed the angle of his penetration of her, her body tightened around him, and she forgot everything except how good she felt and how close she was to falling apart. But he stopped again. And this time he held her tight, so tightly, and he whispered in a low, hard voice, "Wait, damn you, wait."

She cried out a protest.

"I am going to make you lose your mind." He held her still, but he continued to stroke her with one hand. From the top of her spine to the bottom, around her stomach and upward to capture a breast. "You're my fucking post, aren't you?"

She hadn't the wit to agree, but then she should never have read Rochester. Bracebridge turned her over, and she feasted on the sight of his body, the hard muscles, the power of him. But now, but now. He was her husband. He pushed her down to the mattress, and she wanted the physical connection between them so badly that when he thrust inside her again, she shouted his name.

He slid a hand along the underside of her thigh, pulling her leg up higher, higher, and he came first, his head thrown back, mouth open now, silent, lost to her at the same time she was lost to herself.

Chapter Sixteen

A TAP ON the door woke Bracebridge from a sound sleep. He was momentarily disoriented. This was not his room. He was not alone in bed. His arm was draped around a warm female body.

Emily. His wife.

No regrets. None at all.

He sat, careful to keep the sheets and blankets covering her. She was asleep on her side, arms crossed with hands clutching her shoulders. At some point last night, he'd released the heavy silk curtains around the bed. He had no idea what time it was, but it must be late given that daylight penetrated the curtains. "Yes?" he said in a low voice.

"My lord." That was Pond, across the room, also soft-spoken. "My apologies for disturbing you." He cleared his throat. "The Duke and Duchess of Cynssyr have arrived. They wish to speak with you immediately."

Bracebridge had a decent idea what they wanted, but really, no matter how anxious they were over Emily's fate, they shouldn't expect to interrupt the coital bliss of a couple newly married. He had half a mind to tell Pond to send them on their way. He couldn't, though. One did not summarily dismiss a duke and his duchess.

More to the point, he'd never send Anne away. Not for any reason, and never when she must be worried about her sister. Of course not.

But he'd rather linger here. The sheets were warm, and if Emily wasn't too sore or tired, a morning bout would be a rousing, agreeable start to the day.

"My lord?" Pond said.

He hung his head. Mightn't they have contrived an afternoon arrival? "A moment."

His butler cleared his throat. "Her ladyship's maid awaits her pleasure."

Bracebridge scrubbed his hands over his face and through his hair. His night had not involved much sleep. Nor had Emily's. He glanced at her, and whatever their difficulties, whatever their future held, she was the most magnificent fuck of his life.

"Shall I tell Her Grace you will see her presently?"

Emily lay on her side, eyes closed. She spoke without moving. "There's no point in making her wait. Cynssyr, either."

He raised his voice. "I'll have tea in my room before I go downstairs. Please convey my apologies for keeping her waiting."

"My lord."

"Do please bring something for Lady Bracebridge to eat." He put a hand on her shoulder. The contact reminded him of the hours they'd spent exploring each other. She was such a delicate, fragile woman, but she made love with an enthusiasm and physicality that matched his own. He had no complaints in that regard. "Tea or chocolate?" he asked.

"Tea, please."

"Tea for Lady Bracebridge, Pond."

"My lord. I have shown Their Graces to the Matins Parlor."

"Thank you." He said nothing further until he heard the door close. He drew aside the covers and kissed Emily's shoulder. The bed smelled like sex, and she looked like his every pleasure about to be fulfilled. "I have to see her."

"I know."

He could not help himself. He stroked a hand along her side to her hip and around to her mons. "Are you sore?"

Emily turned onto her back. A shiver of arousal centered in his belly. She was absolutely exquisite. Her hair was now a wave of curls and tangles he found quite fetching. "No," she whispered.

"Are you certain?" He slipped his fingers between her parted thighs. She was wet, and her breath had become shallow. "I seem to recall taking you hard enough that you ought to be."

Her smile was secret, satisfied, and for him only. "It feels good."

"Yes?"

In answer, her hand wrapped around his stiff cock and urged him forward while she leaned toward him, one leg over his hip. "Quickly, if you don't mind," she said.

He brushed aside the thought that she'd said that to give him an excuse to rush, but then again, he was randy, and a quick fuck was entirely to his tastes just now. He slid inside her, and it was better than all the times before. He didn't even try to keep the separation between his appreciation of her physical form and his awareness of her as Emily.

He fucked her hard and fast, exactly as she'd asked. Speech became unnecessary and impossible. He chased his climax with the expectation that he would not reach the peaks of last night, but the world narrowed to the two of them, and then he came hard enough that for a brief moment he was completely gone. He could not breathe. He could not think.

Eventually, his brain did manage to register that he wanted to feel that way again. And again.

Her lips brushed his collarbone. "Anne is waiting for you."

He tightened his arms around her. "I promise you I'll make up for leaving you unsatisfied."

"Unsatisfied? Hardly." Her reply was amused. She did not sound like a spoiled young lady. For the moment, he was content to think it true. "However," she said, "if you feel you must make amends at a later date, I shan't dissuade you from the attempt."

He rested his head on her shoulder and laughed. This was her gift, that impertinent joy. "On my honor, I shall make amends."

"Go," she said. "You mustn't keep her waiting much longer."

Some time later, he entered the Matins Parlor to find only Anne seated on a chair near the fire. She set down her tea and stood. His heart lurched with a familiar ache. He loved her still. He would always love her. He would have destroyed every shred of his honor for her.

The present Duke of Cynssyr had been that rare boyhood acquaintance who had not turned his back on Bracebridge after his father threw him out. How ironic that it had been Cynssyr who had brought him to Rosefeld. There, Bracebridge had met and fallen in love with Anne. But for Cynssyr, he would never have met her. But for Cynssyr, he would never have lost her.

Anne settled her glasses firmly on her nose. He knew the gesture well, and it made his heart turn over to see it.

"Good morning, Bracebridge. Thank you for seeing me."

Objectively, Anne was merely pretty. Her sisters were undisputed beauties, but Anne's calm resolve and passionate intellect, her earnest devotion to her father and sisters, her kindness and character made her beautiful and dear and beloved by him. They had spent hours in conversation. Hours of what amounted to courtship.

"Where's Cynssyr?" The question was too abrupt, but then, this was not a social call, was it? He knew why her husband was not in the parlor. It annoyed him that Cynssyr was wise enough to let his wife handle the first round of questions. Recriminations would come from Cynssyr.

"He's gone for a stroll." She managed a smile, but her mouth soon firmed. "Corth Abbey is such a beautiful property. He bid me tell you good day."

He was not often on the receiving end of her disapproval, and he keenly resented it. Did she hope he hadn't been upstairs making love to her sister? They both knew he had been. He did not owe her sexual fidelity. She could not possibly expect it of him.

She smoothed her skirts once and gestured to another chair. "Please."

"I'll stand for now."

"Mary wrote me."

"Oh?"

"Is it true? You've married Emily?"

"I have."

She jumped to her feet and began to pace. He'd never declared himself to her, nor she to him. Never in words. Aldreth and Cynssyr had known he intended to propose to Anne. The imaginary life he had constructed for the two of them was as familiar to him as this house. His imagination. Not hers. He'd wanted her, loved her passionately, and he'd imagined a life with her. But that was as far as the two of them had got. "You must believe I want only the best for you."

"Thank you."

"I have always wanted you to be happy." She took a step toward him. "But *Emily?*"

"Did Lady Aldreth tell you that your father lost the Cooperage?"

She sat down hard, elbows on the nearby table, and leaned her forehead into her upturned palms. She sighed. "No. No, she did not mention that. Oh,

Papa. Papa, what have you done?" Since she'd said that mostly to herself, he did not reply.

"As it happens, the Cooperage is safe."

She lifted her head. "How?"

"I obtained the deed."

She understood what that meant. "Cynssyr will repay you."

"There's no need. I intend to transfer the property to your sister." *This* was the reason he'd proposed to Emily. So that Anne need never worry about her sister's future. Imagine what the conversation would have been if the discussion had instead centered on Emily's marriage to Walter Davener. "To make up in some small part for there being no settlement."

Her shoulders relaxed appreciably, and she resettled her glasses. "That is generous of you."

"I'm sure by now you've guessed your father took a familiar route to resolving the situation he was in after he put the Cooperage at stake."

She closed her eyes briefly. "Yes. Of course he would. I thought he was better. I thought he was. She never complained about him."

"Did you expect she would?"

"No." Her shoulders sagged. "I've never known anyone so convincingly happy when she is not. But Papa seemed so much better. He stopped writing me for money."

All along, he'd intended to tell Anne how he'd prevented an intolerable marriage for her youngest sister so she'd know just how deeply his emotions ran, but as he assembled the words, he was shocked to discover he had hitherto unexpected scruples. Emily was his wife, and he owed her both loyalty and discretion. "Your sister acted to put herself beyond his reach."

Her head came up, and her eyes widened. Anne understood what that meant, too. "By eloping with you." Her eyes narrowed, and he let the silence continue. "How like her to act in the heat of emotion."

"In that," he said gently, "you are much mistaken."

Anne wilted on the chair, and he saw the woman with whom he'd fallen so deeply in love. Always looking after her family. Always putting them first. "Oh, Emily. Emily." She took a handkerchief from her pocket and removed her spectacles to dab a corner of her eye. She pressed a hand to her heart, handkerchief clutched in her fingers. "Who was this other man?"

"Does it matter?"

"I suppose not. But what am I to say to you now?" Even the sound of her voice was dear to him. "I was prepared to lecture you for whatever foolishness led you to this, for we all know you and my sister do not suit. But now." She squeezed her eyes shut. Her anguish was so transparent, he was hard pressed not to take her in his arms and comfort her. She was resolute when she opened her eyes again.

He felt . . . odd. Unsettled. Conflicted. Not half an hour ago, he'd been in bed with the sister of the woman he loved, a circumstance he had never once thought would be a reality. More baffling still, his until-now unwavering loyalty to Anne had bifurcated. He had never put anyone's interests or well-being before Anne's.

She waved him off again. "You need not answer."

He bowed. "No doubt you wished a better fate for her than me."

"My dear friend," she said. "If anyone but Emily were your wife, I would scold you for uttering such words. Please do not misunderstand me. No matter my opinion of your marriage, I must thank you. All of us who love Emily owe you our gratitude."

"She did me a great honor by agreeing to marry me."

"How gallant of you." She waved a hand as she stood. "I regret that you became entangled in Papa's difficulties." She extended a hand to him, and when he took it, she pressed his hand between both of hers. "I shan't ask your reasons for marrying her over returning her to Aldreth or to me. I know she would not have been safe in any other case. Not from Papa." Her voice shook. "I cannot forgive him, Bracebridge. Not for this. My heavens." She pressed his hands. "What if you had not discovered Papa's plans for her?"

"Your sister would have managed an entirely different scandal."

"No doubt." She let out a breath. "I do not wish for either of you to be unhappy."

"I am aware."

"But, Bracebridge, my dear friend, your feelings are so very different from hers."

He gripped her hand, but there was a distance between them now that had never been there before. "How can I be unhappy when I have done what honor and my heart demanded?"

She touched the side of his face. He turned his cheek toward the contact. "My dear, dear friend," she said. "I would never have wanted you to sacrifice your future happiness on my account. I don't deserve it."

His chest tightened. This was the closest she had come to acknowledging the depth of his feelings for her, and it was a remonstrance after a fashion.

She was steadfast and serene, as always. "But I am glad you did, and for that I am sorry." She walked away from him to stare out the window. Presently, though, she faced him again. Years of heartache gathered in the center of his chest. "I have so wanted you to find someone you could love. Marriage is . . . nothing any of us can anticipate, no matter what we believe. You must know, I have long wished for you to be as happy as I am."

He lifted his hands and let them fall to his sides. She wasn't his. Anne would never be his.

"My sister . . . Emily is . . ." She threw up her hands in exasperation. Emily would not have held back whatever words Anne did not pronounce. "Bracebridge. You have been my friend and confidante. A gentleman in every respect."

"You may speak freely with me, Duchess."

She bit her lower lip once, then slowly shook her head. "I fear you have never appreciated my sister's many admirable qualities."

He ignored the guilt that streaked through him.

"She's so very young, and she has been spoiled and cosseted. By me. And Papa. By Mary and Lucy, too. But she is intelligent and as accomplished as any other young lady. If she seems flighty and unserious, well, I can only say that she is also joyful and generous and the most loyal friend one might hope to have."

"She's more levelheaded than you give her credit for." He'd chosen the colors of this parlor because he knew Anne would like them. Walls the same blue-grey of her eyes, a carpet the color of a summer sky. Elegant and restrained, like Anne herself.

"Say you of the girl who eloped with but a moment's consideration!"

"You must say the same of me."

She shook her head ruefully. "If it were anyone but you, I'd say you were dazzled out of your wits."

Bracebridge laughed. "In her defense, Anne, our scheme succeeded. She is safe from your father."

"But, Bracebridge, is she safe from you?"

Her hard question sent his heart pounding. He did not want to quarrel with Anne. "I hope you do not intend to insult me."

"No, never." Anne softened, and he was relieved. "You know what I mean."

"Have no fear on her account. I intend to see that she is." His next words were as astonishing to him as they were true. "I promised her that much and more when I married her. I mean to see this through."

Chapter Seventeen

E MILY HEADED DOWN the stairs as quickly as she could, Frieda with her. With her sister in the house, she needed to be as far away as possible. She wanted fresh air, the sky overhead, and her legs moving so fast she could hardly catch her breath. Then, perhaps, she might wrest her thoughts away from Bracebridge falling even more hopelessly in love with her sister.

At the bottom of the stairs, Frieda danced toward the door with Emily hurrying after. Escape was a mere ten feet away. Then the front door opened.

Cynssyr entered, hat in his hand, greatcoat buttoned. Frieda was ecstatic at the opportunity to meet a new friend and began her wriggling, enthusiastic greeting. Emily plastered on a smile while the duke hunkered down to greet the dog. He kept his face out of range of overeager kisses. Her brother-in-law was as impossibly handsome as always. "Who is this?" he asked.

"Frieda. She is my dog." She paused in the hope the lump in her throat would go away. Her hopes were dashed.

"Good day, Frieda." He glanced at her, his green eyes piercing and far too kind. She did not want his pity. "If I'm not mistaken, she is a relation of Roger's. Sit." She could not disagree. Roger was her sister Lucy's dog, a mongrel like Frieda, but with obvious wolfhound heritage. The duke pressed a hand to Frieda's haunches. At least the dog dipped her bottom toward the floor. Unfortunately, she then immediately pressed herself against his legs.

"She's young yet." There. Emily had managed to speak without bursting into tears. She and Cynssyr almost never spoke when only the two of them were about. She didn't care about him as a former suitor. She did care whether he made Anne happy. So far, the answer was yes.

"Emily," he said when Frieda settled down. She resigned herself to a lecture from him. "Are you well?"

"Yes, Your Grace." When all was said and done, he was Anne's husband, and his rank meant everything he said and did carried more weight. One did not contradict a duke.

"None of that," he said with a quick frown. "Not at a time like this." He held out a hand, but she avoided the contact by holding Frieda's leash with both hands.

"It would be more efficient if you and Anne spoke to me at the same time," she said. "Then I've only one lecture to endure."

His eyes softened, and she very much distrusted that. "Your sister and I have agreed to disagree on the subject of lectures."

"Very well. Two lectures then." She smiled as if she thought that a lovely prospect. "Please commence. I'd like to get this over with."

"I am the last person to lecture anyone in such a case as this." He fingered the brim of his beaver hat. "No lecture from me." He was not judging her; at least there was that. Kindness and warmth might be worse, though, for the lump in her throat returned.

She didn't know which was worse, Cynssyr pretending to celebrate her marriage or him only leading up to a discussion of all that might go wrong. "Anne may have other ideas," he said. "However, I am here to ask you how I may be of assistance."

Tears welled up again, unwanted and resented. She longed for him to mean those words but feared they were mere platitudes to soothe a situation that was wrecked beyond repair. Her husband did not love her, because he was in love with Anne. Everyone knew that. Only now did she realize how badly she wanted someone, anyone, to believe she hadn't made a complete hash of her life and, by implication, of Bracebridge's, too.

To have anyone, even Cynssyr, extend the slightest kindness to her personally, as if she mattered, broke her resolve that none of this would touch her. To her dismay, when she opened her mouth to thank him, she burst into tears.

The duke's eyes widened, but then he made everything worse, for he extended both arms, and she, still crying, walked into them. He held her close and rested his chin on the top of her head. "There, there, my dear. Cry until you needn't," he said. He gave over his handkerchief, and she took it.

"What about your shirt?" she said through sobs.

"I've dozens of clean shirts. Tell me everything. Is he unkind to you?"

She shook her head.

"Yet here you are in tears."

Frieda pushed her nose between them and licked Emily's hand when she reached to pet her. "I don't mean to upset anyone," she said between sniffles. "It's been . . . difficult recently." Too late, she realized Cynssyr would misinterpret that. "Not because of anything he's said or done. It's everything else. Papa, and, and . . ."

"I understand."

She looked at him through tear-filled eyes and saw that he *did* understand. An unexpected, scandalous marriage had also thrown his life into disarray. The reasons may have been different, but the immediate result had been shock and gossip. "Did you feel this awful when it was you and Anne?"

The duke hugged her once. "Shall we walk with this fine young dog of yours?"

"Yes." She sniffled again and covered her nose with the handkerchief until she was confident her tears were safely at bay. "I should like a breath of fresh air."

"I as well." He tucked her hand into the crook of his elbow, and they walked outside. They headed around the side of the house toward the iron gate that opened onto a groomed path that led toward one of the many groves of trees on the property. The stable block was behind them and to their right. "Shall I drive you and Frieda to Hinderhead?" he asked. "Let's have tea and visit the confectioner's, if that is agreeable. We might visit the butcher, too."

She blew her nose as discreetly as possible. "I've had enough of driving, if you don't mind."

"Ah, yes, of course. Scotland. Then we shall stroll about this beautiful property of your husband's." They walked in silence for several minutes, not heading any particular direction, until he pointed at a thick stand of pines. "There's a spectacular view through there. Shall we?"

Frieda went ahead until the leash stretched to its fullest, forcing Emily to either pull back or walk faster. She darted forward and caught up long enough to release the tension on the leash. Cynssyr easily kept up. "She's trying very hard to be a good dog."

"I can see that she is."

Silence fell between them again, but ten feet from the trees, she summoned the nerve to ask, "Why are you being so kind?" Cynssyr stopped walking and took the leash from her. "Be careful, Your Grace. She does not know the property."

"Understood. I'll not let go of the leash, on my honor." They resumed their stroll. Once they reached the shade of the pines, her brother-in-law said, "It's no small matter when a young lady of good family elopes. Surely you understand this."

Her stomach somersaulted, then tied itself into a knot. "Others might dispute that the Sinclairs are good family."

"None of that, Emily," he said. "Even if you were not my sister-in-law, there is no dispute on that subject. I shan't tolerate such talk from you or anyone else." He swung around to face her and shake his finger in her face. "Your sister is my duchess. You Sinclairs are of the best stock, so not another word of deprecation from you, my lady."

For a long moment, she wondered at his ironic use of *my lady*, and then she realized he'd used the honorific with full respect. She summoned the smile she used to assure everyone all was right with her. They continued through the trees. "Yes, Your Grace. My apologies."

He set a hand to her shoulder, and they stopped just short of the clearing at the edge of the trees. Frieda sat at Cynssyr's feet. "I meant what I said earlier. What may I do for you?"

She sighed. "Buy me a castle in the sky?" *Tell me how to make Bracebridge love me the way you love Anne.*

"Something more practical, perhaps." He removed his hand from her shoulder and stooped to pet Frieda. "I don't mean to shock you," he said as he did this, "but have you considered the possibility of divorce or annulment?"

"No!"

"Perhaps you should." He straightened. Heavens, he was serious.

"Is such a thing even possible?"

"Given sufficient resources and connections, time, and a willingness to accept the consequences, most anything is."

"Husbands divorce their wives, Your Grace." A return to her old life was impossible. She knew that. But was there hope for a future in which she and Bracebridge were not trapped in what she now realized was a certain disaster of a marriage? "Where would I go?" she asked. "How would I live? Papa would never have me back."

"Nor should you return to your father. That is out of the question. Now, it's true either option, divorce or annulment, would displease anyone who loves you." Cynssyr leaned against the trunk of a massive pine. "But if your situation is intolerable, as I suspect it is, I cannot allow you to continue in it. Not if there is something I can do."

"But, Your Grace," she said on a breath that trembled along with her heart.

"Marriage is not a state to set aside lightly." He plucked a twig from overhead and slowly stripped off the needles, heedless of the damage to his gloves.

"You did not divorce Anne."

"No."

"Why not?"

He looked skyward for a moment. "The circumstances of my marriage to your sister were materially different than yours. I was at fault for what happened, and I had political and social ambitions I wished not to be ended. So." He held her gaze. "For me, there was no question of ending the marriage. None." With a self-deprecating smile, he said, "There may well have been times when Anne felt otherwise."

"I'm sure not."

He chuckled and shook his head. "To the best of my knowledge, Bracebridge has no political ambitions. His interests lie elsewhere."

"But the scandal," she said, barely above a whisper. "The scandal is not to be borne. Anne would never forgive you, and she would know your role in the matter. You know she'd guess."

"Do not think me incapable of taking a position with which others, including my wife, would disagree. You are family and, therefore, my responsibility. Your future happiness and security matter to me. I have no wish to see you miserable or in harm's way. The question to be settled is what *you* wish to do."

"You think Bracebridge and I are doomed to be unhappy."

"I did not say that."

She wilted inside because it was true. Cynssyr's solemn mood solidified for her the depths of her mistake in following her heart instead of her head.

"Everyone says we do not suit each other, and if you, of all people, think that, then there is no hope. None." Her intentions of finding a way for them to get on dissolved. "Even you believe there is no hope."

"Nor did I say that."

"You are one of Bracebridge's closest friends. You know when he's done something he ought not to have." She loved Bracebridge to the point where she'd glossed over all the obstacles facing them and hadn't thought what it meant for him to be married to her. Whatever joy he took from his revenge on her father would not last. "You feel it. Suppose I said yes?" she said, tearful again. "What then?"

He tossed aside the twig and pressed her hand. "Bracebridge is not alone in his ability to remain informed," he said dryly. "You have not married in the Church of England, is that correct?"

She nodded. "He has a certificate, and the priest filled out his log."

"There's no question the marriage is legal, but if there is to be a solution, we may well find it in the fact that your marriage is not Church of England. It's a pity this happened after you reached your majority. But here we are."

She looked around. "Here, where I should never have been."

"Parliament, the courts, and the church alike may well compel you to remain in the union. You understand that, I hope."

"You must believe that I do."

Frieda had found a stick and was now happily chewing it to bits.

"Multiple grounds possibly offer a path forward, particularly if he cooperates with the effort."

Nor had this occurred to her: that Bracebridge would have come to the same conclusion she had and cooperate with this. Why, he might even decide to sue for divorce himself.

"Are there grounds for an annulment?" His matter-of-fact question shook her. He made the possibility sound inconsequential, yet she knew that was not so.

She shook her head without meeting his eyes.

"Has he been cruel or violent with you?"

"No, he hasn't. He hasn't. He never!"

"Have you?"

She wanted more than anything to sit down, for Cynssyr had just turned the ground beneath her into a quagmire. "Have I what?"

"Have you given him grounds to divorce you? As in infidelity or a refusal of his marital rights?"

"No, Your Grace," she whispered. "I haven't. I haven't. I never would."

"Gathering crim con may well be required—yours, his, or both depending upon the tack we choose. If we proceed, you must be prepared to hear disagreeable conclusions about his character and conduct, as well as yours."

Nothing was real. None of this was real. Except she knew without doubt that Bracebridge did not want to be married to her. She fully believed they would reach a time and place when all their differences and grievances would become intolerable to them both.

"A list of the inns you stayed at while you traveled to and from Gretna Green would be of great assistance."

She swallowed hard. "Yes, Your Grace."

"It is my understanding you did not have your maid with you."

"I did not."

"Were you at any time alone with a man other than Bracebridge?"

She shook her head. But no, that was not so. "From time to time I may have been alone with a male servant."

"Make a list of each of those occasions too. Name and appearance, if you recall them."

She reared back. "I've done nothing. I would never!"

"Hardly the point. We may find it to our benefit that you did not have a maid accompanying you. I daresay you were noticed at every stop. It will be simple enough to find witnesses whose recollections would be advantageous. Even with all that, we may be compelled to give undue emphasis to incidents that might cast you or your character in a poor enough light that he is persuaded to sue for divorce."

Her stomach tied itself in knots.

"While you are here at Corth Abbey," he went on, "please be aware you are surrounded by those who might speak of impropriety on your part. Make a note of who is reliable and loyal to Bracebridge and whether anyone is loyal to you."

"This is Corth Abbey. They are all Bracebridge's servants."

"You underestimate yourself greatly if you think no one here will find you worthy of their loyalty."

That made her laugh. "I'll keep a list of my enemies among the staff, for it's they whom you'll want. My God, Cynssyr, what are these words? Enemies among the staff, divorce?" She leaned her head against his upper arm, and when he folded her once again into his arms, she shook so hard she didn't dare let go of him. Bracebridge would learn to hate her, and the thought devastated her. "He does not want me. We've not been wed even a week, and he wishes he were rid of me. What will it be like a month from now? Six months? A year?"

"Best to understand one's choices," he said. He stroked her shoulder. "As well as what hurdles you might face if you wish to end the marriage. Or if Bracebridge elects to do so himself."

She pushed away from him and headed for the clearing. Cynssyr, still with Frieda, easily kept stride. They reached the path that led to the lake and headed down the gentle slope.

"Bracebridge has been my friend for a very long time," the duke said by-and-by. "I shan't regale you with tales of my misdeeds before I married your sister, but he's the reason I didn't drink myself to death or get myself killed from sheer carelessness of my person."

She stopped walking and faced him, aghast to realize she had not understood that her foolhardiness affected him, too. And Aldreth. And Lord Thrale. All her sisters. Her nephews and nieces, too. "I have no desire to be the cause of a break in your friendship with him. I cannot do that. Not to him or you."

A breeze brought up a swirl of dead leaves. Several wrens flew out of the surrounding trees, made a circle, then settled down. "My dear," he said. "I am aware you have long had feelings for him. Just as I am equally aware of his feelings for Anne." He held up a hand. "I don't mean to imply that you do not know these things. You do." He fell silent a moment. "I did not love your sister when we married. Nor did she love me. Quite the opposite, as you know. But I came to love her, passionately and with all my soul. Anne made me a better man than I was."

"That was inevitable."

"I cannot disagree with you." He smiled. "Your sister is a remarkable woman. However, my point is that it may not be impossible for Bracebridge to develop some degree of affection for you."

"What he did, marrying me, everything to do with the Cooperage, he did for Anne. Not me. He'll oppose a dissolution or divorce because of her. Because he won't have her hurt by the scandal."

"Perhaps."

She walked away from the duke, closer to the top of the hillock from which there was a sweeping view of Corth Abbey. Bracebridge was inside there, with Anne, being reminded of all the ways Emily was not like her sister. "He'd live a lifetime with a woman he cannot love in order to protect the one he does. I can do nothing to change that." Tears welled up. Horrible tears of pity for the future she had created for herself and imposed on Bracebridge. "Nothing at all."

Cynssyr and Frieda joined her. "Bracebridge has been my friend for years. Decades. He stood by me in difficult times."

"He could do nothing else. But you have stood by him, too."

He smiled slightly. "Such is friendship."

His imperturbable manner was worse than any lecture she would ever have from her sister. Cynssyr put before her an unexpected kindness and the possibility of freedom from the marriage Bracebridge did not want. Her freedom from a life spent with a man who would never love her.

Then why, why, did she want so badly to be near him when that was a certain path to despair? She wanted to be near him. She wanted those nights of his body and hers together, of forgetting all that was wrong between them.

Cynssyr found another stick and gave it to Frieda. While they watched her destroy it, he said, "Having dispensed with all that we have said to one another and you being assured of my support in whatever decision you take, tell me, what may I do for you now?"

"Nothing. There's nothing to be done."

"Not so." He ran his fingers through his hair before resetting his hat. "If I'm not to travel to London to consult with my lawyers, very well. Groundwork might be laid while we wait. Nothing irreparable, I do promise you. Meanwhile, would you agree to a lavish party to celebrate your union? Invite as many people as you like. Jubert would look forward to the challenge. I am happy to turn my home into a woodland scene for you."

Jubert was his chef, and his offer of Jubert's services was a rare honor. "Or a gambling hell?" she said.

His eyes lit with a devilish light. "*Rouge et noir, vingt et un*, dice. We'd dress the servants as Mollies and Black Legs and serve blue ruin and champagne. What a sensational party that would be."

She pretended to hit his arm. "Anne would never allow it."

"It's not for Anne to say yea or nay." His attention sharpened on her. "It's your wedding celebration. You need only send the bills to me."

"I don't think Bracebridge would approve of either offer, however kindly intended." She stopped smiling. "Not a party and certainly not me sending you bills."

He remained amused. "A wise husband allows his wife to entertain as she sees fit. That's a lesson I've learned."

"Bracebridge would never."

"Why? You forget I've seen the cost to outfit you for Town. It's not nearly what it might be. You Sinclair women are a frugal lot."

She laughed. "I don't feel a party with the theme of a gaming hell is the impression Bracebridge ought to make."

The duke put a hand over his heart and adopted a puppy-dog look. "You're certain?"

"Yes."

He blew out a breath. "I confess to some disappointment. However, I stand ready to assist in whatever you plan, here or in London."

"No party. He would not want one."

"If you are to be a wife soon set aside, an extravagant party would provide an opportunity to build helpful rumors."

She kicked away a pebble on the path. "There is no reason Bracebridge and I must live together. Many married couples do not."

"After they have been fruitful, yes."

She stared at her feet. Certain mysteries of life had become clearer with personal experience. Cynssyr and Anne. Good heavens.

"You might refuse him that."

The back of her neck and her cheeks flamed with heat. She could not look at him. "I doubt I have the will for that."

He cleared his throat. "There is one matter in which I intend to meddle, no matter what you say, and that is providing for your future security. It's difficult to protect your interests after the fact. At this point, it might even be impossible. However, I do intend to settle property upon any children you might bear, legitimate or otherwise, for your use in your lifetime."

She continued to stare at her feet. He meant if she were unfaithful to her husband.

"I don't expect Bracebridge to be unreasonable about this. Please believe you will not be left without resources."

"That's very generous."

"I've a moldy castle or two somewhere, I'm sure. You might find one of them will do."

"Have you got one with a ghost?"

He waved as if describing a fortress on a hill. "The one I am thinking of has been haunted since the days of the illustrious Henry VII."

She righted herself in this most unbelievable of conversations and smiled with the express intention of setting Cynssyr on his heels. His eyes did widen. She knew the look well. "It sounds delightful," she said.

"I always intended for you to have a settlement when you married. I put aside funds for you and Lucy shortly after Anne and I were wed. My idea, not Anne's, by the way. Or at least, if I'm to be entirely fair, I had the idea before Anne came to me with the same request. I'll not have any man wishing his wife had brought something to the marriage besides her heart."

She was absurdly grateful he hadn't said *beauty*.

"A most generous spirit." He took her hand in his again. "You are a delightful, lovely woman. There is a reason you are so well liked. I know Bracebridge. I know him well." He released her and put his hands on her shoulders. "Not every man deserves the woman he marries. If your marriage becomes intolerable, tell me. I will do what I can. Will you promise me that much? That you will tell me if your situation becomes unendurable?"

Chapter Eighteen

❦

W*HAT THE DEVIL?* The morning following the arrival of the Duke and Duchess of Cynssyr, Bracebridge stood at the side of his house in breeches and shirt, mouth open. A line of carriages stretched from the front door and around the first curve of the driveway and past. Two footmen were outside assisting passengers from carriages, pointing drivers toward the stables, or directing other servants to drive the same direction.

He'd gone out for a morning breather, an essential part of his training regimen, then into Hinderhead to spar, and now this? He wiped his forehead with his sleeve.

He ought to have expected this. His neighbors had descended upon Corth Abbey because the long-unmarried, scandalous Earl of Bracebridge had secured a countess. That, and the fact that the Duke and Duchess of Cynssyr were present. Word generally got around when Cynssyr called.

The length of the line suggested that gentry from well beyond Hinderhead had called, too. He glanced at the front parlor window and saw the owners of those carriages crowding the room. Thank goodness Anne and Cynssyr were here to handle everything. Not that he thought Emily incapable, but for a second night, neither of them had slept much. One could hardly expect a bride as young and inexperienced as Emily to cope with a crush of visiting strangers.

A drop of sweat trickled down the back of his neck and reminded him he was not appropriately dressed and that he ought not allow anyone to see him. His valet swooped in the moment he entered his quarters via the private entrance at the back of the house.

"My lord," Keller said as he caught the shirt Bracebridge stripped off and tossed at him.

"How long have the vultures been here?" He peeled off the rest of his clothes and touched a sore spot on his upper chest. When he was at Corth Abbey, he frequently sparred with a fighter who had retired to ownership of a tavern in Hinderhead. While he had bruises to show for the outing, so did his sparring partner.

"They began arriving promptly at ten o'clock, my lord."

It was now going on noon. Emily had been alone with those people for going on two hours.

"Thank goodness the duchess is here to see that all is in order."

Keller stropped a razor while they spoke. They had their routine. A fresh suit was laid out; polished shoes, ready. He stepped to the basin and picked up the cloth next to a jar of fragrant salve. "His Grace and the duchess departed shortly after you went out this morning."

Bracebridge stared at his valet. "Do you mean to say she's down there alone with every woman from the parish and Lord only knows how many others?"

"Yes, my lord." Keller took over washing away the dirt and sweat of Bracebridge's training.

"Someone should have sent for me."

Keller looked horrified, and under any other circumstance, this would have been the appropriate response. The entire staff was used to staffing a bachelor's household and, subsequently, knew his training was not to be interrupted.

"I do *not* wish to be interrupted. Nothing has changed about that. But I am a married man now. The rules must necessarily be relaxed."

"My lord."

"I'll have a word with Pond." He thought of that line of carriages. Emily must be overwhelmed. "News travels quickly."

"Indeed, my lord."

Further conversation was delayed while Keller shaved him. No doubt Bracebridge's marriage had become common knowledge within an hour of their arrival at Corth Abbey and grew widespread once Pond engaged that young woman as a lady's maid. Not to mention purchases had been made for Emily.

Of course everyone knew. Of course callers descended. Whatever disaster was unfolding in the parlor, the fault was his and his alone.

Keller wiped the remaining lather from Bracebridge's face. "Her ladyship herself assured us there was no need to fetch you."

He declined to inform Keller that Emily was in over her head. If the staff had not already realized that, they soon would. She had no experience with a household the size of his. The Cooperage was in no way comparable. "The cream waistcoat, I think," Bracebridge said. "With the gold stitching."

"An excellent choice, my lord." Keller retreated to the wardrobe to fetch the garment Bracebridge normally wore only for formal or official events.

He entered the parlor unnoticed, wondering whether the din signaled a success or something more ominous. Pond had opened the doors to the connecting salon to accommodate the crowd. Bracebridge recognized many of the guests, but not all: his immediate neighbors, anyone from Hinderhead with pretensions to gentility, and several from nearby villages.

Most everyone seemed to be smiling and holding glasses and plates of food. The kitchen must be an absolute madhouse now, for footmen strolled among the guests with trays of food and drink or discreetly removed abandoned plates and glasses. Farther inside the parlor, the scene was familiar to anyone who had ever been at a London crush attended by the Divine Sinclair.

His wife was the center of attention, absolutely radiant.

Fortunately, it appeared, the single men with whom he kept company knew better than to call without an indication from him that he intended to continue the acquaintance, but there were others who were obviously sons or scions of the leading families.

Despite the crowd, somehow Emily knew he was here, for she stood and caught his eye. He'd seen her in that gown nearly every day for the past fortnight, and still she took his breath. A flash of empathy for her got caught up in his reaction. He'd taken her from a situation not to her liking and put her into one where she would not have what she deserved. Plenty of better men than he genuinely loved her.

If he hadn't taken her off to Scotland to make a point to her father, one of those men would eventually have been her husband. Someone who loved her; someone who appreciated her intellect, her wit, and the joy with which she approached life. He'd denied her that.

His regret was complicated by vivid memories of her naked and in his arms. Her mouth. The taste of her. Her whispering his name. Her utter abandon to the act of marital intimacy. Being inside her while she clung to him. He yearned to take her aside right now.

They would find a way to make a life together. There would be no grand love, no exalted emotion, but there were grounds for mutual respect.

Someone tapped his arm. "My lord?"

He swung his head to his left to see Mrs. Iddings, the matriarch of one of Hinderhead's leading families and a woman who thoroughly disapproved of him. She sank into a curtsey. To her credit, her greeting managed to convey respect without pretending they were on good terms. For Emily's sake, he could do the same.

The Iddingses lived on the opposite side of Hinderhead from Corth Abbey. Mr. Iddings was not the sort to frequent the likes of Two Fives, or to attend parties to which Bracebridge had also been invited, so Bracebridge had mercifully little to do with either of them. The Iddingses had a daughter, but he knew only that she existed and was roughly Emily's age.

"Mrs. Iddings," he said with a bow. "Welcome to Corth Abbey."

"I am here," she said, "because of your wife."

He maintained a pleasant smile. "How delightful."

"We are exceedingly fond of Lady Bracebridge at Fontain." Fontain was the Iddings' estate.

"I appreciate your kind words."

Her attention focused on him. Mrs. Iddings was a handsome woman who had once given him a direct cut and had not addressed him since. "When we heard the news of her marriage, we came immediately."

Her marriage. Did she mean to insult him? Emily hadn't got married by herself, after all. He knew how to smile at people who thought they were better than he, so he did just that at Mrs. Iddings. "I was not aware you were acquainted with Lady Bracebridge."

"We consider her a dear friend." Mrs. Iddings cleared her throat, and he gave her his attention once more. She drew him aside, away from the crowd forming to greet him. "My lord." She curtseyed again, and the reprobate in him hoped she hated the necessity of all that bowing and *my lord*-ing. He was Bracebridge, and she had best not forget that fact. "May I beg a moment of your time?"

Nothing would have given him more pleasure than to send her away with a curt *no*. "Certainly."

"Thank you, my lord."

He restrained himself from asking her to get on with it. Emily would need allies if she stayed in at Corth Abbey, and Mrs. Iddings would be an important one.

"Your condescension is appreciated," she said. "Do please accept my heartfelt congratulations on your marriage. Mr. Iddings and I wish Lady Bracebridge all the happiness in the world."

Her sincerity took him aback almost as much as her exclusion of him from her wishes of happiness. For an absurd moment, he actually thought, *I shall be very bloody happy, thank you*. "I shall relay your sentiments to Lady Bracebridge."

Mrs. Iddings clasped her hands beneath her chin, gathering herself for the continuing effort of being polite to a man of whom she disapproved. "You are exceedingly lucky to have won her heart."

"I am indeed." He put his hands behind his back and curled his fingers around one wrist. The poor woman was floundering, and he took pity on her. For Emily's sake. "You are perhaps unaware that I have known the Sinclair family for many years."

"Lady Bracebridge mentioned her acquaintance with you once she learned we lived in Hinderhead." She took a short breath, obviously coming to a decision about what she intended to say to him. Thank God. He'd been in the parlor hardly ten minutes, and he was at his limit of good behavior.

"My lord. Mr. Iddings and I have not pursued as warm an acquaintance with you as we might have, given how close Corth Abbey is to Fontain. You came here a bachelor, and your frequent visitors were of a sort we were unused to seeing in Hinderhead."

He crossed his arms over his chest. He would not ruin Emily's friendship with this woman. He would not. Pray God, he would not. "I commend you for keeping better company than I."

She squinted across the room, but when he followed her look, he saw nothing there to pique her interest: several young ladies and a corresponding number of fathers, brothers, and other male relations. She returned her attention to him. "You have married the most generous, caring, and loyal young woman it has ever been my pleasure to know. I do confess to you that when she was introduced to us, I was concerned about her influence on my daughter. Given her family, I am sure you understand."

"We shall quarrel if you mean her sister, the duchess."

"I consider it an honor to know Her Grace." She lifted her chin. "But her father, the scandal of her sister's first marriage—"

"You mean the present Lady Thrale?"

She swallowed. "Lady Bracebridge has been an excellent friend to my daughter, and I could not, in good conscience, fail to pay my respects or tell you of our regard for your wife."

"Indeed?" He knew how to behave in public, but he was hard pressed not to tell Mrs. Iddings that he did not consider her opinion much of a recommendation. Emily, however, deserved his discretion. He had no wish to be the cause of difficulties between Emily and her friends.

"Our regard for Lady Bracebridge knows no bounds. She is all that is charming and gentle. So intelligent. Such a delight. Say what you will about her father, her character is exemplary." Mrs. Iddings pressed his arm. "All of this is familiar to you, I am sure, and I do commend your good sense and judgment. You have married an exceptional woman. All of us at Fontain hope to continue our acquaintance with your wife."

He gave her a half bow. "I leave our social calendar entirely to Lady Bracebridge." True or not, the words rolled smoothly from his lips. As for him, well, if he must tolerate a house full of people more often than he liked, he would. He would even tolerate Mrs. Iddings.

The woman beamed at him. "Very wise of you, my lord. I think you shall find a wife convenient in many ways, not the least of which is managing one's social calendar."

He inclined his head. "Thank you for your good wishes. Lady Bracebridge and I appreciate that very much." He took a breath and adopted the most ingratiating manner possible. "We are fortunate to have the support of a woman such as yourself."

Mrs. Iddings considered him for a long moment, and smiled in a way he had not seen from her before. He almost believed she meant it. "You are too kind, my lord."

She curtseyed and made her escape while Bracebridge stood, bemused and confounded. Guests descended upon him, eager to pay their respects. For the next half hour at least, he shook hands, greeted people he barely recalled, and was introduced to people whose names he'd never known and promptly forgot. He had not been the best neighbor; he was the first to admit that.

Eventually, he made his way to the sofa where Emily sat. The crowd around her parted when he reached her. The young woman beside her proved to be none other than Miss Iddings, whom he liked against his inclination. She strongly resembled her mother, but her face was open, agreeable, and sincere.

He kissed Emily's cheek amid swooning *ahs* from onlookers, and was swept into another wave of introductions. He recognized the besotted admiration of the company around his wife. Men and women alike fell under her spell. For the next hour, he chatted with strangers who had long wished to know him better and who now plainly admired Emily. He had several conversations about land usage, hunting and hunting dogs, and entertained one or two sly jokes about gaming hells, which he pretended not to understand.

The crowd eventually began to disperse, with Emily or himself escorting one or more of their callers to the parlor door. And then, somehow, he was alone with his wife, and their first social event as Lord and Lady Bracebridge was behind them.

Having seen out the very last caller, she returned to the sofa and sat with her head leaning back. She pressed a hand to her forehead and let out a long breath. "We have survived."

He wondered whether he ought to sit beside her but ultimately did not. "I apologize for leaving you here to deal with most of Hinderhead and beyond descending upon the house."

She sat straight. He had no idea how to deal with Emily as his wife. Should he be demonstrative with her when there was no prior affection between them? Was that not in some way dishonest? The state of their marital relations suggested otherwise, but satisfying intimacy was not the same as a years-long friendship, which they did not have. He again considered sitting beside her, but his thoughts went immediately to holding her in his arms. Was that not proof that what he had with Emily was something other than friendship?

"Pond was wonderful," she said, oblivious to his thoughts. "My compliments to him and your staff. As for the rest, you Hinderheadians are a charming lot. I enjoyed meeting them."

Two footmen silently removed the detritus of the party while another closed the connecting doors, returning the parlor to its usual dimensions. The servants completed their work, and he and Emily were truly alone.

"I was surprised you joined us." She curled her legs underneath her. "I told everyone you would not return in time."

After all, he did sit beside her, closer than would have been proper were they not married. This was his house. His home. She was his wife. "I'm glad I did."

She leaned back, chin tilted toward the ceiling. "I saw Mrs. Iddings take you aside. I was about to come to your rescue when you managed to get free. I am sorry. She can be a difficult woman."

"We arrived at an understanding."

She shot him a quick look. "About?"

He had no habit of confiding in Emily. She wasn't Anne, with whom he had so much in common. He and Anne shared favorite poets, their opinions on many subjects were similar, and they were often amused by the same things. He had always found her serenity to be a soothing counterpoint to his volatility. When he was with Anne, he always came away convinced he could be a better person than he was. But Emily? He'd spent the past year actively avoiding her because he was not a better person around her.

As he sat beside Emily, he acknowledged a prick of resentment. Anne was the woman he loved, and he did not want his marriage to interfere with that. He did not know Emily even half as well as he knew Anne. "Mrs. Iddings and I have agreed to hold our mutual dislike in abeyance."

"That is a relief."

"I was not aware that you knew her."

"Why would you be?" She rearranged her legs and the distance between them, surely by happenstance, increased. "I like Miss Iddings. We've always got along. I was resigned to being obliged to call on her at Fontain, rather than invite her here, for I know her mother disapproves of you. She's another Mrs. Glynn."

"There is no shortage of women who disapprove of me." He stretched an arm along the top of the sofa. "You may entertain whomever you like."

Emily shifted to face him. "I ought to tell you before I forget, I've promised the vicar I shall assist him with a school he is attempting to organize. I hope you don't mind. If you do, I can make an excuse."

"No need. Do just as you like." He pressed his hand against her far shoulder, and she moved closer to him until her shoulder touched his chest. They'd done this all backward. Lovers before the kind of encounters that led to respect and friendship. How on Earth did one begin?

"Mrs. Miller promised to send us her famous raspberry cordial, by the way."

He bumbled about in his memories for a recollection of this Mrs. Miller but came up blank.

"Your neighbor to the north. Grey hair going white, very spry, but like Pond, she has a painful knee."

"Did you recommend a similar poultice?"

"Yes. She walked here, and Pond tells me she is five miles distant. I sent her home in one of your carriages with everything she needs to improve her knee."

"That was thoughtful of you." Mrs. Miller, he now recalled, was a widow of some years. Exactly the sort of lady who avoided a man like him.

He contemplated taking Emily's hand again but didn't. She was wearing a pair of white kid gloves more suited to morning calls than the pair he'd bought her. Several shops in Hinderhead had already sent on bills for accouterments of the sort ladies required. He had put them in line for immediate payment.

He took her hand and toyed with the buttons on her gloves. "Until your things arrive from Bartley Green, purchase whatever you need from Hinderhead. Or send to London, if there is someone there you prefer."

"Thank you, I shall."

He unfastened the buttons at the wrist of her gloves and stripped them off.

As if he hadn't, she said, "I should like to have Mrs. Elliot come here. You need a housekeeper, and Mrs. Elliot will do quite well. Pond would appreciate the assistance. May I write to her?"

He worked off her other glove. He approved of the suggestion, and not the least because Mrs. Elliot would be her ally. "Yes, please. There must be someone to deal with female staff."

She moved closer. "I rather thought Maggie might be the first and last."

He kissed the tip of her first finger. "Mrs. Elliot shall be an exceptional housekeeper. If you had not suggested it, I would have. Write to her at Rosefeld. If she's not there, Aldreth will know how to reach her."

"Thank you."

With his fingers lightly around her forearm, he kissed her second finger, then the third, and finally the smallest. Her skin was so soft. From experience, he knew this was true everywhere. He moved closer and, at last, she ceased staring at the ceiling.

"Miss Iddings told me you were the most intimidating gentleman she'd ever seen and that she never dared look you in the eye."

"I am the terror of Hinderhead." He moved closer, twisting so he could look into her face. She was simply exquisite. There was a deathless silence between them as he gazed into her face. His focus settled on her mouth, and he slowly drew her close. Why shouldn't he kiss his wife?

She came willingly, arms around his shoulders, smiling, inviting. He kissed her, and she relaxed into his embrace and answered his lust with desire of her own. All his uncertainties and regrets faded away, to be replaced with a spreading lightness. There was no one less suited to him than Emily, except in this one thing. As a lover, she had no equal.

But he did not want this opportunity to know his wife better to be lost in dalliance, however appealing the idea. "Did Cynssyr or your sister say why they left?" He did not realize how treacherous the subject was until he'd broached it, and then he wasn't certain how best to recover. "I regret I was not here to bid them goodbye."

Emily's response was smooth, entirely unexceptional. "No, they did not. I asked them to stay, but Cynssyr said they never intended to stay long."

He did not trust her heart-stopping smile. She used her smile the way a knight used his shield. "Anne might have helped you entertain."

Silence fell, and still she was smiling as if at this very moment, the world was the best of all possible worlds. *Us.* He ought to have said *us.* What a blunder.

"I am capable of entertaining callers," she said. "As for being prepared, you could not ask for a better manager of your staff than Pond. He and York rose to the challenge."

"Indeed, they did."

"Even if you cannot trust my competence, you ought to have trusted theirs." She stood. "I've had a long morning. I'm tired."

With a sinking heart, he watched her leave. He'd bungled that badly.

Chapter Nineteen

EMILY STAYED WHERE SHE was when she saw Bracebridge come around the corner. Behind her, the path forked. To the left the path would take one to the house; to the right was the lake. He did not see her yet, so she took the opportunity to steady herself.

Frieda, now aware Bracebridge was headed their way, strained at the leash, but Emily said, "Sit," in a determined voice, and the dog obeyed. What a good girl.

Hinderhead did not have an academy like Mr. Johnson's in Bartley Green, but a retired pugilist owned a tavern in town, and Bracebridge often sparred with him. He took his fighting condition seriously. Every day he engaged in some form of training, whether it was a morning breather, sparring, or lifting heavy objects.

Bracebridge was at last close enough to see her, and Frieda left her seated position with a yelp, surging forward to the full extension of the leash. Emily stood to one side of this shady section of the path with a bottle in one hand and an umbrella in the other, which was necessary as a ward against the sun since her effects had yet to arrive from the Cooperage. She did not want to spend money on a new parasol when she had so many of her own. She closed the umbrella when he was close enough to know it was her.

Today must have been only a breather, as he called them, an exercise intended to improve one's wind and bottom, in the pugilistic parlance. He wore only a shirt, shoes, stockings, and his breeches, the latter being held up by a sash.

Despite the clear sky, the weather was cool, so in addition to her borrowed umbrella, she wore a woolen coat recently procured for her in

Hinderhead. Her half-boots were the same brown leather ones she'd been wearing since she'd left Bartley Green. The same bonnet that had made the trip to Scotland and back was on her head.

Bracebridge came to a stop several feet away. Her pulse sped up. She did like his height and the breadth of his shoulders. At the moment, his hair was a riot of black curls, and that dishevelment appealed to her as much as the rest. He never failed to make her pulse race. She'd had the idea that her relationship with Bracebridge might become something like her friendship with Harry Glynn, but it wasn't that at all. Harry never smoldered the way Bracebridge did.

He put his hands on his hips and took in and released several breaths before he spoke. He didn't seem annoyed or angry that she'd met him out here. "Em," he said with a nod.

She came close enough to hand him the bottle, which he accepted with an appreciative nod. "Have you been waiting for me, or is this happy coincidence?"

"Not coincidence."

One side of his mouth lifted. "I'll warrant you're the prettiest bottleman I've had at my side." He referred, of course, to one of a prizefighter's attendants during a bout.

"Mary says Mr. Rachagorla is very pretty." As soon as the words were out, she wished them back. They made her sound as if she only cared about his looks. Nothing could be farther from the truth. Mr. Rachagorla was one of her husband's closest friends. There was far more to him than his looks, whatever they might be.

"He is." He leaned down to pat Frieda. "What a good girl you're being. Gopal, however, never distracted me from a fight." He unstoppered the bottle and drank deeply. "You would, though."

She smiled. During her two seasons in London, she had successfully conversed with gentlemen and noblemen, cabinet ministers and members of Parliament, and she had never felt awkward or at a loss at any time. Bracebridge made her feel both. All the time.

He frowned at her, eyes narrowed. His lashes were thick and as black as his eyes. She had, in the privacy of their bedroom, kissed his beautiful eyes. She wondered what he'd think if she walked right up to him and did that now. "I should not have said that," he said.

"That Mr. Rachagorla is pretty? Why not, if it's true?"

"Not that."

She patted Frieda's shoulder. "What a good dog you are. She's behaving very well, don't you think?"

"When I compliment you, it is impossible to tell whether you take any pleasure in what I say."

Her heart sank. This would soon be another mark in the column for failed conversations. "I assure you, I am always pleased."

He handed the bottle back to her, then crouched down, hands cupped. She understood what he intended, for she poured water into his hands so that Frieda could drink. "You do not like flattery. That is my conclusion. What I don't understand is why."

"I do not want to argue. Not again. I apologize for making you think I do not appreciate your compliments."

"This is a discussion, not an argument. I want to understand." He stood and took back the bottle. He managed to wash off his face with what was left. When he was done, he rubbed his fingers through his hair.

"I suppose I could lie and tell you I wish to be flattered every moment of every day. But it isn't so." She waited until the lump in her throat was gone. "I appreciate your kind words, but are there not other things you might say to me? You might comment on the weather or something you have recently read. Anything."

His expression moved from concerned to amused to something that made her think she really ought to kiss him. He looked at her from beneath half-lidded eyes. "Sometimes I tell you 'more' or 'harder' or 'this spot over here.'"

"Yes," she said, willing to have him divert her in this manner. "Sometimes you do say that." With her most innocent expression and voice, she said, "I always follow your instructions."

"You do." He took a step toward her. "When we are intimate, I wish to tell you what I feel. Whatever your opinion about all the gentlemen who flatter you, you are an extraordinarily beautiful woman. May I tell you that, in those circumstances, without worrying that I am displeasing you?"

"Yes, of course." She took a step closer to him.

"I'm not fit company for a lady when I've been training."

She looked away from his face, from his soulful, expressive eyes. She had the right now to stare at him as much as she liked. Slowly her gaze moved downward. Her attention lingered at his chest and then at his hips. "Yes, look at you," she said in a voice full of the white-hot spark of desire arcing through her. "What a sight you are."

"Em."

"I am not in the least offended by you."

He grabbed the front of his shirt in both hands. "When I'm like this?"

"True, I like you better when you haven't a shirt at all."

He peeled off the shirt, revealing his heavily muscled chest. He gave her a wicked grin when he stood there, bare chested, his shirt clutched in one hand. "Like so?"

"Just so." His smile melted her inside. She did like the way he looked. "There's shade here," she said, indicating a spot between several trees, three or four steps past the opposite side of the path and into the surrounding trees. "Wouldn't you prefer to stand in the shade?"

Her entire being focused on Bracebridge when he glanced that direction. When he looked back, it was he who examined her from head to toe. She'd do anything for him when he looked at her like that, like he wanted to devour her. He took Frieda's leash and tied one end to a branch suitable for the purpose.

"You prefer a disreputable man?"

"No doubt you're ashamed to have a wife such as I am," she said.

He grabbed her hand and walked them both off the path. "You're correct. I had much rather be in the shade."

She faced him, and he placed his hands atop her shoulders. She lifted her hands and set her fingers lightly to his chest. His skin was warm. She pressed her palms to his pectorals and slid her hands down. His body was hard, and she wondered why that did not frighten her, when he was so much larger than her.

"Give me your coat," he said in a voice that was half growl. He stood behind her to assist her.

Her memories of that day a year ago when he had disabused her of the idea there could be anything between them pained her still. He had not been kind. But she had never been able to forget the moments leading up to those words.

She closed her eyes. This wasn't Bartley Green, but all the same emotions burned through her. Bracebridge touching her, kissing her, his hands on her in places no one else had ever touched. Drugging, glorious, kisses. Her heart's desire within reach.

When the garment was in his hands, he kissed the top of her shoulder.

That infamous day, they had been outside in the woods near the Cooperage, like now, on the edge of physical paradise. She had not known then what she did today, and she understood now why he had been so horrified. He had known that they were on the edge of unrecoverable ruin.

She was not the same woman now; how could she be? She was married, no longer innocent of all *that*, and the one thing she knew without any doubt at all was the two of them were physical creatures. Perhaps that was all they'd ever have.

He spread her cloak on the ground between the trees and helped her to sit. Once he was beside her, he kicked off his shoes. Her heart jumped because his smile was genuine and private, meant only for her. Only her.

"Hurry," she whispered in a passion-roughened voice.

"Here." He guided her to his lap and made short work of the fastening of his trousers. She was wet between her legs, ready for him. He brought himself to her, and once they got her skirts out of the way, she adjusted herself, hands on his shoulders, until he was inside her, stroking upward. "Lord, Em."

His hands tightened around her hips. Holding her hard. This was more than paradise, though it was a paradise she lived in by herself. Plenty of men who were handsome and kind, or amusing or admirable for any number of reasons had begged for her attention. But her body had known all along that Bracebridge was the only man who mattered.

She bent over him and kissed him, hard, deep, passionate, and he returned her passion in kind. She adjusted herself and the rhythm of her hips, so that he came in deeper, and she pressed her hands to his chest, all the hard muscle of his stomach, each ridge, down lower. "I adore your body."

"Wait, Em."

She forced her eyes open. "What?"

He was grinning; she had absolutely no idea why, until he said, "Touch me a little bit over here."

She didn't mean to laugh, but she did, and it seemed a miracle to her that he laughed, too, and it was a moment so perfect that her heart broke. She let go of her resentment and guilt and accepted what she felt right then, which was a deep and abiding love.

When it was over and they had each found their private bliss, he put his arm around her shoulders, drew her close, and whispered, "I repeat what I said earlier. You're the prettiest bottleman I've ever had."

She turned her face away from his, resting her cheek on his chest near his shoulder. She laughed, because it was amusing at the same time it wasn't. "Thank you."

Chapter Twenty

THE CLOCK ON the mantel struck three in the morning, then settled into a low tick-tock. The house was otherwise silent, yet an unaccustomed ache in his heart kept Bracebridge from falling back to sleep. His disquiet was not his sorrow over losing Anne—no, this feeling was new and unsettling. It was a disturbance in him that made him feel a stranger in his own home. The sensation had begun as the faintest of whispers, easy to dismiss. And now it wasn't.

He was in Emily's room, where he had been every night since his return from Gretna Green. Emily was sleeping with her back to him, curled up just barely in reach of his outstretched arm. Her legs were tucked up, her arms wrapped around her upper body.

The closed bed curtains enveloped them in darkness and kept out the nighttime chill. As he'd learned, she was a restless sleeper.

They'd begun in each other's arms, him holding her, both of them sated and in that state of physical and mental languor that followed their lovemaking. He liked to hold her while she slept. She was such a small woman compared to him that he easily cradled her in his embrace. He liked her company in bed, Lord, yes. He liked falling asleep with her.

He'd soon discovered that she routinely gravitated away from him until she was sleeping as she was now, alone. He'd wake up because he missed the warmth of her, her curves against him, and there she'd be, several feet away while he lay where they had fallen asleep.

And now here he was, awake in the middle of the night with Emily asleep far from him, and him with this sense that time was passing with him not doing what he should. Why, when as a married man, he was doing exactly as he ought? He was here, with his wife. He turned his head toward her again and shifted enough to brush his fingers over her shoulder. God willing, in the normal course of things, they would have children.

What if this new space in his heart was a permanent change? He could not help but worry that the feeling building was regret for the marriage. He did regret depriving her of a more normal marriage. He regretted that he did not feel about her the way he had felt about Anne when they'd met.

In the dark, he reached for her and drew her back to him. She came willingly, not really waking up. He drew a strand of golden hair away from her cheek. He'd never expected to feel any degree of tenderness for her, but he did. He would at least admit that change.

She sighed in her sleep, and he held her close until he fell asleep again. In the morning, that space in his heart was still there, and Emily was once again on the far side of the bed when he slipped out to meet Keller and prepare for his morning training.

Later in the day, Bracebridge was in his private office when Pond knocked lightly on the open door. Bracebridge set aside the correspondence his secretary had sorted for him and gestured for Pond to enter. Given the infuriating contents of one of those letters, he was glad of the interruption.

"My lord." Pond bowed and extended a salver on which there lay a letter that had been delivered privately rather than by the post. Reports from Gopal were scattered across the desktop, all of them detailing the status of their several joint businesses. The documents required his attention and his eventual replies with questions, instructions, suggestions, and he was not even a quarter of the way through them.

"Thank you." Alas, the letter was from Thomas Sinclair and could only add to the frustrations of his day. Pond cleared his throat as Bracebridge broke the seal. He hoped to God Sinclair was fully enraged and completely impotent. "Something else, Pond?"

"Her ladyship requests a moment of your time."

He tapped a finger on his desk to give the impression he needed to think about this interruption when in fact he had every intention of seeing her. True, he was busy, but he was not too busy for his wife. "Send her in."

"My lord."

He read Sinclair's letter while he waited for her to arrive. With a muttered curse, he dropped the page on his desk. Indeed, an unpleasant read.

A smear of ink on his finger caught his attention. Another streak marred the outside edge of his palm. Emily would be here any moment. A cursory rub with his handkerchief had no effect. He dipped a corner of the silk into his cold tea and rubbed harder. The stains turned greyish.

Still behind the desk, he unbuttoned his waistcoat and adjusted his shirt. No matter how much care Keller took with his attire, Bracebridge was always disheveled within a few hours. From his long-suffering valet, he knew his neckcloth took the most abuse. He used the window to check the state of his knot and adjust the folds.

Footsteps in the corridor outside signaled Emily's approach. He ran his fingers through his curls. No hope there, though he took some consolation in Emily having told him more than once how much she liked his hair. He neatened a stack of correspondence.

She tapped on the doorframe. "My lord?"

He squared the corners of the papers as if he had only now noticed her. "Come in, come in."

She sat on the chair nearest the window. Today she wore a gown he hadn't seen before: bronze dotted with smaller, darker flowers. A matching ribbon held back her hair. Her shawl was a gold wool he did recognize.

He picked up Sinclair's letter, then let it drop. "Your father has sent me an invoice."

"For what?" She leaned over and took the paper. "What is this?"

"His accounting of the cost of your upkeep over the past three years."

"Good heavens." She scanned the figures. "He puts a dear price on me."

"You'll not like the rest any better."

"Why? Is he suggesting we ought to have eloped sooner?"

He laughed. Say what you would about her youth, their history, or the circumstances of their marriage, he was often amused by her. "He informs me that since we are married, I am responsible for all your debts."

She threw the paper on his desk. "What debts?" She gave him a shrewd look. "Oh please, no. He does not mean the debts he incurred whilst I lived at the Cooperage, does he?"

"He demands that you return what you took with you when you departed Bartley Green. He has thoughtfully provided a separate inventory of that. He's invented things from the ether. He also includes in his accounting the funds he expected from Mr. Davener, and his bill from the lawyer he has consulted to recover said funds. In addition, he intends to sue me for Walter Davener's disappointment."

She leaned against the back of her chair. "Mr. Davener's disappointment cannot be worth more than sixpence. Send it to him and be done with it." She frowned. "He is harassing you. For that, I apologize."

"Never apologize for your father." Not long ago, he'd been convinced Emily had no idea of her father's faults. He had been wrong about that, too. "I shall deal with him, never fear. If he wants a fight in the courts, I shall give it to him." He picked up another letter, one that had arrived in the post. "In happier news, Mrs. Elliot has accepted the position of housekeeper here. She has been visiting various relations in the north. My letter to her had to be forwarded several times before it found her."

She broke into a smile. "That *is* good news."

"We are to expect her directly." He tapped Mrs. Elliot's letter. "She also writes that your maid was discharged from the Cooperage and has since found new employment."

Her fingers were laced tightly on her lap. "One can hardly blame her."

He smoothed the front of his waistcoat. "There is additional unpleasant news."

"Papa does not intend to send on any of my things, does he?"

Bracebridge shook his head.

"I expect he's already sold them."

"I would not be surprised." He unlocked the drawer that contained petty cash and took out several banknotes. "In any event, I have been remiss. You ought to have money of your own. I'll formalize the amount when we are in London."

"London, but why?"

He tugged on his waistcoat again. The plain blue wool fit well, but perhaps he ought to adopt something more like the Rachagorla style. He might be a beast compared to her, but more color in his dress would harm nothing. "You are the Countess of Bracebridge. You must dress accordingly." He smiled to take the edge off his too-serious tone. "I won't have people wondering why my wife goes about in the same three or four gowns."

She touched the skirts of her frock. "I'm hardly in rags. Maggie is an excellent seamstress, as you can see."

"Nevertheless, we shall go to London where you are to properly outfit yourself for Town *and* the country." He gave her a wicked grin. "I like you well enough in your skin, but that does not mean I cannot appreciate you in an evening gown or draped in jewels, for that matter. A noted beauty must dress the part."

She drew her eyebrows together in a devastatingly angelic frown, then stood, gripping the top of the chair. He stood, too. The silence was dreadful. Somewhere in this conversation, he had made a mistake.

He came around to the other side of his desk. She blinked several times, and it seemed a lifetime ago that he'd believed her a spoiled, frivolous young woman incapable of masking her emotions. He put a hand on her cheek. She turned away from the contact.

"What?" he said, thoroughly confused. "What is it? I've put off addressing the issue of your wardrobe because I believed your effects would be sent on. Now that we know otherwise, you cannot possibly expect me to do nothing."

"Of course not."

He was in quicksand and sinking fast. "Tell me, Em. I want to understand."

"I'm bored, is all."

"Is that all? You want an occupation?"

"Yes," she said.

"Anne has several charitable works. As does Lady Aldreth." She didn't look any happier, but what she required from him was a practical solution, not a comparison to her sisters. Luckily, just such a solution was to hand. "I'm told the vicar has opened a school for the children of Hinderhead. If I asked, I'm certain he would agree that you may assist him in some capacity."

At last, she looked at him. He ought to have died from that look. But why? "The idea is an excellent one," he said. "I'm sure you agree the cause is worthy."

"I am on the committee that oversees the school." She lifted her eyebrows in a way that strongly reminded him of Anne. "I told you so the day everyone called."

"Did you?" Now that he thought of it, he did vaguely recall her saying some such thing.

"I did."

"Very good timing, then, that the project was just getting off the ground when we arrived."

"Yes," she said in a voice that lifted the hair on the back of his neck. It was astonishing, really, how she looked as if she thought he was the most brilliant man in the world yet sounded quite the opposite. "Why, it's almost as if someone only recently proposed such an endeavor to him. Imagine that."

The ground continued in its unstable condition. "I'm sure the ladies of Hinderhead have been mulling it over for some time."

Her eyes opened wide, and he absolutely could not fathom what he had done to deserve a look of such incredulous scorn. "I had no idea your opinion of me was quite so low."

"What do you mean?"

"The vicar and the ladies of Hinderhead had no such plans until I proposed it."

The ground beneath his feet was treacherous indeed. He saw the trap but not the means of escape. He was completely out of his depth and did not understand why or how. He extended his hands to her, but she ignored him.

"Tell me, my lord. Which do you object to more? My youth or my stupidity?"

"Neither." Emily's quick wit and quicker tongue always found their mark with deadly aim. "I object to neither."

"I thank you for your time and generosity." She bent a knee and was halfway to the door before he could settle on a response.

"That isn't what I meant." But she walked away without a backward look. He watched her leave, at a loss. Was this regret he felt at his mishandling of their conversation? He was annoyed and irritated, of that he was certain.

That aching hole in his heart got bigger. He thought he knew her, but lately it seemed that at every turn, he faced proof he did not. He knew nothing of the young woman who had made a friend of an awkward young woman. He knew nothing of the woman who was a dear and lifelong friend of Clara Glynn or who had earned the steadfast regard of Harry Glynn. He knew nothing of the Emily who had rescued Frieda and worried so constantly that something would happen to her dog. He did not know the woman who understood her father would steal from her and, indeed, expected he would do so.

"Emily," he said moments before she reached the door.

She faced him, angelically composed. Frozen. Nothing he said or did could touch her, and it frightened him that she could be so remote. So completely belonging to herself and him with no way to connect to that person. "My lord?"

"I intended no insult. I apologize if I've upset you."

"I accept your apology," she said with no change in expression.

"Yet," he said, "you do not appear assuaged." He lifted his hands toward her. "Whatever I've done, I assure you it was unintentional."

"That is the entire point." The ice in her voice could freeze water on the boil.

"I cannot improve myself or our situation unless you tell me. Please."

"You believe I am stupid."

"Inexperience of life is not stupidity." He crossed the room, and when he stood before her, he attempted and failed to take her hand. She was having none of that.

"You have no more experience being married than I."

"You must admit I have a good deal more experience in life."

"I've had a letter from Cynssyr," she said.

Alarm shot through him. Pond had said Emily wanted to see him. He realized now that she had not told him the reason for her request.

"Go on."

"He's purchased a cottage in Little Merton."

A twisting sense of dread joined his alarm. The village of Little Merton adjoined Bartley Green. The village was charming and, relevant to his concern, had the distinct advantage of being close to Rosefeld yet not convenient to the Cooperage.

Her enthusiastic smile had to be a sham. It simply had to be. There was no reason for her to be so eager to leave him, or so certain he would agree to such thing. Surely, he had not been *that* ham handed with her. Had he? "Cynssyr is agreeable to me living there. At no expense to you, I should add."

"Are you seriously suggesting that you remove to Little Merton? To a house owned by Cynssyr?"

She cocked her head and speared him with an infuriatingly peaceful smile. "You do not want me here."

"That is not so." She could not leave him. He did not want her to leave him. Good God, she meant this.

"I am not suggesting a permanent break." She took and then released a breath. "You may visit whenever you like."

"No." He closed the distance between them and cupped the side of her face. "No. Emily. No. You've got it wrong."

She closed her eyes. He could feel her despair, and still he remained at a loss to understand why. She knew him. She knew what had happened with Anne. She knew. To his astonishment and near complete undoing, a tear trickled down her cheek. He swept it away with the side of his thumb.

She opened her eyes slowly and without looking at him directly. "I'm me, Bracebridge. Me. Not Anne. Nor Clara. Nor Mary or Lucy, and I can do no right where you are concerned. Please, let me go to Little Merton. It's for the best."

"No." No, no, a thousand times no.

"Why, when you do not want me here?"

"I never said that."

"You did not have to." She gripped the lapels of his coat again. "I see your resentment of me every day. Why should we both be miserable when I can live in Little Merton and never trouble you? I understand why you wish no changes here, so let me go elsewhere. What I do there cannot possibly offend you." She drew away, and could he blame her? "I ask nothing from you but this." She gestured. "Spend all your time here or at Two Fives or anywhere you like."

How the hell did he politely tell her that he could not imagine becoming tired of taking her to bed, or that Little Merton was too damned far, or that he wanted her here at Corth Abbey? "Emily."

"I can do whatever I like at Little Merton." She was a stranger to him, this earnest young woman. His heart turned over at her tremulous smile. "I shall have a cheerful parlor with flowers and plants, and walls painted whatever color pleases me. Frieda and I can walk miles and miles every day. I can paper the walls with watercolors by my own hand if I wish."

"You can do that here." Where that deep and heartfelt response had come from he did not know, but now that he'd said it, he felt it was true to his very bones. "Paint a watercolor every day. I'll hang them on every wall in the house if it pleases you."

"It ought to please you." Her eyes glittered with incipient tears. "You don't even know that I happen to be better artist than Anne."

"Are you?"

"I could be Michelangelo, and you'd think, 'That's not what Anne would have drawn.'"

"You exaggerate." Did she? The was an uncomfortable ring of truth in her accusastion.

She continued to smile. Only a few weeks ago he would have believed she was amused. "Not much."

Now, he knew better than to believe the surface she presented, but he did not know how to get past the polished perfection to reach the real and true Emily. He put a hand on her shoulder, and as he did, he felt he'd stepped out of time and place. Who was she, if she wasn't the woman he'd had fixed in his mind all this time?

He wiped another tear from her upper cheek. "I've wanted my life to continue as it was before we were married." He took a steadying breath, but his heart beat too fast. She was a person separate from her sisters. She had hopes and dreams, likes and dislikes that were her own. "You are correct. I am an inexperienced husband, and I have been unfair to you."

She pushed away his hand and wiped both her eyes. "I don't mean to be a water pot. It's just, this isn't at all what I thought it would be like."

"If either of us thought we knew that, we were wrong."

This time, her smile seemed more genuine, but again, he was out of step with the world, for she was not merely Anne's sister. She was someone he ought to get to know, someone, he thought, he might actually like a great deal. "Indeed," she said in a damp voice. "Indeed, we were."

"We are new to our married life, and there must be bumps along the way. But, Emily, Emily, my dear, I mean to do better by us both. Please. I do not want you to remove to Little Merton. Stay here. With me."

The room became quiet. She'd retreated behind the armor of her perfection, and there was no getting past to the real Emily.

"We should not be here." She meant Corth Abbey. Lord, but his heart ached because his thoughtless assumptions had hurt her badly. "Not yet. Not so early in our marriage."

Her insight was acute and intensely discomforting. She understood their situation better than he did. "All the more reason for us to go to London."

"I don't see how that would be any different."

He took a deep breath. "I never imagined her at Cavendish Square. It was only here."

She smiled sadly and briefly cupped the side of his face. "Don't be sorry. Don't be. We cannot change the shape our hearts take when we have loved grandly. I'd never ask that of you."

"God, Emily, I am sorry. So sorry for what I've done. You deserve better."

Chapter Twenty-One

B RACEBRIDGE STOOD TWENTY YARDS from his Cavendish Square house as he so often did before he went inside. His greatcoat was buttoned against a dreary and foggy day, and water dripped from the brim of his hat.

He hadn't realized until he came here with Emily how thoroughly his feelings for Anne shaded every part of his life. The ache of losing her remained; his admiration of and respect for her was unchanged. Even here.

With the fog thickening, he peeled away the layers around his heart. As Emily had said, the shape of his heart had been forever altered, but he and Anne would never be, and that, too, had changed him. Emily had walked through his despair, bright and joyful, consuming him, capturing his notice, distracting him. *He* had been the one to act. He was the one who'd kissed her. Him. He had rejected his feelings for her at the same time he drew her in and blamed her for his sorrow.

Emily was there, inside his London home, and because of that, a pinprick of joy unfurled in the center of his chest, unaccustomed, unwarranted, but there. A fair part of his boyhood had been spent in Margaret Street. With ease, he called up memories of his brothers laughing, his mother whispering his name while she hugged him close. The scent of her perfume. The echo of feet on the stairs. The smell of beeswax and polish. The way the light came through the windows, the brilliant red of the roses his mother so loved. His father coldly informing him he would never be welcome here again.

Bracebridge gripped his umbrella. The sheer weight of those ghostly recollections ought to have brought the house down to its foundation, but the building stood as a monument to his resentment, his failures, and his duty to centuries of the dead and those yet to live. He and his father had always been at loggerheads. A dutiful son would have done what was expected of him, but that wasn't the life he'd wanted for himself. He'd left with angry words to match his father's and made his own way.

However vivid his recollections, or sharp the ache in his soul, his parents and brothers would never be inside. Within a fortnight of falling ill, his mother, father, brothers, and many of the servants had perished, and Bracebridge hadn't known until the family solicitor arrived at Corth Abbey with the news.

Now, though, he was married, and the house held more than memories of his family or the bittersweet memory of the ball he'd held to show the world his support of the new Duchess of Cynssyr and the love of his life. Now he also had memories of Emily looking up from a book or needlework and smiling when he walked into whatever room she was in.

Emily, stretched out on his bed, spectacular to look at, but so very attuned to the mood of their intimacy: tender, serious, at the edges of crude and rough. She was there, rearranging, reordering, changing everything, with each breath sweeping away the past.

He could have gone to his club for dinner as he often did when he was in London. Or to Two Fives, or to his townhouse in Marylebone where Emily had burst in on him when he was still reeling from Anne's marriage to Cynssyr. He understood now, years after the fact, just how much he'd lost during that encounter. He chose none of those, damn it to hell.

That moment in the house in Marylebone was the cause of his troubled relations with Emily. He understood that now. At last. She'd burst into his rooms, but he was the one who had transgressed. He was the one who had continued to cross lines of propriety. That moment, above all others in respect of the former Miss Emily Sinclair, had cemented the discord in him that persisted to this day. Unshakable, unwanted, and permanent, he feared. He had long resented her because his body recognized her and overruled his reason and, so he'd believed, his loyalty.

She wasn't quiet, peaceful Anne, who smoothed all his rough edges. His wife was the fire that matched his own. Anne would never be his. He could do nothing to change that, not travel back in time, not change anything he had said or done. But oh Lord, Lord in heaven, he did not want his heart at war like this.

If he went inside, Emily would be there, all lightness and grace, and he would tell her about his day while he thought of how he would fuck her later, because more than any other lover of his, she had no trouble navigating both sides of his life, the polite and the crude. His wife liked his rawness in bed, though she appreciated tenderness, too.

So. No. Not his club. Not Two Fives. Not his townhouse, but here, where Emily was. He came in the front door rather than the side entrance. The quiet immediately told him his wife was not home. His disappointment was a visceral thing.

Pond glided in to take his things. "My lord."

"Pond." He dropped his umbrella into the receptacle and handed over his hat.

The chairs that had lined the walls for as long as he could recall had been replaced with a walnut table on which there sat a vase he'd not seen since he was a boy too young to have fatally offended his father. The cream porcelain was painted with lemons and at present, filled with yellow peonies and irises. Such memories. The vase had been a favorite of his mother's.

There were other changes besides the flowers. The entry seemed larger because there was only half the usual number of chairs. Where a painting of a prancing white steed had once been, there now hung a gilt-framed mirror.

He took stock of the transformed space. "I ought to have let you have your way years ago." If he had, he might have come to feel the Margaret Street house was truly his rather than a place he shared with the memories of his family and the resentments of his father.

Pond practically glowed. "Lady Bracebridge has exceptional taste."

"Lady Bracebridge?"

"It has been a pleasure carrying out her suggestions." Pond tugged on the dangling sleeve of Bracebridge's coat, and Bracebridge realized he'd been staring at nothing for several seconds. He drew his other arm from his sleeve, and Pond draped the coat over his arm.

Bracebridge glanced across the space and, now that he knew to look, saw Emily here. Like her, the entryway was light, cheerful, and elegant. "How much has this cost me?"

"Time and labor." Pond's smile faded. "Shall I bring you the ledgers? Her accounts are meticulous, as you'll see."

"Yes, please." He was not ready to accept this. He did not want Emily to be accomplished or sensible when he needed her to be volatile, thoughtless, and frivolous. He'd told her to do as she pleased here, never expecting he would admire what she'd done. She wasn't supposed to be competent, to uncover a favorite vase of his mother's, or to arrange a room that made him feel emotions long suppressed.

He missed his mother. He'd give anything to see his brothers again. He'd even consider a reconciliation with his father. He did not want this ache in his heart.

Pond seemed to have learned Emily's trick of using a smile as a shield. "As you wish, milord."

Bracebridge touched a fingertip to the top stretcher of one of the remaining chairs. These weren't the uncomfortable seats his father had put out for guests. These were different chairs entirely.

Childhood memories flooded back. When his father was alive, every chair had been filled with people seeking access to the Earl of Bracebridge. No longer. Anyone who wished to importune him for money or favors knew to find him at Two Fives. "These used to be in the music room."

"'A treasure,' Lady Bracebridge said when she saw them."

"Where did you find them?" His father, for reasons he'd been too young to understand at the time, had done his best to erase his mother's impact on the house. By the time he'd been old enough to be of interest to his father, there were no more of the outings his elder brothers had so fondly recalled: rides down the Thames, excursions to the zoo, afternoons spent demonstrating talents and accomplishments to their parents. As the youngest of the children, Bracebridge had known mostly silence and strife between his parents and too many years of his father's cold regard.

"The second attic, my lord. She has an unerring eye. Even in the dim light and with all the dust, she saw the beauty of these chairs." Obviously, Pond was completely under Emily's spell. As were York, the head groom, the head footman, and, if he were to be honest, most all the servants. Mrs. Elliot, too, now that she was here from Bartley Green, which went without saying. "I had my doubts, but she was correct. A cleaning and some vigorous waxing, and you see the result, just as her ladyship predicted."

She was taking over the house, and him, too, changing him in ways he did not understand or like. He did not love her. He might have a degree of tenderness for her, but nothing more. How could he let go of his love for Anne when it was she who had made him a better person? Anne, not Emily.

He pointed. "That vase used to be in the Lemon Parlor."

"The Lemon Parlor, my lord?"

"No longer exists." He shook his head. No one knew that but him. "It's my father's smoking room now." But no. The house was his, and his father lay in his grave. The smoking room was his now and could be whatever he wished to make of it. He could turn it into a billiards room or back into a parlor, or he could have the doors nailed shut.

"I was a boy when he took over the room." What a memory, and one he'd rather not have. He'd been six or seven at the time and already taller than the shortest of his older brothers. "My mother shed a great many tears over losing its use." He'd come to his mother's defense, and that had enraged his father.

He looked around the entryway, hating the reminders. "None of this belongs here." She wasn't supposed to do this to him, touch him like this. "Not the chairs, that vase, or the table."

Pond gave him a sideways look, then snapped his fingers. Instantly, a footman stepped from the shadows of the servants' door. Pond pointed to the various items. "Take those downstairs."

"I do not recognize the mirror either. Where did that come from?" These changes stole his ability to walk into the house and see the dark and ugly chairs he hated and say to himself, *Here is Devon Carlisle, my lord father, may you rot in hell.*

"I'll have the room returned to its original state within the hour."

"Thank you." He heard his father in that curt response, but was he not justified in his objections? His wife, who was so unhappy with the marriage in which she'd not lasted a month before she was begging to be free of him, had run right over the limits he'd set. *Within reason,* he'd said. He'd told her that, and this was surely not within reason.

He headed upstairs and saw more changes on his way to his rooms. That cobalt blue vase was another possession of his mother's, long hidden away and now striking in the niche at the top of the stairs. She couldn't know she was destroying his private revenge on his father. She couldn't possibly know. He slowed, staring at the vase. How the devil had she known?

But . . . but.

What if he'd married Anne or Clara? Would either of them have stood up to him as directly as Emily did? He thought not. He admitted, as well, that he would not have resented their changes the way he resented Emily's. He would have allowed either of them to take the Margaret Street house down to the foundation and rebuild it from scratch.

He stopped walking. Why Anne or Clara, but not Emily?

Because Emily wasn't the wife he wanted. Because, because, because, he resented her changing him. And what did that make him but the same petty tyrant his father had been? In Anne and Clara, he'd chosen women of quiet reflection who would have found other ways, quieter ways, to confront him were he to behave badly or unfairly. Emily was direct. She always had been. Not better. Not worse. Merely different.

He picked up the cobalt vase, running a hand over the smooth surface. Emily spoke to the very worst parts of his nature, and that fact explained too well why they were incendiary in bed. There was no restraint or decorum with her. He did not have to hold anything back.

How odd that Emily had chosen so many of his mother's favorite possessions from among the centuries of items stored in the attics. In his head, he saw himself smashing the vase to pieces. He could lift it overhead and dash it against the wall and then, without explanation, tell Pond to take care of the mess. No one would question him if he did.

Emily had plucked this vase from some attic crate and, seeing its beauty, had put it here so that one took in its presence almost without noticing, and yet he had been struck by the shape, the pulse of color, and a sense of calmness.

"My lord?"

Mrs. Elliot stood on the stairs below. For an instant, he was convinced she knew he'd been about to hurl the vase against the wall. He replaced it in the niche. "Yes?"

The woman hurried up the stairs and, at the landing where he waited, put a hand over her heart. "My lord, may I have a word in private?"

"You may." He hoped she did not intend to give notice. She'd only just arrived, and Emily would be beyond unhappy at her leaving. Admittedly, their almost immediate departure for London had been disruptive, but there was no help for that. It was absolutely necessary that they leave Corth Abbey.

"My office, then." She nodded. Once they were inside, he gestured to a chair. "Please."

She did not sit. "My lord. Thank you for agreeing to see me."

"I am glad to have you on staff." Anne had never had anything but high praise for Mrs. Elliot, and from all that he had observed, the praise was well deserved. He sat at his desk, leaning back in his chair. "What may I do for you?"

Her mouth firmed and he was immediately put in mind of the last time he'd seen her at the Cooperage: resolute in the face of Thomas Sinclair's rage. Had the man behaved so with his daughter? "I won't abandon that poor girl. I won't. No matter who pays my wages." She touched the key chain dangling from her waist. "I'll go to her sisters and beg their assistance if I must."

He was taken aback and thoroughly confused. "May I ask why you think such a choice is before you?"

Mrs. Elliot narrowed her eyes. Since she'd joined his staff, their relations had undergone a distinct chill, and he was not quite willing to put that down to his being her employer now. "Your lawyer called on me this morning. Maggie, too, I soon learned."

"If you spoke with a lawyer today, it was not mine." He folded his arms across his chest but found himself unable to remain still. He walked away from his desk and paced the distance between the window and the fireplace. A lawyer had called at Margaret Street, and the man had not left a card for the head of the damned household? "He came to the back door, did he?"

"Yes, my lord."

"Did he tell you he was *my* lawyer? That I'd engaged him? I assure you, I did not."

"I assumed he was, milord." She fished a card from her pocket and handed it to him.

He did not recognize the name, but the address was in the Temple Bar. "May I keep this? Thank you," he said when she nodded. "I presume he interviewed you about Lady Bracebridge, else you would not have opened this conversation with a restatement of your loyalty to my wife."

"Yes, sir."

"I have not engaged this man." He gripped the top of the nearest chair. Could this be Cynssyr's work? The duke was responsible for the cottage in Little Merton, after all. "What did he ask you?"

Her stiffness with him eased. She nodded. "He asked what I knew about your marriage and whether Lady Bracebridge is mistreated here. He asked whether you were a faithful husband and whether Lady Bracebridge is a faithful wife."

If not Cynssyr, then Aldreth. Sinclair, for all his threats and pettiness, hadn't the money for lawyers. Thrale was another possibility, though a remote one, since he was, to the best of Bracebridge's knowledge, still at Blackfern with his wife. Was he to find that all her relations were aligned against him?

"I told him the truth." She lifted her chin. "I'll say the same to anyone else who asks. I mean no disrespect, but I was as shocked as anyone when I heard you'd married her. I never thought you cared for her that way."

"You were wrong," he said with undue curtness. Mrs. Elliot stiffened, and he forced himself to soften his manner. "What," he asked as gently as he could, "is the truth you relayed?"

Mrs. Elliot sat at last, hands clasped on her lap. "I told him Lady Bracebridge is unhappy, but not mistreated."

"Thank you for that."

"I told him that I've not been with you long and might be mistaken."

His heart thudded hard when he took in the rest of what she'd said. "You believe Lady Bracebridge is unhappy?"

"Yes, my lord, I do."

"What makes you say such a thing?" He was afraid he knew the answer.

"There is a melancholy about her I never saw before. She had spells at the Cooperage, but that's to be expected, given her father and his own particular *spells*. There's no denying marriage is an adjustment for any woman, but, my lord, I know that girl. I know her. I watched her grow up and become the woman she is now. It breaks my heart to see such sadness in a woman so recently married."

He released the chair he'd been holding so hard and sat. He had only ever considered his own side of this situation, and that was true even when he told himself he was thinking of Emily. In actual fact, he only ever considered how Emily reacted to him and never why she might react as she did. She was an expert at hiding her emotions; he'd certainly learned that.

The thought of her going through this marriage showing him only what she thought he wanted to see carved a crater deep into the center of him.

Where his heart ought to have been, there was nothing. He had never seen this sadness Mrs. Elliot had noticed from the start.

"I told him she would never be unfaithful," Mrs. Elliot continued, as if she hadn't put a mirror before him and forced him to see an unpleasant truth. "In the time I have been in your employ, I've seen nothing in her behavior to convince me otherwise."

Emily loved him. He knew she did. This damned house, so full of memories of his father he had done nothing to banish. He closed his eyes and saw a future in which he was a different man. Perhaps even a better one.

"A good many husbands take little notice of their wives," Mrs. Elliot said. He opened his eyes in time to see her shaking her head. "You're not alone in that regard." She looked away, then back. "Many a union exists without passion. She'll adjust her expectations of marriage and find, God willing, should she be a mother, other sources of joy."

The word *mother* was a bucket of cold water in his face. Emily a mother meant him a father. Emily a mother transformed his life entirely. Mrs. Elliot meant was that Emily would settle into a version of their marriage in which there was no affection between them, and that he wanted such a result. But that wasn't what he wanted, was it?

"I did not like that lawyer. He insinuated unpleasant things, asking whether she was faithful to you." She clutched one side of the seat of her chair. "Her ladyship has shown you unwavering support, and I don't mean just since I came here. Time and again, she defended you to her father." She interlaced her fingers and leaned toward him. "Did you wonder why she has no wardrobe, after all the money Lord Aldreth and His Grace spent outfitting her and her sisters?"

"He's refused to return them."

She sat back. "I should think so, since he sold them the day after he discovered she was gone." She snapped her fingers. "Like that. Everything gone. It's not the first time he's stolen from his daughters."

"God willing, it shall be the last."

"You saw her father, my lord, that day you came to the Cooperage, and I'll tell you now what her ladyship never will; that such was a common condition for him. More than once I begged her to leave, to live with Lady Thrale or one of her sisters. But she had the duchess for a pattern, and Lady

Thrale, and Lady Aldreth, who all did their Christian duty toward their father. She did the same as them."

The world unmoored itself from everything he knew and desired of it. "You believe she's unhappy."

"She'll settle in, my lord."

He steeled himself. "I'm no paragon among men. But I am no Thomas Sinclair, either. She is a countess. Whatever she desires, it is within my means to see that she has it. What reason has she to be unhappy?"

"Why, none at all, my lord."

"I have brought her to my home. Here and at Corth Abbey. We are in London so that she may obtain a wardrobe that befits her new rank and position. Lady Bracebridge is young. She has no experience with a household the size of mine. No experience with the duties that come with being Lady Bracebridge."

Mrs. Elliot only shook her head. "Who do you think managed the Cooperage after Lady Thrale was married? The same accounts, the same bills, the same father as her sisters, only by the time it was your wife who tried to hold the household together, it was that many more years of hardship and mismanagement. That many more years of his bitterness."

"That is my point entirely." Desperation filled him, threatened to choke him. "Her life with me is immeasurably better."

"I watched you fall in love with the duchess and prayed the two of you would find the happiness you deserved. I am sorry you did not. But none of that means Lady Bracebridge is less."

"That goes without saying."

Slowly, Mrs. Elliot stood, her disappointment in him a wound across his heart. "You'll break my heart again if you aren't the man to see that."

"She knows me," he said. "She knows me."

"I don't doubt for a moment that you and Her Grace would have had a life of love and happiness. We all wished that for you, for you both. But I'll tell you what I've always thought since your wife grew up to be the young woman she is: She is a better match for you than the duchess ever was."

Chapter Twenty-Two

꧁ꕥ꧂

As BRACEBRIDGE STOOD at the Margaret Street corner of Cavendish Square, a woman came around the opposite corner, a maid and footman trailing after her. She moved with a purposeful stride, not hurried, just determined. Emily moved like that. Full of joy and energy. Even from a distance, she was compelling.

His heart thumped when he realized that the woman was no stranger at all but his own wife. The shock of seeing her in this new way momentarily paralyzed him. She wasn't the past he regretted, but his future. His wife.

She took the stairs to the door but did not immediately go in, even after her maid and the footman went downstairs to the servants' quarters. Instead, she crouched at the threshold, protected from the rain by the portico. Had she dropped something? Had Pond forgot she was here and left the door locked, and now she was searching for a hidden key?

He headed toward the house. She was still crouched when he arrived at the steps. If she'd lost her key or some personal possession, the item must be well and truly misplaced. He mounted the steps and heard her speaking in a cajoling croon.

"Poor little thing. Hush, hush. Shh. Kitty, kitty. There's a sweet one."

He stepped underneath the portico. Pond had planted flowers in the urns on either side of the door: yellow, purple, and blue. For years prior, they had stood empty.

"Shh. Kitty, kitty. Aren't you sweet? Are you calm now?" Emily, now aware he was here, looked over her shoulder at him and then upward, because he was standing while she was not. She put a finger across her lips and moved so he could see what she was cooing over.

A cat. Considering its size, more a largish kitten. Whichever it was, it mewed and hissed as if it saw a portal to hell.

"It's only got three legs, and it's a baby, the poor thing. Aren't you brave?" she said to the kitten. She got a hiss in response. "Oh, the poor thing. It can't survive out here. Not by itself."

"It has so far."

"Pond said the kitchen cat has vanished," she said.

"That isn't the missing kitchen cat."

She rolled her eyes at the implication she would mistake a sickly, three-legged kitten for a full-grown mouser. "We could have another cat in the house. Even if the other comes back."

First Frieda, now a misfit cat? He put his hands on his hips and shook his head, knowing he would give in. What man could possibly resist that pleading look? "Bring it inside, then."

"I don't want to terrify it more than it already is, and besides it's got sharp claws."

The pitiful beast was jammed into the hollow formed by the side of the house and the stone urn that now held those flowers. Geraniums, he believed, and some sort of daisy. He propped his umbrella against the side of the house and removed his scarf. He folded it twice over as he moved toward her and the kitten. "Allow me."

She made room for him. The moment he hunkered down beside his wife and made eye contact with the cat, it calmed, though without ceasing its yowls. She was right about it being a kitten still, though it was far too thin to be healthy.

"Do be careful," she said.

"I shan't hurt it." He dropped his scarf over the animal and scooped it up. He held it tight to his chest.

"I meant," Emily said from behind him, "that I did not want *you* to be scratched or bitten."

Absently, he rubbed the kitten's head. It purred loudly. "Poor little beast-ie."

She grabbed his umbrella, then opened the door for him, and in they went. Pond appeared from the corridor that led to the servants' quarters, ready to take coats and hats, then went wide-eyed at the sight of Bracebridge and his burden.

A dull *thunk* broke the silence; the metal tip of his umbrella hitting the bottom of the canister provided for the purpose of holding it. Emily hurried ahead of him, brushing through the ghost of his recollection of the day he and his brothers had played at soldiers in the foyer. Bracebridge had been at his turn with the sword they'd taken from the suit of armor that was no longer in the corner. His father had lit into him for that. *You could have taken someone's head.* A ridiculous accusation. They had all of them studied with a swordmaster. He bloody well knew how to handle a weapon, then and now.

"Look what we've found." Emily pointed to Bracebridge as she addressed Pond. "A kitten! It was by the door when I came home, and Bracebridge rescued it just now." She made it sound as if he'd fought off the demons of hell rather than bent down and picked it up. Damned if he didn't feel as if he might have done so, if what he got in return was that awed voice.

"Valiant of you, my lord."

"Thank you." He held the kitten securely against his chest. "We'll take it to the kitchen and see if York will let us raid the larder."

As ever, Pond remained calm in the midst of the excitement. "Straightaway."

Emily moved closer to him, rubbing a finger gently along the top of the kitten's head. "It's still purring."

"Indeed, it is."

"I believe it's taken a liking to you, Bracebridge." The animal had settled into its fate as a captive of his arms and scarf. He caught the edge of a breathtaking smile when Emily bent in for a closer look. There was no denying she was a tenderhearted woman.

He lifted the kitten in front of his face for a better look. An awkward-looking creature, from what he could see. Black with white blotches and a head too large for its body. "It's got one blue eye and one green one," he said.

"Is that so?" She went up on tiptoe to look, and he lowered the kitten to show her. He breathed in the scent of violets and remembered the softness of her skin, the warmth of her when he entered her. For half a second, she held his gaze with the promise of lust to be explored at their leisure. "So it does. Isn't that curious?"

Pond led the way to the kitchen, opening doors and ensuring the way was clear for them. Bracebridge was aware of Emily looking at him as if he'd saved God himself instead of a starving, bedraggled, three-legged dab of a cat.

They had some distance to walk since the kitchen was in the far-left wing of the house. His cook came to attention the moment they walked into the space, a wide, low-ceilinged room of whitewashed walls and the tiniest of windows at the top of the rear wall.

"Mr. York," Emily said with a wide gesture. The poor fellow looked as if he feared the worst from this invasion of his domain. "Lord Bracebridge has rescued a kitten."

Pond smoothly said, "Might there be cream and some of last night's chicken?"

York crooked a finger at one of the kitchen maids, but the girl was already heading for the pantry. Another fetched a small bowl and filled it with cream.

Bracebridge set the kitten down, keeping a hand on its back to prevent its escape, should it attempt such foolishness. His fear proved unfounded. Even after Emily reached in and gently pulled away his scarf, the kitten pressed against him and purred. The bedraggled, maimed cat hovered at the edge of hideous. Ugly and scrappy, like him, the kitten had persevered.

"Here we are, Lady Bracebridge." One of the newly hired maids set down the cream and stepped back to watch Emily with worshipful regard. Meanwhile, York chopped and shredded chicken into suitably sized bits and arranged the meat on a plate.

Emily beamed at York when he set the plate before the kitten. His famously ill-tempered cook was transfixed by her. "Thank you, York. You are a hero."

The animal investigated the chicken first. Its foray revealed that it was male and that the injury to its right rear leg must have occurred early in its young life, since the wound was mostly healed. How it had survived such an injury seemed both mysterious and miraculous.

Moments later, after a first, tentative bite, it snarled and tore into the chicken, absurdly fierce. Bracebridge's heart pinched.

"Poor, poor creature," Emily said over the sound of the kitten growling as he ate. "You need a home, don't you? Would you like to live here?" Immediately, she looked to Bracebridge. "Mayn't he? For now."

Without thinking, he stroked the kitten. It purred and snarled at the same time. The servants stood in various attitudes of attention, but it was plain as day he would never be forgiven if he broke Emily's heart. "I have no objection."

"He needs a name. A grand name."

The misfit cat finished the chicken and licked the dish twice over before turning to the cream.

Emily put her arms on the table, eyes on the kitten. "Ajax? Plato? Pythagoras?"

"Cicero?"

"Hypotenuse." She laughed, and he smiled despite not wanting to. He didn't smile often enough; that was his trouble. He'd got out of the habit of smiling.

"That's a mouthful. Isosceles? Because he's only got three legs. Or Socrates," he said. "He was wise enough to choose our door as a refuge."

She narrowed her eyes in thought, oblivious to him saying *our door*. "Socrates. I like that name. Yes. He is a profound thinker, just as you have observed." Emily left off gazing at the kitten to look at Bracebridge. Mrs. Iddings had called Emily kind, and that was true. Emphatically true. Frieda. Socrates. Miss Iddings. Clara. Mrs. Elliot, too. His wife took care of those whom she loved.

The kitten finished off his cream and hopped over to him. Bracebridge picked him up. "Socrates, my friend, welcome to your new home. You shall enjoy living here, you lucky beast." He held up the kitten and looked into its different colored eyes. "I like the little fellow."

"You'll keep food on hand for him, won't you, York?" Emily said.

There was silence while Pond and York looked to Bracebridge for confirmation of her request. He grinned, but the awkwardness expanded. "Please lay in a supply of delicacies to tempt our young philosopher."

A pang of guilt burned its way through his heart. Had he just made a stray cat more welcome in his home than his wife?

Chapter Twenty-Three

ANNE WROTE IN a hand that was neat to the point of artistry.

Dear Friend—

As I write, Mrs. MacInnis is here at Portman Square and is once again being exceedingly disagreeable to your wife. Well do I understand that you are a gentleman with great responsibilities, and I should never suggest that you neglect those. It grieves me to tell you that others speculate about your regard for my sister. It is unseemly, unkind, and hurtful to my sister. But what is one to think when, where one would expect to see a husband with his new wife, we do not see *you?*

She'd underlined *you* three times.

Others have remarked, my lord. Others have wondered if you intend—I can scarcely write these words—to abandon your marriage. It has been said in this very house. I have personally overheard those very words.

If you have any regard at all for my sister, please come to Portman Square at your earliest convenience. That woman has always been susceptible to your charms. Other thoughts of mine in this regard are reserved for some future time.

—A

A month ago, Bracebridge would not have bothered knocking at the door to Portman Square. He would have gone straight in, confident of his welcome. Now, he was not so certain. There was growing evidence that the lawyer who had interviewed his servants was connected to Emily's family.

Aldreth's butler opened the door. After a pause, the servant opened the door enough to admit him, though without the warmer welcome he would have expected before his marriage. The coolness was disheartening. "Good day, milord."

"Smith." He stepped inside and handed over his hat and coat. Cynssyr or Aldreth. One of them must be responsible for the damned lawyer. Smith's reaction made him put Aldreth at the top of the list. "I am expected."

"Upstairs, milord. In the parlor."

Animated voices and laughter increased in volume as he climbed the stairs. Not a few guests, then, but many. Was Emily truly the target of scorn? If so, why had she said nothing to him about this when she must have encountered such reactions before today?

He knew the answer to that, didn't he? He'd given her no reason to believe he would care to know. Almost every night, he told her about his day and his business affairs, sometimes at great length. Only rarely did he ask about her day, and he realized now he had been foolish to assume she would say anything other than what she believed he wanted to know.

The conversational noise increased. Whoever was playing the piano had only the virtue of enthusiasm to recommend the performance. A flute chimed in, also not played well. Out of sheer habit, he stood in the parlor door until he found Anne. Cynssyr stood at her side, one hand on her shoulder, listening intently to what she was saying. Old and familiar feelings welled up: respect, admiration, heartache, a sad longing for what might have been.

Just as he had feared, the tenderness he felt for Emily tempered his response to his feelings about Anne. His life and Anne's had taken different paths. Why should he resent the path he had taken?

Lady Aldreth sat on the sofa nearest the fire, surrounded by the usual cadre of ardent admirers. He did not yet see Emily. As he made his way into the room, he saw Mrs. MacInnis in conversation with a woman he did not recognize and a gentleman who was a fixture at Two Fives. All three were smiling. All in all, a normal gathering at Portman Square.

He located Emily via the usual means: by finding the largest crowd of young bucks. They appeared as besotted with her as ever. Her entourage included Mr. Greenleigh, a man with a well-deserved reputation for pursuing women known to be unhappily married, and the disappointed Mr. Walter Davener.

Mrs. MacInnis broke off conversation when Bracebridge passed her on his way to greet Lady Aldreth. He held her gaze a moment too long before he nodded in acknowledgment and continued. Across the room, Emily came to her feet. Anyone looking at her would think she had nothing on her mind but how many of the gentlemen had yet to compliment her. But he knew now, that wasn't so.

He was very much aware of others watching him, which proved Anne had not exaggerated. Emily was his wife and, as such, deserved his public respect and support. That was true whether he had moments of tender feelings toward her or not.

Anne intercepted him before he reached Lady Aldreth. He bowed over her hand. The warmth of their long friendship remained, but the ache of his disappointment was not as sharp as it had been. Time had passed.

"You came," she said softly.

"Of course I did." He *had* come because of Anne. But he had done so for Emily.

"My dear Bracebridge." Lady Aldreth joined them and gave him her hand. Her smile lacked warmth.

"Lady Aldreth." He bent over her hand. Emily had retaken her seat and was listening to some young buck who ought to have known better than to make cow eyes at a married woman. Her expression was dangerously smooth.

Lady Aldreth lowered her voice and addressed her elder sister. "Duchess, I hope you don't mind, I need a word with Bracebridge. In private."

"Certainly not."

"Lady Aldreth, I hope you will allow me to first greet my wife."

She met his gaze. "The subject is urgent."

"Then I am at your disposal." He glanced at Emily again, but a fellow in a naval uniform had her attention.

Lady Aldreth walked him out of the parlor to an office at the back of the house. She faced him, arms crossed underneath her breasts. "What's to be done, Bracebridge?"

"About?"

"This." She gestured with frustration. "You and Emily. Papa and Mr. Davener! And Mr. Greenleigh."

"Forgive me, Lady Aldreth, are we quarreling?"

She took a long, deep breath. She was a Sinclair; therefore her anger was magnificent. "What have *you* done?"

"Today?" He intended to provoke and did. "Nothing that would interest you. Might you answer my question?"

"Yes." She threw up her hands. "Yes, we are quarreling."

"Why?"

"I am not amused." She speared him with a look he'd not seen from her in some time. "Not at all."

"Nor am I. Perhaps you might get to the point."

"You and Emily. What on Earth possessed you to do such a thing?"

"Your esteemed father and his habit of arranging marriages for his daughters provided he receives a suitable price."

Her fine eyes glistened with incipient tears, and the corner of her mouth trembled. "You have been a friend for years. A dear friend." She squeezed his arm. He refused to react. "I was so sorry about you and Anne. Truly I was."

"Thank you for your sympathy. However, as we both know, Anne is married, happily so. To be clear, you would have approved of my marriage to your elder sister but not to your youngest? Why?"

Her eyes widened. "You know why. You love Anne. You do not love Emily. You married Emily to revenge yourself on our father. Please," she said, the word dripping with scorn, "do not make the mistake of underestimating my understanding of you, my father, or any of my sisters."

"Believe me, I do not."

"I shan't forgive you for putting your satisfaction before her happiness. You must have known she would say yes."

"I do not underestimate any Sinclair sister, including Emily." His chest tightened unpleasantly because for quite some time, that had not been true. At least now he knew who had sent the lawyer. "It seems I overestimated your husband, though. I shall tell you, Lady Aldreth, what I shall tell him to his face. I shall not tolerate his interference in my marriage."

"Why not? If there is a way to be free of your marriage, why not pursue it? You are no stranger to scandal."

"No." The ferocity with which the sisters defended each other humbled him and made his heart ache for his brothers.

"Your heart cannot be won. Not by her. If there exists a woman you can love besides Anne, then free yourself to find and marry her. I do not wish you unhappiness. Nor does Anne. But Emily deserves a husband capable of loving the woman she is."

He did not reply. He agreed, though. Oh, how he agreed.

"You have many fine qualities, I do not dispute that. I admire you. I respect you. You have been a valued, important friend to me and my husband, and to Anne and Lucy."

"But not Emily."

"No. Not Emily."

"I am her husband in the eyes of the law and in the eyes of God. She is my wife, Lady Aldreth. You won't convince me to stand aside. Not for anything."

"Not even her happiness?"

"Why do you assume she is unhappy?"

She laughed out loud. "Your question only proves me correct. You have always resented her joyful spirit. Your interactions with her have always had an element of condescension to her. It did not matter before. It does now. Believe you me, my lord, it matters now."

"I do not resent her."

"You do," she said softly. "I am sorry, but you do, and you had best learn to see your marriage and your wife with open eyes. You resent what makes Emily beautiful inside because it's not what Anne is like. If there is the slightest chance the marriage can be set aside, why not take it? You do her no good by remaining in this farce of a marriage." She lifted a hand to prevent his interrupting. "Your loyalty to Anne came at Emily's expense." She drew a sharp breath. "I don't know that I shall ever forgive you for that. You can only make her unhappy. She's been through enough. Enough."

Understanding dawned. His enemy was not Aldreth or Cynssyr. "It's you who sent a lawyer to interview my servants."

"Cynssyr has bought a property for her. In Little Merton. Did you know that?"

"She told me."

"Let her live there while others work to free you both."

"You have no legal standing to interfere in my marriage. It would be ludicrous even if Aldreth were acting on your behalf."

"Marriages are set aside often enough that I know it can be done. Emily has powerful connections, and I assure you they can and shall be brought to bear against you."

"Have you told Emily what you've done?" The deadness inside him expanded. "Does she approve?"

"She hasn't any idea." Lady Aldreth was blithe and unrepentant. "I did not take my decision lightly. I am fully cognizant of the scandal that attends an annulment or divorce. But I would rather endure the scandal of the decade than see her trapped in a marriage that cannot make either of you happy. I should think, my lord, if you have any regard for her at all, that you would want the same."

"There are no grounds for divorce. Or annulment. You shall not have any cooperation from me. The marriage is legal. Your sister is my wife. Best resign yourself to that fact."

"That is your pride speaking. Your stubbornness. It's a trait you share with your late father, by the way."

"She may have conceived by me already. Do you see nothing wrong with putting our future children at risk of illegitimacy?" The words came off his tongue hot as fire, and his mind processed what he'd said only after their utterance. *Our children. Ours*, not *my.*

"If that's so, my lord, congratulations. She should retreat to Little Merton as soon as her condition is confirmed." She smiled. "She can have her lying-in at Rosefeld, attended by those who love her and want only the best for her. If she gives you a son, you need never see her again."

"How long have you been my enemy? Since Anne? Or before then?"

"Don't be ridiculous." She was chillingly calm. "I would have been pleased beyond measure if you had married Anne. Aldreth and I hoped that you would." She gave a small shrug of her shoulders. "Think on what I've said, Bracebridge. It's not too late to make this right."

"I have already done what is right." Not entirely true, but close enough.

Lady Aldreth fell silent for several moments. "I became your enemy the moment you married Emily knowing that she loves you when you do not."

The parlor door opened, then closed, with a purposeful click. Whatever the reason for the interruption, he was grateful, for he was close to words that would likely have ended in a permanent rupture between him and Aldreth's wife.

When he turned, he saw Emily with her hand on the doorknob and her attention on her sister. "Mary." She pushed away from the door and walked toward them. "Please do not speak so to my husband."

Lady Aldreth wheeled on her sister. "It's for your own good."

"I believe you mean that. I know you do." Emily crossed the room to him and linked arms with him. "In this matter, you are wrong. I shall always be the youngest, but I am no longer a girl who needs direction and advice at every turn. I have not been for some time now. I beg you to please accept that and to keep in your mind that I am not a child, not legally and not in fact. You insult me with your assumption that I was powerless to refuse his offer. You insult me again when you assume I did not understand the state of his heart and mine when he proposed marriage. I assure you: I did know, and I took that into consideration."

"Emily."

The parallels between him and Lady Aldreth were ironic indeed. They had both failed to give Emily the respect she deserved. He, too, had treated Emily as if she were too young to understand.

"I am his wife," Emily said. "You must respect that."

"It's not necessary for you to remain in a loveless marriage. It's not. Not with me and Lucy and Anne to watch out for you. We care about you. We only want the best for you. You needn't stay in a marriage that makes you unhappy."

"But Mary." She let go of his hand to take her sister's and press it against her chest. "Mary. I am happy. I am happy that I am not married to that dunce, Mr. Davener. I am happy I am no longer obliged to live with Papa and his threats—you understand what I mean. I know you do."

Lady Aldreth's voice thickened. "I ought to have insisted you come to Rosefeld once Lucy was married. I never should have allowed you to stay there with him."

"I would have refused to come. I am happy now, and Bracebridge is the reason. Both of us know full well the state of our respective hearts. It is not for you to judge or to decide that either of us should have different sentiments than we do. You may have whatever opinion you like, but it is, after all, only your opinion."

"Emily, you do not—"

"Mary!" Emily drew herself up. "Bracebridge and I understand one another. If you persist, we shall quarrel. Do not interfere in our lives. Give advice, yes, if I ask it of you. But if my husband wishes to end this marriage, that is his choice. Not yours. Not mine. Not Papa's. Not Aldreth's or anyone else. Should he come to such a decision, I assure you, I will seek assistance. Respectfully, I ask that you withhold your advice until I feel myself in need of your wise counsel."

Lady Aldreth, a formidable foe to have made, looked between the two of them. "I want the best for you, Emily, and this marriage is not best for you or him. I want you to be happy, and how can that be? I ask you, with all that we know about him, how can that be?"

"I know you want the best for me, and I thank you for that," Emily replied gently. Her fingers tightened around his once again. "What is best for me is that my sisters allow me to live the life that is before me. The one I freely chose."

Lady Aldreth threw her arms around her sister. He heard her whisper fiercely, "Emily, Emily, our mother would not want this for you. She wouldn't."

His wife hugged her sister and stepped back. She was still holding his hand. "If anyone knows my faults, it's him." Her smile was stupefyingly brilliant. "I say with confidence that I cannot disappoint him, and that there is no one else about whom I may say such a thing."

"Harry Glynn loves you, Emily. He loves you, and if you were free, he would marry you."

"Enough, Mary. I've had quite enough. We shall have an irreparable break if you persist." Emily turned to him. "My lord. If you do not mind, I would like for us to go home."

Chapter Twenty-Four

H E SPRAWLED NAKED on his bed, pillows piled between him and the headboard, knees bent, one wrist dangling off his knees as he watched Emily return to him. Naked and smiling, she moved toward him on her knees. He spread his legs wider and enjoyed the rousing response of his body at the sight of her.

She stopped just past the gateway created by his knees, hands on his thighs, focused on his torso. "You have another bruise."

"It's nothing." He glanced at the spot she meant. The bruise wasn't large, but it was just now a very dark blue. She'd already kissed a healing scrape across his knuckles that had resulted from him sparring without first wrapping his hands or donning gloves. "I visited Gentleman Jack's this morning."

"Does it hurt?"

"Not when I look at you." He reached for her, keeping his back against the pillows. He slid his fingers from her collarbone, down and over her breast. He was convinced he would always find Emily arousing to the point of his own stupidity. Her groan when his fingers slid over her nipples brought a smile to his heart. She was his match in this. Perfect for him. Perfect with him.

He continued downward until his fingers were on her belly. He adored the texture of her skin, the shape of her, the way she responded to physical contact. They'd learned each other better, and now they were incendiary together. She did like him just as he was. Rough, crude, tender, or something in between.

"Mm." She let her head fall back, and for several seconds, the pain of her beauty filled him. He did like a woman who showed what she felt during bed play, and Emily felt a great deal. It was immensely satisfying that she so thoroughly appreciated his physicality. He certainly appreciated hers.

He stroked her stomach. Ever since he'd so bluntly told Lady Aldreth that it was possible Emily was with child, he couldn't stop wondering if she was. "Em."

"Yes?"

"Shouldn't you have had your courses by now?"

She straightened and for a beat or two looked confused. Then her expression turned cautious. She pressed the side of her fist to her lips and shook her head in a slow, thoughtful manner. "I don't think it means that."

He hadn't realized how intensely he wanted children until his confrontation with Mrs. Elliot and then Lady Aldreth had brought the possibility to the front. The idea that he might soon be a father had refused to let go of him. Several times, he'd counted the number of days they'd been married and the number of days they'd been together. He continued stroking her. "Why not?"

"Because," she said, "I don't feel different. Anne and Mary say they always know because they're so miserably ill." She met his gaze and touched a finger to the side of his face. "I'm disappointed, too," she said. "I know you're anxious to have your heir. I as well."

"I'm not disappointed." An heir, yes, but he would not mind a daughter. He moved his legs so his calves were behind her. He was disappointed, though. He'd got it into his head that they'd managed to start on their progeny right away. The very first time he took her to bed. "We've not been married long."

"Not long at all." She put her hand around the base of his cock. "Except here. Here, you are quite long."

"Yes. Love. Yes, please, just so." He forced his eyes open, and his stomach tightened with anticipation when he saw her arch smile. As he lifted into her grip of him, he said, "Two months, Em. This almost every night. No interruptions other than those few days at the beginning of this adventure. God, Em."

She tightened her hand around him. She had long ago proved a quick student; she was enthusiastic about his big body, his strength, and his predilection for crude fucking, to the point where he wondered, not without some irony, whether her appreciation of him was physical alone.

A few moments later, she put her mouth where her hand had been, and there wasn't another woman who compared to what she did to him. He concentrated on holding out, on drawing out his pleasure. He swept her hair to one side and fisted a handful. He'd taught her how to take him like this, and she now mastered him utterly. What she did with her tongue destroyed him.

It happened that he did not want to finish in her mouth, and when he was uncomfortably close, he drew away. She braced her hands on his shoulders and gave him a look that burned. He still had his hand tangled in her hair. He let out a coarse grunt as he cupped her bottom with his free hand and brought her to him.

"Now," he said. "Now, but slow. Take me in slowly." He let go of her hair and threw his hands back to grip the top of the carved bedstead that had been in the Margaret Street house for two hundred years.

She smiled in a way that sent him hurtling toward climax, but she knew his body well and held back. He hadn't precisely taught her that, but she'd learned the benefit of a moment's denial. They froze, teetering on separate peaks of bliss. He drew a slow breath and concentrated on not losing control. Yes. Yes. Done.

He hitched himself up enough to flex the muscles of his arms and upper body, and she seated herself on him. Controlled, except for her sigh of contentment. He was near out of his mind with lust by now. She rocked her hips on him, and every so often, he angled himself so the head of his cock went deeper in her. So close. Killingly close. Fucking her was like nothing else. Nothing.

He, Devon, Lord Bracebridge, had what every other man in London wanted: the most beautiful woman in England in his bed. The Divine Sinclair was his, unreservedly and wholeheartedly.

The coal in the fireplace shifted, and there were several long moments when the light changed and flickered through the room and there was silence between them; his heart expanded in his chest in a peculiar manner that had begun with his walking out of Aldreth's house with her hand still in his. But by God, she was his wife, and no matter the difficulties of their past, she was his. His and only his.

"Emily."

She leaned forward and put her hands over his. Her hair fell past her shoulders, unfastened because he'd grown to like her hair free when they were like this. He watched her face; her eyes were closed, and she was breathing harder, harder. Secret Emily, unknowable. His.

He pushed up, and she cried out.

"Tell me," he said. "Tell me."

Her eyes opened. There simply wasn't a name for that pure, intense, lust-laced blue. He released one hand from his grip on the headboard, wrapped it around the back of her neck and brought her closer.

"Say it," he said. There weren't going to be more words for him. He was so close to the peak he might not last another five seconds. "Say what's in your head."

His body broke, and he whirled away to her whispered confession.

"I wish I didn't love you."

Chapter Twenty-Five

M AGGIE ANSWERED THE TAP on the door to Emily's room and admitted Mrs. Elliot. "Milady," the housekeeper said with a quick curtsy.

"Yes?" Emily slid a piece of paper into her book to mark her place. At home—that is, at the Cooperage—she'd had a lovely ivory bookmark that had been a gift from Anne last year. Gone forever now, since Papa had surely sold it. She constantly encountered the need or longing for items she no longer had. A bookmark. A fan. Paintings she'd done and was rather proud of.

"His lordship begs me to inform you that he is downstairs with guests and hopes you will join him."

"How many guests?" Behind her, Maggie headed for her dressing room. That day at Portman Square, she and Bracebridge had reached peace, if one defined peace as an acknowledgment of the lack of mutual sentiment. *I wish I didn't love you*, she'd said, to which he had said nothing. But they understood each other now, and that made it possible for them to get on with whatever sort of marriage they were going to have.

"Four, milady."

"Please tell him I shall be down shortly." She'd spent most of the afternoon home rereading *Waverly*. She wasn't dressed for dinner since she'd expected to dine alone in her room. There was no reason for the flutter of her heart, but with their respective positions out in the open, she could acknowledge the reaction and not have it tear her apart. "Do you know who he's brought here?"

"No, milady."

Maggie approached with an armful of gowns. "The grey, the burgundy, or the dark blue?"

"The dark blue."

Her maid hurried away to fetch the rest of the ensemble. By now, Emily trusted Maggie implicitly, and thank goodness for her unerring taste and attention to detail.

Between the two women, Emily was quickly dressed and outfitted in matching slippers. Maggie had the lint brush in hand and was brushing the blue velvet overdress.

The maid stepped back, brush aloft in one hand, then walked a circle around her. "Perfect, if I do say so myself."

Emily straightened her skirt and the silver lace shawl Maggie handed her, and was on her way. She found Pond first, though, for more information on the meal being prepared and the guests Bracebridge had brought home. She relaxed when she heard Mr. Rachagorla's name. There would be at least one person she knew and liked.

According to Pond, Mr. Simmons was an actor who managed a theater in partnership with Bracebridge and Mr. Rachagorla. His companion and very dear friend was Mrs. Quinn, a noted actress. The fourth name sent a thrill of recognition through her, for this guest was none other than the diva Signora Ciolini. Mrs. Simmons, Mrs. Quinn, and Signora Ciolini had made her husband's acquaintance in his days as a prizefighter and operator of Two Fives.

Emily was well acquainted with the rumor that Ciolini and Bracebridge had once been lovers. In the early days of that relationship, gossip had reached as far as Bartley Green.

Outside the anteroom where Bracebridge and his guests were gathered, she took a deep breath, smoothed her skirts once, and walked in. She knew how to entertain and enthrall. No matter what anyone thought of her, in this regard she was entirely competent.

Mr. Rachagorla was nearest to the door and already standing when she came in. If his suit was not from Weston himself, then it had been made by someone equally skilled. His waistcoat was exquisite, too. She'd never seen anything as lovely as that crimson and saffron silk. Wouldn't Bracebridge look handsome in colors like that?

Across the room with Bracebridge, another man stood; he must be the theater owner, Mr. Simmons. The woman next to him, a blonde whom she did not recognize, must therefore be Mrs. Quinn. The woman on the sofa was none other than the infamous, gloriously talented, Ciolini.

At first glance, Signora Ciolini was smaller and much more ordinary than she appeared on stage. Except there was nothing ordinary about her.

The singer rose with languid ease, then crossed toward Emily as if she were entering stage right. She took Emily's hand in hers and pressed it tenderly. Her eyes were large, a dark brown both expressive and liquid. Her nose was hooked, her eyebrows thick and black, and her chin was too strong. She spoke in heavily accented but exceedingly charming English.

"What a beautiful young woman you are."

"Thank you." Ciolini was exactly the sort of woman Bracebridge would admire: talented, interesting, and fascinating.

"My delightful young beauty, tell me, what is your name?" Ciolini stepped back and looked Emily up and down, then glanced over her shoulder at Bracebridge. "*Caro mio*, you did not tell us you had another guest."

Oh dear. The woman had no intention of making herself agreeable. Emily withdrew her hand with just enough force to make her point. She waited until she had the woman's full attention before she said, far too sweetly, "Lady Bracebridge, at your service."

"Indeed?"

"Yes. Indeed. Signora Ciolini, how delightful to meet you."

Ciolini whirled without much grace and arranged herself on the sofa to great advantage. She gestured with one hand. "Everyone is delighted to meet me."

Bracebridge had by then realized he had social duties to perform. He came to Emily's side and introduced her to Mr. Simmons and Mrs. Quinn. At last came her official introduction to Signora Ciolini.

Emily maintained her smile. "I heard you sing when I was a girl. I'm sure you don't remember, but you came to Bartley Green at the invitation of a neighbor of ours. My sisters and I were permitted to attend, and your singing was—" She put a hand over her heart. She had no difficulty at all being genuine. "—the most astonishing, captivating thing I have ever heard in all my life. Ever since that day, I have been mad about opera."

Ciolini shot a glance at Bracebridge. "Do you go to the opera often?"

"As often as possible." From the corner of her eye, she saw Ciolini's lip curl. "Last season, Signora, I attended the most astonishing performances. My sisters and I have heard you sing several times, to our great delight and honor."

"Have you many sisters?" the Italian asked.

"Three," she said.

"So many?"

Mr. Rachagorla broke the tension that followed. "Bracebridge has always spoken highly of the Sinclair sisters. Ciolini, I am astonished that you do not recall this."

Emily waved a hand. "If he spoke of me at all, the word 'brat' figured prominently in his complaint. I thank you for omitting that, Mr. Rachagorla."

"I am sure he never complained of you." Despite his warm smile, Mr. Rachagorla had the same hardness she so often saw in Bracebridge. She had no more idea how to bridge that gap with him than she did with her husband. "His praise most certainly encompassed all the Sinclair sisters."

"Say no more, sir. I wish to hold that thought dear."

"You doubt me?" he asked with a smile.

She seated herself midway between the fireplace and the sofa where Ciolini reigned. "How fortunate for me, Mr. Rachagorla, that your memory is faulty."

That reply earned her a more genuine smile. "I am glad to have met all the Sinclair sisters. Bracebridge is entirely correct. You are all charming, delightful, and accomplished women."

Mr. Simmons had retaken the chair he'd vacated upon her entrance and now tipped his head to one side, one hand dangling off the end of the chair arm. "One thing I know, my lady, is that your husband did not exaggerate your beauty."

With feline grace, Ciolini rose from the sofa and walked to Bracebridge. She opened the fan hanging from her wrist and held it so that only her liquid brown eyes showed. "My lord, I congratulate you on your marriage to this perfect little woman."

He took Ciolini's hand and kissed her knuckles. The woman swept into a graceful, only slightly too respectful, curtsey. He raised her hand higher, and she took a step back. But their gazes locked, and he was smiling at the woman with genuine affection. "Devastating as always."

Emily's heart sank. Ciolini was fascinating, and gifted, and interesting. She was everything Bracebridge preferred in a woman and that Emily could never be. The diva's self-possession was reason enough for a man to find himself besotted. Emily believed absolutely the rumors that the woman's lovers had included men from the highest reaches of fashionable London. The very highest.

At last Bracebridge released Ciolini's hand. Emily sat on her chair and felt useless and dull while her husband escorted Ciolini back to the sofa. Once again, she arranged herself in regal fashion. It was impossible not to stare at her.

"Now that we are all here, tell us, Moll," Bracebridge said to Mrs. Quinn, "what role has your admirers enthralled now?"

"Desdemona, darling man." She gave an overdone sigh intended to amuse, which it did. Like Ciolini, she left her seat to approach Bracebridge, wrapping her arm around his and leaning close. She, too, was a woman who was much more than her appearance. Mrs. Quinn might not have Ciolini's penchant for the dramatic—odd in an actress—but she was not without the ability to move one to emotion. "You have not been to see me in the part. Everyone says I'm brilliant. Isn't that so, Mr. Simmons?"

"It is." Mr. Simmons brought together the tips of his fingers, kissed them, and released that kiss to the air.

"I do not doubt for a moment that you are brilliant in the role," Bracebridge replied.

Emily had never seen him with friends other than Mr. Rachagorla from his disreputable days, but this was what she had imagined: compellingß, talented men and women whom she would not have been permitted to meet under any other circumstances but these, Mr. Rachagorla excepted, since he was often invited to the very best parties and gatherings.

"I must remedy this most deplorable lack."

"When you do, I hope you will bring Lady Bracebridge." Mrs. Quinn released Bracebridge's arm. "You said you enjoy the opera, Lady Bracebridge. Do you also enjoy the theater?"

Emily could easily answer with a genuine smile. She very much liked Mrs. Quinn. "*Othello* is a favorite play of mine."

Mrs. Quinn gave her an encouraging look. "One of the great tragedies."

"As children, my sisters and I performed the play several times." She let her gaze slide to Bracebridge, but he was watching Mrs. Quinn. "We were perfectly awful, but it was great fun."

"You were cast as Desdemona, I presume?" Mrs. Quinn asked. "You would be, with your astonishing beauty."

"You played Desdemona?" Bracebridge swung around to her. "Why was I not invited to such a spectacle as that?"

Emily waved him off. "We were actresses long before you had ever heard of Bartley Green. And no, Mrs. Quinn. My sister Anne had the role of Desdemona." She counted off on her fingers. "I played the Duke of Venice, Iago, Roderigo, and various others whenever there was a need for soldiers."

"You are a versatile actress, then."

"Out of pure necessity. I fear no one but we Sinclair sisters enjoyed our productions. But I promise you, we had our moments with such material as Shakespeare gives us. I sobbed most horribly whenever Anne died."

"Who played Othello?" Mr. Rachagorla asked.

"My sister, Lady Aldreth."

"Indeed?" Bracebridge said.

"Yes. I'm surprised you did not guess that."

"My lord," Mr. Simmons said. "You must bring her to our production. I insist. Come any night you like. I'll reserve a box for you."

Emily did not dare stop smiling. "Mr. Simmons, how very kind of you. However, it's more likely I shall attend with one of my sisters. I have three times the opportunity to persuade someone to accompany me. Since we have all acted the play before, we have a singular affection for the work. It won't be difficult at all to convince one of my sisters to attend with me."

"The duchess, perhaps?" Mr. Simmons looked dazzled by the thought of the Duchess of Cynssyr in attendance at his theater.

"Oh, very possibly." She would do him a good turn if she could persuade Anne. She was more than willing to try.

"Lady Bracebridge, you are as charming as you are beautiful."

"Thank you."

"You said you have heard Ciolini sing?" Mr. Simmons asked.

"Yes, several times, but as I said, the first was when I was a girl."

"Bartley Green, did you say?" Ciolini tapped her chin.

"Yes. It would have been for the Glynns. They live at Withercomb in Bartley Green."

Ciolini glanced at Bracebridge. "Yes, yes, I remember. A private performance. For intimates only. There was a terrace. You were not there, *caro mio.*"

"I was not," Bracebridge said.

Indeed, not. At the time, he would have been merely Mr. Devon Carlisle and, though he was not yet officially unwelcome at Withercomb, Emily could not imagine Mrs. Glynn allowing a prizefighter at her home.

Emily's life then seemed so uncomplicated. None of the Sinclairs had yet met Bracebridge, Aldreth's father had still been alive, and her own father hadn't succumbed yet to the daily call of spirits.

"My dear child," Ciolini said. "How old were you? No more than five or six, no?"

"Twelve or thirteen, I think."

Ciolini looked at Bracebridge with one eyebrow arched as she murmured, "So young."

"Alas," Bracebridge said, "I missed *Othello* at the Cooperage and Ciolini at Withercomb."

Emily smiled at Ciolini as if she hadn't heard her husband's murmurs. "You were in such fine voice, I came away in tears."

Pond rescued her by calling them to dinner, for which Emily was quite grateful. There was no reason she could see for Ciolini to behave as she was. Mrs. Quinn, who had an equally long and likely intimate past with Bracebridge, was perfectly pleasant and agreeable.

The meal was a masterpiece and the service flawless. Conversation among the six of them was easy and intimate. Everyone but her shared wonderful, amusing stories about their lives or referred to stories of events from the days of Mr. Devon Carlisle. Plainly, they were fond and close acquaintances, with a shared past she knew very little about.

Other than stories of the plays she and her sisters had staged, quite dreadfully, or the many times she'd been in trouble with one of her sisters for one reason or another, she had little of interest to say. She could, however, give her opinion of recent events, of politics, or of the novels and poetry she'd read. She had Mr. Rachagorla to thank for bringing up subjects such as that.

The last course was served, and now they were merely lingering at the table. In a transparent attempt to bring Emily into the circle, Bracebridge told the others how she had taken in Frieda and Socrates and bluntly ended with, "My affection for that dog goes far beyond reason, and if the cat does not sit on my lap when I'm reading, I am entirely out of sorts."

Ciolini put her elbow on the table and rested her chin between her thumb and forefinger as she slowly blinked her magnificent eyes at Bracebridge. "I do not recall that you had any great liking for animals before."

"I have now. Hearing what mischief she's been up to—" Bracebridge winked at Emily. "—the dog, not my wife, when I've returned home, amuses me no end." He helped himself to more wine. "There is much to be said for the salutatory effect of a devoted dog on one's mood."

"I promise all of you," Emily said, "that I am rarely up to mischief."

Bracebridge hoisted his glass in her direction. "But when you are, darling, when you are."

"Ooh, la, la," said Mrs. Quinn, fanning herself.

Mr. Rachagorla chuckled. "What husband would not be desperately in love with such a delightful and charming woman as Lady Bracebridge?

Mrs. Quinn, being seated to Bracebridge's left, put her hand on his arm and said, "You've done well for yourself, my lord."

"I have."

Mr. Simmons and Mr. Rachagorla shared stories about Bracebridge that gave Emily a different view of her husband. He was well liked by these people, and not because he was Lord Bracebridge. They liked him because he had been their friend during times and circumstances she had always assumed had been the most trying of his life. Perhaps not. Perhaps not in the way she'd imagined.

They soon after removed to the withdrawing room, and Bracebridge headed for the side table. Several decanters and bottles were lined up with the various glasses suited to each of the liquors. A footman in a somber suit of black wool stood ready to serve.

"There's brandy." Bracebridge looked over his shoulder at Mr. Rachagorla. "What you sent me from your private stock, so perhaps that's too familiar, my friend. Sherry. Hock? Something else?"

He meant, Emily realized, brandy that had been smuggled in from France during the war.

"Brandy, please," Mr. Rachagorla said. "Whatever you have on hand."

"Simmons, I have Green Chartreuse for you. Ciolini? Moll?" The women made their requests, and Bracebridge busied himself playing host.

Mr. Rachagorla lifted his glass in Emily's direction with a quizzical look. "Nothing for you, Lady Bracebridge? The brandy is excellent, I assure you."

"Nothing, thank you."

"Your husband does not permit you spirits?" Signora Ciolini raised her voice. "A wise decision, my lord, with a wife so young as yours."

Bracebridge lifted a hand before Emily could settle on the best response. An amused smile hovered on his mouth as he handed Ciolini the drink she'd requested. "Believe me, my wife has a mind of her own."

"Does she? I mean no disrespect." Signora Ciolini put a hand on Bracebridge's chest and gazed up at him. "But she is so young."

"Please, Ciolini," Mr. Rachagorla said. "Will you sing for us? I am happy to accompany you." Fortunately, this suggestion was eagerly applauded.

Five minutes later, Emily was in absolute raptures. She would forgive Ciolini anything in return for the joy of her hearing her sing. After a fourth sublime song, Ciolini relinquished the floor to Mrs. Quinn. She performed a scene from *Macbeth*, and another from *Richard III* with Mr. Simmons, who proved he had no little talent himself, with a subsequent and riveting performance of Falstaff.

In the silence that fell at the conclusion of Mr. Simmons's enactment of Hamlet's soliloquy, they all heard Bracebridge say in some frustration, "I am married now."

Chapter Twenty-Six

B RACEBRIDGE SETTLED ON the sofa in his father's smoking room, once the Lemon Parlor so beloved by his mother. He plucked the most recent issue of the *Edinburgh Review* from a table and stretched his legs toward the grate. He did not open the magazine; instead, he stared at the ceiling. Uneasiness interfered with his ability to concentrate. He did not care for the feeling yet did not know what to do about it.

Gopal sat beside him with a charcoal pencil and a sketch pad, drawing intricate patterns. They weren't smoking despite the name given to the room. They had luncheoned at Two Fives, then moved to the Margaret Street house all because Bracebridge had hoped Emily would be there. As it turned out, she was not. She'd gone out for the afternoon. He refused to dwell on his disappointment.

"Are you staying in London much longer?" Gopal asked. In the normal course of things, Bracebridge spent extended summers at Corth Abbey with frequent stays at Rosefeld or with Cynssyr. He only went to the Lords if it was absolutely necessary, though he did enjoy casting votes for reform.

"Undetermined at this time." He flipped through several pages of his magazine without reading a single line of text. "Have I told you her bloody father refused to send on her possessions?" He remained outraged, which was something of a surprise. "I have considered engaging a lawyer."

"The question is whether the cost is worth the aggravation."

He could always rely on Gopal's honest opinion. That honesty was a benefit of a friendship that predated his stepping into his father's title. "The more aggravated Sinclair is, the better."

"The pettiness is mutual, then."

"Have you been speaking with my wife? For she's told me the same."

Gopal chuckled as he drew. "Lady Bracebridge is a wise woman."

"My point is, why should her father engage in such despicable behavior without consequence? As her husband, I ought to stand up for her."

"I agree it would be satisfying to have a court compel the return of her possessions." This pencil moved across the page. "However many years hence, I am sure you shall be quite satisfied."

"He left her with nothing. Nothing but her dog and what she had in her pockets when she left Bartley Green." He tossed aside the magazine. "I tell you, I have yet to hear one word of complaint from her."

Gopal shot him a glance, and Bracebridge felt a twinge of guilt. Emily kept too much to herself, and he knew that was his fault. "Fortunately, you are more than capable of providing her with all she requires for her comfort and sustenance."

"We are in town for that reason entirely. It's not as though I do not do my duty to her. In any event, she ought to have a new wardrobe. As befits my countess."

"Certainly."

"Because of her father's pettiness, she has forever lost mementos and other items she holds dear. Even when you and I hadn't a shilling between us, did we not have possessions that meant a great deal to us, items we would have been devastated to lose?"

"I do not disagree with you."

"Is that not worth some pettiness from me?"

"A man is wise who considers the opinions and counsel of one's partner in life."

Bracebridge shook his head, but he didn't know whether he was disagreeing or simply acknowledging the situation was more complicated than he wanted to admit. "What man does not think himself fortunate if his wife is beautiful?"

"Is that all you see?" Gopal stopped sketching. "Her beauty? I tell you I see much more. A woman who is kind, and thoughtful, and forbearing. Ciolini behaved badly to her, yet your wife welcomed her. Your destiny is most fortunate."

"Yes, of course." Was hers, though? He was more than willing to admit his good fortune. But would she say the same about hers? He had no idea. "I fear she is unhappy."

Gopal put aside his paper and pencil. "You believe that because you loved another woman once, you can never love another, but I tell you that is not true. Fate has brought you here, to this time and to this place. Fate has brought you together with the wife you were meant to have. She is your destiny. Cease looking back on what did not come to pass and accept what did."

He knew what Gopal meant. Emily had told him as much herself: that when he looked at her, he saw only the ways in which she was not Anne. He had loved Anne, and there would always be a place in his heart for her. That did not mean there wasn't a place for Emily. "I don't know her."

Gopal looked down his nose at Bracebridge. "Is this not something you should remedy?" He consulted the clock on the fireplace mantel. "I ought to have been at Two Fives half an hour ago. My dear Bracebridge, I leave you to contemplate the life you have."

He stood, but Gopal raised a hand.

"I'll show myself out." He put a hand on Bracebridge's shoulder and squeezed once. "Open your eyes and ears, and you may find that you have also opened your heart."

When the door closed behind him, Bracebridge sat on the sofa facing the fire. What if Gopal was right? What if?

Socrates sauntered in and jumped on Bracebridge's lap. How a three-legged cat could saunter was a mystery, but there was no doubt the cat managed it. He'd gained weight in the short time he'd been here and was looking to be a proper tomcat one day. Within moments, Socrates was fast asleep, his fur soft beneath Bracebridge's fingers.

Emily came home not long after he and Socrates had settled onto the sofa. He listened to the unmistakable stir of her arrival: her greeting Pond, Frieda's nails clicking on the marble. That dog loved her. But of course she did. Emily had saved her, given her a home, and loved her unreservedly.

He thought of Frieda never having been rescued, or Socrates here never having been noticed. The idea opened a crack across his heart, and part of that was grief pouring out for the woman he had loved and the woman he did not. He was flawed, too flawed to love where he ought to.

He ought to get up and go to her. He ought to tell her how sorry he was and that he would try to do better. The moment before he came to his feet, intending that somehow between now and when he found her, he would have the right words, Emily tapped on the door.

"My lord?"

"Enter," he called out. He closed his eyes and pictured her in his mind. What came to him was a recollection of her joyful smile. How tenderly she held Socrates. The two of them in bed. He pictured Emily in fullness, with depth, shadow and light, in color and in joy, all spreading a tenderness in his heart.

"I'm sorry to disturb you." Concern threaded through her words, and he sat up straight. Her skirts swished as she walked across the room. He tried to see past her smile and couldn't because she intended her smile to be a shield. "Have you seen Socrates?"

Who was she, besides the Divine Sinclair?

Owing to the high sides of the sofa, she could not see the cat asleep on his lap. "They've not seen him in the kitchen," she said, "and I can't find him anywhere."

He did not know much about his wife, but he did know she'd convinced herself some horrible fate had befallen Socrates, just as she continually worried that something might happen to Frieda. Her father had done that to her. Thomas Sinclair had raised his daughters in a household where they must constantly worry about what they might lose next. Was it any wonder Emily armored herself against disasters imagined and real?

"Here." He lifted a hand and gestured for her to come the rest of the way in. As ever, he was struck by her beauty, but they now shared the familiarity that came with intimacy. "All is well."

She cared deeply for those whom she loved. She lived most of her life dreading, anticipating, and preparing for the next disaster. All the incidents and challenges Anne had described about her life applied to Emily. She had lived all that, too.

She came around just to the side, so that she could see him and now the cat. Relief spread across her face, followed quickly by chagrin. "It's ridiculous, I know. I can't seem to help myself. No, no!" She lifted her hands, palms out, then bent to pet Frieda, who had followed her into the room. "Do not stand, my lord. You cannot."

He remained as he was. For now at least, they were a married couple at their leisure, and it was entirely appropriate for them to converse when they were together and for them to relax the rules of propriety. "Then sit here beside me."

She retreated farther behind the mask of her perfection and settled her weight on one hip. "There's no reason for me to disturb you." She saw the magazine he'd thrown, now just out of his reach. "Shall I fetch that for you?"

"Not necessary."

He placed the cat on the sofa and stood. "Emily."

"Yes?" She waited patiently, hands clasped before her.

"Did you have a pleasant day?"

Her eyebrows rose. His wife was a person entire in herself, with a heart, emotions, likes, and dislikes. Just like Anne or any other woman. Except with Emily, he had made mistake after mistake. He had assumed the least of her rather than the most.

All the air in the room vanished.

She was not happy.

Emily was not happy, and the fault was his.

"I did, thank you," she said.

He had no way of knowing whether that was true. She had been protecting herself from his neglect and disinterest for some time. She told him what he wanted to hear instead of anything personal about her. His chest tightened, and he drew a breath.

"Emily. I was wrong to instruct Pond to return Corth Abbey to its previous condition. Not just wrong, but wrongheaded and ungentlemanly. You have every right to make your stamp in our home."

She maintained her smooth, pleasant expression. "You disliked the changes. It was your right to revoke them."

"The entrance was bright and cheerful." He had badly underestimated her, for she understood that he had ordered the changes undone simply because she had made them. "I liked what you did, and it was unforgivable of me to behave as if I did not."

Her eyes widened, and she backed away from him. His heart cracked open wider. "Don't go," he said. Objections swirled around in his head. She meant to leave him; he was afraid it would kill them if she did. "Please. Do not go."

"Little Merton isn't far. Come whenever it pleases you."

"I apologize to you for Ciolini's behavior. She was petty and jealous. I don't know why she behaved that way, but I assure you there is nothing between us. There has not been for years. Since before I ever met a Sinclair."

"Honestly, you needn't worry about that. You must have your own life."

"By which you mean?" There was more, he knew it. He could see she was deciding how to reply, and he did not know whether to wait for her decision about what more to say or ask or insist or plead with her to tell him.

She sighed. "It's no wonder you were lovers."

"Years ago. We are not now, no matter what she wanted you to believe." He walked to her and took her hand and he tried, he tried so very hard to see her for herself, but all he saw was the woman he'd wanted her to be. "I do not know how to be the man you deserve." He touched his chest. "I am broken here. I have been broken for years. This house. This house haunts me. Your sister haunts me, and I do not know how to love anymore. I'm sorry, Emily. So sorry. If I were capable, I would love you. If only I could."

She drew in a shaky breath and took another step back. "Do not do this. Do not. I beg of you, my lord."

"I have been disrespectful of you and your position as my wife and countess. I have not treated you as a partner in our union. I was wrong to do so. For all that and more, I beg your forgiveness."

She blinked several times.

He was not a man to be impotent in the face of strong emotion, but he struggled to find words to convey the chaos of his heart. "You deserve more than I can give. You are so much more than I ever imagined of you. I want to love you, Emily. I want to love you as you deserve to be loved. I want to love you the way I loved Anne. I want to more than you can imagine."

"I haven't asked you to love me that way." She retreated another step. "Never." There was a tear in the veil she kept over the untroubled facade she presented. He saw through it now and was shaken by her sorrow. *This* was what Mrs. Elliot had meant. He'd made his young and joyful wife unhappy. "Your love for Anne was real and true. Hold that in your heart, for she deserved your regard. She deserves it now."

He closed the distance between them. "I have denied you the respect you deserve. There is my confessed fault, renounced from this moment. I shall inform Pond that your instructions are to be followed without question. Here and at Corth Abbey."

Slowly, she shook her head, and he confronted the abyss of a failure worse than any his father had accused him of. Not mere failure but personal dishonor. He had no idea how to repair this. "Stay. Please stay. Stay and make this house into a place where my father does not lurk in every corner. Please." His throat grew thick. "Please stay. Please stay with me, and let me try."

"Oh, Bracebridge."

He brushed a hand across her cheek and congratulated himself for finding a bridge they could both cross, however tentatively. "Let's begin now as we should have from the start. We're in London. Let's entertain as Lord and Lady Bracebridge ought." She relaxed into that contact, and the heat between them was instantaneous. "Allow me to show off my beautiful wife."

"You see," she said without irony. He was delighted that he had found a way to begin. "I am useful."

He slid his arms around her. Thank the stars above, he'd found a way to start.

Chapter Twenty-Seven

THE MOMENT HER HUSBAND'S lips brushed across hers, her stomach burst into shivers of longing. In his arms, her unhappiness vanished. She adored kissing him, was lost entirely whenever he did. Her body wanted his, craved the devastation of his touch, the exquisite bliss of completion in his arms. Though his every touch eroded the safeguards she'd erected around her heart, she was safest at times like this. Pleasure crowded out everything else.

He maneuvered them to the sofa, and she came to life as she always did with him. One thing she'd learned all on her own about Devon Carlisle, Earl of Bracebridge, was that however ingrained his disregard for her, he held back nothing in their intimacy. She did not doubt for a moment that he would have been more circumspect with some other woman as his wife. Not with her, though. She was his match.

When they were like this, she could be herself. There was safety in their mutual lust. He never saw her, not truly, and so he would never know that she had given him her soul. She threaded her fingers through his hair, so thick and soft. She loved those dark curls, just as she loved his lust and the rawness of their physical joining. She pulled back, not far, and pressed a palm to the center of his chest. "Dare we here?"

He pulled up one side of her skirts, and his fingers slid around her thigh, just above her knee. "Yes," he said in a low, silky voice of desire. "Dare all. So say I."

She adjusted herself to give access to his wandering hands. "Dinner is at half past seven. Someone might come looking for us."

"If they do, they'll delay the meal." He held her closer, smiling in that wicked way of his. Her heart flew away with the butterflies that inhabited her stomach. "Allow me to convince you."

He pushed her shoulder until she lay on her back, and she had the rare pleasure of watching his expression as he slowly pushed up her skirts, past her calves, past her knees. His gaze fixed on her legs, following the slide of his fingers on her, toying, for a moment, with her garter, then upward, over her knee, then along the inside of her thigh.

"So beautiful," he said. "So bloody beautiful. You can't help yourself."

Every word was an unintended condemnation. If all that mattered was her appearance, what future had they? One day, inevitably, her youth would fade. She would grow old, and no one would ever know she'd been considered a beauty. What use would she be then? Of what value?

She squeezed her eyes closed. That day was not now. Today, he found her beautiful, and if that was what pleased him about her, then she must take her pleasure now. She stretched, arched her back, and absorbed the cascade of need through her. One day, he too would be old and grey, but whenever she imagined her future, she was always in love with him.

His fingers reached her sex, and she bit her lower lip until she couldn't hold back another moan. He stroked along her, pressing and sliding, caressing that area that never failed to fetch her. "Like so?" he asked, low and wicked.

"Yes." She released herself into her body, surrendered to the ruin of his kisses. Nothing mattered right now but this.

He pressed his lips to the side of her thigh, just above her knee. His mouth was hot and damp, and she fell deeper into the storm of him touching her. "I wish you were naked," he said in a gruff voice. "Spread out for me to worship."

Her eyes popped open and another shiver shot through her at the sight of his dark, dark eyes. He was looking at her body. Looking with lust and longing. "Lock the door, then," she said, perfectly willing.

In a flash, he was on his feet and then back to her with the door locked. That impish, sensual grin killed her every time she saw it. She lay on the sofa, one leg dangling off. His mouth curved, such a ruinous grin that she was lost all over again. He would shatter her heart into pieces, and with that smile, she did not care in the least what happened to her later.

He sat and, with a grunt, pulled her over him so that she straddled his thighs. While she lifted her skirts out of the way, he unfastened his trousers, and then she sank down on him, and there was nothing in this world like him sliding inside her. She trembled, half coming just from this.

"Yes?" he said, full of pride and lust, but with an edge of something else there that she did not understand. Truly, though, when it came to this, what was there to understand but the pursuit of pleasure? "Have I pleased you?"

"Yes. Yes, my God, Bracebridge, you cannot imagine how pleased I feel just now."

"Might you make the attempt?"

She met his thrust upward. When they were intimate, she could say words denied to her any other time. "I adore your cock, but I also wish you were naked and that I could touch and kiss every inch of you. Now, stop." She rocked her hips into his. "Enough talking, and more of *this*."

He had his hands under her skirts and around her bottom, setting a rhythm for them. "I'd rather we were naked on a mattress so you could touch and kiss me everywhere."

"I thought you meant to undress me now."

"There's not room. "He leaned forward to kiss her, and by the time he drew back, she was nearly mad with lust for him. "*You* fit here, I do not."

She shifted her hips, taking him deeper. "But, my lord, you are wrong. You fit perfectly."

He pressed the back of his head against the sofa and laughed. "You never in your life said a truer thing." He grabbed her hips and held her still. "Let's finish this upstairs where we can both be conveniently naked. I'll fit you just as well there as here, but we'll have more room to explore."

"Make me spend now, Bracebridge."

"Yes, my lady." He sounded oddly tender, but that could only be her imagination. "Whatever your heart desires is yours."

Not long afterward, he made his clothes minimally decent, then took her hand and they fled upstairs, laughing. For whatever reason, he proceeded to his room rather than hers. No matter, there was a bed there, too.

He closed his door with a crack and shot the bolt home. "I don't need you, Keller!"

She heard a discreet cough and then Bracebridge spun her around so she ended up facing the wall. He unhooked the first fastening of her dress, then the next and the next. "I like this color on you."

Emily looked down, for she momentarily had no idea what she was wearing. "I like this gown better when it's off."

"Agreed." He pressed his mouth to the back of her neck, and she braced her palms on the wall. "When you wear this shade of blue, I can see your eyes from across the room." His fingers moved down her back. "Hooks. Too many hooks. But there is a reward at the end."

"Tapes and laces, too."

"This gown, which I liked excessively only moments ago, has too many hooks."

"My apologies, my lord."

His fingers were as agile as the rest of him, and he was nothing if not determined. "There will be a reward for us both at the end. That's all that sustains me during the toil of stripping you down. Oh, bugger it." He pushed her dress to her waist. Somehow, he'd managed to unfasten enough of the tapes and hooks to accomplish that. Bracebridge dispatched the rest of the fastenings, and her petticoats and frock pooled at her feet.

She stared at the fabric and breathed in the scent of him, absorbed the nearness of him so that when this ended she would have memories of a time when he had not wished she were Anne. Deft hands. Strong. Such soft lips when he pressed them to her exposed skin. Before long he'd stripped her to her chemise.

"Don't move," he said when she backed away.

She remained facing the wall. If she were to stretch out a hand, her fingers might just brush the plaster. His quarters here were not as dark and ponderous as much of the rest of the house. This was fresher paint than elsewhere in the house. More like Corth Abbey. Thank God. At least here he wouldn't be thinking of how he'd disappointed his father.

Bracebridge put his hands on her shoulders and slid them downward, then to the sides of her hips, then up to cup her breasts, and she groaned because with the way he touched her, almost reverently, she could imagine he wanted her as intensely as she wanted him. That he wanted not just a woman like her, but *her*.

She let her head fall back and groaned as he continued stroking her. Every inch of her, along her arms, fingers lightly dancing, both hands down either side of her spine, fitting into the dip of her lower back.

"So soft." His fingers curved around her hips to her belly. "Luscious." His voice was rough. The real Bracebridge, not the cold and distant man he was when they weren't in bed. Raw with need and with no reason to be polite. "I could fuck you a dozen times a day, and you'd still take my breath away."

She was a sea of want, and his fingers discovered that. His other hand found her breast and, my God, she would never have guessed those two things would steal away her wits. Yes. Yes. This was Bracebridge touching her, kissing her shoulder, his fingers sliding inside her. She would melt from want of him.

He left off touching her to pull the pins from her hair, finding them deftly and dropping several to land wherever they might. She tipped her head forward to balance the weight of her hair as it shifted and came free. He took a step closer, his front to her back, and threaded fingers through her hair.

"Like gold," he whispered, but though she reacted to that soft whisper, all she could think was that she had once overheard him say no woman's hair compared to Anne's. She squeezed her eyes closed and pushed aside the memory.

"Soft, so soft." He drew the mass of her hair to one side and pressed his mouth to the side of her shoulder. She turned her head toward him, and he slid his mouth along her jaw then captured her mouth, and she melted into that meeting of their mouths.

There were times she felt she'd betrayed all her sisters just from having loved him for so long. She'd always felt guilty for not wanting to marry the Duke of Cynssyr. Even before they'd left for London, she hadn't wanted the duke, only the safety she and her sisters would have if she married him. She felt guiltier yet for thinking, if only for an instant, that, with Anne married, Bracebridge might at last notice her. He hadn't. At least not in any way that mattered.

His fingers flexed against her lower back. "Turn around. I want to look at you."

She turned. The tips of his fingers slid along her shoulders, and she sighed with the desire of this moment and her anticipation of the next. Better that she keep her eyes closed. Better for them both.

"Emily," he whispered, drawing his hands down her sides. "Emily, you slay me. I did not know a woman could consume me this way. You are perfect. I adore your body, your hair, your skin, the shape of you, the taste of you. The way you feel when I am inside you."

All that, but not her. He did not adore her.

He kissed her shoulder. "You take my breath, and then you make me laugh." He kissed her other shoulder. "I do love a saucy wench."

She turned and tipped her head to his and shivered from his hands touching her. She had never thought him unhandsome. Never. She'd heard women say they found him too brutal to be called attractive, but more than one woman had declared him monstrous with a sly smile that belied the overt meaning. Several older women recalled his father and lamented the loss of such a proper, handsome man of principle, all the while shaking their heads in dismay at the current holder of the title.

She'd listened so hard and intently to any conversation involving him. As a boy and a young man, Devon Carlisle had been wild. Wicked. A disappointment to his family for refusing a commission. But at Bartley Green, he'd been so unbearably sweet and attentive to Anne, and how could she not love him for that?

"Come here." He gripped her hand and headed for his bed, and when they stood beside it, he pulled her into his arms again. "Shall I make you come again? Better yet, make me laugh."

"Oh, now that I just, I shan't be able to."

"You shall, Em." He spun them in a circle. "It's part of you. You're quick-witted."

"Heavens, Bracebridge, you'll make me dizzy with this nude waltzing."

He picked her up and got them both onto his bed. "Nude waltzing."

"It's the very next rage. If you think tickets for Almack's are difficult to get now, wait until they approve nude waltzing."

Between gulps of laughter that seemed miraculous to her, he said, "That might get me in the door."

"Well," she said, throwing her arms around his shoulders. "It shall get you in somewhere."

"Saucy wench."

She let the moment take her away from possibilities that would only likely end in heartache. He would never love her the way she needed him to.

Chapter Twenty-Eight

AT THE EDGE of Cavendish Square, lights glowed in the rooms Emily had transformed to bright and elegant. He *wanted* to go inside. He *wanted* to be in rooms that were light and colorful and filled with touches of beauty and whimsy. He liked a dash of living green on the tables, in corners or niches. He wanted to sit before the fires with his feet by the new screens. Never mind Two Fives. Never mind nights spent in the green room of opera houses or theaters. No more staring out the window of his club at the parade of women passing by.

When he came in, Frieda dashed down the stairs, wiggling with joy. While Pond waited to take his things, he petted her and scratched her ears and only just managed to avoid having his face licked. The dog followed him to his room, happy to be in his company. He'd dined at Two Fives, but it was early for London. Not even eight yet.

"I'll change my clothes," he told Keller.

Keller, having learned that Frieda calmed down when she was made much of, was enthusiastically stroking her. "You are going out, milord?"

"No. One of my new waistcoats, though. The green and gold one." Gopal's tailor did superior work. Emily had complimented Bracebridge when he'd worn the first of the three he'd ordered. He was coming to prefer colorful waistcoats and was considering purchasing more.

"Very good, milord."

"See if you can do something about my hair." He rubbed his chin. "A shave, too." Forty minutes later, he walked into the parlor where he'd been told Emily was and found her asleep on the sofa by the fire, needlework abandoned on her lap. A book was tucked spine down into the space between her leg and the side of the sofa. Socrates was purring on her lap. She did not stir when he approached.

He stood before her, transfixed by the heartbreaking arrangement of her features. His chest tightened for no reason that he wanted to understand. At every turn since she'd first come to London with her sisters, she had challenged him, refused to stand down. Amused him. Annoyed him. Aroused him. And now, her presence here made him eager to come home, happy to see her smile, beyond avid to hold her in his arms.

She stirred, passed a hand over her face, then slowly opened her eyes and blinked several times. She squinted in his direction. Still, he had no name for the tightness in his chest. Why not? Why did he not know what this feeling was?

"Is that you, Bracebridge?"

"Yes." He pushed away the tightness. She was a creature of ethereal beauty. Naturally, he enjoyed looking at her. Naturally, he reacted to her beauty. Every man in London was lovesick over her.

She sat straighter and rested a hand on Socrates's back. The kitten stretched and settled back to its nap. "I fell asleep."

"Indeed, you did."

She let out a breath. "My apologies. I don't know when I've ever been so tired."

"Are you well?"

"Perfectly fine." She busied herself with putting away her needlework. She was wearing an ashy blue that made her eyes particularly piercing. "I don't know what's the matter with me today. I feel as if I've not slept in a month." She smoothed her hair and took a long, slow breath that she let out when she looked at the clock. "Nearly nine! I'd not meant to sleep that long." With a sheepish smile in his direction, she added, "Or at all."

"I am glad to find you home."

"Where else would I be?" Her sewing was stowed away now. She brushed a curl of golden hair from her face. "I took Frieda for several walks in the square today."

"I'm sure she was thrilled by the outings."

"She was." She shot him an inscrutable look. He did not want to feel this crushing guilt and upset that she had yet to confide in him. "That's a handsome waistcoat. Is it new?"

"Yes, do you like it?"

"I do."

"Perhaps you ought to go out. Visit your sisters. I'm sure they'd love to see you."

"I had rather not. Not just now." She fussed with the lace at her sleeve. "In any event, I had no plans today or tonight. Quite by design. I'd prefer to spend the night reading. It's what I intended, rather than falling asleep."

"You?" He immediately understood the enormous error of that reply. "But you enjoy parties." Lord, he'd dug the hole deeper with that reply, hadn't he? "No, no. I've got that wrong. That is, don't you enjoy parties? It always seemed to me that you do."

"Not especially," she said with a shrug. "I do once I've arrived, but I never want to go."

"Never? But . . . How can this be? You've always enjoyed yourself at gatherings."

"It's expected of me." She burst out laughing, and he could not help smiling back. "You look as though I've just told you I want to keep a live bear in the house. I like parties when it's friends, and I don't mind larger parties. It's just that I find them tiring." She patted the sofa, quite far from her. He sat closer than she'd indicated. "I prefer small parties with people I know. Sadly, in London one is expected to invite whatever number of guests will exceed the available space."

"True," he said, settling himself beside her. He reached over to scratch Socrates's chin. "We'll stay in tonight, then."

"Don't on my account."

"I don't mind a quiet evening." He pointed at the book at her side. "Is that *Waverley*?"

"Oh, no. That's finished twice over now." She looked at the volume. "I've been reading *Rob Roy*."

"Shall I read to you?"

Her eyes opened wide. "Would you?"

"Yes." Should he be chagrined or pleased by her surprised delight?

She handed over the book. "Chapter five, but I don't mind if you'd rather start from the beginning."

He opened to the chapter and began reading. Halfway through the second page, Socrates moved onto his lap and curled up. Emily leaned into him, and he put an arm around her shoulder.

When he reached the end of the chapter, she said, "That was lovely. Thank you."

"Perhaps another chapter tomorrow."

She swallowed once. "I'd like that."

He nodded.

"By the way," she said, "Mr. Simmons delivered tickets to *Othello* for this Thursday. I should like to go, unless you have plans that require me to be elsewhere. I should like to bring Miss Iddings with me. She and her mother are in London, and Miss Iddings likes the tragedies."

"I am free that evening." If he wasn't, he would make sure he was.

Again, she was taken aback. "Yes, of course. Mrs. Quinn is your friend, after all."

"And you are my wife." He put Socrates on the floor and stood. "I shall wear one of my new waistcoats and be quite splendid."

"I shall write to her mother to ask whether she'll allow Miss Iddings to join us." She yawned, covering her mouth just in time. "My goodness. I don't know what's come over me." She took *Rob Roy* from him. "Fortunately, I've plenty to read tonight."

"You're going to continue without me?"

"Do you really want to read the book together?" She yawned again.

"I'd like that." He moved in and swept her into his arms, surprising himself as much as her.

She cried out, "Oh!" and swung an arm around his neck to keep her balance. "What are you doing?"

"Taking you upstairs."

She let her head fall back and laughed. "I can walk, sir."

"I can carry you, ma'am." She was such a small woman. He towered over her, outweighed her by nearly eight stone. Compared to her, he was a brute and a monster, and what a lucky man he was that she liked that about him. He grinned at her. Amusing his wife was no betrayal of himself or anyone else. "Do you doubt me?"

Though she smiled in return, there was no answering rise from her. "Never," she said.

"You don't, do you?"

"No," she said softly before she looked away and rested her head against his shoulder. "I never doubt you."

He carried her all the way to her room, through the anteroom and to her dressing room. Her maid came in from the other room but retreated when she saw him. He set her down slowly, letting his hands linger. "You must admit, Lady Bracebridge, I am no weakling."

She busied herself straightening out her skirts. "I never said otherwise."

He knew his weakness where she was concerned, so if he was to learn more about his wife, he ought to keep his distance. Until tonight, it had only been during intimacy that he caught even a glimpse of who she was. That too, he suspected, was but a facet of the woman to whom he was married.

"Sit, my love." He walked them toward her dressing table but gave her a quick look when he realized what he'd said. Had she noticed? No, he decided. She hadn't, and that was for the best. He'd misspoke, that's all. "Since I've frightened away your maid, I'll prepare you for bed."

"Very well." She sat, hands folded on her lap. There was a plain wooden box at one corner of the dresser. Next to that were the brush and comb he had bought her in Scotland. He had been in enough boudoirs to know there was not half of what a lady of fashion kept at hand. One bottle of scent, one small bottle of lotion of the sort one got for a penny. On the opposite side was a battered leather-bound book small enough to fit into a pocket. He could read only a portion of the text imprinted on the spine: *Wordsworth.* So. Poetry.

He began with her hair. He touched the filigree of one of the combs he'd bought her on their way back from Scotland. "Do you like this?" he asked. He had brought her to London to outfit her, but he did not recollect seeing any receipts from a jeweler, and now that he thought about it, he couldn't recall her wearing anything but her garnet ring. "Do you wear these often because they're all you have?"

"Does it matter? I like them very much."

He pulled out the other hair comb and placed it beside the other. "It matters if you feel, for some reason, you cannot purchase things you like. I intended that you would start anew. I wish I could replace the pieces that had private meaning for you, but perhaps between the two of us, we can see about making new meaning for what you have yet to replace."

She folded her hands before her. His heart sank because he had learned to recognize when she was presenting a facade that all was well. "You needn't concern yourself, though I appreciate the sentiment. It happens that I am a most fortunate wife. To have a husband of such bracing size."

He said nothing more until he had removed hairpins and unraveled the braid at the back of her head. Then he moved aside her hair and brushed his fingertips over the nape of her neck. "I am a fortunate husband to have a wife who likes a bracing husband."

"Very much."

She sounded sad. Why? He let the silence stand, for he recognized now that she had deflected his attention, and he needed a few moments to reflect on that. The process of brushing her hair was soothing. He liked the intimacy. "Women of fashion and society have tiaras, rings, earrings. Necklaces and brooches."

"Does it matter?"

He leaned down and braced his hands on either side of her on the dresser. "My dear. I want you to have beautiful things that make you happy. I like to see you smile. A proper husband thinks of what shall make his wife happy." He picked up the brush again and returned to work. Gently, he untangled a spot where her hair was partially plaited. "In this very house is a safe with jewelry that belonged to previous countesses. I ought to have put those into your hands before now. I'll have them brought up for you to choose what you like. Some of the pieces must remain in the safe if you are not wearing them, but others can certainly be here. You ought to know your choices."

"Thank you. I should like to see."

"I suspect I shall have to personally remedy your lack of adornment."

"As you wish."

"Yes, precisely. In the meantime, tell me about your day. What did you do and see when you were out?"

In the mirror, he saw her blink several times. He could not read her expression. At least now he knew she had retreated from him. A year ago, six months ago, three months ago, he'd never have known.

"We walked around Cavendish Square. I met Mrs. Strand. She lives across the square. She and Frieda became acquaintances. She and her husband have just returned from Argentina, of all places. Tomorrow, I am engaged to call on her to hear more of her adventures. Her husband is one of the Devonshire Strands. Aldreth knows him."

"It would be pleasant to have a friend so close. Perhaps we should invite them to dinner."

"Did I tell you I've had a letter from the vicar in Hinderhead? They've hired a teacher for the school."

"Do you approve of the choice?"

"I do. He was my preferred candidate." She picked up one of the combs and turned it over and over in her hands. "He is a recent graduate of Cambridge. He is bright and ambitious with excellent references, and he does not disagree with the education of girls."

"How did you come to hear of him?"

"We advertised. He was one of five whom we interviewed. That was right before we left for London. He had glowing recommendations from two of his professors at university."

"What else did you do today?"

She continued turning the hair comb from one side to another, stroking a finger just under the filigree. "I wrote letters. Read. Consulted with Mrs. Elliot and Pond. I think Mrs. Elliot is doing an excellent job."

"I did not doubt that she would. She is an invaluable addition to the staff."

"She is, isn't she?"

"I've made my calls." He referred to the custom of a newly married man leaving cards with acquaintances he meant to continue as appropriate to his new status in life.

"Have you?" But her smile did not reach her eyes.

"Is there anyone you recommend I call on? I'll await your recommendation about Mr. Strand."

Her fingers went still. "I'll ask my sisters for a list."

"You know as well as they, perhaps even better, who would be advantageous for me to know in this new phase of my life."

"For reasons of politics or finance?"

"Either, I suppose."

"Cynssyr or Aldreth can advise you better than I of what clubs you ought to join. Those two and Thrale make you more connected than most anyone."

"I should like your opinion."

She spoke carefully and without much inflection. She was being cautious with him, and the fault for that was his and his alone. "I suppose I might prepare a list."

"Thank you." He braided her hair, and when he came to the end, she handed him a ribbon. When he had assisted her out of her clothes and into her nightrobe, she went to the basin and scrubbed her face. While she did so, he picked up the book of poems she'd left on her dresser.

When she turned, still patting her face dry, she stared at his hands and the book he held. He said, "I like Wordsworth, too. Shall I read to you?"

"Yes, please." For an instant, her delight at his suggestion turned his heart too big for his chest. Almost immediately, she smothered the reaction. "I should like that."

Chapter Twenty-Nine

T HE NIGHT BRACEBRIDGE read Wordsworth to Emily was the start of a ritual. It happened that they shared several favorite poets but also disagreed sharply on others. Sometimes she read to him, and one night she read him a scene from *A Midsummer Night's Dream*. That too, he learned, was a play she and her sisters had enacted. She was really very good at reading out loud.

The pace of their evenings together changed. And though there was still an essential part of her she did not share with him, he had learned a great deal about her that he had not formerly known. About a week after this, he joined Emily on his bed and lay on his side, propped up on his elbow, while she read from the works of Keats.

When she finished, he took a handful of her hair and curled the tresses around his finger. Anne's hair was straight and so pale it was nearly white, but Emily's pure gold hair was so perfectly suited to her that he had no complaints.

She moved toward him.

"Mm," he said, flattening his hand on her shoulder. "Let me look at you awhile." Light from the lamp Keller had left on the table threw shadows across her delectable, delicious, divine body. True, she was not as tall as he would have liked, but all the rest? A man would have to be made of stone not to appreciate her form and the unexpected lushness of her bosom.

Her eyes were bluer than Anne's, but just as darkly lashed, and no less beautiful or lively. As he drank in the perfection of her form, he smoothed a hand along her curves. Such soft skin. She stretched, pressing upward with his touch. He knew her better now, just from listening to the way she read poetry. He wondered whether she learned half as much about him when he read to her.

He'd learned to recognize when she was hiding her emotions and when, as she was now, she was open to him. The several and varied ways he'd been wrong about her expanded into a moment of time that placed him at the edge of a river with currents too fast to navigate. He'd been so certain he knew how she felt, and he'd been wrong. Not just wrong, but blind. He'd been blind to the real Emily Sinclair for years. She wasn't spoiled or frivolous. She read enough poetry to have an opinion on Byron and Rochester. She had a brain, and she used it. God help him.

"You have on too many clothes," she said.

"Madam," he said with mock sternness and a swift glance at himself. He was randy beyond belief. "I dare not stay another moment in such a state. Shall I remove my coat? Will that be sufficient?"

"I don't believe so, sir. Let's remove this and see." She unbuttoned his coat.

He ought to have taken over the process, but he didn't. He was captivated by the idea of her undressing him. He backed up to the headboard, and she sat up to continue. Every so often as she worked, he caressed her because he could not help himself, and that was arousing, to touch her so freely. To have his palm filled with her breast or the curve of her hip. He'd had so many wicked, unconscionable thoughts about her, and all of them were proper now.

Nimbly, she unfastened his watch and chain and threw herself diagonally across the mattress to set them on the bedside table. He set a hand to her lower waist and followed the curve of her from waist to hip to bottom, such a luscious curve, and she lay there, on her stomach, for several enjoyable minutes before she returned to work at the buttons of his waistcoat.

Coat, gone, fled to he did not care where. Waistcoat vanquished. Neckcloth, stickpin. Braces next, and then his shirt, too, no longer covered him. She blinked slowly, staring at his torso.

"What do you make of me?" he asked as if she were the sort of woman who visited him at Two Fives or at the house where she'd once found him in the bloody middle of fornication with a married woman.

"You know I find you magnificent." She drew her hands down his chest, and he watched her face, transfixed and so hard now he wasn't sure how much longer he wanted to wait. He drew a breath. Then another while she touched him. Savored him.

She leaned in and licked his nipple, the fingers of her other hand lightly touching his thigh. The contact sent a shiver of arousal straight to his balls. He spread his legs to accommodate the change in his state. He was disappointed when she drew back, but she kissed his stomach just above the waist of his trousers, with all that implied about travels south. She removed his shoes and stockings and, good God, she traced a finger from his toe along the top of his foot, his shin, up to the waist of his trousers and sent his sanity into a whirl of lust.

"God, yes," he said.

What remained of his clothes was disposed of, and he too was naked. She gazed at him as if he were the only man in existence, and it made his heart feel too small for his chest. He was no stranger to women who liked what he had to offer, and he was beyond grateful that she fell into the category because it meant she wanted the hard irreverence of fucking.

His heart raced away as he brought her close enough to thread his fingers through her curls once again. He kissed her without holding back. She clung to him, forgave the demand of his mouth, and he felt the rise of desire. He could no more stop this descent into fire than he could choose to stop the beat of his heart.

He learned the shape of her body through touch. Soft at first, then not. A harder grip on her breast. Fingers between her thighs, finding the soft wetness of her desire. He drew back, but only enough to rasp, "This is what I like, Emily. No regard for this delicate body of yours."

Her arms twined around his neck, one hand curving over the back of his head. "Poor Mr. Devon Carlisle," she murmured, but when he opened his eyes, there was an unmistakable glint of amusement. "You understand so little of your wife."

He was unable to smother a laugh even though it was uncomfortably true. "I am greatly to be pitied."

Several reactions flickered over her face, and then she settled against him, into his hand still between her legs. "I am about to faint away from the disregard your manhood has for me." She put a hand over his sex. "It's so—" She curled her fingers around him. "—substantial where I am not at all."

"Where do you mean, my dear wife?" He put his hands around her waist and lifted her onto his lap. When she straddled him, he pushed three fingers inside her. The tension of arousal burned him from the inside out. "Here, do you mean?"

She held his gaze. "Yes, my lord." With that expression, those words, in that tone, the words *my lord* became a promise that released the final shreds of his decency. "Just there." She settled her arms around his shoulders. "I am bereft of you. Dying for proof of your disregard of my delicacy."

He lifted her up and thrust into her in a moment of unspeakable need. He lost the faculty of speech. There was only their bodies, and his cock inside her, and her passage around him. She separated her thighs until her knees were on the mattress. She held his shoulders, as desperate and needy as he was. More, perhaps, for her arms tightened around him.

The room disappeared; his senses narrowed until he knew nothing but her body, her responses, his body, and his need for her. He slipped a hand beneath one of her thighs, out of his mind with the softness of her skin. Beneath his fingers, he felt the flex and relaxation of her taut muscles.

He kissed her hard and deep while he thrust into her, wild and on the edge, and he believed utterly what she wanted was the beast he was. She groaned with abandon when he wrapped his arms tight around her and held her in place while he pushed hard into her. They ended up with her on her back, hips straining toward him, and with him, Jesus, God, him slamming into her. "Good, so good."

She set her fingers to his cheek. "Look at me. I want to see you."

How he managed to pry his eyes open, he had no idea. But he did, and he was stunned at the sight of her. The need conveyed in the curve of her mouth and her half-open eyes. He slowed, a little, because he wanted to last longer. He wasn't a selfish lover, and she hadn't come yet, and he wanted to be certain she did.

"I want you to lose control." She put her hands on the mattress and pushed up, eyes storm-cloud blue, so perfectly blue, her golden hair spread over the mattress.

A response required more coherent thought than he was capable of, but he managed to ask, "You want me to fuck you with no regard for your pleasure?"

She braced a hand on his shoulder and pushed back. "Yes." She let out a breath. "You have no idea how that would please me."

He moved over her again and grabbed her wrists, pinning them above her head on the mattress as he shoved into her. Once again, he was gone. He knew no language, no civility, nothing but him putting his cock into her again and again and again. She came just from his savage fucking. She groaned his name.

At the last moment, while she was still at the peak, he began again hard and fast and not all gentlemanly. As his crisis approached, he began to think of the timing of pulling out of her before it was too late, only to remember she was his wife and there was no need.

When he came, he really did feel he died just a little.

Chapter Thirty

WHEN BRACEBRIDGE CAME to her dressing room holding the copy of *Rob Roy* they were reading together, Emily felt the impact of his presence like a blow. *It's him, him, him, and I have come alive.* The reaction wasn't new anymore, but it still took her breath. He was here in her room, not two feet from her.

"Good evening," she said once Maggie had put down the hairbrush and made her exit. Every time she saw him, the same shivery anticipation shot through her. She was tired again, but never too tired for Bracebridge. Their relationship had settled in and become more comfortable.

Book in hand, he moved close and brushed the back of his first two fingers across her cheek. She did so adore the way he looked at her as if he were imagining the wickedest things possible. She certainly hoped so. "Good evening to you, too, Em."

She set her hands on his stomach, and he reached down to slide his hands under her forearms and lift. She moved happily into his arms. Her breath caught before she could rein in her feelings.

He brought her close, and she reveled in the hardness of his arms and chest. He cupped her head and began a search for hairpins that he discarded without thought of the mess or the work for Maggie. Before long, he was combing his fingers through her loosened hair. "Like gold," he whispered. He filled his hands with her hair. "Such a color might inspire a man to poetry."

She laughed. "You're not going to go on about Byron again, are you? I prefer Wordsworth or Shelley. I like their poems. Now, no more nonsense about my hair. I've always wished I were dark-haired like Mary or Lucy."

"You'd be exquisite no matter what color your hair." He returned one arm to her waist.

"I dyed it once."

"You didn't," he said.

In all the time they'd been married, she'd never shared anything but the most superficial of stories about herself, but he did not look as if he was asking merely to be polite. In fact, his smile was eager and encouraging. "I did, indeed."

"How old were you?"

"Fourteen or fifteen, I think."

"What color?" He took a lock of her hair between his fingers. "Ginger, was it?"

"Brown, though that was not the color advertised. A peddler came to town and among his wares was a hair dye guaranteed to provide the most miraculous, most excellent, and blackest of hair color. I bought his concoction, and that very afternoon I went to my room and followed the instructions exactly." The memory of her excitement that day made her laugh. "It smelled awful and made the most terrible mess. To this day, there is a stain on the floor where I spilled some. I was so pleased I would have lovely black hair, just like Lucy's."

"I cannot picture your hair any color but this. It was brown, you say?"

"Not raven's-wing black at all but a horrible brown. Like dirt. All one color. I would have been pleased to have hair like Mary's. Glorious chestnut would have pleased me almost as much as raven's-wing black. Alas, the peddler's miracle dye did not produce anything close to either color. Anne was furious when she saw, but I was heartbroken."

"What happened? Obviously, it was not permanent. How long was your hair that color?"

"Fortunately, it washed out with a week of daily washing. My hands were stained for days afterward too." She laughed and was relieved to see him smile in return. "What a waste of my hard-earned sixpence. I learned my lesson well. The next day, I went out with my head wrapped in a turban to demand my money back, but he was already gone." She touched the silk of his black hair. "If I couldn't have Lucy's hair, I would have wanted yours. Curls every which way across my forehead and the nape of my neck."

The corner of his mouth curved. "Your hair is perfect just as it is."

She kept her smile.

He put both hands to her waist and frowned at her. "I know that look," he said. "You don't believe me. Why not?"

"I believe you meant to compliment me, and I thank you for that."

"I haven't poetic words for you about your hair." He drew her hair over one of her shoulders. "Just my sincere appreciation of the color, how soft it is in my hands. How randy I am when I see you like this."

"There has to be some use for my looks."

He frowned again. "Em . . ."

This was no time to argue. She wanted him in her arms, his body against hers, in hers, his drugging kisses, and the climb to passion. She leaned against him, thinking the most reprehensible thoughts. Him naked, her hands on his person, her mouth on him. "You like my looks. Do not deny it."

He laughed and rested his forehead against hers. He had to slouch a little to do so. "I shan't, for it's true. I like how you bring me to a cockstand, and now I've told you as poetically as possible for a brute like me."

"That's very good, considering your execrable taste in poetry."

"My God, sometimes you do make me laugh."

"I like it best when you make me scream."

"Emily." He whispered her name, rasped the syllables, and her response to that was a jolt of arousal. "When you look at me like that . . ."

"What?"

"I want to know what you are thinking."

She leaned into him. "No great surprise there. I want to see you without the encumbrance of these fine clothes. Have I told you how much I like your new waistcoats?"

He took the bottom hem of the garment in both hands and pretended to rearrange the fit. "Yes, but tell me again."

"I do like this color." She traced the shape of one of the embroidered leaves. "It reminds me of Mr. Rachagorla's waistcoats. Not everyone can carry off the look, but you do."

"I went to his tailor." He slid his hands around her shoulders and fumbled with the hooks at the back of her gown.

"I approve," she said. "I would approve even more if you removed all your clothing so I might gaze upon Adonis."

He lowered his head and pressed his mouth to the side of her throat. "Adonis, you say?"

"Mm. Yes."

He drew just far enough away to murmur, "What a wicked woman you are."

She tipped back her head to look into the inky pools of his eyes, and while she stared into those depths, she unbuttoned the topmost button of his coat. Her heart beat as if it had wings that meant to fly her soul out of her chest. "Strip off, my lord."

Somehow, he'd managed to unfasten enough of the back of her dress to make it gape at the neckline. He moved behind her in one smooth motion. "Your every wish is my command. As soon as I have you naked."

He worked quickly until her gown fell to her feet. She kicked off her slippers and stepped free of the fabric. He stripped off her chemise but left her in her stockings. She turned and said, "I wanted to see you and . . . this is the result?" She spread her arms. "Unfair."

He drew two fingers down the center of her body, reverently. "You give a good account of yourself in your skin."

"I am attempting to recall if you do as well." She shook her head. "You'll have to strip off to refresh my memory."

"Soon enough." He withdrew a parcel from his coat pocket.

"If only you wished to oblige me, my lord. What a shame you do not."

"I want you to have sufficient time to admire me in my waistcoat. But first—" He opened the package and withdrew a strand of aquamarine beads and another of pearls. He gave her a searingly wicked grin. "I should like to see you in nothing but these."

"Are they from the safe?"

"No." He put both around her neck, double looping the pearls. "They are lovely on your skin. Quite suitable for Lady Bracebridge, if I do say."

"Thank you." She was more touched than she ought to have been. The aquamarine beads were faceted just enough to shimmer in the light when she held some of them on her palm. She fingered one of the buttons of his waistcoat. "I should hate for your lovely waistcoat to be damaged, my lord. Surely you agree you must remove this."

He shrugged off his coat and, while she watched, he undressed without hurry. His waistcoat, neckcloth, braces all landed on the floor. With every item removed, she saw the man who made her empty with longing. Rough. Disreputable. Unbearably masculine. She was transfixed. Breathless with anticipation.

He dropped his shirt on the floor, then bent and removed his boots gracefully. Muscles flexed up and down his arms and across his torso. He pushed down his trousers and smallclothes in one smooth motion and tossed them one-handed on the floor with the rest of his clothes. He stood with his hands on his hips, a smile glinting in his eyes and around his mouth. "Do you like what you see?"

Her reply caught in her throat because she did. Too much. "Yes." She longed to touch him, to curl her fingers around his upper arms, to drag her hands down his torso. "I always have."

"Touch me, Em."

She could not speak. Words were lost to her. And of course, Bracebridge misunderstood.

"Are you feeling well?" He put a hand on her stomach, then turned his hand so his fingers pointed diagonally down. "If you are feeling delicate . . ."

"Not in the least." She *was* tired, but her exhaustion had faded away in the heat of this encounter. She closed the distance between them and put a hand on his torso. The beat of his heart transferred to her palm. "Do not move." She glanced toward the cheval glass, then back, careful not to meet his gaze. "I can see your back from where I stand. And lower."

"And?"

"You're magnificent, as well you know." She leaned in and pressed her mouth to the spot where her hand had been.

"I like to hear the words." He'd tipped his head back, eyes closed. She gazed at him, drank up the structure of his face. The crooked nose, strong features, and though he could never be called beautiful by a dispassionate observer, to her, he was. Painfully so. "You don't care for compliments, but I do."

She drew her palm down the center of his torso. Whatever the state of their marriage or of his lack of feelings for her, there was always electricity between them when they were like this. "You *are* magnificent," she said with heartfelt sincerity.

He opened his eyes and looked down at her, and as always, she was drawn into the depths. Mystery lived there in his eyes. Lust. Desire. "How magnificent?"

She pushed him toward her bed, and he took a step backward in the direction they both intended to go. "You make me weak. I tremble with this . . . passion." She could not say the word *love* even though that was the word she meant. He did not want to hear that from her, and she did not want to spoil the one aspect of their marriage that pleased them both. "Allow me to demonstrate what I mean."

"Tell me, too."

"I'm not a poetess."

"You are," he said with an odd bluntness. "Every day you bring beauty into my life." He wrapped his hand around hers and kissed her knuckles. "Have I told you how grateful I am for that?"

"Why, Bracebridge, that's most poetic of you."

"Yes, it is, isn't it?" He grinned. "It comes of my reading Byron."

"No, it doesn't." She gave him a gentle push. He sat on the edge of the mattress, his feet firmly on the floor because so much of his height was in his legs. She placed her hands on his thighs and stepped between his legs. He smiled, and it made her heart twist up. She drew her fingers along the inside of his thighs toward his sex. "I adore how big you are." She swept her gaze downward, then back to his face. "Everywhere."

"More poetry. Do go on."

When he was like this, attentive to her during intimacy, she was freer than at any other time. She left one hand on his thigh and put the other on his pectoral, tracing the shape of the muscle, sliding a finger over his nipple because she'd discovered he liked that.

"Em." He cupped the back of her head in one hand and stared at her. "Why would a woman like you prefer me over any other man?"

"Because you are my husband."

"Before we were married." His voice sounded thick. How odd. "Before I was Bracebridge. Before and after Anne. Why would a woman as perfectly beautiful as you want a man like me?"

She didn't mean to sound cross, but that's how the words came out. "My looks have nothing to do with my heart or my affection for anyone. If looks are all that matter, why did you prefer Anne? Why did you and Ciolini become lovers? Why we fall in love has much more to do with what we are inside. You know that as well as I."

"I know why I fell in love with Anne." He wrapped a length of the pearls around his hand. "Why did you fall in love with me?" He slipped his other hand down her body, and she sighed because the way he touched her was so delicious. "It doesn't make sense."

She bent her head for a moment. "Don't do this. Please don't. What difference does it make?"

He slid his fingers between her legs, and she made sure to accommodate him. "Why a brute like me?"

"I like you as a brute."

"That's no answer."

"I can't think when you touch me like that."

"Try."

"I've known for years I prefer large men. Tall and brawny." She rubbed her hands up and down his arms. "Even before I met you. Of course I did not learn the reason I like brutes like you until recently." She brushed her other hand along his shaft and smiled when he drew in a breath. "I adore the shape of you. The feel of this hair in my hands, this skin, this part of you." She met his gaze. "The way you cover me. You. Inside me."

He gave her an arch look. "Are you saying you love me because of my looks or because of my cock?"

"Both, of course. Oh, more of that, please. I loved you because you were kind to all of us Sinclair sisters. You were amusing. Are amusing. You had been through so much. Losing your family the way you did. The fact that you fell in love with Anne." She drew a shuddering breath. "Enough talk. Let me see you."

He glanced down. "I stand ready to accept your appreciation." She burst into delighted laughter that made him smile. "The two of us are a better match than I ever anticipated." He put his hands on her waist and brought her onto the bed with him. "You make me smile and laugh. You make me glad to come home, and I never thought I would ever be glad to come here."

She expected him to enter her, wanted him to badly, but he did not. Instead, weight on his forearm, he stroked his other hand down her body, from the top of her throat to her knee. "Your skin is soft," he murmured.

She knew the litany of compliments, and she wasn't displeased by them anymore. He found her beautiful, and that was nothing to complain of. They were not, alas, two people who cared deeply for each other. She was well aware the feelings were one sided. She was bitterly relieved there was something about her he found worthy of admiration.

His hand wandered over her body, touching, caressing, bringing her to a peak of arousal, to the edge of losing herself to him. "Be Emily with me," he said.

Her eyes popped open, but he was absorbed by her breasts at the moment, and as she watched, he bent to take her nipple in his mouth. Her thoughts were swept away.

Some moments later, he lifted his head and positioned himself over her. As ever, her body responded. "Be Emily with me," he whispered.

As he pushed inside her, she could not help but say, "Why, when you do not like Emily?"

Chapter Thirty-One

A WOMAN'S TERRIFIED SCREAM shattered the quiet repose of the smoking room. Bracebridge dropped the newspaper he'd been reading, and Gopal, who had his legs stretched out to the fire, sat up straight and turned toward the windows. The cry had come from outside, on the Margaret Street side of Cavendish Square.

"Cease and desist!"

Alarm streaked through Bracebridge because that was Pond's voice.

Outside, another woman loudly sobbed, "No! Oh no, oh no!" Her moans turned to a shout. "They've taken her!"

Bracebridge shot to his feet as the front door slammed and at least two people raced up the stairs. Gopal had left the window and was now heading for the door. More voices joined the commotion. His heart slammed against his chest; he did not hear Emily's voice in the tumult.

Mrs. Elliot burst into the room, sobbing, "My lord, they've taken her, and she's gone after them! They're making away with her now!"

He grabbed the woman's shoulders, terrified to the point of panic. Emily. Lord above, Emily. He could not lose her. Not now. Not now. Not ever. "What's happened? Where is Lady Bracebridge?"

Pond stumbled into the room, half his head crimson. His coat was torn at the shoulder, and blood dripped down his cheek and from his nose. He brushed at his face and spread blood across his cheek and into his hair. "Milord. Milord—"

Gopal leaped for Pond, guiding the man to a chair and pressing his handkerchief to Pond's bloody head even though that dab of silk was inadequate to the task of stanching the wound. "Were you set upon by thieves?" Gopal asked.

Still holding Mrs. Elliot's shoulders, Bracebridge looked into the corridor. He did not see Emily. She had to be here. Downstairs, still, perhaps dealing with Frieda. He roared, "Emily!"

There was no answer.

"Lift your head." Gopal pushed Pond's chin up and pinched the bridge of the butler's nose between two fingers.

Pond batted away Gopal's hand, but Gopal was not deterred. He continued to press the wadded-up handkerchief to the back of Pond's head. "My lord." Pond raised his voice. "Her ladyship's father—"

"What about him?"

Mrs. Elliot wrung her hands. "She went after them, my lord."

"What the devil do you mean?" His heart stopped beating. "Do you mean to say she's pursuing thieves?"

One of the footmen who'd dashed in answered between gasps. "Lady Bracebridge was returning home when just outside the house someone snatched Frieda, milord."

"Madam," Gopal said to Mrs. Elliot, "we require a basin, water, and some cloths. If you would be so kind as to fetch those items for us."

Emily had yet to appear, and amid the chaos, Bracebridge boomed out, "Where is Lady Bracebridge?"

Pond twisted toward him, his hair wild and soaked brilliant red from the bleeding cut on his head. "My lord, she raced off in pursuit of the blackguard who took her dog."

That fairly stopped Bracebridge's heart again. She'd not been snatched from the streets, and that was a bone-shaking relief. They would find her, then, but how bloody like her to do something so reckless. He pointed at the footman in the doorway. "Have Keller fetch my pistols."

Pond said, "Her ladyship's father is responsible for this outrage. I saw him in the carriage as it drove away."

"What carriage?" He was hurled once again into the possibility that Emily might be taken away. A carriage? If she got into a carriage, she might travel too far and too fast for him to find her. He could not lose her. He couldn't. He couldn't bear the thought.

Mrs. Elliot burst into tears, and it was clear the woman was hearing this news for the first time and was having the same panicked reaction as he was. "I knew in my heart he'd do something like this. Just to spite her. Oh, that poor, dear dog!"

His butler took a shuddering breath. "When her ladyship arrived home, there was a carriage nearby. Two men jumped from the vehicle as she came up the stairs. One pushed Maggie to the ground and shoved her ladyship away while the other took Frieda."

The more disheveled of the footmen took up the narrative. "We ran to their aid, and there was a set-to." He nodded at Pond. "The man who took the dog raced away, and her ladyship followed and Maggie with her, and then the man who bashed Pond in the head got away and the carriage took off, and we came to fetch you."

Three more footmen came in, dressed to go out. Bracebridge made a point of hiring former prizefighters whenever he could, and these three were impressive specimens. Thank God, they'd understood they'd be needed. "What did they look like?" They needed to be after her, but haring off without sufficient information about who and what to look for might doom them to failure. "Keller! Where the devil are you?"

Behind him, the footman said, "The one who stole away with Frieda was almost as tall as you. Brown coat and a green felt hat. Dark hair. They headed down Harley Street toward Queen Anne Street."

Keller hurried in, coattails flying, with Bracebridge's greatcoat, hat, and the box that held his pistols. Bracebridge took the box from the servant and shoved his arms into his coat. "What was Lady Bracebridge wearing, did anyone notice?"

"A dark cloak, milord," the footman said. "Green frock, I think." He motioned putting a hood over his head. "Maggie had a hood."

Bracebridge handed the first loaded pistol to Gopal.

Gopal nodded and held the pistol muzzle to the ceiling. Bracebridge headed out, Gopal and the three footmen at his heels. Once outside, they set off along the edge of Cavendish Square, then took a right onto Harley Street.

Bracebridge's fear was that Emily had caught up with Sinclair's henchmen and been met with violence. If the fellow was his size, he could easily overpower Emily. A thousand horrible outcomes flew at him. There was no time to lose.

At the next corner, he yelled at the top of his lungs, "Frieda! Frieda, come!"

They listened intently, but all Bracebridge heard was the usual sounds of this part of the city. They continued down Harley Street until Gopal came to a halt and said, "A moment of silence, please?"

Again they heard nothing, but Gopal held him back. "That. A dog barking, yes?"

Nothing. He heard nothing. He cupped his hands around his mouth. "Frieda! Emily!"

There was no reply. They raced along the street with the footmen taking side streets and returning, having found nothing. There was too much bloody damn noise to hear even Frieda's distinctive bark. Once, his heart fairly jumped out of his throat at the sight of a woman Emily's size, but when he caught up with the startled woman, she wasn't his wife at all.

A mile from Cavendish Square, and there was no sign of Emily, her maid, or a man with a dog.

"There it is again." Gopal cocked his head. "Barking. Most peculiar."

This time, he heard the sound too, and they set off at a dead run, pushing through the increasingly crowded walkway. He did not see any women who could be Emily or Maggie, nor anyone with Frieda. Then Bracebridge heard, much louder now, that half bay, half bark that was undeniably Frieda.

They rounded another corner and in a split second took in the scene. At the other end of the street, a man in a green hat was attempting to heave a large dog into a waiting carriage. A woman sprawled on the walkway scrambled to her feet while another woman yanked on the carriage door. The man struggling with the dog shoved the woman now on her feet hard enough to send her stumbling back.

Bracebridge put on a burst of speed. "You there! Halt!"

The man in the hat looked over his shoulder as he pushed the dog into the carriage. The other woman was Emily. Bracebridge had only the time to think, *Oh, thank God, thank God.*

She slammed a folded pink parasol into the side of the man's face while she shouted at the top of her lungs, "Help, help! Frieda!"

Gopal and one of the footmen split off down the street, aiming for the front of the carriage to prevent an escape. The green hat flew into the air, and the carriage door swung open.

Maggie grabbed the now hatless man by the coattails and pulled hard. Just as Bracebridge came even with the rear of the vehicle, Emily leaped inside the carriage. The vehicle rocked and shook, and the door slammed shut. Maggie grabbed hold of the door.

One of the footmen grabbed the bridle of the lead horse. Gopal leaped into the driver's seat, pistol drawn, and pointed at the driver. "On your life, do not move!"

The man who'd shoved Maggie was back on his feet. Bracebridge brought his clenched fist straight up from his waist and slammed into the bottom of the man's chin with all the strength he had. The man's head snapped back. As his legs buckled, Bracebridge followed with a punch to the ribs.

Maggie moved away from the carriage door when the man hit the pavement, and Bracebridge whirled. With a shout of inchoate rage, he yanked open the carriage door and reached in, half his torso inside. He grabbed Emily's arm and pulled her toward the door.

"Not without Frieda!" His wife, too fierce to be frightened, looked furious.

With his other arm, he grabbed the dog by the collar and dragged her out. One of the footmen snatched the trailing leash. Only then did Emily jump to the street, her broken parasol clutched in one hand.

"Maggie," Bracebridge called over his shoulder, "see to your mistress."

He reached into the carriage again and hauled Thomas Sinclair onto the street. With two fistfuls of the other man's coat, Bracebridge slammed Sinclair against the side of the carriage. The stink of alcohol was overpowering.

"Help!" Sinclair got one arm up and into the air. "Murder!"

Bracebridge dragged Sinclair upward until he was on the tips of his toes. "If ever you come near Cavendish Square again, I shall have the law after you so fast, your head will spin."

Sinclair threw up his hands in a mockery of surrender and snarled, "I'm taking back what's mine. Emily got that dog before she was married. The dog is mine. Not hers, and never yours."

Bracebridge maintained his grip on her father. *Careful*, he told himself. *Careful*. Sinclair was much, much older, and he was angry enough to do unintentional harm. "My forbearance with you is at an end. I own your house. I own your debts. Anything you kept from my wife out of spite or for any other reason belongs to me. If you sold them, the money is mine, and I expect you to remit it immediately." He slapped his palm on the side of the carriage near Sinclair's ear. He spoke slowly, ignoring the crowd gathering on the walkway. "I want it back. All of it. I own this vehicle and the horses drawing it. The clothes on your back belong to me. Whatever income the Cooperage produces belongs to me. Including the damned dog."

Sinclair sneered. "I'll soon have your marriage annulled. See if I don't. You won't be so high and mighty then."

"Emily is my wife, and she will remain so."

Sinclair grinned. "She'll leave you soon enough. You know it as well as I. You aren't worthy of one of my girls. You never have been, and you never shall be."

"Go to hell, Sinclair." Bracebridge picked him up by the front of his coat and shoved him into the carriage. He slammed the door with such violence, the vehicle rocked.

He looked up at the driver. The man was ashen and staring at Gopal's pistol trained on the center of his forehead. "You," he said. "Driver. If you value your life, get down."

Gopal grabbed the reins as the driver scrambled to comply. Bracebridge pointed to the footman holding the lead horse and dug in his pocket to give the man enough to cover tolls and expenses that might arise. "Drive the blackguard back to Bartley Green and return here with the carriage."

"Milord." The servant climbed up and took the driver's place. Gopal engaged the safety on his pistol and descended. Moments later, the carriage was on its way out of London.

Without Sinclair or the carriage to engage him, Frieda wriggled her way to Bracebridge, whining, hanging her head, and lowering her body. He crouched, put his arms around the dog, and buried his face against her massive shoulder. She pressed against him, wagging her tail and half her body.

He held the dog tight, overcome with panic and dismay and a thousand other emotions warring in him. What if something had happened to Emily? What if, what if, what if? He shook hard enough he didn't dare release the dog. "You are safe now," he whispered, still shaking. "You're safe, you bloody great beast. Praise God, we've got you back."

Gopal put a hand on his shoulder the way he had in his fighting days, and Bracebridge immediately regained his calm. He shook himself, stood, and handed Frieda's leash to Gopal. His gaze locked with Emily's, and everything disappeared but her and the spreading ache in his heart. Without conscious thought, he pulled her into his arms. He held her close, breathing in the scent of her. "Are you all right?"

"Thank God we got her back," she said.

He held her tight, afraid to let her go, afraid of what was happening to him—had already happened. Nothing less than the utter transformation of his life, and one he'd fought for years. Years.

Before long, though, Emily pushed him back.

"Are you safe, Em? Did he hurt you?" He looked her over for scrapes or bruises and saw no obvious injuries. "He pushed you. I saw you fall."

She lifted her parasol with a regretful gaze at its condition. "This is the harm. I fear it's destroyed."

He looked to Maggie. One of his footmen had an arm around the young woman's waist. "And you? He shoved you, too."

Maggie burst out with, "I knew you'd come, milord. I knew you'd hear the ruckus and come to our aid."

"Lady Bracebridge seems to have had things well in hand," he replied. "You're certain you're not injured?"

"No, milord."

"My dear," he said to Emily, "I assume you are armed. Why the devil didn't you shoot the fellow?"

Gopal handed him a small pistol, disassembled. "I found it there." He pointed several feet distant.

"I was prepared to." She spoke in a cool voice. He knew she would have. His wife had nerves of steel. "But I did not have a clear shot. I was afraid I'd miss and hurt a bystander."

"My lord," Gopal said, "I've hailed a cab for you and the ladies. I'll walk back with the men while you see to your wife."

"Yes, yes. Thank you." He held out a hand for Frieda's leash. Emily would worry if they didn't take the dog with them, and he had no desire to let either of them out of his sight. He got Emily, Maggie, and the dog into the hansom cab and got in himself. Maggie, bless her, had already left room for him next to Emily. Frieda lay her head on Emily's lap, who kept a tight grip on her collar while she stroked the dog's head.

He kept his arms around Emily for the entire return to Cavendish Square. At one point, he pulled out his handkerchief and brushed away flecks of dirt clinging to Emily's cheek. Too many words jammed in his throat, too many emotions.

Back at Margaret Street, Mrs. Elliot met them at the door, and Emily let go of his hand to run straight into the housekeeper's arms. "He found us, he found us in time. Oh, I thought we'd lost her."

"Hush, my love," Mrs. Elliot said. "Hush, now."

"You should have seen Bracebridge. He saved her. Mr. Rachagorla, too. Oh, Mrs. Elliot!" Emily dissolved into tears.

Mrs. Elliot looked at Bracebridge over Emily's shoulder. "Thank you, my lord. Bless you."

He gripped Frieda's leash hard and found his throat was too tight with emotion to reply. He'd fallen in love with the damned dog.

Emily released the housekeeper and bent down to hug Frieda. Her shoulders heaved. "You trust too much, you silly dog," she said in a damp voice. She wiped her eyes with one hand. "No more running off and assuming everyone loves you."

Bracebridge hunkered down beside them. He slipped an arm around Emily's shoulders and drew her close. "We got her back, Em."

"You did. You did."

"With the help of your parasol attack."

She looked at him, eyes open wide, then she half laughed and half cried and threw her arms around him. He brought them to their feet, and she took a step back and went up on her toes to put her hands on either side of his face. "Thank you. From the depths of my soul, thank you."

She made him feel like a bloody damned hero.

Chapter Thirty-Two

B RACEBRIDGE ROSE WHEN his wife entered the parlor off the dining room. No guests of his. Never any of hers. She knew exactly when to be punctual and when a late arrival was most effective, but tonight, early, late, or punctual did not matter in the least. She was here. When she came near, he held out a hand, as a gentleman did for a lady and one's wife.

You don't like Emily.

Too many people had told him that. Because they all loved Emily and cared about her happiness. All of them had doubted his ability to love her as she deserved. For too long, that had been true. He hadn't seen how to love Emily.

How did one dislike a woman as brave and loyal as her? How could he dislike the woman who was a true friend to so many others? How could he dislike a woman with whom he had so much in common? They liked many of the same poets and had spirited discussions when they disagreed. They enjoyed stories of adventures. Her presence in his life had made Corth Abbey a warmer place and had turned every damned ghost out of the Margaret Street house.

He wanted to hold her in his arms. He wanted to hear her laugh, and he wanted to argue with her and agree with her or land somewhere in between. Yes, she was his match in bed and out. He loved her abandon with him, and the truth, the stark truth, was that with her, he'd reached levels of physical satisfaction he hadn't known were possible.

All the time he was learning about his wife, he'd denied what was happening. He'd told her nothing of his feelings once they began to change. He'd not told her how terrified he'd been that she would come to harm or that he would lose her, nor all the ways he'd learned to admire her.

He watched her enter, and already his heart was lighter. She wore white satin and the aquamarine beads he'd given her. Was she happy with them? Had he chosen a gift she wanted from him? Her beauty was always stunning, but there was more now. His heart lurched and changed shape, and he closed his eyes and examined the difference. What a dunce he'd been. What a stubborn, resentful fool he was.

"How handsome you are tonight," she said into the silence caused by his loss of composure. Short of her stripped bare, there was no more arousing vision than his wife at this moment. Eyes so blue he could see the color from across the room, joy and lightness that brightened his soul, too.

This was not the marriage he thought he'd wanted, nor the woman he'd imagined would be his wife. But sometime between their marriage and now, his heart had settled into a different place and shape, and it was wonderful and terrifying.

He was happy. Emily made him happy. And he had not told her.

"My lord." She curtseyed when she reached him.

"Lady Bracebridge."

She seated herself on the chair where she kept her knitting and took out her needles and yarn. She worked her needles without looking. These, too, were new.

"Allow me to tell you how lovely you are tonight." But no, that was not what must be said.

"Thank you." Not a whisper of a smile curved her mouth. Compliments were so rarely successful with her. But of course. She believed herself unworthy of regard for any reason but her looks.

He removed the slender box he'd slipped into his pocket before he came downstairs to wait here for her. Fancy that. He was nervous about whether she would like his gift.

She cocked an eyebrow at him. He kept his attention on her face as he opened the box.

"Aquamarines, again," he said when she continued to say nothing. "To match those. They remind me of your eyes."

She touched the gems nestled on the velvet-lined interior. "They're lovely."

He picked up the bracelet of the set and placed the box on a nearby table. "Allow me."

She held out her hand, and he fastened the piece around her wrist. Did she like it? He had no idea.

"They go well with your gown," he said. He reached for the matching necklace, and she obligingly turned around so he could fasten it for her. She put on the earrings herself, then walked to the pier glass on the adjacent wall. The gems made her eyes as blue as a sunny sky.

He stood behind her. The two of them were a stunning contrast. Him so dark and rough, with hair that never behaved. Her so exquisite, breathtakingly lovely, and that cascade of perfect golden curls over one shoulder. More, though, was how the thought of her smile cheered him.

She touched the necklace and turned her head to watch the light refract from the gems at her ears. "They're beautiful. All of it. Beautiful." She turned, chin tipped so she could meet his eyes. She was smiling, and it pierced his soul.

"You said you liked aquamarines."

"I did say that." She adjusted the bracelet. "They're perfect, and they're perfect with this gown."

"Perfect for you." That coaxed more of a smile from her. A real one this time. "What have I done to deserve you but live a reckless, disreputable life?"

She tried to suppress a smile. "You know I adore that about you."

The girl who'd inhabited his brain and resentment these past years was rash, impetuous, and vain. The Emily he held in his mind was an exaggeration of the woman to whom he was married. He'd built up what was unflattering to her and refused to acknowledge her qualities.

She retook her seat and arranged herself on it. Graceful and serene. Where was the fast-moving hoyden of his memories? True, she'd raced through Mayfair to rescue her dog, but if she hadn't, Sinclair might have succeeded in stealing her away.

She bent to bring her sewing basket closer and picked up her needles again. She'd been working on a pair of stockings for some time. He watched her, and his heart turned over. Why? Why had he been so unfair to her? Because. Because. Because the truth threatened to destroy the man he had become after he met Anne. As if that were the only sort of man he could be.

"Emily."

She looked up, questioning.

"Is there a reason you've never invited any of your acquaintances for dinner? The Iddingses, for example? The Strands across the Square?"

She bent over her project and examined her work, counting off several stitches. For longer than was necessary, he thought. "Dinner should be announced soon."

"Your sisters, perhaps? You've not had them here since we came to London."

"I see them often enough at Portman Square."

"Are you not holding at-homes?"

She rested one hand on her leg and held her knitting in the other. "I understand we haven't the usual sort of marriage."

His stomach tightened unpleasantly. He hadn't thought about it at all. He'd not insisted, and he ought to have. He ought to have sat her down and asked her to plan a grand party for them here. "It was never my intention that you should not entertain. I should have told you I should like us to entertain."

"Very well. Give me a list of people to invite and we shall. Or the reason for the party. I'll see that the right people come."

The words he'd been thinking of saying for some time rushed from him, hot and fast. "Yes. Thank you. Excellent." She smiled. "Emily, I have arranged for us to be married in the Church of England."

"Whatever for?"

"Because I wish it. Because I do not trust your father. If we are also married in the Church of England, it will be harder for anyone to mount a challenge to our union."

Her expression went blank. "Whatever you require of me."

"And what do you require of me, darling?"

Her hands, still holding her knitting, were still. "What do I require of you? I require that you not tell me lies."

He was taken aback by the retort. "I've told you no lies."

"Don't say 'darling' when I am not darling to you. Don't. It makes me unhappy when you tell me lies."

"It's no lie." He stood tall. "You are darling to me."

"How is it we are speaking at such cross-purposes?"

"I've no notion of that either. I say words that have a clear and unambiguous meaning, and you persist in telling me I do not mean them. Emily.

Please listen to me." He was going to come apart. What if it was too late? What if his stubborn refusal to see the quality of the woman before him had cost him her love? "I owe you an apology."

"What for?" Already, she was retreating behind that wall. She'd built it for her own protection, but he meant to convince her to take it down. He must. He must.

"For refusing to accept you. For pushing you away as I have. For not telling you sooner how much I care for you." He went down on one knee, took her hand in his, and held tight.

"I know your heart," she said. She brushed a finger across his cheek. "I know. I am at peace with that. There is no reason for this. I am content."

"I thought I could only ever love but once, that my heart was incapable of a similar emotion. But I was wrong. Wrong, I tell you. There is a place for you here, a place where you and only you fit." He brought her hand to his chest where his heart beat too fast. "You fill that space. You, Emily."

She shook her head. "Don't say such things to me."

"It's time I stopped being a damned fool." He shook his head. "I wanted you. I think I knew all along there was more between us than lust. From the first moment I kissed you. From the moment you walked in on me that day, to the day I pushed you away with words that did me no credit. All of it. I blamed you for my desire. I blamed you for making me feel I was betraying Anne for wanting you."

She put her hand around the back of his neck. "I am so very sorry."

He gripped her hand and brought it to his lips. He kissed her knuckles gently. "You have nothing to apologize for. It is I who should apologize, and I do, Emily."

She turned her head away from him. Her shoulders moved oh so slightly because she'd taken and released a slow breath. Whether he was too late or not, she deserved the truth.

"Emily?"

"Apology accepted."

He touched her shoulder, then let his hand fall away. "When you told me that I see only what makes you different from Anne, you were right. I should have listened to you the first time you said it. I should have listened to what my heart has been telling me."

Her hand came up and made a motion out of his sight that suggested she'd wiped away tears. "What, Bracebridge? What has your heart been telling you?"

"If I go out, I am happy to come home because you are here. Don't cry, or please stop if you are. With child or not, I love you, Emily. I don't know when it happened, but I do love you. I have been falling in love with you for years, and I've been too stupid and stubborn to admit it. Worst, worst of all, I've hurt you because of it. I don't love you as I once loved your sister because you are not her. I love you for the woman you are. A woman who has become dear to me, as necessary to me as the very air I breathe."

She made a sound halfway between a sob and a gasp, and he moved close enough to bring her into the circle of his arms. At first she resisted, but he smoothed her back, and she leaned against him. "How do you know?" She lifted her face to his. She *had* been crying. "How do you know you love me?"

"I feel it here." He thumped his chest. "Here. I thought—I told myself if ever I fell in love again, I would feel as I did with Anne. But you and I are not like that. You are a different woman altogether." He held her close and told himself he would not cry either. "What a fool I've been. Such a fool. All this time pushing you away." He stared at her, the woman who had given him a home, her love, her admiration, and her respect. "I love you, Emily. I do love you. With all my heart. There is no more fortunate man in the world than I, if only you still love me."

Her eyelashes sparkled with the remains of her tears. "Not a fool," she said in a damp voice. "Only stubborn."

"Both." He tightened his arms around her. "What have I done to deserve you?" He kissed the top of her head. "Nothing. Nothing at all. But I mean to change that, if you'll let me."

The smile that always made his heart turn over flashed on her mouth. "I could be persuaded."

"What would persuade you?"

She put her hands on either side of his face. "A kiss."

"You shall have that. As many as you like. I'll spend the rest of my life proving myself worthy of you."

When their lips parted after another kiss, she sighed and said, "I tried to stop loving you. I tried."

"Praise the heavens, you failed."

"Miserably. I do love you. How could I not love you after all the poetry you read to me? Even poetry you did not like."

He kissed her again, slowly, tenderly, and when they parted, he said, "This is us, Em. We're a lusty, lively pair, and I am the most fortunate man alive."

"Yes," she said with a wicked grin. "You are."

"Promise me you'll never let me forget it."

Her arms tightened around him. "I promise."

He held her close and embraced not just her but the way she fit into his heart. "My brothers would have loved you. I wish they could have met you. I wish my family could have met you and seen how happy you make me. I think even my father would have told me I had at last done something of which he could approve."

She pressed her hand to the side of his face. "I wish I could have met them, too. I'm sorry I cannot. But, Bracebridge, my darling, my dear, dear love, don't regret the past. If your father was anything at all like you, and he must've been, for you are his son, he would have approved of the man you became. And if I'm wrong, and he would not have, that does not diminish who you are now."

"I love you, Emily. I'd love you if your hair was brown as dirt." He took her hand in his and placed it over his heart. "Every beat for you."

"For us."

"Yes, my love. Every beat for us."

Epilogue

EMILY'S STOMACH KNOTTED the moment her sisters walked into the parlor at Corth Abbey. In the next moment, she relaxed because her life was now all that she had dreamed it would be. The tension wasn't entirely gone. The memory of how desperately she had needed to protect herself left her with the conviction that she had best be armed for disaster. Which was, she knew, absurd.

Mary and Anne came in together, followed by their respective nurse-maids and the children. Aldreth and Cynssyr came in one after the other. Lucy, Emily's gorgeous black-haired sister, came in on the arm of the man she'd married. Lord Thrale had size and height in common with Bracebridge. After that they were not similar at all. Thrale was handsome enough to rival Aldreth or Cynssyr, and there was always at least a hint of polish about him. Not so with Bracebridge.

Mr. Rachagorla had arrived yesterday, shortly after the Strands, who had become close friends of theirs. At the moment, Mr. Strand was making much of Frieda. The children ran in to greet Emily and ask whether they might, please, play with Frieda. After accepting a hug and a kiss from each of them, she told them that yes, they might. Cynssyr's eldest had his father's green eyes and mahogany hair, but even as young as he was, the boy possessed Anne's serenity. The children greeted Bracebridge quite prettily, and each of them admired their new cousin.

Mrs. Iddings and her husband were also here. For Emily, Bracebridge had declared he would tolerate the couple. Fortunately, they seemed to have made a similar sacrifice.

Papa was not in attendance. She had no regrets about his absence. Unbeknownst to her father, Bracebridge had transferred ownership of the Cooperage to their son, with Emily having the use of the property for her lifetime. He'd said nothing when she allowed her father to live in the house with whatever servants could be persuaded to stay in service.

As for her father's expenses, Bracebridge had control of every penny of income the Cooperage produced. And so, to appease Anne, Emily sent her father money every quarter. She had no doubt he would find a way to gamble more than he could afford, but at this point, it was well known among the bookmakers of Bartley Green and most places in London that Thomas Sinclair would be unable to pay debts incurred.

Mary visited him from time to time, and to Emily's knowledge, Anne had been once, but not Lucy. Lucy was more like Emily—not prone to forgiveness. She would have been happy to see the father she remembered from her girlhood, but that man no longer existed.

Shrieks of joy and delight accompanied the children's departure with Frieda and their nursemaids, both of whom had been told that under no circumstances was the dog to be released from her leash.

Emily had made peace, of a sort, with Mary. They had come quite close to a permanent break until the day Mary had dissolved into tears on a day early in Emily's confinement. Her sister had made a rambling, tearful explanation of her actions that had, at last, concluded with a heartfelt apology. She and Mary had never got along, but now there was a friendship building between them.

"Have you ever seen a more handsome infant?" Bracebridge asked the gathering, smiling like the proud papa he was. He cradled their month-old son in his arms and leaned over to kiss Christopher's forehead for what had to be the dozenth time.

"Never in all the history of children," Cynssyr said with a grin.

Bracebridge looked ready to agree, but Emily gently elbowed him and said, "Shh. They have their own children, you know. Never make them admit their own aren't as perfect and lovely as ours."

He kissed her cheek. "You are a wise woman, my love."

"Yes, I am, aren't I?" She leaned her cheek against the side of his arm. She was happy, deliriously, wonderfully happy, and she was almost, almost, getting over her fear that Bracebridge would change his mind.

Lucy left Thrale's side to embrace Emily and put her mouth by Emily's ear. "I am so happy for you, my dear, dear sister. I have always wished that you would find happiness."

Emily hugged her sister. "Thank you."

Lucy stepped back, a vision in rose silk. "How far we've come, we Sinclair sisters. Look at us. All of us married to fine and wonderful men who love us and whom we love in return." She put a hand on her stomach. As Emily had recently learned, Lucy was pregnant with her first child.

"When we heard the news . . ."

"You were as concerned as everyone else, I know."

"No," her sister said. "My first thought was that at last he'd come to his senses."

She tilted her head. "Whatever do you mean?"

Lucy took Emily's hands and drew her away from Bracebridge. Mary, meanwhile, approached Bracebridge with her arms out. Bracebridge did not quickly relinquish his son to the coos and fond kisses of his aunt.

"I always thought you two would suit each other," Lucy said.

"If you did, you're the only one." They headed to a corner of the room, and it was like old times, with the two of them whispering secrets to each other. "Was I that obvious?"

"You?" Lucy touched Emily's shoulder and laughed. "Bracebridge was just as obvious. I know he had his hopes for Anne broken, but afterward, well, it was plain to me he was doing everything he could to deny his feelings for you."

"You never did think such a thing."

"I assure you I did."

Thrale joined them and slid an arm around Lucy's waist, then leaned in to kiss his wife's cheek. "Good afternoon, Lady Bracebridge. You are as radiant as ever."

She curtseyed. "My lord." Thrale was nearly as big and tall as Bracebridge. He, too, practiced the art and science of pugilism and had the physique of someone who was serious about his condition. Overcome by how grateful she was that Lucy had found happiness of her own after her first husband's passing, Emily threw her arms around Thrale and said, "Thank you. Thank you for loving my sister."

When they separated, he said, "I could do nothing else. I am quite convinced Bracebridge soon found himself in a similar predicament." He kissed her cheek. "Congratulations on the birth of your son. He's a fine-looking boy."

"He is, isn't it?" Her entire life had changed again the moment she held her son in her arms. Bracebridge had been so sweet in his relief that she and the infant had come through the delivery, then they'd both been overwhelmed by the responsibilities of parenting. Part of her had feared that once he had his heir, Bracebridge would withdraw from her, but he hadn't at all. Quite the opposite.

"He loves you," Thrale said. "I see it in his eyes and hear it in his voice whenever he speaks of you."

"I know he does." She needed a moment to keep tears at bay. "He loves me, and I love him, and I am so wonderfully blessed."

"What's all this whispering?" Bracebridge joined them and drew Emily to his side. "Christopher is in Anne's loving hands," he said.

She looked over her shoulder to see her eldest sister cooing over the baby. Cynssyr was tickling his feet. "Thrale was telling me tall tales," she said.

"Oh?"

Thrale looked askance at her. "Hardly, my dear sister. Hardly. My lord, I told your wife you are head over heels in love with her, that's all."

"I am." Bracebridge took her hand and kissed it. "I love her more than my own soul. She is my partner in life and in love. There is no man more fortunate than I, for I resisted for too long. I ought to have surrendered from the very start."

Emily's heart overflowed, and this time, the tears came freely. "Oh, Bracebridge," she said.

He took her into his arms. "What's this?"

"I do love you," she said, and that was a truth she was only too happy to accept.

THE SINCLAIR SISTERS SERIES

Lord Ruin – Book 1

Anne and Cynssyr

He hunted for beauty. He wasn't prepared for love.

A Notorious Ruin – Book 2

Lucy and Thrale

She hides her heart behind a thick skin. He's the only one who sees right through it.

Surrender to Ruin – Book 3

Emily and Devon

She's loved him forever. He's still in love with her oldest sister.

Excerpts

SCANDAL

Havenwood, near Duke's Head, England,
NOVEMBER 2, 1814

THE FIRST THING GWILYM, Earl of Banallt, noticed when he rounded the drive was Sophie perched on the ledge of a low fountain. Surely, he thought, some other explanation existed for the hard, slow thud of his heart against his ribs. After all, he hadn't seen her in well over a year, and they had not parted on the best of terms. He ought to be over her by now. And yet the jolt of seeing her again shot straight through to his soul.

He was dismayed beyond words.

Beside him, Sophie's brother continued riding toward the house, oblivious.

She heard them coming; she left off trailing her fingers in the water and straightened, though not before he caught a glimpse of the pale nape of her neck. Just that flash of bare skin, and Banallt couldn't breathe. Still seated on the fountain's edge, she turned toward the drive and looked first at her brother and then, at last, at him. She did not smile. Nor, he thought, was she unaffected.

Nothing at all had changed.

"Sophie!" Mercer called to his sister. He urged his horse to the edge of the gravel drive. Banallt took a breath, prayed for his heart to stop banging its way out of his chest, and followed. He wasn't afraid of her. Certainly he wasn't. Why would he be? She was a woman and only a tolerably pretty one at that. He had years of experience dealing with women. "What luck we've found you outside," Mercer said, leaning a forearm across his horse's neck.

Anxiety pressed in on Banallt, which annoyed him to no end. What he wanted from this moment was proof she hadn't taken possession of his heart. That his memories of her, of the two of them, were distorted by past circumstance. They had met during a turbulent time in his life during which he had perhaps not always behaved as a gentleman ought. They had parted on a day that had forever scarred him. He wanted to see her as plain and uninteresting. He wanted to think that, after all, he'd been mistaken about her eyes. He wanted his fascination with her to have vanished.

None of that had happened.

Banallt still thought he'd do anything to take her to bed.

Sophie lifted a hand to shade her eyes. "Hullo, John."

She was no beauty. Not at first glance. Not even at second glance. Bony cheeks only just balanced her pointed chin. Her nose was too long, with a small but noticeable curve below the bridge that did not straighten out near soon enough. Her mouth was not particularly full. Thick eyebrows darker than her dark hair arched over eyes that blazed with intelligence. The first time he saw her he'd thought it a pity a woman with eyes like hers wasn't better looking. Not the only time he'd misjudged her; merely the first.

She stood and walked to the edge of the lawn. Behind her, nearer the house, mist rose from emerald grass, and above the roof more fog curled around the chimneys to mingle with smoke. Havenwood was a very pretty property.

"My lord." Sophie curtseyed when she came to a halt. Her smile didn't reach her eyes. Banallt saw the wariness in the blue green depths. She didn't trust him, and she was still angry. Considering his reputation and their past interactions, a wise decision. She knew him too well. Better than anyone ever had.

Banallt relaxed his hands on the reins. Really, he told himself, his situation was not dire at all. He preferred tall women, and Sophie was not tall. In coloring, his bias had always been for blondes, and she was a brunette whose fine-boned features added to one's impression of her fragility. Delicate women did not interest him. She was in every way wrong for him. Havenwood might be a gentleman's estate, but despite the wealth and property, despite the fact that Mercer had important connections, the truth remained that Mercer and his sister were only minor gentry. Sophie's marriage had most definitely been a step down for her. His dismay eased. He would get through this ill-advised visit unscathed. He would tell her good morning, or afternoon, or whatever the hell time of day it was, express his surprise at seeing her, and be on his way, having just recalled an important engagement.

"You haven't changed," he told her. Good. He sounded stiff and formal. It was not in his nature to abase himself to anyone. Not even to Sophie Evans. His Cleveland Bay stretched its nose in her direction, remembering carrots and sugar fed from her hand, no doubt.

"You've met?" Mercer asked. His mount danced sideways, but he settled his gelding quickly. He was a competent horseman, John Mercer was. And far too alert now. Mercer was a dutiful brother looking out for his sister. Well. There was nothing for it. Banallt was here after all, and Mercer had reason to be suspicious.

"Lord Banallt was a friend of Tommy's," Sophie replied when Banallt did not answer. She pressed her lips together in familiar disapproval. Sophie had seen him at his worst, which was quite bad indeed. Legendary, in fact. Heaven only knew what was going through her mind right now. Actually, he thought he knew. It was not much to his credit.

"I didn't realize," Mercer said. Now he had the same wary eyes as his sister. The line between connections that were tolerable and connections that were not was sometimes all too fine. Mercer must have been wondering if that slender gap had been breached. A widowed nobleman with a long-standing reputation as a rake was one thing. A gentleman might overlook a scandal or two in the career of such a man. But a rake with a heretofore unknown acquaintance with one's sister was altogether different. Particularly when said sister was already well connected with scandal.

A look passed between Sophie and Mercer that made her mouth go thinner yet. If she was unhappy living with her brother, Banallt thought, this was something in his favor—*if* he went through with the madness that had begun flirting with him the moment he saw Sophie sitting at the fountain. That same compulsion had brought him here, all the way from Paris by way of London.

"We met once," she said. "Only once in eight years."

"Twice, wasn't it?" Banallt said in a lazy voice. If she was lying to her brother, which she was, then he had hope that she would not dismiss him out of hand. In fact, he had visited Rider Hall exactly four times. Three times that her late husband had known about.

"Was it?" she replied. Her voice could have frozen hell at noon twice over. He knew that voice well, and hearing it again made him want to smile. So many memories. She was the first woman ever to arouse his intellectual interest. Suffice it to say he typically admired women for other attributes than the quality of their minds. Perhaps his downfall had begun the moment he heard her speak with crisp indifference for his consequence. She spoke her mind. She wore her hair differently now, smoothed back from her forehead with fewer curls than he remembered. How like her to do so little to enhance her looks. "I don't recall."

"Sophie," her brother said with eyes that narrowed as he looked at her. But Mercer was no match for his sister's chill. No one was. "I should think you'd want to mention that."

She rolled her eyes. "John, for goodness' sake." Her familiar no-nonsense tone fit perfectly with her features. Prim. Modest. Completely unremarkable. She was like a governess scolding some young charge.

Banallt stared at her, more fascinated by her than he'd been by any other woman. His obsession with her bubbled up from wherever it was he'd tried to lock it away. He had been in the intimate company of women of undisputed beauty, but not one of them, not even the most exquisite, had made his stomach drop to the bottom of the earth as did one glimpse of Sophie.

"What does it matter," Sophie asked her brother, "if I met Lord Banallt before you did or, for that matter, whether we met one time or three?" She threw a hand in the air, and Banallt felt smugly certain she recalled exactly how many times they'd met. "Or even a dozen?"

"Mercer," Banallt said. He shifted on his saddle. "I'd no idea your sister was Mrs. Thomas Evans." The lie rolled from his tongue like warm butter.

The thing was, Mercer was right to be suspicious. Banallt and Sophie were both lying, for one thing. For another, any woman who confessed to knowing him stood a good chance of having been to bed with him. John Mercer was not fool enough to think his sister would be excluded from the likelihood. Well. And so. The truth was he wished Mercer's suspicions were well-founded.

"That much I understand, my lord." Mercer smiled. "It's my sister's silence I wonder at. You're all anyone has talked about since first we heard of your arrival at Castle Darmead. For pity's sake, she practically lived at

Darmead when we were children. Your hair would curl, my lord, if you'd heard even half the stories she told about you and your ancestors."

Sophie shrugged as if the talk—more like gossip—was a matter of no importance. Her attention was on her brother, which gave Banallt an unrestricted view of her inelegant nose and the slant of her sharp cheekbone. Today's cold and foggy weather suited her; the gray brought out the bronze in her dark hair and gave the faintest pink to her cheeks. Had he not come to Havenwood to discover whether the unthinkable had, indeed, befallen him? He was far more than bewitched. Damn the world to hell and back for it, too.

"Sophie," Mercer said. "Let's serve tea in the conservatory, shall we?"

"As you like, John." She spoke coolly, and Banallt didn't know if she did so to allay her brother's suspicions, unfounded though they were as to any past sexual connection, or whether because she was bitterly displeased that Banallt had come to Havenwood. God knows she was justified in thinking him here for no good purpose.

Banallt urged his horse up the drive ahead of Mercer so as not to reveal his uneasy state of mind. Whatever else he did, he owed her an apology. Would she forgive him? And if she did not? He might well regret his decision to come here. He'd made a mistake. They'd never have met, not in a thousand years, if she hadn't been married to that bounder Tommy Evans. Met they had, and Christ, he'd fallen hard. Precisely, he thought, because she was so unexpectedly the opposite of everything. The opposite of his expectations, the opposite of his desires, the opposite of any woman ever to flit into his imagination.

She was still dainty. Still slender. Still with eyes that made a man think of nothing but looking into them a moment longer. Still wary and reserved. He knew her as he had never come to know any other woman. He knew she longed for love and that her life up to now had not been one to make her think she would ever have it. He still wanted to take her into his arms and swear she would never want for anything again. None of which he had ever done, despite the fact that he never had considered a woman's marital status an impediment to an affair. Nor his own, either. Her opinion on the matter was quite the opposite.

Rather than catching up to Banallt, Mercer stayed behind to say something further to his sister. Banallt heard the tension in their voices but not the words themselves. He gave his Cleveland Bay the signal to stop when he heard Mercer riding after him. Damn. A man of his experience of life was too old for butterflies. The question now was whether Mercer had been tasked with sending him on his way. He mastered himself, and the control felt comfortable, like a favorite coat. From the corner of his eye, he saw Sophie cross the lawn, heading toward the house.

"Sophie never mentioned she knew you," Mercer said when he'd caught up.

Banallt gave Mercer an icy stare. "Should she have?"

"You tell me."

"Like any good rake, Tommy Evans kept his mistress in London and his wife in the country." He tried to recall whether Sophie had ever talked about her family and concluded he'd known only that she had an elder brother who lived at Havenwood. "London was where he preferred to be. In those days, so did I."

Mercer said nothing, and Banallt didn't know what to make of the man's silence. How unfortunate that Mercer was easily as intelligent as his sister.

"I was in Kent twice, as I recall. Perhaps three times. I met your sister then, when Evans brought me to Rider Hall to hunt." They had not, to his memory, done much hunting, unless one counted choosing a whore at the local bawdy house as hunting. More like shooting fish in a barrel.

"I see."

Banallt sighed. Mercer most assuredly did not see. "Forgive me if I am blunt. But Evans was more interested in whoring and gaming than in his domestic bliss. As was I. In those days," Banallt said.

"But you met her."

So, Mercer did suspect they'd been lovers. He wished they had been, because then he'd not be here, making a fool of himself.

"Naturally, we met. I thought her—" What was he to say? Heartbreaking. And then intriguing, and at last, utterly beguiling. "—charming." He had not for a moment expected Tommy Evans's wife to be anything but a foolish, empty-headed female of the sort that kept a man in London month after month. He had arrived at Rider Hall a rake unfettered by scruples of any kind, blissful in his ignorance that his life was to be set on end.

"There's scandal attached to her," Mercer said. The bitter way he spoke made Banallt look sharply at him. Mercer had a knowledge of Sophie's past that Banallt did not. He knew a different Sophie, a woman Banallt had but glimpsed through a door left ajar, then swiftly and decisively closed. He envied Mercer the knowledge. Deep waters here, treacherous to navigate. "Were you aware they eloped?"

"Evans mentioned something about that." Crowed about it. He'd eloped with an heiress. Some dull and starry-eyed seventeen-year-old who was his before they crossed the Scottish border into Gretna Green where the laws were so amenable to eloping couples. Even if they'd been caught, he'd have been forced to marry her. Respectable heiresses did not run off in the night with men to whom they were not married.

"It was a scandal here."

"Elopements generally are," Banallt said. Poor Sophie. She'd squandered her love and her money over the anvil. Tommy put her away in Kent and dedicated himself to spending seventy thousand pounds sterling as fast as he could.

"And then there was Evans's death," Mercer said, opening that distant door again and offering another glimpse of Sophie. Banallt was fiercely opposed to learning anything to Sophie's detriment. "If he was an acquaintance of yours, I'm sure you heard."

"No, actually. I've only recently returned from Paris. He died while I was away." His curt reply seemed to satisfy Mercer. Thank God.

When they got around the corner of the house and were heading for the stables, Mercer pulled up. Banallt did the same. He knew what was to come, and, like Mercer, he did not care to have the servants overhear. This was a discussion best had quickly and in privacy. One of the grooms came out of the barn but retreated when he saw them in conversation. Mercer leaned forward. "I know your reputation, my lord."

Banallt waited to hear if he was to be sent away. His mount, well-trained beast that it was, remained utterly still. There was no defense possible for his past. He'd been warned off more than once in his life, and by men with more reason than Mercer to be angry and fearful. But Mercer surprised him by meeting his eyes directly, and for that Banallt liked him.

"You've come to Duke's Head for the first time in your life." There was steel in Mercer's voice. Another groom turned a corner from the rear of the stables, glanced their direction, and disappeared inside the outbuilding. "People talk about a thing like that."

Banallt cocked his head in acknowledgment. Mercer had no choice but to connect Banallt's presence here with his sister. He was right to do so.

"I hope," Mercer said softly, "that scandal does not come down on us again."

Oh, well done. Mercer's oblique warning ranked among the best he'd ever had from a concerned relative. More than oblique enough to be taken for concern about Sophie's behavior rather than his. Banallt said, "My wife has been dead for some time now. I have no heir and no desire to see the title go elsewhere. A man in my circumstance must put his mind to marriage." That, he thought, was rather well done of him.

Mercer's green eyes were unforgiving. "From among the young ladies of Duke's Head?"

From where they'd stopped, Banallt could see servants moving inside the conservatory. He was amused that Mercer could not bring himself to ask the obvious. Well. He'd had enough of warnings and insinuations. He met Mercer's eyes. "I did not come to Duke's Head on a lark."

"I thought not."

Banallt took a breath. One never liked to show one's hand too soon. But there it was. "I intend to marry your sister."

Mercer's eyes widened, but he had something of Sophie's fortitude. "My lord." He inclined his head. "Just so we are perfectly clear, are you asking for my consent or my blessing?"

"Either will do." His heart thudded again. If only the matter could be resolved so easily. What he wanted, though, was for Sophie's too-intelligent brother to stay the hell out of his way.

Mercer leaned forward then resettled himself on his saddle. The leather creaked as he did. "They say you're likely to be raised in the peerage."

"I am quite content with my present title," he said. If he went from earl to marquess or even higher, then he was content with that, too.

Mercer frowned, and for an instant, Banallt saw him as the young man Sophie had spoken of. But only for an instant. Mercer returned to what he was: an impediment to something Banallt desired. "Suppose you marry Sophie."

"Yes," he murmured. "Suppose I do."

"Setting aside my conviction that such a marriage would make no one happy, least of all my sister, my nephew might be a marquess or perhaps even a duke."

"Or merely a lowly earl."

"With fifty or a hundred thousand a year in his pocket."

"Closer to a hundred thousand," Banallt said. Triumph flashed through him. He urged his horse toward the stable. "Console yourself, Mercer, by writing her a settlement to ease your conscience."

"I'm sure you've bought women for far less," Mercer said.

Well, yes, actually. But having Sophie as his wife was worth any price.

MOONLIGHT: A FREE SHORT STORY
CHAPTER 1

June 3, 1815, The ballroom at Frieth Hall, The Grange, North Baslemere, Surrey, England

BY THE TIME ALEC MCHENRY FALL, who had been the third earl of Dane for a very short time, made his way around the ballroom, Philippa was by herself. She sat on a chair backed up against the wall, her chin tipped toward the ceiling. Her eyes were closed in an attitude of relaxation rather than, so Dane hoped, prayer.

Her position exposed the slender column of her throat to anyone who might be looking, which was almost no one besides him since the room was nearly empty. Her hands lay motionless on her lap with the fingers of one hand curled around an ivory fan, the other held a corner of a fringed shawl the color of champagne.

He continued walking, not thinking about much except that Philippa was his good friend and that he was glad to have had her assistance tonight. He stepped around the detritus of a hundred people jammed inside a room that comfortably held half that number. A gentleman's glove. A bit of lace, a handkerchief, silk flowers that had surely started the evening pinned to some young lady's hair or hem.

Dane stopped in front of her chair. "Philippa."

She straightened her head and blinked at him. Her shawl draped behind her bare shoulders, exposing skin as pale as any Englishwoman could wish. Her legs were crossed at the ankles and her feet were tucked under her chair. Dane was quite sure she smiled before she knew it was him. He didn't remember her eyes being quite so remarkable a shade of green. An usual, light green. How interesting. And yes, disturbing, that he should notice any such thing about her.

He grinned and reached for her hand. He'd removed his gloves for the night, but she still wore hers. "A success, my little party, don't you think?"

A concoction of lace, ribbons and silk flowers covered the top of her strawberry blonde hair, a fashionable color among the young ladies of society. That he was now the sort of man who knew such things as what was fashionable among the ladies remained a source of amazement to him. He'd known Philippa his entire life. Her hair had been that shade of reddish-gold before it was fashionable.

Philippa was no girl. She was a mature woman. Thirty-one, though she could easily pass for younger. Her features were more elegant than he had called to mind during the time he'd been away. The shape of her face and the definite mouth above a pointed chin balanced out her nose, and her eyes, as, for some reason, he was just noticing tonight, were striking. Her smile, in his opinion, came too rarely.

"My lord." Her eyes traveled from his head to his toes, and he quirked his eyebrows at that. She meant nothing by the perusal, after all. Another smile played about her mouth. "How dare you be so perfectly put together after dancing and entertaining all night."

Dane knew he was in splendid form. His clothes fit with the perfection only a London tailor achieved for a man of means. He wasn't a sheep farmer anymore, except by proxy when his steward forwarded the income, and he was inordinately pleased that Philippa had noticed the change. Made him feel a proper sort of aristo.

"I was about to ask you the very same question." He bowed, returning her smile with one of his own.

Philippa had agreed to act as his hostess tonight because he was a twenty-five-year-old bachelor, his mother was in Bath with his eldest sister, and he was alone at Frieth House for the first time since leaving four years ago. He made a mental note to send her flowers tomorrow. Was there even a florist in North Baslemere? Gad. He might have send to Guildford for roses. Pink or white, he wondered? Or perhaps tulips if they could be found.

"Flatterer." She opened her fan and waved it beneath her chin. Her eyes twinkled with amusement. He did like the sound of her voice. Definite, controlled. And yet, there was a fullness to the tone that made him wish she'd keep talking. "Do go on, my lord."

He laughed, but that he'd said such a fatuous thing embarrassed him. He'd been in London long enough that empty words came to his lips without thought. There was no good reason for him to flatter Philippa, particularly when doing so made him look a bloody damn fool.

Was it flattery if what he'd said was true?

The only other people in the room now were servants, most of them hired by Philippa on his behalf since he no longer made Frieth House his primary home. He'd come back to North Baslemere for a number of reasons. This was his birthplace, for one, and he had deep and lasting connections here despite the changes in his life. For another, Philippa was going to remarry, and he wanted to celebrate the happy event when she and her prospective groom formally announced their news.

"Not too tired to walk a little more, I hope?" He cocked his head in the direction of the terrace door and looked at her sideways. She'd taken a great deal of care with her appearance tonight. Something he hadn't noticed before, what with the excitement of a party so perfectly managed he'd had nothing to do but enjoy himself. Pink roses. "Did I remember to compliment your appearance?" This wasn't flattery, he told himself. "If I didn't, you have permission to shoot me."

"No, Alec, I don't believe you did." These days Philippa was the only person to call him by his given name. He rather liked the informality. From her. She held out her hand, and he took it as she rose. "A breath of air would be delightful."

Now that he'd spent time in London, he saw Philippa with a more experienced eye. She was not quite beautiful, but she had something that appealed. Her looks were in no way inferior, but her confidence, her utter satisfaction with herself as she was, made her interesting for more than her face and figure. During his time away, he had learned that even perfection was tedious in a woman one did not otherwise admire. She glanced at him, mercifully unaware of his inventory of her physical attributes. Christ. London and its courtesans had made him a letch before he was thirty. What business had he noticing her that way? Before she tucked her hand in the crook of his arm, she adjusted her shawl and in the process gave him a flash of bare shoulder. He hadn't seen her in an evening gown before, and, well, this close to her and with none of his earlier distractions he could see her skin was perfectly smooth and white from her forehead to her bosom.

They continued to the set of double doors that led to the terrace, leaving the servants to the task of cleaning up. If it were daylight they would be able to see the roses that had been his mother's pride while she lived here, before his sisters had given their mother grandchildren upon which to dote.

"I've asked a maid to make up a room for you," he said. They were outside now and crossing the terrace. He'd also never realized she was as delicate as she was, thought one also had to take into account the fact that he was a bigger man now, taller and broader through the shoulders than when he'd left North Baslemere.

"It's not so late," she said. "I'll walk home."

"Nonsense." He put his hand over hers. "I won't hear of it."

Philippa tilted her head in his direction. "I'm not sure that's wise, my lord."

"What isn't wise?"

"My staying the night."

"Why ever not? You're family." Even before the words were out, he understood, with a disconcerting thump of his heart, what she meant. He'd thought of her as an older sister for years and years. Twenty-five years, to be exact. But she wasn't his sister. Appearances were everything, and if she stayed the night, a youthful widow in the home of a London buck, there might be unpleasant speculation.

A rather explicit image popped into his head. Him covering her, thrusting into her, while she held him tight against her naked body.

Good God. Had he gone entirely mad?

"And yet, not family." She adjusted her shawl.

"If not family, then fast friends." Dane had the oddest conviction that he'd somehow stepped out of time and that now nothing was familiar to him. Not his childhood home. Not this terrace or the garden he'd grown up with. Not even Philippa, who he admired as a friend.

"Yes," she said, tightening her hand on his arm. "We are friends, aren't we? Lifelong friends." They stopped at the furthest edge of the terrace. She took a deep breath of the night air.

Dane who, by coincidence, happened to be looking down, saw the swell of her breasts against her neckline. In his out-of-place mood, he thought of sex. With Philippa. And that sent another jolt of heat through him.

Thanks for reading *Surrender to Ruin*. I hope you enjoyed the excerpts.

About Carolyn Jewel

Carolyn Jewel was born on a moonless night. That darkness was seared into her soul and she became an award-winning and USA Today bestselling author of historical and paranormal romance. She has a very dusty car and a Master's degree in English that proves useful at the oddest times. An avid fan of fine chocolate, finer heroines, Bollywood films, and heroism in all forms, she has two cats and two dogs. Also a son. One of the cats is his.

Visit Carolyn on the web at:

carolynjewel.com

Twitter: @cjewel

Facebook: facebook.com/carolynjewelauthor

Goodreads: goodreads.com/cjewel

Sign up for Carolyn's **newsletter** (http://cjewel.me/nlWS39) so you never miss a new book and get exclusive, subscriber-only content.

Made in the USA
Las Vegas, NV
02 December 2022

60962315R00173